I0713376

MARKED BY FORTUNE

APOCALYPTIC URBAN FANTASY

ANN GIMPEL

CONTENTS

MARKED BY FORTUNE

By

Ann Gimpel

Apocalyptic Urban Fantasy

Tumble into a world where magic rules and hope is hard to find

Copyright Page

All rights reserved.
Copyright © July 2013, Ann Gimpel
Cover Art Copyright © September 2019, EerilyFair Designs
Edited by: Angela Kelly
Names, characters, and incidents depicted in this book are products of the
author's imagination, or are used fictitiously. Any resemblance to actual
events, locales, organizations, or people living or dead, is entirely coincidental
and beyond the intent of the author.
No part of this book may be reproduced or shared by any electronic or
mechanical means, including but not limited to printing, file sharing, e-mail,
or web posting without written permission from the author.
ISBN: 9781948871273

BOOK DESCRIPTION, MARKED BY FORTUNE

Magic levies a steep price on anyone brave enough or stupid enough to dabble in it.

Wizards never forgave Ned for not being one of them. They didn't exactly come out and say his life was expendable, but they didn't have to. He figured it out fast enough when they conscripted him into their long-running war the second he was old enough to fight. Isolated, different, he puzzled out how his brand of magic worked on his own.

Fleeing the tide of doom wiping out humanity, Amanda and her family escape to a remote corner of California, where they eke out a hardscrabble existence. With her parents at each other's throats and her brother mysteriously gone, Amanda encounters malevolent power beyond her wildest imaginings. Captured by the Undead, she's about to join their ranks when Ned shows up.

Defying a direct order from his wizard battle lord, Ned dives into the fray. He might not know Amanda, but it doesn't matter. She's in trouble and needs his magic.

It's good enough for him.

READER PRAISE FOR MARKED BY
FORTUNE:

If you are looking for action, betrayal, smelly bad guys, gods, mythical creatures and a really good reading experience, this is the book for you. While you are looking at this story be sure to pick up some of her other wonderful books, you won't be disappointed.

Action, Adventure, Magic, and love come together in a dystopian world that will make you question everything you know!

Ned is a great character and I truly enjoyed watching him grow into a fine young man. I recommend Fortune's Scion to anyone looking for a fast paced fantasy with a touch of romance.

I wade into Ms. Gimpel's books cautiously, only to fall completely and totally into her stories. I'm a fan of her parallel universes, fantasy worlds and curious creatures. I travel back and forth between worlds in her transportation system called "the Ways." Her characters are always completely formed and compelling in their individual challenges and journeys, pushing against the powers of evil and prejudice, against sudden jerks in their action. A very good read, new adult or old.

Ann's world-building skills truly amaze as she bounces from dystopian San Francisco, to the wizard's stronghold, and to an evil god's lair. Be prepared for multiple POV's, but being in the major character's heads gives you a great sense of the story. This was a totally different read for me, even from Ann's previous works. The ending was actually quite dark and surprising, but totally realistic despite the fantasy aspect of the story.

Romance, magic, adventure, and a devastating war fill this story and kept me enthralled! I loved the wizards, mages, and their magical travels to alternate worlds. Even though this story is on the dark side, ultimately there is a profound sense of hope through its entirety.

HISTORY PRIMER FOR THE UNINITIATED

Humans never knew about wizards until it was too late, and even then most didn't believe magical beings existed. Wizards, on the other hand, have always known about humans. Contrary to the olden stories, they never liked them very well, and they liked them even less after humans damaged Earth beyond redemption.

It didn't happen overnight, but fuel sources dried up, and the oceans rose as the planet grew warmer. Water and air became progressively more toxic. Earth's population—the human one—continued to grow at a relentless pace.

Wars broke out as people fought over increasingly scarce resources. Countless battles solved the population problem and kept right on rolling. Cities lay in ruins. People died in droves from bad water and rampant disease. Communications systems failed, and a once-interconnected world devolved into isolated pockets of humanity.

Wizards watched the tableau unfold amid much teeth-gnashing. It wasn't the disaster for them that it was for humans. They could pull up stakes and travel to other worlds after Earth failed. Still, Earth was their primary home, and their antipathy for all things human escalated, driven by a dying Earth.

Attracted by chaos, the wizards' ancient enemies breached Earth's veil with greater and greater frequency. Conflict that had gone on as long as most wizards could remember—and that mortals knew nothing about—became far more brutal. Human energy once had a modulating effect. With the vast majority of humans dead, the dark gods became bolder than they'd been before.

Wizard losses escalated, causing more teeth-gnashing.

It's tough to deliver a message to mortals who didn't believe wizards were real, who mocked the magic shimmering around them as smoke, mirrors, or a clever trick employing trapped electrical energy. Still, wizards made more of a good faith effort than many believed was warranted, before finally giving it up for a lost cause.

NED'S WAR

$\mathcal{N}$ed crouched amid the remains of what was once downtown Sacramento, using a convenient, partly-decimated building as cover. The rest of his unit hid in close proximity—at least he hoped they did. A low, whistling noise ratcheted his heart into hyper drive. Enemy magic. Maintaining his crouch, he spun, searching the late afternoon gloom for clues. Not quite sure what tipped him off, he leapt out of the way just before a concrete block exploded, showering him with debris.

"Whew! Way too close." The words tore out of him before he could stop them.

He drew his lips into a disgusted snarl and wondered for the thousandth time how he, a human mage, ever got mixed up with the wizards' war.

Because the bastards didn't give me a choice.

Sweat trickled down his forehead. His leather headband caught some of it, but a few drops fell into his eyes. They stung like hell, and he shook his head to disperse the salty liquid. The beginnings of a headache throbbed behind one temple.

"Landarik." Ned spoke his commander's name into his mouthpiece. "Where are you?"

"Right behind you." A voice dripped sarcasm into Ned's ear.

"Son of a bitch."

Ned whipped around. Landarik stood so close, Ned's braids slapped against the wizard's helmet. "I wish you wouldn't do that," Ned sputtered through clenched teeth. "I hate when you sneak up on me. Especially when it could have been one of *them*. You're lucky I didn't blast you."

"Your puny human magic wouldn't have made a dent. Cut the shit. What do you want?"

Speaking through the slit in his bronzed helmet, Landarik looked like a robot. Only his blond braids, with debris tangled in them, ruined the automaton image. He must have noticed Ned's stare because Landarik gathered his ratty braids and tossed them over his shoulders.

"I'm beat. Request permission to return to the caves."

"Mage or no," Landarik grunted, "you humans are more work than you're worth. I have no fucking idea what the goddess had up her sleeve when she created those like you."

"Fine. Neither do I. Now can I go?"

"I release you—but only because you're more worthless than usual. Return no later than first light." Whistling sounded again. Without apparent thought or effort, Landarik raised a hand. A bolt of power flew from his fingertips and vaporized a small building a hundred yards away.

"How can you know so...precisely?" Ned sputtered.

Landarik tipped the visor of his helmet up. His shrewd blue eyes shot darts at Ned, and the sharp-boned features characteristic of the wizard race twisted in irritation. "I've told you and told you," he lectured in a patronizing voice that grated on Ned's nerves. "Hold your inner parts still, human. If you managed yourself better, you'd hear where the enemy is hiding." He snorted. "Sometimes I find it difficult to fathom how you're still alive."

"You and me both," Ned mumbled.

Sketching a rectangular portal in the hot, dusty air, he jumped through into the Ways, picturing the wizards' caves as he did so. Wizards developed the Ways thousands of years ago so they could travel to distant locations. Their harmonics were so well matched to galactic magnetics, they remained fully functional despite minimal maintenance.

As he sped through the dimension carrying him to a few hours of safety, Ned's empty stomach clenched in anger. It wasn't fair for Landarik to expect him to know everything the vetted wizard warriors did. Most of them were hundreds —if not thousands—of years old, while he was a mere...well, something. Young, anyway. In truth, he wasn't precisely sure of his age. Wizards lived so long they didn't bother keeping those types of records.

Ned didn't know if it was fortune, or her opposite, but he'd drawn his first breath in a wizard stronghold. He had little memory of his first few years, but around the time he turned five, one of the wizards—the acolyte master, Karras

—took notice of the little human who carted power after him the same way other youngsters dragged beloved toys.

The discovery he held magic within him turned out to be a two-edged sword. His mother was a normal human, and the wizards kicked her out of their stronghold after she refused to divulge his father's name. Ned offered her points for courage. If she'd given up his father's name, the wizards would have hunted him down and probably killed him—for having the temerity to be intimate with one of their servants.

Once his mother was out of the way, his lessons in mage craft took off like a shot and never really stopped. Catching up with the wizards proved impossible, particularly since they reminded him of his inferiority on a regular basis.

Things may well have gone differently had his teachers been other human mages. Perhaps they might have been more sensitive to his skills—and less critical of his efforts. Come to think of it, maybe their teaching style would have suited his magic far better. It took several years, but Ned finally figured out that his gifts manifested quite differently than the wizards'. He fought off a wave of bitterness and severed his line of thought. Surely other human mages existed—his father, for example—but he'd never met one in the flesh.

He sent magic spiraling outward to make certain he was still on course. Infernals might try to sabotage the Ways, despite maintaining their own traveling portals. "They'd have to get in here, first," Ned said, talking to himself. "It wouldn't be easy."

The Ways required special spells and an affinity established by one of the wizards. Without those things, they'd refuse to open. Ned wished he knew more about other races, like humans for instance. Or elves. All his history lessons had focused solely on wizards, which made sense because everyone else in his classes was one. He'd felt quite the misfit. Worse, wizards weren't fond of humans and rarely missed an opportunity to pound the point home.

The deceleration presaging his arrival began, tugging at his midsection. Ned summoned magic to call up a portal. It formed slowly because he was so tapped out. How long since his last rest? He did some quick calculations and came up with sixty-five hours. Wizard physiology was different. They could last five or six days on the battlefield without a break. No matter how hard he tried, Ned had never managed much more than three. Even then, the last hours turned into such a struggle, they were hardly worth it. Ned set his teeth in a grim line. Like he'd told Landarik, he was surprised he was still alive too.

His portal glowed. Warm and inviting, it radiated a soft blue light, the color of many of his workings. Ned peeled the door back and jumped through, so dead on his feet his eyes were half-shut.

The minute he stepped into the flickering, magic-driven torchlight of the sloppily excavated cave the wizards used as a re-supply station, Ned knew something was wrong. He felt the subtle presence of something malevolent in the air currents moving through their subterranean quarters. He didn't close off the portal—just in case. Sibilant swishing from deep in the shadows dragged a last bit of adrenaline into his bloodstream. He felt sick, jittery, but at least he was wide-awake again.

A horny snout came into view, accompanied by a hissing shriek as the thing raced out of the darkness right at him. Running on nerves and instinct, Ned didn't stop to examine his adversary. The thing intended to kill him. He jumped backward—body surprisingly nimble given his exhaustion —and sealed off his portal before he resurrected the spell that had carried him from the battlefield. Because the Ways required a destination, he visualized Sacramento. He could always correct his course en route.

What in the nine hells was in the cave?

Ned cleared his mind. He examined the feel of the wrongness. He didn't sense Infernals. Not exactly. No, it was more like one of the trogs: a cross between trolls and warthogs. Infernals kept them for pets. It was a safe bet if a trog was in the entry hall of the wizards' cave, its masters weren't far distant.

Ned shuddered. He'd fought trogs more than once in this war. Their highly poisonous bite could kill on contact if it hit a key spot. His Comparative Zoology instructor at the wizard stronghold in the Carpathian Alps had taught him about genetic catastrophes developed in the Infernals' labs. Trogs were only one of the perverted creatures born from those unnatural experiments. Closing his eyes, Ned visualized the wall chart with trogs, wargs, the undead...

Why bother?

Can't change any of it.

Where can I go? Not back to the battle. I'd be worth about as much as a drowned dragon.

He needed to pick a destination, and fast, so he could grab a couple hours of badly needed sleep. Sacramento wouldn't do it, even if he skirted the worst of the fighting. The large urban areas were worse than anywhere else, and he'd need to stay sharp to avoid danger. Right now, he wasn't.

Ned racked his mind, calling up the geography of California. He'd almost decided to head for the Sierra Nevada Mountains—a place Karras took him years ago—when he rethought things. No matter how much he wanted to retreat somewhere safe, he needed to let Landarik know about the breach in their cave. With a great deal of reluctance, he linked what was left of his magic to the frequency of the Ways, and reiterated his command for them to take him back to Sacramento.

Ned didn't like the wizards any more than they cared about him, but they were the only family he'd ever known. Despite all the times he'd wished Landarik would die a slow, painful death, he did value the concept of duty. Ned shook his head to jar himself into a more wakeful state. Thinking pain might rouse him, he bit his lower lip until he tasted blood, but it didn't help much.

He still felt like one of the undead.

Gradual slowing meant he was almost there. Squaring his shoulders, Ned summoned a portal. He scanned the countryside with cautious eyes before he stepped out of the Ways. "Landarik," he hissed through the wizard-crafted communication system still jammed between his ear and his mouth. Although the wizards claimed credit for the device, Ned had his doubts. Research in the extensive stronghold library suggested the design originated with the United States Special Forces.

"I thought you left." Landarik's voice boomed in Ned's ear, but the wizard was somewhere out of sight.

"I did, but..." Using as few words as possible, he described what he'd found in the caves. The harsh rumble of Landarik breathing right into his mouthpiece made Ned's headset crackle. Wizards could be insensitive, and the battle lord was worse than most.

"Good work. We'll send a few select warriors to handle it." In an uncharacteristic burst of empathy, Landarik added, "You must still be tired."

"Ah, yes, I am. Actually, I was hoping for permission to go into the mountains to sleep for a bit."

"Denied." The wizard's crisp voice echoed in Ned's headset. Landarik was used to commanding wizard troops. Maybe he'd already forgotten Ned was dead on his feet—or he just didn't care. "I must confer with the other battle lords. Don't leave before I release you."

Head bobbing with weariness, Ned cast about for a protected spot to wait out Landarik's orders. Sending tendrils of magic outward, he hunted for a secure place where he might not be killed instantly if his heavy lids got the better of him. Try as he might, he couldn't detect their enemy nearby. Had they gone elsewhere? Or was he just too tired to be sensitive to their presence?

Head pounding, eyes like sandpaper, Ned staggered to one side of what had once been a shopping plaza and wedged himself under the remains of a metal dumpster butted up against a cinderblock wall. An army of rats challenged him for the choice spot under heavy steel. Ned tried reasoning with them. When that failed, he vaporized the biggest one with his stun gun.

They left him alone after that.

Taking stock of himself, he noted tattered leather breeches, a scarred leather vest, and the Celtic tattoos on both arms marking him a warrior. He remembered the wizards' arguments about those tattoos. All the warrior wizards had them, but many were loath to see the symbol of their courage inked onto one like him, who wasn't of their blood.

Somewhere in the midst of his memories, sleep claimed him. Ned wasn't sure how long he slept, but Landarik hadn't called him. The wizard would have used a louder voice if he didn't answer. What awakened him was the wind. It gusted out of everywhere and nowhere, culling up bits of grit and debris. They turned into small projectiles and tore his skin. Scrunching his eyes against the onslaught, Ned forced his logy, sleep-saturated brain to focus.

Should he call Landarik?

Time had passed since the wizard told him to wait— maybe quite a bit. The wind worsened, howling as it snatched at his clothing. Ned's headache, forgotten while he slept, came back in force. Bellying out from under the dumpster, he looked at the sky.

Fear flooded him, its taste sharp and metallic. The last vestiges of sleep fled. Green and blue light flickered through the clouds, punctuated in places with black. The world was disintegrating. Had someone managed to get hold of one of the long-since-banned atomic weapons? Remembering the potentially toxic levels from nuclear debris, Ned tried to hold his breath until he could figure things out. It didn't work very well. In the end, he decided the wrongness felt more like magic than something manufactured by men.

He didn't need his mage senses to feel unnatural displacements in the air. Curiosity sparred with dread as he cataloged what swirled around him. Except it didn't fit any patterns he knew about. Maybe he was being cowardly, but only flight mattered now. If he waited, he wasn't sure he could summon enough power to leave.

"Human—" Landarik's voice sounded raspy.

"Yes. I'm still here."

"We're retreating. You must leave."

"I can't go back to the caves," Ned protested.

"Agreed." The wizard's voice grew weaker. "We have an assignment for you. East of the mountains is a woman with power akin to your own. She may be part wizard or part mage. We're not certain. She's at grave risk. The Infernals already have her children. At least we think they do."

"What do you want me to do once I find her?"

Why can't I just go back to the wizard stronghold along with the rest of you?

An explosion boomed, loud against his ears. Ned pulled the communications device away from his head and stared mutely at it before settling it back into place.

Landarik's voice, muffled by static, crackled, "Goddess blast it. For once in your sorry life, human, figure *something* out on your own. I must leave while I still can."

Adrenaline pounded through Ned. His heart beat a tattoo against his ribs, and sweat dripped down his sides. He reached for his magic, stunned to find it shrinking away by the moment. Panicked, he pulled a weak portal out of the ether, forced it shut behind him, and entered the Ways without an absolute destination in mind. He felt them balk but pushed inside anyway.

The lands east of the Sierra Nevada Mountains spread across an immense distance. It might not be possible to find a single person in thousands of acres. Reining in hopelessness so it wouldn't overwhelm him, Ned called up an image of Mono Lake.

He shook so hard his teeth rattled together, but fatigue trumped fear. He hunkered down, wrapped his arms around his knees, and prayed to the goddess to get him out of this one. When he thought about the journey later, he figured he must have passed out because he didn't remember much until he sensed deceleration. Before the Ways could jettison him, Ned scrambled upright. He raised a hand to summon a portal, but hesitated.

What would he find?

"It doesn't matter," he growled. "I can't stay in here forever. I'll starve." He tried to estimate how long it had been since he'd eaten. Better than twenty hours. Between no food and no sleep, small wonder he felt so depleted.

His portal opened—thank the gods his magic wasn't totally dead—on fading daylight. Ned peered out, ready to take flight if something—anything—didn't feel right. Satisfied to find only sagebrush and desert, he stumbled from the Ways, spoke a command, and felt the vague release of suction as his gateway vanished.

Ned searched for a spot to spend the night. It was safer here than in the midst of the wreckage of California's central valley. This part of California had been sparsely populated even before the oil ran dry and climate change eroded the polar ice caps. The lack of humanity meant the worst of the squabbling over scarce resources was less of an issue here than in more developed areas.

The wizards blamed humans for Earth's devastation, and for once, they weren't far off the mark. Humans burned up all the fossil fuels without a shred of foresight and poisoned the seas. They destroyed the rain forests and the ozone layer, sabotaging the atmosphere and making the Earth far too warm. Wizard warnings had been too little and come too late to change anything.

Ned found a feeder stream within a grove of scrubby trees. Kneeling, he opened his mouth at the water's surface and drank. It tasted pure and sweet, so he pulled off his tattered green backpack, dragged out a couple of water skins, and filled them.

Almost afraid to test his abilities, Ned reached within himself to the spot where his power lived. Relief raced through him as he tapped into the rich vein holding his magic and it pinged back. Nowhere near whole, but not as washed-out as he feared, either.

He mouthed a quick prayer of thanks to whomever watched over poor sods like him and sent his mage senses outward, questing for danger. He was far more thorough than he'd been leaving the Ways, but the only life force he found, aside from small rodents, was his own.

Relief sluiced through him.

He settled into the shadows of some overgrown manzanita bushes about fifty paces from the grove where he'd found the stream. Pulling a fur-lined cloak out of his rucksack, he arranged it over himself against the chill of the desert night. He set a ward. Since he'd done everything he could to ensure his safety, he tucked his pack under his head, stretched out, and fell into an exhausted sleep.

THE SUN in his face and his communications device jabbing the side of his head brought him around. He opened his eyes and saw he wasn't alone. Sometime during the night, a herd of wild horses in every color of the rainbow had joined him. They pushed against the perimeter of his ward, accompanied by a cacophony of *neighs*.

Ned grinned. For the first time in weeks, he felt truly alive. Loosing his ward to the morning breeze, he yanked the headpiece out of his ear and stuffed it into a pocket.

He bent to gather his few belongings and toyed with asking the horses if any Infernals skulked close by. Watching the carefree way the horse herd played with one another argued against the presence of the wizards' ancient enemy, so he decided not to bother them.

For long moments, he breathed in clean air, enjoying the chill bite of morning in his lungs. The blue-green waters of Mono Lake, half a mile distant, held a starburst reflection of the rising sun. Toward the west, the terrain gained elevation, sagebrush giving way to timber. He'd gotten plenty of rest. It was past time to head into the mountains.

An inner voice—the naggy one—said he needed to hurry, find the woman, and return to Landarik and his regiment. Ned ignored it. He was sick of war. It wasn't a calling for him like it was for the warrior wizards who ate, breathed, and sang battle lore, broad smiles on their faces as they recalled past glories and spoke of victories to come. With a final farewell to the horses, Ned shouldered his pack and started uphill with the rising sun to his back.

A forest of evergreens and aspens sheltered him from the growing warmth of the day. Berry bushes and an abandoned orchard with withered, late-season apples provided snacks. Insects buzzed. Relaxing his tightly held fists, he flexed his fingers, enjoying the simple movement. A chickadee's song grabbed his attention, and he stopped walking to listen.

How long had it been since he'd heard *any* bird singing? He couldn't remember, and sadness tugged at him. His life was war, duty, and absolute adherence to whatever orders some wizard barked his way. Nothing was likely to change, so Ned reached beyond himself into the day. The beauty of a place not yet tainted by Infernals seeped into him.

After a while, it displaced self-pity.

He pulled his solar-powered stun gun—used by wizards when their own powers waned—from its holster. Ned mouthed a hasty prayer to the goddess for the food he was about to take and hunted in earnest, luring game with his mage senses. Apples and berries weren't enough to fill the empty space in his belly.

Ned knelt in tall scrub grass to dress two fat rabbits. The sun beat down. Flies buzzed, but he drew magic to keep them away from his kill. A flash of blue caught his attention. Ned glanced up and spied a small lake through the trees. It looked so inviting, he picked up his bounty and headed toward a rocky beach at one end.

He sat on some ratty vegetation near the water's edge. Tugging at the sweat-hardened leather of the band he wore around his head, he jimmied the knot loose with difficulty. Ned dropped the filthy scrap of deer hide into the shallows of the lake and worked water into it. After a while, the leather became supple and he laid it in the grass to dry.

He went to work on his hair. Done up in the wizard custom, it was braided close to his skull in tightly woven rows. Unbraiding it took a long time. The wizards—at least the warrior caste—washed the braids in place without bothering to undo them since it took another set of hands to get them done up again. Unused to the feel of his hair hanging around his face and cascading down his back to his waist, Ned shook his head to loosen it. Greasy, dark strands fell across his eyes.

He laid his leather vest, boots, and breeches in the grass and waded into the lake with the rest of his clothes on. They were so filthy he might as well wash them right along with himself. The water was cold enough to be uncomfortable. Casting a quick spell, he warmed a tight circle close to his body and sighed with pleasure as the water came close to bathing temperature. He dunked his head and grabbed handfuls of sand from the bottom to scrub himself. Nubbins of soft whiskers met his fingers as he cleaned his face. Unlike the wizards, it didn't appear he was destined to ever have a beard to tend.

Clean as he was likely to get without soap, he waded from the pond and stripped off his soaked smallclothes, laying them over nearby tree branches to dry. He could hasten the process with magic, but the scraps of cloth might dry enough while he cleaned, cooked, and ate his rabbits. He could almost hear one of his old teachers lecturing.

Never use magic if you don't have to. It squanders the goddess's resources unnecessarily.

He checked for the presence of others—or, goddess forbid, an Infernal—again, but found nothing amiss. Satisfied, he went to work preparing his first real meal in days.

Ned turned the rabbit meat on green sticks over a small fire and sifted through the short years of his life. For probably the millionth time, he wondered what had become of Karras, the acolyte master who first noticed his magic. It was a sad day when Karras found him in the warren of rooms behind the library to say goodbye.

Stricken to see his one true friend amongst the wizards departing, Ned asked if he could go too. The wizard looked at him through dark eyes filled with compassion. "I'm not certain I shall return," he said, his voice soft. "Life in the stronghold is not the life for all of us, and it grates on me after hundreds of years." Karras had paused for long moments before adding, "There are many ways to fight Infernals."

Ned had asked—no, actually begged—Karras to take him along, but the wizard demurred. "You're not done with your training, lad. 'Twill take a few more years afore you're ready to leave the stronghold. Mayhap..." But Karras fell silent then, and Ned never knew what his old friend and mentor decided not to say.

Life at the stronghold grew quite a bit worse after Karras's departure. Many talked of forcing Ned to leave. When he'd packed his few clothes one warmish spring day, sick to death of the wizards' constant posturing, he found the doors barred. Furious, Ned retreated to his small room above the kitchens, planning to find a length of rope and use one of the many open windows as an escape route.

Hreth, blind seer and one of three wizards of the High Council, stood waiting in Ned's room. White hair cascaded about him like a mantle. Turning his greenish, milk glass eyes toward Ned, the wizard came as close as a wizard could to apologizing. He said something like, "'Tis not safe beyond these walls. Not for us, nor for thee. We shall not, of course, hold thee against thy will. Nonetheless, 'twould be better for all if thou stayed."

Over time, Ned noticed a marginal improvement in how the wizards treated him. More like a bastard stepchild than an actual pariah.

Wiping grease from his fingers, he exerted effort to not grind his teeth together in frustration. Wizards. Fuck all of them.

At least his belly was full. Landarik flitted through his mind, along with his assignment, but for once, he buried his responsibilities deep. Things were so much better here than where he'd come from, he didn't know if he'd be able to force himself to go back, no matter how hard he tried.

"Duty," he grumbled. "Duty be damned." Once he found the woman, he'd have to do something. Exactly what was vague. Hadn't Landarik told him to figure things out himself? Maybe he could just take his sweet time hunting for her.

It was unlikely the wizards would spare the manpower to come looking for him—or an unknown female, no matter what kind of magic she possessed. If he were another wizard, they'd move heaven and earth to find him. As things stood, they might be just as happy he was gone. He could almost see the smirk on Landarik's face and hear him say, "Mayhap we should leave well enough alone."

Come tomorrow, he'd start walking toward the west again, into the mountains. If he stumbled across the woman, he'd deal with it when it happened. If he never found her, that would suit him just fine. For the first time in his life, Ned felt free, and he rather liked the sensation.

MY DAUGHTER IS LOST

*L*ori Haraldssen urged her mare forward. It had taken close to half a day to round up the animal from her summer pasture a thousand feet below the house. Because she was in a hurry, Lori hadn't gone back by the house to pick up her saddle. The blanket she'd tossed over the horse's withers slipped, and Lori clutched at the reins. She'd never been much of a horsewoman, and her lack of skill was coming back to bite her in the ass.

A sudden gust of wind blew hair into her eyes. Unable to see through the curtain of golden-brown curls, she gathered her tresses into a queue and tucked what she could inside her sweater. She shivered. All of her was cold. She barely felt her fingers or toes. Woolen pants, hand-sewn from material woven on her loom, clung to her legs. She wished she'd worked harder to achieve a tight weave—or that she'd worn something beneath them. They were the same sheep-color as her sweater. Dyes were a waste of time, even if she could find plants to yield colors. A sudden lurch jarred her when Nellie stumbled into one of many uneven declinations in the rough mountain terrain.

"Easy, girl," she murmured, keeping her tone soothing. "You can go slower. The worst thing would be if we didn't get there at all."

Bad luck. Nothing but bad luck, reverberated through her weary mind.

Five years ago, she and Rolf, and their two teenaged kids fled from what looked like the wholesale collapse of society. Those five years had been filled with nothing but backbreaking labor and heartbreaking loss. Jon, her oldest, disappeared toward the end of the first year. Without a damned trace. Now Amanda was gone. More shivers coursed down Lori's sweaty back. Her hands slipped on the reins. The sweat just made her colder as wind whistled through her clothing.

One minute, her daughter—beautiful eighteen-year-old Amanda with her long blonde hair and ever-so-blue eyes— was there and the next she'd vanished. The same thing had happened to Jon four years earlier.

She and Amanda had been in the barn milking goats this morning. Lori picked up the pail and carried it into the house, expecting Amanda to come along any moment with the eggs. She never showed. When Lori went back to look for her, her daughter wasn't there. The wolves hadn't barked or howled, so whatever happened hadn't alerted them.

An ugly truth hit her. Jon was eighteen when he'd been taken, or abducted, or whatever the hell happened to him.

Was it something about the age? Lori did some quick mental math.

Not just eighteen, eighteen and three months.

A chill scurried down her spine like a small, unwelcome animal with very sharp claws.

Lori wished for her husband—both his presence and his quick mind—but he'd gone hunting the previous day with Naia, the only female in their resident wolf pack. Winter wasn't far off, and they needed more meat to see them through the cold months.

Nikki and Kua, her other two wolves, ranged off to one side. They sensed Nellie's discomfort with them and were considerate enough to keep their distance from the mare.

"Are you certain you didn't hear anything?" she asked Nikki for the tenth time.

"Nothing. I would have told you if I did. Pack puppies are everyone's responsibility."

His reply held such injured dignity, she hastened to apologize. Lori understood how much he loved Amanda. The wolves came to live with them after Jon's disappearance, but Nikki was aware another of the pack's puppies had gone missing years before. He occasionally licked her chin, offering sympathy, but wolves apparently held a more pragmatic view of missing children than humans.

Still a pup himself at a little less than a year, Kua was immersed in his own world. Lori wondered if he even knew Amanda was gone.

The track steepened. They passed Gibbs Lake, and then negotiated a rough hillside. A jeep road once wound its way up here, but the miners abandoned it when they left the

Eastern Sierras in the nineteen thirties. Seriously eroded, it disappeared under deadfall in a lot of places.

Lori wanted to talk with Karras badly enough to risk the sketchy track on the flanks of Mount Gibbs. He lived in a rustic cabin a few miles from theirs. It would have been a trivial journey but for the two thousand feet of elevation gain.

What if he's not there?

Lori didn't know much about the old man—other than he was some sort of shaman or witch. She wasn't even sure why she thought he was particularly old. Gray streaked his hair, but his face remained relatively unlined. Like something out of *Lord of the Rings* with his flowing black robes and long hair and beard, he even used a staff carved with runes. When she asked him about it, he told her each symbol meant something in his native tongue.

He was the one who taught her to talk with the wolves. He offered her additional lessons in other arcane pursuits, but Lori wasn't interested. It still freaked her out to hold a conversation with Nikki. Never mind any of the other things Karras wanted to teach her. Like bringing fire or creating light out of thin air. When Naia and her pup, Kua, showed zero interest in communicating with her, Lori felt relieved, pure and simple.

One talking wolf was quite enough, thank you.

There hadn't been a rational explanation for Jon's disappearance. Amanda's held the same ghoulish feel. Lori swallowed hard. Despite her antipathy for paranormal phenomena, she needed Karras's magic. She'd suspend almost any belief she held about how the world worked if it would bring her daughter back. The thought no sooner crossed her mind than she knew she'd written off her son. He'd been gone far too long for her to still hold any hope.

Her hands froze into place around the reins. She uncurled one and stuck it under the opposite armpit to bring some sensation back. Then she did the same with the other.

Thank God I'm almost there.

She'd left a note for Rolf telling him where she'd gone. After considering exactly what to put in it, she'd been vague but left it in his shop where he'd be sure to find it. Rolf had a temper. She feared he might do something...ill-advised since he wasn't overly fond of Karras. For all Lori knew, Rolf might blame him for Amanda's disappearance. Made sense. After all, the three of them were the only ones for miles around.

Nellie was blowing hard when she stepped up the last steep part. Her back hooves slipped and slid as they crested the high plateau where Karras lived. Just a little farther and they'd be there. Travel was easier now over relatively level terrain. The Sierras were like that—steep parts interspersed with broad, high altitude meadows—until the crags just below the crest of the range.

Tugging at the reins to get Lori's attention, the mare angled her head toward a stream. Lori understood and gave the horse her head. She shouldn't drink too much on top of being lathered up, but a little wouldn't hurt. When Nellie didn't show any inclination to pull her snout out of the water, Lori slid off her back. She flipped the reins over the mare's head and strode toward Karras's cabin, using the reins as a lead rope.

After a bit of token resistance, the mare followed along.

"You can hunt, but stay close," Lori called to the wolves. A quick nuzzle from Nikki, then he and Kua took off, disappearing over a ridge.

Lori wasn't certain Karras could help find Amanda, but if not him, whom? He was their only neighbor. The only other person she'd seen since she and Rolf relocated to the Sierras. Maybe he could use the magic fairly oozing out of him, since her all-too-human efforts had failed miserably. Yelling hadn't located her daughter. Neither had hunting for her footprints. Lori wasn't bad at tracking, but there'd been nothing to follow.

She saw smoke before she saw the cabin and breathed a sigh of relief. Karras was there. He had to be. His cabin was close to timberline at ten thousand feet. Precious little wood grew so high, certainly none to waste heating an empty house. Quickening her pace, she trotted into the clearing around his homey log cabin and let go of her horse. Lori swarmed up the short flight of steps and knocked on the door.

No one answered, so she knocked again.

Snapping her jaws together in frustration—seasoned with a healthy dollop of fear—Lori glanced at the horse grazing in a patch of scrub grass. Night was falling, the sun already below the western horizon. Navigating the steep, rocky path on horseback would be impossible if she couldn't see. If Karras didn't show soon, she'd end up walking home in the dark. The horse would come along. She always did, with her built-in homing instinct for the barn and feed trough. As an afterthought, Lori retrieved the blanket and bridle, draping them over the porch railing.

She pulled the latch and let herself inside the cabin to wait. Smoky warmth surrounded her, and she reveled in it. How stupid to rush off without a hat or gloves—or a coat. It always got cold high in the mountains as the day faded. She was woefully underdressed.

Lori tossed a chunk of wood into the stove blazing in a corner and took in the small, neat space. The cabin was one room with a loft, which presumably held a bed. The downstairs included a kitchen with a pump and a sink. Racks and shelves of dried and drying food rose in evenly spaced layers all the way to the ceiling in the corner nearest the stove, exactly like they did at her house. A wooden table with two chairs sat in the middle of the cabin, and a well-creased, leather, easy chair was pushed under a window, its placement taking advantage of daylight to read.

Walls not dedicated to food were lined with overflowing bookshelves. Except the books included scrolls and other ancient-looking tomes. Lori thought about her e-reader and all the computer equipment she'd abandoned with the wreckage of her old life. Avid readers, she and Rolf brought plenty of books with them when they fled civilization. In the intervening years, they'd read each of them many times over, and wished they had more.

She'd just settled herself at the table when Karras's footsteps sounded on the stairs, and he strode into his home. "I saw your horse outside. What brings you here?" His bushy, gray brows drew together into a worried line. He was dressed in his usual black robes. Today he wore a wool hat against the cold, but his hands were bare.

Lori sprang toward him. "Amanda's missing," she blurted. "You have to help me find her. It's just like it was with Jon. One minute she was—"

"Stop right there." Karras held up a hand. "You say she's vanished. Just like your other child did."

Lori nodded. The tears she'd suppressed ever since losing her daughter threatened to spill over. Hot and bitter, they pricked her lids. Not trusting herself to speak, she looked imploringly at the shaman—or whatever he was. His dark, bottomless gaze met hers—and held it. When she tried to look away, she couldn't. Sudden panic eclipsed her sorrow.

Coming here was a mistake. I should have tried to find Rolf.

"Breathe," he suggested, his voice mild. "I wouldn't harm you. Surely you know as much by now."

Something shifted in the small room. It suddenly felt far too warm, and Lori looked down, studying the cabin's floorboards. "I wish you'd be more normal." She drew a shaky breath. "All this is bad enough, without me trying to figure you out."

He raised an eyebrow and twisted one corner of his mouth into a wry expression. "If I were *normal*, you wouldn't have come. I was gathering information. Sometimes the easiest way is to pluck it out of your mind. Saves quite a bit of time. I forget how finicky you humans are about such things."

Turning away, he moved toward a bookshelf and pulled a scroll out from under several others. Dust motes scattered. Lori, who'd followed close on his heels, sneezed. Karras blew on the parchment, and still more dust flew everywhere. "There." He rattled the vellum softly. "I suppose I ought to clean more, but it's quite a low priority."

He untied the faded, bluish ribbon securing the roll, and its sides sprang outward. For a moment, the thing looked alive. Startled, Lori took a step back.

Karras laughed. "It doesn't bite."

He pushed a couple books and a partially filled mug out of the way before settling the scroll front and center on the tabletop. He looked absent-mindedly at Lori and shook his head, almost like he was reminding himself of her presence. "Would you like to make us some tea?"

Curious about the scroll's contents, she edged closer. "Sure, but first—"

"You won't be able to read it."

Oh, stupid me. Of course not. Probably written in one of those runic languages.

"I do speak German, French, Italian, Russian, and Mandarin Chinese in addition to English." She bristled. As a medical researcher, her facility with languages had proven priceless. Many of the journal articles in other languages lost much of their nuanced meaning in translation.

"Yes, but you do not know *this* language," he said, his voice soft and patient. "Tea?"

Exasperated at being relegated to coffee, tea, or me status, Lori stomped to the stove. She picked up the kettle and filled it at the kitchen pump. That done, she looked about for tea leaves.

"Third canister on the right. The blue one," Karras said helpfully.

He hadn't even looked up from the scroll. How the hell had he known what she needed? Rolling her mental eyes, she tossed leaves into cups and added water once it got hot.

So worried about her daughter, she was about to jump out of her skin, Lori set a steaming mug in front of Karras. She opened her mouth, but he waved her to silence, marking his place on one of the lines of scribbling with a finger. It looked like Ancient Minoan, but Karras was correct —she couldn't read it. He wrapped a long-fingered hand about the mug and returned to reading.

She emptied her own cup without her remembering much about drinking its contents. Lori looked out a window and wasn't surprised to find it totally dark. Thinking she should check on her horse, she rose.

Before she got to the door, Karras murmured, "Your horse found her way into my barn. She's fine for now. You can let the wolves in if you'd like."

Lori turned to face him. "How much longer—"

His face held a disturbing, ancient expression. "I don't know. These things take as long as they take."

Lori pulled the cabin door open and whistled for Nikki and Kua. They came running, right along with Shyla— Karras's wolf and littermate to Kua. The three had been playing hard. Their eyes shone, and they crowded atop one another, taking up all the spare floor space. Where her two were black and silver with white bellies and amber eyes, Shyla was pure silver with a greenish cast to her gaze.

The young female wolf sidled up to Lori. *"Food?"* she inquired, her tongue lolling.

"For me." Lori looked hard at the young wolf. *"You can hunt."*

"If there's anything extra—"

"You'll be the first to know."

The interchange reminded Lori of when her children were young, and a sad, slow tide moved through her. She pushed past Kua and rummaged through the kitchen, looking for something to eat that wouldn't require cooking. Her stomach churned, sour from worry, but it would probably feel better if she put something into it. Karras's shelves held the same things hers did: goat cheese, bread—probably made from pine-nut flour—and dried fruit. She sliced a hunk of cheese and a piece of bread and put them on a plate with a handful of dried blackberries.

"Do you want some?" she asked over one shoulder.

"Whatever you're having." Karras's voice sounded distant, like he was a long way away, concentrating hard.

Time slid by, but it probably wasn't more than thirty minutes before Karras looked up. His face was screwed into a bitter expression as if he'd bitten into a piece of rotten fruit.

"What?" Lori's heart beat far too fast, and breath refused to fill her straining lungs.

He looked speculatively at her, but didn't say anything.

Out of her seat like a zephyr, Lori flew to his side and grabbed a handful of his robe. "Tell me," she demanded in a strangled voice.

"You must overcome your antipathy to your...other side," he said at last.

"What other side?" Her voice rose to a shriek, and she jerked on Karras's arm for emphasis.

"Stop!"

Something like an electric shock traveled up her fingers until the fine hair along her arms stood on end. She jumped back, her eyes wide and startled.

"Don't touch me unless I give you leave." Something almost menacing darkened Karras's tone. This was a side of the man—or whatever he was—she hadn't seen before. Fear intruded. She stalked to the door and grasped the latch, intent on flight before common sense intervened.

Reluctantly, she stood her ground and turned to face the old man. If Karras knew something, he had to tell her. Then she'd go.

"Okay." She worked to keep her voice from trembling. "Sorry."

"Better. I was referring to the side of you that talks to animals—though why you chose to stop with the wolves is beyond me. You hold power within you. You should have been nurturing your magic since childhood. I fear you have a very long way to go."

"You're mistaken. You have to be. I'm not magical. Not at all. No way," Lori muttered. Rattled by his attitude that seemed to expect instant compliance, she switched gears. The topic of supernatural anything spooked her. "Where's Amanda?"

"I'm not mistaken about you, and I'm not certain where your daughter is. Those who took her did so because she has your abilities. Your son is probably in the same place."

"They're together?" Lori was incredulous. "How could you possibly know? I figured Jon was dead."

"I don't really know anything," Karras admitted. "'Tis

more conjecture on my part than absolute truth. Yet, 'tis likely, particularly given they were both taken at the same point in their lives."

Lori paced the length of the small room, zigzagging to avoid the wolves. "Not that I'm considering it, mind you, but why does me learning about magic have any bearing on finding Amanda?"

Inhaling deeply, Karras blew out an exasperated-sounding breath. "You know so little, 'tis difficult to know where to begin explaining things. Blood links are the strongest. Because of those ties, you have a much better chance of locating Amanda than anyone—other than that husband of yours." Karras hesitated. "He is her father, is he not?"

Lori colored. "Of course he is," she sputtered. "What do you take me for?"

Karras waved a dismissive hand. "Get off your high horse. I could have snagged the information out of your mind as easily as asking. If I recall, you didn't like that approach overmuch before."

Lori balled her hands into fists at her sides. "Why'd you ask about Rolf?"

"Because," Karras replied, impatience coloring his tone, "I'm still trying to figure out why the Infernals wanted your children."

His words slammed into her like a kick in the guts. Lori fell back into her chair. "Infernals? Who—or what—are they?"

A crack of lightning split the night sky. Thunder

followed, shaking the cabin. Hail spattered on the metal roof, making an incredible racket.

Karras raised a curious eyebrow, got to his feet, and went to peer out a window. "Odd," he murmured. "The sky was clear— Oh, I think I understand." A shrewd expression played over his sharply-hewn features.

"Well, I don't." Annoyance ate at her like acid. Karras was talking in riddles.

"Your husband is coming."

Springing from her chair again, Lori pulled the cabin door open. Wind swooshed into the room like a live thing. An accommodating flash of lightning illuminated an empty yard. "No, he's not." She slammed the door and spun to face Karras. "Besides, what the hell would Rolf have to do with a thunderstorm?"

The wizard shook his head. "You're so literal. What I meant is he's on his way. He should be here quite soon. In the meantime, sit back down, and I'll try to answer at least one of your questions."

"If Rolf's on his way, I should go meet him."

And smooth his ruffled feathers. He'll blow in here like a latter day avenging angel.

"Sit down," Karras thundered. "Next time I won't ask. You'll just find yourself in a chair, and you won't care for how it happened."

Lori drew her lips back into a snarl. "You wouldn't."

"Try me." His tone was mild, but something behind it got her attention.

To calm her rampaging nerves, Lori plucked the kettle simmering on the back of the stove and poured more hot water over her tea leaves. How could a lightning storm alert Karras that Rolf was on his way? It didn't make any sense. Battling burgeoning resentment, she glanced sidelong at Karras, but he took his time replenishing his own tea. Pacing wasn't helping, so she perched on the edge of a chair, balancing the cup between her hands.

"Ready?" He settled in his chair and nodded to himself before taking a draught from his cup.

"Probably not, but don't let that stop you." Lori sounded surly, but didn't waste energy modulating her tone.

Karras ignored her last statement and began talking, except he didn't look at her.

"Infernals encompass many entities, some human, some not. They are the evil and wickedness in the world. We," he spread his hands wide, "have fought against them for millennia. 'Tis a battle I fear we cannot win. Yet we can't give up, either. It's a bit like the myth with Sisyphus and the rock. There was a time—"

Karras was still talking half an hour later when all three wolves barked. An answering howl came from without. Looking at the door, Karras smiled just before it flew open. A very bedraggled Rolf stood in the doorway, scowling. At well over six feet, he had to duck to enter the cabin. His leather riding pants shone with water. Lace-up boots squelched when he walked. His worn sheepskin jacket was tossed over an equally threadbare flannel shirt. Both dripped rain. Long, blond hair was plastered against his head. Fury sparked from his ice-blue eyes. The ends of reins dangled from one hand. Rolf shook himself like a dog might, and water droplets flew everywhere.

"Are you planning on bringing your horse in here?" Karras got to his feet. He strode toward Rolf, a hand extended in greeting.

"Don't know what I'm planning," Rolf snapped, taking the wizard's proffered hand with the same distaste he might use to handle a snake. He dropped it almost as soon as he made contact.

"Your horse?" Karras asked again, quirking a brow.

"Need to put Noah in your barn. It's a miracle he didn't break a leg getting up here in the dark."

A whinny from Noah seconded the opinion, followed by an outraged neigh as Naia squeezed past Rolf into the cabin. Water streamed off her coat, and the reek of wet wolf entered with her, thick and cloying. She made a beeline for the other three. They tipped their muzzles upward and howled, clearly delighted at being together.

"Stop it!" Lori shouted, her ears ringing. All four wolves broke off mid-song and stared at her with *what did we do?* expressions. Nikki took a step forward, growling softly.

Lori felt chagrined. *"Sorry,"* she told the wolves, *"I'm just tired and worried."*

Nikki herded his mate and their two pups against one wall. Soft whines and muted barks held a joyous undertone. Naia licked Shyla effusively, and Lori recognized a fellow mother.

Wonder what she'd do if any of her children disappeared?

"Noah's welcome in the barn." Karras pried the reins out of Rolf's hand and left the cabin. Lori heard him cluck to the horse in a language she didn't recognize.

Pushing the door shut, Rolf crossed the small space to

where she sat. He folded his arms over his chest. "What the hell?" he demanded. "I get home with an elk, and I had to leave it in the shop. If coyotes don't get in and eat it down to the bones, it'll be miserable to butcher since I couldn't get to it right away."

"Amanda's gone." She rose, locking her gaze on her husband's. "I didn't want to put it in the note—"

"What? No, she's not." Rolf took a step backward. He looked at Lori as if she'd lost her mind. "She was making dinner when I got home. Offered to work on the elk, but she's never dressed out anything that big. I needed help, and you're up here. You knew I'd be back sometime today—"

Relief so poignant it almost sickened her raced along Lori's nerve endings. Amanda wasn't gone. She was fine. Her beloved daughter was just a few miles down canyon.

How could she be? I looked and called for over an hour before I went to get Nellie.

"Jesus fucking Christ," Lori muttered. "Am I going crazy? Developing Alzheimer's?"

"You can figure it out later," Rolf growled. "We need to get home before the elk freezes." He took her arm and pulled her toward the door. It opened before they got to it.

Karras stood framed in the doorway, his wet robes clinging to him. "Not quite yet," the wizard said quietly. "Neither of you are leaving until we've had a chance to talk."

BATTLE WITH THE UNDEAD

*E*arlier *that day:*

Ned ran along an upward-sloping track. The previous day had been so uneventful, it was easy to let his guard down. He chided himself for sloppiness and resurrected his wards. A few minutes later, distracted by the wonders of autumn with no wizards to remind him of his deficiencies, he loosed his hold on them. Traveling unprotected—again—Ned reached a once-lush meadow. The grass was dying, but he could see how thick it had been.

Late season lupines dotted the gentle terrain. He stopped to pick one, feeling a bit foolish. A few more steps and he came to an abrupt halt. An empty paddock stood off to his right. Ned reached out with his mage senses and felt someone's presence from not too long ago. He wondered if it were the woman Landarik had sent him to find and then prayed it wasn't.

The flower fell from his hand, forgotten. He snapped his

wards back into place. He hadn't sensed anything but the lingering, hours-old presence of someone. Still, he needed to be more careful. Landarik and the regiment weren't here to bail him out if he made a stupid mistake. Gathering invisibility about himself, Ned faded into an aspen grove where fallen leaves had turned the canyon floor a rusty orange. He stretched his senses as far as he could, kicking himself for being nervous as an old woman.

Something pricked the edges of his projection, so faint he convinced himself he'd imagined it—until he sensed it again. The vague presence barely registered, but he recognized Infernal energy. It had a particular, scorched feel he'd know anywhere.

His heart beat faster. His mouth went dry. Ned considered his next moves, but he was so rattled it wasn't easy. If Infernals were near, they'd sense him as well. Whatever just stumbled into his information-gathering spell was probably spreading the word even now. For a panicked moment, he raised his arms to call a portal to escape into the Ways. Instead, he forced himself to breathe. Maybe nowhere remained to escape to.

He stared at the tattoos on his arms and felt ashamed. No wonder the wizards balked at him getting the markings. Were the things they'd said about him true? Was he nothing but a coward?

Ned drew himself tall, hoping a commanding posture might solidify his courage. Even if the wizards never knew about this, he'd face whatever was out there in a way to make them proud. He wove a protective spell about himself to strengthen his wards and was nearly done when he heard a faint scuffling, like animals trooping through the thick carpet of leaves. He paid out a thin stream of magic. No point in alerting the enemy with a large blast.

There it was again. The same touch of evil. Except now it felt a whole lot closer—and it was way more than a hint. Ned's eyes widened; bitter bile coated the back of his throat. Did they know about him? Were they coming to kill him? He poured more magic into the invisibility illusion, merging it into his ward. It wouldn't work as well against magical creatures, but he couldn't think of anything better. Shutting his eyes briefly, he sent a silent prayer to the goddess to protect him.

The rustling grew louder. Barely breathing, he sank into the shadow of a large tree and pried one nervous eye open. Ned stifled a gasp.

Two undead clutched an unconscious woman between them. She was utterly lovely, and very much alive, but she wouldn't be for long if those two got her to wherever they were going. Double-checking his initial impression, Ned took in skeletal fingers gripping the beautiful blonde maiden. The pair skimmed along a few inches above the ground, no doubt draining their captive's life energy to propel themselves forward. After a while, all the undead looked the same: insubstantial, with pasty complexions and long, stringy hair. They sucked essence from the living to maintain themselves. Ned hadn't seen one of them since leaving the Old Country. He didn't think they even existed here in America.

Ned could almost hear his old instructor back at the stronghold. *When Infernals co-opt humans to do their bidding, the partnership always sours. Once that happens, demons or goblins—whatever seduced the humans in the first place—turn them into an abomination. Neither living nor dead, they exist in a half-world dependent on pulling life energy out of others' souls. They could make do with animal energy, but far prefer to prey on other humans. Unlike vampires, they have absolutely no interest in blood...*

For a moment, he wished Master Blalock were here to review his facts. Ned refocused. He had to do something. No way would he allow demon spawn to waltz away with the most beautiful creature he'd ever seen—or anyone for that fact. Trying to remember everything his teacher in war craft taught him about this species of Infernal, Ned bit his lower lip. He needed wizard magic, but all he had was his own. It would have to do. He didn't know if he possessed enough energy to cast the spell of unmaking all by himself, but it was definitely the one needed to destroy the undead. It separated them from their putrid souls and forced them into the underworld where they belonged.

The meadow fell silent as the undead approached. Even the small chitterings of forest animals and birds ceased. They recognized the threat walking their lands and made themselves scarce. An idea formed in Ned's mind. If he could distract the pair, he'd stand a much better chance. Using his silent voice, he called out to marmots and hawks, outlining his problem.

"...I cannot promise no casualties," he explained. *"Yet, action is critical to rid your meadow of Infernals."*

Despite his nervousness, Ned grinned. He sounded just like Karras. Maybe all those years in the wizard stronghold had rubbed off on him after all. A rush of wing beats from the skies and rustling from the meadow told him his animal allies had heeded his call. No going back now. Determined not to waste their sacrifice, Ned raised his hands and began the chant to strip the undead of their power. The trio was quite close, so at least he didn't waste energy projecting his spell over distance.

A piercing, inhuman shriek split the air. Smoke spiraled from one of the undead. Ned ratcheted up his spell. He didn't have time to be elegant. He needed them to be well and truly dead. As in dead and not coming back—ever.

A pair of hawks tag-teamed the other abomination and pecked out its eyes. It dropped its hold on the girl about the time its fellow ghoul caught fire, blazing like a torch.

Ned worried about the girl getting burned, but couldn't divert his attention, not even for a moment. Another hawk, caught in the inferno, squawked pitifully. Ned said a quick prayer committing the bird to the goddess. Hundreds of fat marmots fell on the other undead with sharp teeth and claws, while crows and turkey vultures closed from above.

Ned drew an uneven breath. This was turning out better than he'd hoped. Magic nearly spent, he dropped the invisibility illusion. Leaving the cover of the aspen tree, he bolted to where the remaining ghoul lay on the ground. Fingers with some of the flesh eaten away were raised to protect its eye sockets from marauding birds.

It made a pathetic mewling noise. Apparently sensing Ned's presence, the thing moaned, "Let me go, human mage. I will cause no more trouble."

It's asking for mercy. What shall I do?

Ned started to tell the animals to release the thing, but had second thoughts. If he let it leave, it would just come back with reinforcements. For the first time, he regretted not paying closer attention to his lessons. Ned always depended on his commanding officers to make the hard choices. Now, he was all alone. Compassion battled with common sense. He came to a decision, set his teeth, and closed his ears to the thing's pleas.

Ned thanked the animals and told them scatter. He marshaled what was left of his fading energy and focused another spell. With the creature's "Nooooooo—" ringing in his ears, Ned consigned it to the circles of Hell. Lungs on fire, he panted with the effort it took to hold his casting, but if he left even so much as a scrap of the thing, it could resurrect itself.

Finally, nothing remained but cinders. Ned staggered with exhaustion, nearly going to his knees. His vision wavered. He was afraid he'd pass out and pitch face forward into the meadow grass.

Can't. What if there're more of them?

He forced himself to where the girl lay, relieved she appeared unharmed. Dropping to the ground next to her, Ned reached out with his magic, only to discover he'd run the well dry. It had happened before. He needed food and sleep before he'd be able to cast so much as a tinker's pattern. The marmots and birds streamed close. Their simple presence warmed him. He'd needed their help, and they'd given it unstintingly.

"Thank you," he called, waving his arms expansively. Then he bowed his head. "I am sorry for those who fell today. I think it was only one brave hawk, yet there may have been others."

"What's going on?" The fetching blonde creature rolled over and struggled to sit, managing on the second try. She had the bluest eyes Ned had ever seen.

"T-thank the goddess you're unharmed," Ned stammered. He'd thought her lovely before, but consciousness lent an ethereal splendor to the maid. That sort of beauty only existed among wizards. Acutely aware of his scruffy appearance, Ned stumbled to his feet and bowed low. "Er… I'm Ned Ameron. At your service." His face heated. He straightened, and his gaze met hers.

"Amanda Haraldssen." A formality in her tone matched his. She looked away and stroked a pair of fat marmots snuggled into her lap. Turning her head from side to side, she drew her brows together. "Wait. I know where I am." She pointed at the paddock. "It's our summer pasture for the horses. How'd I get here? Last I remember I was in the barn."

"You were kidnapped," he said. "By a pair of undead."

"Huh? Undead? What do you mean? This is real life, not some zombie movie."

"They're what are left when humans become servants of the Infernals."

"What? This isn't getting any clearer." Confusion marred her perfect features. "Who are Infernals? What do they want with me?"

Ned's head swam. Between her exquisite beauty and his depleted state, conversation felt quite beyond him. He pulled his rucksack off his back, got himself a drink, and rummaged for some of yesterday's apples. He bit into one, then remembered his manners and thrust the water skin and an apple her way. "Got to eat," he explained. "No more energy."

"No thanks." Amanda waved his offering away. "Home's not far, but it's all uphill." She pushed to her feet. "We have lots of food. Come with me."

"Are you sure?" Ned's voice cracked. "It's not necessary, really...uh...ma'am."

"Ma'am?" She laughed and rolled her eyes. "Call me Amanda. Please. I feel about a million years old when you say ma'am. Of course I'm sure. You saved my life. Or at least I think you did. Little enough for me to feed you. Besides," a corner of her perfect mouth twisted down, "walking will do me good. I feel...odd. Like I should be more scared, except I missed most of what happened."

Ned considered fleshing out the details of what had almost befallen her, but couldn't get the words out. She'd had a hell of a shock. Later, when she'd put some distance between her and her abductors might be a better time for *that* discussion.

"Coming?" She made a beckoning gesture with one hand.

Home. She's really inviting me home.

Ned pushed the Infernals from his mind—for now.

He could scarcely believe his good fortune. He trailed after Amanda, mesmerized by her swinging hips and firm stride. She was tall, of a height with him, and her hair hung past her waist. Her skin was deeply tanned, with freckles dotting a perfect nose and arching cheekbones. She wore breeches not unlike his own, which surprised him. Female wizards always wore robes, except on the battlefield where a few preferred leathers. A shapeless, sloppily knit sweater and battered leather boots split along one seam completed her attire. Any other woman would have looked frumpy, but Amanda could have passed for a princess.

Despite his weariness, Ned felt his body respond to the lissome creature a hand span ahead of him. Grateful she couldn't see him, he struggled with unfamiliar emotions and a stiffening cock. The wizards were incredible prudes about sex. Since they didn't mate until they were at least a hundred, wizard maidens paid scant interest to a youngster like him. Human girls' parents told them to stay away from magic. Between those two poles, Ned had barely held a conversation with a woman his age, let alone doing something like kissing.

Whoa ho ho. She invited me for a meal. Let's try to be polite and chivalrous here. She didn't invite me to her bed. Not that I'd know what to do if she did.

"Earth to Ned." She stopped and turned to glance back at him.

His head snapped up. "Uh, what?"

She laughed again. That wonderful sound had come close to being snuffed out forever. Ned shivered. Her uninhibited joyfulness, especially after what had nearly happened to her, told him how innocent she was. A fierce desire to protect her from all the evils in the world warmed his belly. For the first time, he understood how the knights he'd read about in history books must have felt.

"I've been trying to talk to you, but it's like you're not there. Come walk next to me."

"Sorry." Ned dragged himself out of his thoughts and caught up with her. "It took all my magic to banish the undead. I need food and rest to return to myself."

"Magic, huh?" She looked hard at him. "My mom has a friend who does magic. I think it's cool, but she doesn't like to talk about it. Says it makes her feel weird."

"It's, uh, pretty common where I come from." He hesitated, and then added, "My lady."

"My lady? What is this, the Middle Ages?" She laughed yet again.

It surprised Ned. Wizards were a fairly dour crew. He tried out a few responses, but they all sounded lame, stupid. What he'd said about being depleted was true enough, and just putting one foot ahead of the other took a ridiculous amount of concentration.

After they'd walked in silence for quite a while, she pointed and said, "See those buildings over there? It's my home. Mom made soup earlier, and I started some bread. Maybe she finished it. Let's hope so. I'm hungry too."

She lives with her mother.

Ned was startled by how elated he felt. Maids who lived with their parents were not yet wed. At least that was how things worked in the world he was familiar with.

"Who lives with you and your mother?" Ned tried to keep his tone casual.

"Just Mom and Dad and me. Leave your boots on the porch. Keeps the house cleaner." She veered toward the largest building and walked up a few steps to a broad area in front of the door that was partially shielded from the elements by an overhanging second story.

Amanda pulled the door latch and went inside. She called for her mother, but he didn't hear an answer, nor did he sense any other people nearby. Ned undid the laces and jockeyed his boots off before following her inside. The shining track of her energy drew him into an inner room. She'd placed a crock of something, which smelled wonderful, on a carved pine table and laid a place for him with a bowl and spoon.

"Strange Mom's not here," Amanda said and drew her well-arched brows together into a worried line. "Eat. I'm going to do a better job looking for her."

Ned didn't tell her he was almost certain no one else was there. For whatever reason, magic didn't appear to be second nature in this world. He cast a longing gaze at the food in front of him. It would be polite to hold off until she joined him, but hunger cramped his stomach—and she'd suggested that he go ahead and eat.

As he tucked into what tasted like venison and vegetable stew, Ned looked around. The cabin was large. He'd come through a front room lined with bookshelves on his way to a combination dining and kitchen area. A ladder off to one side suggested second story sleeping quarters. It made sense, since upper levels were generally warmer. Dried herbs hung from rafters, and apples and berries were spread across racks. The butter churn sat in a corner. A curtained alcove off the kitchen probably housed some sort of pantry.

Ned ate mechanically and emptied his bowl. He supported his head on one hand and worked hard to keep his eyes open, but his full stomach dragged him toward sleep. He helped himself to a little more stew. Chewing would help him stay awake.

"It really is odd. I can't find Mom anywhere." Amanda came through the curtained alcove, carrying another bowl and a pitcher. She plunked them down. "Be right back." Ned heard rattling. She handed him a glass then settled across the table from him. "Dad's not here either, but I didn't expect to find him. He's hunting." She poured amber liquid from the pitcher into his glass and her own. "I have no idea where Mom's got herself off to, but both horses are gone. Dad had Noah, and Nellie wasn't in the paddock next to where you found me."

"Would your mother have taken, ah...Nellie to go somewhere?" Ned was tired enough, remembering new names wasn't easy.

"Maybe." Amanda dished stew into her bowl. Even though she looked anxious, she shrugged. "Not much I can do about it. Mom always says there's no point in worrying. Besides, Dad should be back before sunset. He'll look for her if she's not back by then."

Something made Ned uncomfortable. "Does your mother often leave like this?"

Amanda shot him an odd look. "No. Why would you ask? You're not making me feel any better."

"Sorry."

This isn't my problem. I shouldn't interfere.

He tried to rein in the knight errant whose sole goal in life was to protect Amanda from harm. Ned took a drink. It tasted like weak ale. He drained his glass and held it out for a refill.

"Tell me about those things that almost got me. Is there some way to protect myself from them?" Amanda's hand flew to her mouth. "Oh, my God. Do you suppose they took Mother?"

She rose to her feet, but Ned motioned her back down. The same thing had occurred to him, but he did *not* want Amada racing about if wickedness were afoot. "Don't think so," he mumbled around a mouthful of stew. Swallowing hastily, he added, "I don't sense evil anywhere close."

She narrowed her eyes. "Even as tired as you are? Didn't you tell me you needed rest to recharge your ability?"

"Even as tired as I am." He laughed hollowly. "I couldn't do much about it if I did detect Infernals nearby, but I'd know they were there."

"How? Tell me."

She fixed him with those sea-blue eyes. It was all he could do not to leap across the table and crush her to him, forgetting everything he'd ever learned about hospitality and manners. His heart thumped against his ribs, and his breeches grew uncomfortably tight. He focused his gaze on his bowl. Maybe if he didn't look at her, it wouldn't be so hard to maintain his equanimity.

"Well?" she persisted. "Aren't you going to tell me how you know my mom's not in danger?"

"I-I'm not sure I can. Tell you, that is." Desperate to change the subject so he wouldn't be forced to try to explain how magic worked to a human—which was absolutely forbidden—he picked up his glass again. Plucking at the shards of his dwindling magic, he attempted a small diversionary spell. "How do you manage to brew this? It tastes like ale."

"It is. Mom uses some from each batch to start the next, so it's pretty weak." Amanda smiled at him.

If he'd been standing, his knees would have buckled. His errant cock jumped, and he wriggled, hoping to settle it into a more comfortable position.

"The ale is quite delicious. So was the stew..." His voice trailed off, Ned felt like a fool. The witty conversation he hoped would sweep the girl off her feet just wasn't there.

Why should it be? he asked himself bitterly. *It's not like I've had much of a chance to practice.*

Ned finished his ale. "Thank you, Amanda," he said stiffly, "for the refreshments. Now I must be on my way." He got to his feet and pivoted quickly so he faced the door. Maybe she wouldn't notice the tented out front of his leather breeches. Maybe. He didn't mean to disrespect her, but his body—particularly that part—wasn't amenable to orders from his brain.

"Oh, but you can't leave. Not yet." She was by his side, hand on his arm, so close he could barely breathe.

He focused a spell, willing her to look anywhere but down. "I-I have to. Got to be somewhere." The lie was patent. She'd almost have to hear the falsehood in his tone.

"I see." She stepped away from him, frowning. "Thank you for rescuing me." Her tone cooled a notch or two, but she still followed him onto the porch, hovering as he struggled to pull his boots on and lace them up.

Never one to pay much attention to his garments, Ned was acutely aware of all the holes in his socks. At least his erection was subsiding. He shouldered his pack and bowed slightly in her direction. "Thank you for the meal, Amanda Haraldssen. I shan't forget you."

The barest of smiles turned one corner of her mouth upward. "Nor I you." With her hair swirling around her like a golden cloud, she turned and went back into her house.

Ned made his way down the steps and across the yard. The missing mother was worrisome. He tried to pull enough magic to fan it around the house and outbuildings looking for Infernals. His spell went about ten feet before it bounced back at him. He blew out an irritated breath. Magic never cut anyone any slack. There was only so much. When it was expended, nothing brought it back but rest, food, and time.

He had to find a safe place to sleep, but he wanted to be close enough to Amanda to help, in case something else happened. "Who am I kidding?" he muttered under his breath. "I couldn't help a flea in my current condition."

Goats *baahed* as he passed the barn, and he heard a pig grunt. Spying the spreading branches of a black oak on the far side of a rushing creek, Ned struck out for it. He'd be close to Amanda, yet not so close his presence would be obvious. The tree would probably add her energy to his to shield him from enemies—if he asked nicely. It was as close to a perfect rest spot as he was likely to find on short notice.

Ned shinnied up the rough trunk and asked the tree for succor. As he'd hoped, she granted it readily. Word of his deeds had spread among the forest animals. Unlike the wizards who always found him wanting, the tree murmured endearments. She called him *brave* and *courageous* and *dear lad.* It was so unlike the way he was used to seeing himself, he thought he must have misheard.

Settling in one of the forks between the trunk and a substantial limb, Ned closed his eyes. The tree wrapped her branches about him so he wouldn't fall, and a warm glow filled his heart. How wonderful to be cared about. He could get used to it. His last conscious thought before sleep took him was to thank his tree guardian.

The tree's deep, rumbly voice crowded into his mind. *"Sleep, young mage. Thou hast earned thy rest."*

olf extended a hand to help Lori down the steep section just above Gibbs Lake. Karras followed right behind them, his mage light providing illumination. The sudden storm had blown itself out while they talked in the cabin, and Rolf's ill temper left along with it. With the help of Karras's light, it was easy to find the good trail leading from the lake down canyon toward their house.

"I shall leave you two here," Karras announced. He moved aside so the horses could walk past him. "It should be safe enough between here and your abode."

Lori batted back disappointment—and something deeper she didn't have a name for. She'd hoped Karras would accompany them home because she'd only scratched the barest surface with her questions. His answers unsettled her enough, she imagined bogeymen behind every tree.

"Never fear, Lori. I shall visit come the morrow. For tonight, there are things I must do."

"How'd you know what I was thinking?" Her voice shrilled, but today's weirdness quotient was already off the charts, and she couldn't modulate anything. Not her voice, nor her inner turmoil.

He didn't bother to answer, just turned and walked back the way they'd come. A muted rumble sounded right before both he and his light disappeared.

Shocked, thinking Karras needed help, Lori raced toward where she'd last seen him, raking the darkness for clues.

Rolf's shouts echoed in her ears. "Come back here. You won't do any good if you break your neck. It's damned dark without that light-thing of his."

Almost as if Rolf planted an unavoidable suggestion, she tripped on something and went sprawling. Lori grunted with pain and rubbed her shinbone. "Oomph! Damn but that smarts."

Rolf settled his hands on her shoulders and then hooked them under her arms. He lifted her to her feet. "Can you walk?" he inquired gruffly.

Lori weighted her foot. Her shin stung, but it was minor. "Uh-huh. What do you suppose happened to Karras?" She leaned into her husband. "You were right. It was stupid for me to take off after him, but I was worried."

Rolf closed his arms around her from behind and, for just a moment, he felt like the old Rolf. The kind, considerate man he'd been before they moved to the wilderness and their son vanished.

"You meant well." Rolf's deep voice sounded next to her ear. "But Karras is a magic man. It's why I'm not fond of him. Hard to trust what I don't understand. He must have used some sort of arcane trickery to return home. Which is what we ought to do—minus the magical display. Here. Let me help you onto Nellie."

As he boosted her onto the horse blanket, Lori recognized the depth of her exhaustion and confusion. What the hell had happened to Amanda? Everything Karras said earlier didn't make much sense. Except to scare her half to death. Lori prided herself on her analytical mind, but tonight it was only capable of running in circles.

The horses plodded single file, easily able to follow the well-delineated trail even in the dark, now that the steeper parts were behind them. Lori thought about what might have been a chink in the armor plating surrounding her husband when he helped her up out of the dirt. Something was desperately wrong between the two of them. She couldn't figure out what it was since she could never get him to talk about it. Every time she asked, he stonewalled her.

Maybe there's nothing left to salvage between us.

Another inner voice piped up and told her she had to keep trying. *Yeah, it's not like I can just divorce him and move to the next town.* The thought was so ludicrous she nearly laughed.

Her stomach tightened, and she prepared herself for one more rejection. "Rolf?"

"Yeah what?" He sounded tapped out too.

She almost stopped there, but this was so important she pressed forward despite her reservations. "What's happened to us?"

"Oh, Lori. For chrissakes not now."

"If not now, then when? We can't very well talk in front of

Amanda. She's worried enough about us as it is. I see it in her eyes."

Silence sat between them like a stubborn mule, ready to kick her in the ass. The muted clip-clop of horse hooves on packed earth sounded unnaturally loud. Sorrow filled her for the loss of their once wonderful partnership, full of love and passion, until she was beyond tears. She didn't understand what had happened to Rolf. He was a hollow shell of the man she met and married over twenty years before.

"I...I'm not sure I can explain it." His voice was low, strained.

Lori sucked in a startled breath. She'd been so certain this would be like every other time she tried to get through to him, she didn't know how to encourage him to open up to her.

Maybe I don't have to say anything...

"It started right after Jon disappeared." Rolf's normally rich baritone squeaked, like guitar strings left out in the weather. "This...thing started talking to me. She—yes, it's a woman—told me to do things. Crazy things like cloud seeding and repairing erosion..."

Minutes ticked by. At first, confusion roiled through her, and then puzzle pieces clicked into place. Rolf was an engineer with specialized training in geophysics and petrochemicals. Weather manipulation and erosion were right up his alley. It had to be more than mere coincidence he was being asked to do something he knew about. What he relayed was troublesome, but she pushed that part to a back burner, focusing instead on Rolf sitting straight as an arrow in his saddle. His blond hair hung nearly to the middle of his back in tangled clumps.

"It must have been unsettling," she said at last, trying to infuse as much warmth as she could into her voice, "to be asked to go back to familiar work by someone you couldn't see. It's like *Mission Impossible* with the tape that self-destructs. Did you worry you were losing your mind?"

"It's not a *did*." He barked a short, bitter laugh. "I still do. She hasn't gone away. She's in my dreams almost every night. I'm almost afraid to go to sleep. At the beginning, she only chided me. Now she shrieks like a Harpy. The worst of it is when I get angry, the weather turns." Once Rolf started talking, words spewed out one atop the other and ran together as if he were afraid he'd lose his courage if he slowed down.

"At first I told myself it was ridiculous. Just a fluke. You saw what happened tonight." He hesitated. "You heard the storm, anyway. Well, there wasn't any storm until I got home and read your note. I'm scared, Lori. Christ, I've never been so terrified in my life. I don't know what to do. I'm scarcely sleeping. Every day I feel worse." His voice broke. "Sometimes I wonder if I'm dying. What will happen to you and Mandy if I'm not here to do the heavy chores?"

Tears gathered at the corners of her eyes. Pain for her husband sluiced through her, but a thought—a longshot—niggled its way to the surface. "When I was up at Karras's, he noticed the storm and immediately linked it to you coming up the mountain toward us. I'll bet he knows what's going on."

"So what if he does?" Rolf's voice grated. "I need for it to go away. I don't know how much longer I can live like this. Someone wants something from me so badly they're willing to flay me alive to get it."

"Karras said he'll be here tomorrow. We'll ask him."

Please God, let him know something.

Lori reined in her horse. They weren't far from their cabin. "Get down," she suggested. "We can walk the rest of the way."

Rolf slid heavily to the ground. Lori put her arms around his comforting bulk. She rested her head on his shoulder. "Thank you."

"For what?" His voice was muffled in her hair.

"Trusting me enough to finally tell me what's going on."

"Didn't want to worry you." He hesitated. "We still don't understand anything about what's wrong with me. The only difference is now both of us know I'm possessed."

She laid a hand on either side of his face and met his gaze. A quarter moon lent enough light for her to see him clearly. "You are not possessed. That's an archaic concept coined by the Roman Catholic Church. I'm just grateful you told me. I...I thought you'd fallen out of love with me after all this time."

He pulled her to him roughly, his heart thudding beneath her ear. "Beloved, you're my life," he murmured. "I don't know what I'd do without you." He bent his head and closed his lips over hers. They clung together, drinking each other in.

She'd stopped keeping track, but it had to have been a year since they'd really hugged one another. The loneliness and desperation of being isolated from him receded, and

Lori swore to herself she'd do whatever she could to free Rolf from whatever wanted him.

Nellie nosed her in the back. Lori stumbled against Rolf and laughed. "Guess she's trying to tell us she wants her cozy barn. Come to think of it, I'm none too warm, either."

Rolf draped an arm around her shoulders and pushed her gently toward home. "Of course Nellie wants the barn. I'm so tired I'm dead on my feet, but the elk's waiting for us. Can't afford to let all that meat rot."

"I'll help you."

"Yes, my love. We'll help each other." He sounded so much like the Rolf she loved, it brought a fresh spate of tears for her to brush away. She twined an arm around his waist and squeezed hard, comforted by an answering pressure from his hand resting on her shoulder.

"I've wanted to tell you for a while now," he admitted sheepishly. "I kept thinking I could figure it out on my own. The longer it went, the harder it got to find words." He brushed her ear with his lips. "I've missed *us*. Even though I've buried myself in work twenty hours a day, there's been this empty spot..."

Joy, bright as a Sierra sunrise, filled her to bursting. "I love you," she murmured. "You just made a pretty long speech for an engineer."

He laughed and pulled her close again. Somewhere in the middle of their kiss, both horses broke and made a dash for home.

They covered the remaining quarter mile in silence, but she found the walk companionable, not strained like before. Noah and Nellie stood patiently huddled next to the barn door. "I'll put them in their stalls," Rolf said. "How about if you make us some of your special tea. It's going to be a long night."

"You got it." Lori headed for the house. She sent her finely honed senses outward in search of her daughter.

Yes!

Amanda's energy pulsed from inside, just like Rolf said, and Lori blew out an anxious breath. Thank God, her daughter was safe, asleep in the house. What the hell had happened earlier today? Why hadn't she been able to find her?

I don't want to wake her. My questions can wait until morning.

She let herself in the back door. After a transit of the pantry, she pumped water into the kettle and set it on the woodstove. Chucking a couple of good-sized pieces of wood on top of the bed of coals, she opened the damper and held her frozen hands to the warmth.

Lori reached into a canister and grabbed the leaves and stems of a plant with stimulant properties. She dropped them into two mugs, along with a dollop of honey collected from their bees. She grinned wryly, wishing she owned a better book about native Sierra plants. Virtually all her learning had happened through trial and error.

The front door opened and swooshed shut. Lori hurried down the short hall to the living room, anxiety gnawing at her. As unsettling as the day had been, everything spooked her. She wrapped her arms around Rolf, relieved it was him and not some unnamed horror entering her house. "Just wanted to make sure it was you."

"Who the hell else would it be?" He sounded exhausted.

"I thought you guys would never get home."

Lori spun and stared at her daughter, who lay swathed in a down comforter on one of the sofas with an open book across her stomach. Amanda gazed back, her eyes heavy with sleep.

"Why aren't you in bed?" Lori asked.

Amanda flung the comforter aside and launched herself first at Lori, then at Rolf, giving each a huge hug and kiss. "Geez, I'm so glad you're home. Maybe it's safe to really go to sleep now."

"Looks like you were already asleep." Lori smiled fondly at her daughter. "Otherwise you would have heard me in the kitchen. I wasn't trying to be terribly quiet since I figured you were upstairs." Her daughter's words sank in, and Lori frowned. "What do you mean? Why wouldn't it be safe to sleep?"

"Oh, that's right." Amanda nodded fuzzily. Her hair eddied about her like sheaves of summer wheat. "You don't know. I had the creepiest experience today. Would have told Dad, but he was pretty spun out when he got home and you weren't here. He got worse after he found that note you left him." A small, uncomfortable laugh burbled out. "Wish I'd found it, I was worried when I couldn't track you down, either."

"What kind of creepy experience?" Lori's stomach tightened, and she eyed her daughter. Waves of apprehension hammered her.

"I had some problems, but a really nice man rescued me."

Rolf had been headed for the kitchen, probably to get his tea, but Amanda's last sentence stopped him dead in his tracks. Spinning to face his daughter, he bellowed, "What man?"

"Calm down, Daddy. It wasn't a man, not really. More like a guy my age. Anyway, he helped me. I wanted him to stay to meet you, but he said he couldn't." Amanda stopped talking to take a breath. "I tried to tell you about him earlier. You know, when you came home with the elk, but you were just so angry 'cause Mom wasn't here—"

Lori held up a hand. "Stop right there. I'm going to get tea for your father and me. How about some of the wild mint for you?" At Amanda's nod, Lori went on. "You can come out to the shop and tell us what happened while we work on the goddamned elk."

"I'm tired," Amanda protested, trailing after her mother toward the kitchen. "Can't I tell you about it tomorrow?"

"Put on some clothes and come outside," Rolf snapped, irritation and worry sharpening his voice. For a moment, two sets of eerily similar blue eyes sparred with one another. "I want to know what happened. Your mother was convinced you'd vanished—just like Jon."

"I think maybe I would have if it hadn't been for Ned."

"Really." Rolf's tone could have etched glass. "Prince Galahad has a name?"

Amanda rolled her eyes. "Fine. I'll go upstairs and get some clothes." She turned to climb the ladder to the loft where they all slept. "Have it your way about dragging me out in the freezing cold," she called down. "You always do."

Lori heard her muttering imprecations. The lid of the antique trunk that held her clothing slammed against a wall.

Tea in hand, Rolf went to the bottom of the ladder and shouted, "None of that. It's been a hard day for everyone. The world doesn't revolve around—"

Lori grabbed his arm and made a chopping motion with her free hand. He pulled away and stomped out of the house, cursing. Lori drank some of her tea and exhaled wearily. She tied a tattered dishtowel around her hair so it wouldn't trail through elk blood and guts. By the time she got to the shed, Rolf had donned the old leather apron he used for butchering animals and started dismembering the carcass with a long-bladed saw. Three large candles provided light. When she saw he'd picked the big pillar ones, she groaned. Those were the hardest to make since most of her molds had broken, crushed by a snow avalanche years before.

"Damn if it didn't freeze," he muttered. "Just like I thought it would. Best to quarter it. Then we can get the hide off. Afterward we can probably quit for tonight. Good thing I gutted it back where I killed it. Might not have if I'd been closer to the house. Pigs really like the entrails."

"So do the wolves." Lori went to work on a part of the elk Rolf had hoisted onto a table, skinning knife in hand. "Speaking of which, what do you suppose happened to them? I haven't seen them since we left Karras's."

"They'll be round once they smell blood. Shit!" He jumped back.

"Did you hurt yourself?" Lori reached his side in an

instant. It'd be easy enough to lose a finger if the saw slipped.

"Nope. I'm okay. Got my hand out of the way in time." Rolf bent to his work again.

Lori chose her next words with care. "Because we left civilization, you never had to go through watching your little girl grow up and date."

"So?"

She smiled to herself. "Back inside, you were pretty upset about Mandy being rescued by a young man."

"Why should I like anything about it? We don't know him." The grating sound of saw against bone filled the small space. Candlelight flickered on the rough-hewn walls, casting everything in an eerie glow.

"If he'd had disreputable intentions, he wouldn't have left—" she began.

"For chrissakes," he thundered. "You don't understand how these things work. He's trying to get her to trust him so next time, or the time after, he can... Well..." Color stained his bearded cheeks.

"You don't know. Not for sure. Just because we spent the first couple of months after we met in your bed, it doesn't mean this Ned wants to—"

"Really?" Amanda, who'd come in unnoticed, sounded fascinated. "You two had sex before you got married? I'll be damned. Here Jon and I thought the only time you got together was when you conceived us."

Rolf cleared his throat. "Watch your language. That's neither here nor there, young lady."

"Your father's right," Lori chimed in, eager to change the

subject. "Have a seat and tell us about today. When I couldn't find you, I was worried half out of my mind."

"I'm not exactly sure I know how it happened," Amanda said, sounding thoughtful as she settled onto a three-legged stool. "One minute I was in the barn and the next I was in the meadow down by the paddock. I'm sure there was much more to it," she added. "I was unconscious. These...things. They abducted me."

"What things?" Rolf laid his saw down and stared at his daughter. Candlelight illuminated deep lines etched into his forehead.

"Ned called them the undead. Said they were what was left when evil was done with humans. Or something like that."

"Like vampires or zombies?" The skinning knife slipped in Lori's suddenly slick palm, and when she glanced at her hand, it was shaking.

"I don't think so. No one bit me or tried to eat my brains, anyway." A nervous giggle escaped Amanda, revealing how rattled she was.

"What happened then?" Rolf strode toward his daughter. She backed away. "Eeeew, you've got blood all over you."

"So I do. Sorry." He retreated to the workbench, his gaze never leaving her. "Talk."

Amanda cleared her throat. "Okay. Once I regained consciousness, the things—undead—were on fire. One of them, anyway. Ned did something, and the other one burned up too. They just sort of folded in on themselves and vanished, all except for a few cinders. There were a bunch of animals. Marmots and birds. It sounds crazy, but I think they helped somehow." She shrugged uncomfortably. "Ned said he'd run through all his magic and needed food and rest, so I invited him here. He left after I fed him."

Amanda looked away. "I really wanted him to stay. Neither of you were here, and I was scared."

"Of course you were." Lori wanted to scoop her daughter up and hold her, but she had almost as much muck on her as Rolf.

"Is there more you can tell us about any of it—or him?" Rolf asked, still looking like he wanted to kill something.

"No, not really. I didn't wake up until I was in the empty paddock. Ned wasn't here very long, but he talked like someone who lived in a much earlier time. Very formal. Can I go back to the house now? I'm cold."

"Sure," Lori said. "We won't be too much longer. Call the wolves. It would be good to keep at least one of them inside tonight."

Their daughter nodded and turned to leave. "Ned was really nice," she said, pulling the latch to open the door. A blast of wind-driven, chilly air raced through the shop and made the candles gutter. Amanda's piercing whistle to summon the wolves was cut short as the shop door banged shut.

Rolf thudded a fist down on his wooden bench, rattling everything that wasn't tacked down. Blue fire blazed from his eyes.

"Yes?" Lori looked at him, her teeth clenched together. She felt like growling but pried her jaws apart long enough to say, "I feel exactly the same way. Furious. You could toss terrified and helpless into the mix too. What exactly are the undead? Why'd they target our daughter? Are they the same ones who took Jon? Do you think they still have him?"

"While we're at it," Rolf muttered. "What does this Ned person have to do with anything? For all we know, he could be in cahoots with whoever took both our kids."

Lori inhaled raggedly, sucking air through her teeth. "I don't get it. I covered the ground between the house and the paddock to get Nellie. If those things took Amanda there, why wouldn't I have run into them?"

"You're asking me?" Rolf shot an incredulous look her way. "This magic mumbo-jumbo crap is just so much shit as far as I'm concerned." He paused a beat. "Maybe they have ways of remaining invisible—if they don't want to be seen."

Conversation grew sparse as they stewed in their own thoughts. Finally, Lori looked up from an elk haunch. "I'm about done." Rolf grunted something incomprehensible, and she laid her knife down and went over to him. "I'm going to take a quick soak in the spring. Want to join me?"

He raised his gaze to meet hers. His eyes held a haunted edge, and her heart ached for him. He managed to gin up a weak smile. "Sure, Lor. It's a better idea than what I planned."

"Which was?"

"A cold sponge bath at the pump."

"I'll see you there." She tried to smile but was too tired and worried to pull it off.

Lori rinsed blood and elk slime off her hands at the pump just inside their back door. Grabbing a threadbare towel, she walked the hundred yards to a natural hot spring behind their house. She'd just shucked her clothes and climbed in, sighing as hot water closed over her, when rustling in the trees made her heart do flip-flops. The acrid taste of fear flooded her mouth, and she gathered her tired muscles for a leap from the pool and a sprint toward the house.

Should have brought one of the guns.

Kua and Naia sauntered out of a grove of Jeffrey pines dragging something between them. Lori peered at the thing. It looked like a fawn.

"You scared the shit out of me," she screeched and sank back into the pool. Oblivious, both wolves ignored her. They haggled over their kill, snarling and snapping.

Rolf's firm tread sounded on the well-worn path. Faced with the squabbling wolves, he cuffed Kua. The young wolf let go of the fawn to move out of Rolf's way. Ever the opportunist, Naia dragged the carcass away. Kua's disgruntled howl filled the night. He bared his teeth at Rolf and snarled.

"Knock it off," Rolf said. "Go find your own kill."

"Maybe it *was* his," Lori said.

"Then he shouldn't have let go of it." Rolf undressed, tossing his clothing in an untidy heap on the ground, and stepped into the spring. "Ahhhh," he groaned. "Feels heavenly."

He leaned toward her. Lori smelled sweat and the musky scent unique to Rolf. She kissed him before settling back against the edge of the tub. "Have you had a chance to think about...? Well, about any of it? You? Amanda? Jon?"

"Uh-huh, but I don't want to talk about it right now. If I

can shut my brain off, maybe tonight I'll actually be able to get some sleep."

The moon had moved far down in the sky, but it still shed enough light for her to see him. A slow, lazy smile lit his tired features. He reached for her. "Come here, wench. It's been a long time."

Heat that had nothing to do with the hot spring raced through her body, and her belly clenched with deep hunger. She melted into his arms. "Yes," she murmured, nuzzling his neck. "Too long."

When he sought her mouth with his, she threw her arms around him, kneading slabs of muscle running along his broad shoulders and down his back. He teased her mouth with his tongue, and her nipples hardened. A sweet ache tightened her belly and tingled between her legs. Love with Rolf had always been urgent, immediate, with the two of them so desperate for one another, nothing got in the way. Not the inconvenience of being in a public place. Not children. Not jobs. It was why his withdrawal from her on both emotional and physical levels had been so inexplicable and so hard to take.

Without breaking their kiss, he spanned her waist with his hands and turned her so she straddled him. When she felt the tip of his cock pressing at the opening to her body, she stopped thinking and gave herself up to sensation and the pure, unbridled joy of her husband's body joined to hers.

OF MAGERY AND MAGIC

Karras knelt in his garden with his mage light hovering off to one side. He'd tried to focus on his scrolls after leaving the woman and her mate by the shores of Gibbs Lake, but was too distracted to concentrate on the arcane symbology. He'd known the woman had wizard blood for years, but he'd only come to recognize something unusual about her husband in recent months. Tonight wasn't the first time he'd searched his library for information. As before, though, luck eluded him. It was almost like something—or someone—didn't want him to discover anything about Rolf.

Lori had been on the edge of asking about her husband —and more than once—through the latter part of the afternoon and evening. He'd subverted her, but she wasn't easy to fool. He wondered how she could possibly have a wizard parent and not know it. Clamping his jaws together, his thoughts flowed in a different direction. He tried to figure out which wizard had dumped Lori after her birth.

He'd just pulled what remained of the season's crop of carrots, laying them in a careful pile, when he felt unmistakable energy, and his eyes snapped open. "Ned," he gasped aloud. "Ned's somewhere, and he's damned close."

Karras stared into the distance, the carrots—and Lori—forgotten. He got to his feet and strode toward a nearby cistern. The wizard raised his arms to begin a casting, but dropped them, creasing his forehead in thought.

He considered the possibility that the Ned sending was a trap, cunningly laid by Infernals to snare him. Even if Infernals weren't out to trap him, once he opened communication with his home stronghold, he'd be giving away his location. He hadn't planned to spend so many years away from his kin. Finding Lori changed things. Over time, the wards he'd woven to mask his presence from his own kind became more-or-less permanent. Once the other wizards knew where he was, they'd demand his return. Something they had every right to do.

The sense he'd gotten of Ned's energy came again, stronger this time. "Goddess blast it." Karras spat on the ground. Resolutely, he raised his arms and began to chant. Minutes passed. He peered into the water, but it remained stubbornly water-like.

"What in the nine hells?" he cursed, changing the tone and timbre of the words in his spell. Finally, from the depths of the cistern, the likeness of another wizard, blond with deep green eyes took form.

"*Who summons me?*" Liefes, one of the three comprising

the wizards' High Council, spoke into Karras's mind. *"Oh, never mind, Karras. I know 'tis thee. Thy spells always were misshapen. Why hast thou called me? It must be important, for now I know where thou art."* Low, rumbling laughter came through the link.

"Where is the human mage? Last I knew he was fighting in Landarik's unit."

Liefes snorted. *"Thou wast always partial to that pathetic scrap of humanity. Hast thou reason to believe he deserted?"*

"No. Well, mayhap yes, since I believe he is close to me, and I am far from the fighting."

Liefes took his time before answering. *"'Tis possible. Our fortifications near the battle were breached. Yet I have much worse news. The ten dark gods who rule the Infernals have come again to our world. 'Tis long past time for thee to return to thy home stronghold. We may well need every wizard afore too much more time has passed."*

"The war?"

"In spite of everything, we appear to be about even. No new strongholds have been destroyed. They did breach the caves near the fighting where thy human mage was, though."

"Mmph... I shall remain here long enough to determine if my acolyte is near. There is the woman too."

"What woman?"

"She's the reason I stayed gone so long."

"Goddess's teeth, Karras, we are thy kin. We need thee. Humans made this mess. Leave them to pick up the pieces."

Karras took a deep breath. *Should I?* Letting it out, he cleared his throat. *"The woman is one of us."*

"Scarcely possible. Surely, thou art mistaken."

"Her blood isn't pure. Yet I suspect she's at least half. Others have noticed her. Her daughter was abducted today, yet miraculously returned. I plan to untangle the conundrum on the morrow. Infernals took her son years ago."

"Oh ho! She must be the one Landarik spoke of. 'Tis coming to me now. He deployed yon human mage to find her. Do you require reinforcements?" Liefes sounded worried, the question of Lori's lineage laid aside—but not for long. *"Hast thou determined whose spawn she is?"* he added slyly.

We'd all like to know, wouldn't we?

But Karras kept that thought to himself. The wizard in question would be severely chastised for breeding outside his—or, possibly her—race.

"Not yet on both counts. No reinforcements or information. Thank you, Liefes. I release you from my...misshapen spell."

Karras lowered his hands and walked back to the pile of carrots. Stooping, he gathered them into a ragged armload and turned toward his cabin. He pursed his lips together as he considered what to do next.

ONCE HE'D SLEPT for a couple hours, Ned tossed and turned in his makeshift bed in the tree. The bark was prickly, even through his clothes, but the odd twig poking him wasn't what kept him awake.

The woman he'd rescued earlier sat front and center in his thoughts and wouldn't let him be.

Now that he wasn't scared to death of the undead and had gotten some rest, something about her—beyond her obvious beauty—nagged at him. His eyes flew open in sudden understanding. She was part wizard. She had to be. It explained the energy he felt pouring off her. Despite her mixed blood, she was innocent, and he'd bet any amount of coinage she didn't realize she was anything besides purely human. Warmth filled him as he thought about how kind she'd been. She'd done far more for him than wizards would have done for a stranger who stumbled across one of their compounds.

Ned dragged his cloak out of his pack. He pushed branches aside to spread it between his body and the tree, draping an edge over himself to stay warm. He'd botched anything even approximating credible conversation with Amanda. Between his exhaustion and her loveliness, he'd been tongue-tied. Yet, she really had wanted him to stay. Go figure.

He wondered about her parents. Her mother was probably the one Landarik had sent him after. After all, there couldn't be very many humans with power in this remote location, which meant he'd have to go back to the house. A smile tugged at his lips, but it rapidly turned to a frown. Why did Landarik want the mother and not the daughter? What about the mother's mate? How did it happen he'd gotten tangled up with a wizard? Even beyond those questions, what was a wizard doing all the way out here? They lived exclusively in their strongholds.

Except for Karras. Who knew where he was these days?

Biting his lower lip in consternation, Ned dug deep in his pack and pulled out the well-thumbed spell book he always kept with him. Wizards didn't need such props, at least not often, but he did. He'd read himself to sleep more than once with the ancient tome, and it was a good idea tonight. He searched for a likely topic to induce drowsiness and thought about Amanda again.

Since she was only part wizard, the other part had to be human. What was it about human-wizard pairings? Or wizard-anything pairings? His forehead scrunched in apprehension, Ned riffled through the book's pages. He found what he sought soon enough and narrowed his eyes, reading quickly.

Lost children.

They were so rare, he'd almost forgotten about them. Amanda—or more likely her mother—had to be one of the wizards' lost children, ostracized from any stronghold and slated for murder once they got old, before their extraordinarily long lives could draw undue attention.

He sighed heavily. Wizards were incredible prudes. They lived so long, they'd developed strict prohibitions regarding the numbers of children they could produce. In fact, they used a lottery system. Not every wizard couple could even have children because if all of them did, the strongholds would be overrun in less than a generation.

Ned snorted. Wizard generations lasted two thousand years. Pairings with other species were strictly forbidden. Wizards who gave birth to racially mixed children were banned from the strongholds, right along with their lost children, and tasked with the eventual destruction of the child.

He thought back to his brief interaction with Amanda. Ned was practically certain she had no idea one of her parents was a wizard. She'd been raised by humans and saw herself as human. End of story. If she even noticed her magic, she probably came up with some perfectly rational explanation for her enhanced abilities. She *had* mentioned her mother being uncomfortable with a friend's magical ability, which also argued against her knowing anything about her own aptitude.

Ned's head spun crazily. He forced his gaze upward from the *Book of Spells,* placed a ward about himself, and cast a calming spell. Sleep caught him as he tried to choreograph what the morning would bring.

"Ned... Ned..."

"What?" Ned sputtered, shaking cobwebs from his drowsy brain.

"I'm not that close. Use mind speech," the wizard said dryly.

"Karras?" Ned's heart swelled. He missed his old mentor. If Karras were able to use mind speech, it meant he couldn't be more than five miles away.

"Who else would it be? Are you awake enough to listen?"

"Yes." He struggled to a sitting position and banged his head on his ward in the process. *"Damn!"* he swore softly and withdrew the magic holding it in place.

"Are you all right? What happened?" Karras sounded anxious.

"I'm fine. Where are you? You must be somewhere close by." Ned spoke brusquely. He did *not* want to tell Karras about

making a neophyte's mistake and colliding with his own ward.

"Yes, I'm close. Stay put, and I'll find you tomorrow." After a hesitation, the wizard asked, *"Do you still have the book I gave you?"*

Reaching over, Ned patted where it was balanced between his body and a tree limb. *"Of course."*

"Be especially careful with it. I've kicked myself for years for leaving the stronghold without one."

"Karras?" Ned waited, but the wizard was apparently done talking to him.

The abrupt dismissal made him feel sad and slighted, somehow. Maybe Karras hadn't been as fond of him as he'd always thought. After all, the wizard left him behind without a second thought. Maybe Karras found out about Landarik's assignment. Any wizard worth his tattoos would have found the woman by now—and figured out what to do with her.

Wizards kept track of the approximate whereabouts of one another. Someone might have raised Karras to ask if he knew where his wandering acolyte was. Ned burrowed back into the nest made of tree branches and his cloak, thinking how odd this journey was becoming. Though he was still weary, sleep took its time coming.

A RED-TAILED HAWK chittered in his face, awakening him to a still, cold morning drenched in sunlight. He found some crumbs in a pocket for the hawk, pushed himself to a sitting position, and reached for his magic. He hadn't had a particularly restful night. Had he gotten enough of a respite to recharge?

When the answer came, relief pummeled him. His stores weren't quite fully replenished, but he had ample magic to face most anything. He untangled his limbs from the tree. Gathering his things, he clambered down. Before leaving, he laid his forehead against the gnarled trunk and thanked the tree's spirit for watching over him.

He had to go back to Amanda's to check out her mother. It was his assignment. At least until he found the woman had no magic. He didn't see how that could possibly be, given her daughter, though.

He could smell himself, sour and rancid from fear sweat, when he stuffed things into his rucksack. He finger-combed the hair he hadn't bothered to re-braid, pulling out twigs tangled in it. Even though it felt like he was stalling, staving off the inevitable, he should clean up before facing Amanda again.

The stream formed a small pool not far from the tree. Ned made good use of it once he'd warmed the icy water to body temperature. He washed his shirt, the smelliest item, and used magic to encourage it to dry. He considered braiding his hair, had even started on it, when the impossibility of the task without so much as a mirror stymied him. He settled for using his leather headband to tie his thick locks into a horse's tail.

Ned got back into his almost dry clothes and was flat out of tasks. Nothing for it but to cross the creek and go back to Amanda's. He wanted to see her so much, a hard knot formed somewhere north of his stomach. Maybe she didn't care one way or the other, but he couldn't stand it if all she felt for him was gratitude—or worse, pity.

He bent to retrieve his rucksack, felt foreign energy rise out of nowhere, and froze. Pack forgotten, he twirled to face whatever was headed for him. Hands raised, he readied himself to pull fire from the earth to defend himself. A tall, powerfully-built blond man strode toward him, fists balled at his sides and color high on his face.

"Who in the hell are you?" the man bellowed.

Must be the father.

Every instinct told Ned to maintain his defensive posture, but he forced himself to drop his hands. "My name is Ned Ameron. I think I may have met your daughter yesterday." Ned quested outward with magic. The man was definitely not the source of Amanda's wizard blood, but something magical lived in him too.

So, she's wizard, human, and something else...

He pushed his magic farther, trying to puzzle out the man's race, but ran into a wall that bit back. Ned winced as his power boomeranged back into him.

"She told us." The man didn't sound any friendlier, but at least his hands relaxed against his sides. His breeches were some sort of badly frayed blue cloth. A loose sweater covered with a leather vest hung off his broad frame. Well-scuffed leather boots kicked at the dirt. Ned could see where Amanda had gotten her wonderful golden hair and sapphire-colored eyes.

He waited. In wizard culture, once you gave your name, the other person did as well. Apparently, Amanda's father had never heard of that rule. The silence became oppressive as they stared at one another. The creek that ran between them made soothing, rippling noises.

"I...ah...was on my way back to your house," Ned offered.

"Really? Why?" Suspicion flared in those blue eyes.

Guess I'll try the truth.

"I'm in the army." Ned rolled back a sleeve far enough to make his tattoos visible. "My commanding officer told me to seek a woman with power living in this area. Since your daughter has wizard blood—and you don't—I need to see if your wife is the one I'm supposed to locate."

Incredulity fairly oozed from the man, and he narrowed his blue eyes to slits. "*What army?* What the hell do you mean about someone wanting Lori? While you're explaining things, what's this about wizards? My wife is *not* like the charlatan who lives up canyon from us, and God only knows what that bastard is."

At least now I know the wife's name.

Ned held up his hands, palms outward and fingers spread in a self-deprecating gesture. "No offense meant, sir. It's the wizards' army. I got tangled up with them since they raised me. I'm not a wizard myself, but a human mage. You've nothing to fear from me. After all, I did save your daughter yesterday." Ned wasn't sure whether he ought to add the last part. If he'd been with wizards, they'd have thought him insufferably pretentious, but this human—or whatever he was—seemed to need reminding.

"Rolf?" A woman's voice sounded from the direction of the house.

"Stay there," the man shouted over his shoulder.

"She has nothing to fear from me, either," Ned pointed

out, exasperation surfacing. Now that he knew the man's name, he used it, hoping to reassure him. "Look, Rolf, if I wanted to harm you—"

Shut up. His inner voice chimed a warning. *I have no idea what type of magic-wielder he is. Could be worse than the Infernals, for all I know.*

Running steps thrummed. Amanda's energy closed the distance between them. She came into view more quickly than he could have hoped, shining far more brilliantly than the new day.

"Ned!" She leapt across the small creek. "I'm so glad you came back." She held out a hand and smiled right at him. He took it, marveling at how wonderful her skin felt against his.

"Get back over here," her father snarled.

"What's wrong, Daddy? This is who I told you about. This is Ned." She beamed at him, ignoring her father, and Ned's heart melted.

"Oh, for Christ fucking sakes." Rolf eyed Ned balefully. "You might as well come along, then. Breakfast is on the table. There's enough to share."

"Are you certain?" Ned tried hard to be polite. Any excuse to spend more time with Amanda was nearly irresistible.

"No. Come along just the same."

"Yes, please join us," Amanda urged. Her deep, musical voice could have induced armies to lay down their weapons and parlay with one another. "You know," she went on, "I didn't sleep very well last night. Those things... What you told me about them was unnerving. Downright creepy, actually."

A chorus of howls interrupted her, and she laughed. "Come on all of you." She punctuated her words with a trilling whistle.

To Ned's surprise, three large silver-and-black wolves charged out of thick tree cover, surrounded him, and snarled in unison.

"Good day to you all," he said, careful to avoid eye contact. Wolves considered it rude for strangers to look directly at them.

The snarls ceased instantly. The lightest-colored wolf, a large male, moved toward Ned. He stopped at a respectful distance. *"You know our customs."*

"Yes, brother. I know them and keep them."

"I am called Nikki."

"I am called Ned."

"Be welcome. Good hunting."

Ned bowed formally. *"To you as well."*

"What did you do?" Rolf sounded like he might be thawing infinitesimally.

"Reassured them I wasn't their enemy." Picking up his rucksack, Ned tossed his thick queue of hair over his shoulder and sprang across the creek. He'd read shaking hands was a human custom, so he held out a hand to Rolf. "I'm not yours, either."

Rolf just looked at the proffered hand, turned, and jogged toward the house.

"Sorry." Amanda moved to his side, speaking softly. "He doesn't mean to be rude. It's just, well, he's worried about what happened to me yesterday."

"He should be," Ned replied, his voice serious. "It was the goddess's will I was there to protect you."

"So that's where you've all gotten yourselves off to." A woman almost as tall as him with waist-length, golden-brown hair and blue-green eyes emerged from an aspen forest growing thickly at the edge of a lush meadow. She was dressed in a homespun skirt and thick woolen sweater. Despite the chill of the morning, her feet were bare. Her words trailed off as her eyes lit on Ned, and a warm smile split her sun-browned face. "You must be the young man who rescued Amanda yesterday. Thank you and welcome."

Ned held his hand out, but the woman swept him into a hug. The shock of it left him breathless. Wizards rarely touched one another outside of immediate family members. He was astonished by how good it felt.

"Thank you so much for what you did," she gushed, moving back a few paces. "I'm Lori. Of course you'll stay for breakfast."

Ned looked up just in time to see Rolf throw a worried look at all of them. The taciturn man sidled to his wife and placed a protective arm about her. "I already invited him."

Ned took advantage of the moment to send his magic questing outward again. He didn't need long. The woman was definitely a wizard. Barely muted power danced about her. Where was the wizard parent who was supposed to do away with her in a few decades?

By the goddess, it must be Karras. It's why he's not far from here—to watch over his lost child.

The revelation was so staggering, Ned struggled to maintain a neutral expression.

He sent up thanks to the warrior god no one noticed his discomfiture. Or if they did, no one remarked on it.

"Come on." Lori laughed. She sounded almost exactly like her daughter. "You can tell us all about yourself over breakfast."

A combination of Lori's conversational skill, and his own relief at finally being with someone who at least appeared to give a damn about him, kept Ned talking through the best breakfast he thought he'd ever had. They sat at the same hand-milled pine table he'd shared with Amanda.

Ned suspected Rolf had built both it and the cabin. He thought about asking a few questions of his own, but decided now wasn't the time. Amanda sat next to him, not across the table as she'd done the previous afternoon. Her energy and warmth were contagious. From time to time, she laid a hand over one of his. If he weren't careful, he could delude himself that she actually cared about him. Her enthusiasm and interest as he talked certainly felt real enough.

The meal wound down, and Ned mulled over the problem of what to do about Lori now he'd found her. It wasn't as if Landarik had given him instructions. The wolves whined from where they lay under the table, and their furry bodies collided as they made a beeline for the front of the house, the scrape of their claws loud against the wooden floor.

A knock sounded.

Amanda stiffened next to him. "Who the hell—?" she began.

"Watch your tongue," Rolf snapped. He stood and

clomped out of the room, covering the short distance to the door. Ned heard it open.

"Must be Karras," Lori said. "He told us he'd come by today."

Karras!

Ned sprang to his feet. Joy pounded through him, and he understood how much he'd missed the wizard's soothing ways and kind heart.

Karras swept into the room, dark robes fluttering around him, followed by yet another wolf. Ned fell into his arms, laughing and trying to talk all at the same time. "You said you were nearby, but..."

"'Tis a sight for sore eyes you are, lad." Karras clasped him close and pounded on his back until Ned longed to remind him the traditional wizard family greeting—more slaps than hugs—was hard on humans.

"Apparently you two know one another." Rolf's finely arched brows raised in twin question marks. "We've lost a lot of today as it is. May as well kill another hour. Sit down, Karras. Tell us how you and Ned are acquainted."

Ned waited for Karras to tell Rolf to lose himself in the nine circles of Hell. Wizards never explained themselves to humans. To his surprise, Karras smiled, sat, and began to talk once he helped himself to what remained of breakfast.

ATTACK!

"So Karras is like a father to you." Amanda leaned closer to Ned.

Watching from across the table, Lori worried her daughter was being too forward. At least Rolf had calmed down. When he first came back with the boy in tow, she worried he'd just run Ned through with a hunting knife and be done with it.

"Actually more of a mentor," Ned replied thoughtfully. "I don't have much idea what it would be like to have a father."

"Lad never knew who spawned him," Karras agreed. "Not that we didn't try to ferret the information out of his mother."

Something about the combination of tone and words caught Lori's attention, and she zeroed in on Karras. "Surely you didn't torture the poor woman."

"Sorry. Poor choice of words. Of course not. What do you

take us for?" Karras's tone exuded injured innocence, but Lori's mental picture of life in wizard strongholds developed a definitely medieval cast.

"Never mind. Shouldn't have said anything." Rising to her feet, she went to one of the windows to figure out how much of the day they'd shot talking.

Karras had wanted details about Amanda's near mishap. Rolf had grilled the wizard about Ned. At one point the wizard winked at Ned and said, "You'll owe me for this, lad. Character references never come cheap." Between the two men's questions, they'd burned up at least a couple hours.

"This has been fascinating, but we've got to get moving," she said. "Rolf and I have to finish up with the elk. Goats didn't get milked this morning, and someone needs to let the sow and piglets out of the barn."

Rolf scraped his chair back and got to his feet. He held out a hand to Karras, who clasped it. After the briefest of hesitations, he did the same to Ned, though he didn't quite meet Ned's eyes.

"Get outside as soon as you can, eh?" He tapped his wife on the shoulder. With a practiced shove, he moved the curtain over the pantry aside and went out the back door.

Nikki rubbed against her leg to let her know he wanted out too, so she got to her feet and held the spring-loaded back door open. All four wolves ran outside. Barks and howls followed their exit. The day was sunny, but cool, and Lori wedged the door in place. Fresh air would do the cabin good.

"I'll take care of the pig and goats," Amanda said. Turning to Ned, she added shyly, "Maybe you could help."

Ned opened his mouth to reply, but Karras shot him a meaningful look before he could get any words out. "I'll be taking you with me," he said. "We have years of catching up to do."

"We'll come back really soon." Ned smiled at Amanda and quirked a brow at Karras. "Like maybe tomorrow?"

"We shall discuss it."

Lori swallowed down a laugh, remembering all the times she'd said exactly the same thing, with an identical inflection, to one of her children.

He certainly sounds like Ned's father, even though both of them deny the relationship.

"Whenever you want to visit, you'll be most welcome." Lori tried to hug Karras, but settled on a handshake when the wizard drew away. Ned came willingly into her arms, and she drew him close.

Poor child, those wizards chased his mother off when he was just past toddlerhood...

Thoughts of her own son filled Lori's mind, and sadness threatened to swamp her. She didn't often let herself think of her missing boy for just that reason. It was hard to pull herself back together.

"...far from done," Karras said. Since she'd missed the first part, she had no idea what he was talking about.

"Uh, you're probably right." Lori covered her lack of attentiveness with a noncommittal agreement.

The wolves' barking escalated to a fever pitch. Had they scared up game so close to the house?

"God damn all you bastards to hell!" Rolf's shout was followed by a blast from his deer rifle.

Karras and Ned exchanged glances before racing out the open doorway with Lori right behind. "You stay here," she screamed over her shoulder at Amanda. "Lock the doors."

"All alone?" her daughter wailed.

Alone and safe, Lori hoped fervently and slammed the door behind her. The report of Rolf's gun rocked her again, reverberating in her guts.

Lori stared past the shop door and stopped dead. Her mouth fell open, and her stomach twisted viciously. It felt as if she'd been run down by a truck, but hadn't been lucky enough to be knocked unconscious. A scene from Dante's *Inferno* spread before her. Horrible, misshapen creatures stood upright on animal legs with cloven hooves. About four feet tall, their bodies were covered in black fur. Piggish, dark eyes glittered from under sloping, Neanderthal foreheads.

They'd been feasting on the elk. Blood and bones lay everywhere. Vicious machete-like weapons clasped in three-fingered hands doubled as projectiles. She ducked as one of the ghastly things chucked something right at her. Rolf fought one of the abominations. It had a grip on his gun, and the two grappled over who was going to end up with it.

How can this be happening? Things like this don't exist.

Karras chanted. The staff she'd always thought of as a glorified walking stick glowed with a blue-white light. Sparks shot from its tip, burying themselves in eyes and fur. Ned held some sort of pistol in his hand. It looked like something out of *Star Wars.* He shot at the things, and they fell in their tracks.

A dark place glistened wetly in the corner of the shop. It

was hard to look directly at the breach because it wavered. For every vile creature Ned and Karras killed, two more crawled through the opening to take their place.

Fuck, no double fuck. We're all going to die here.

Lori's head spun dizzily. A part of her wanted out. She knew that side of herself. Privately, she called it her dark side. She'd never told anyone about it—not even Rolf— because she was afraid it meant she was certifiable. She'd always been able to stuff it back to wherever it lived when it wasn't haranguing her.

Not today.

With the Lori part of her aghast and drowning, the other side blazed bright as diamonds. Her hands came up of their own accord, and heat erupted from her palms. Bolts of energy flew at the intruders, focused particularly on the one locked in a death-struggle with Rolf.

Karras moved behind her, staff in hand. "Finally," he snapped, his tone sharp. "Let it flow through you. 'Tis far too late to fight against it." He placed his arms around her from behind. She felt something like a protective shield focus the unnatural energy surging through her and funnel it toward the wriggling darkness in the corner.

Ned joined them and added his power to theirs. He and Karras chanted in a language she'd never heard. Yet she understood the words. More than anything, that turned the marrow of her bones to ice. Freezing from the inside out, her connection to her physical body truncated.

Someone else's blood turned to ice water. Not hers.

The chanting reached a crescendo. The freezing

sensation gave way to heat, and she felt like an electrical wire transmitting a load so strong one more electron would scatter her cells through the galaxy. A shriek tore from her throat, followed by another. Finally, the dark place folded in on itself. She forced herself to look harder.

The shop was just the shop again.

Rolf stood a few feet away, gasping for air. A jagged cut ran down one side of his face. His eyes—deep, troubled, haunted—looked like a phalanx of ghosts had marched over his grave. She sagged against Karras. At least it was her body again. The other presence inside her was gone.

"Lori?" Rolf held out a hand uncertainly, but didn't come any closer.

"Yes, it's me again. God only knows who I was a few minutes ago." She pushed away from Karras, staggered a few steps, and fell into Rolf's arms. After a pause that felt too long, he closed them around her.

She tried to make sense of what just happened, but she couldn't. It was like forcing herself to jump out of an airplane without a parachute. She heard Ned panting and Karras muttering as he walked the perimeter of the small space. An energy field she now recognized as power flowed from his hands and the staff. "W-what are you doing?" she asked shakily.

"Closing the portal so the Infernals' spawn can't return— at least not through this passage."

"What in damnation were those?" Rolf asked. Fear roughened the edges of his voice, and he tightened his hold on Lori.

"Not sure. Probably another of the Infernals' genetic experiments. Better if you come outside." Ned still sucked air so rapidly he sounded like a bellows. "I'll check on Amanda, and then I'll join you." Out of the corner of her eye, Lori watched him hurry out of the shop.

"Yes, outside," Karras said gruffly. "We're done in here for now. The dead can wait. We'll have to burn them."

"Come on." Rolf guided her after Karras. Once they cleared the barn, he flipped a log end over and helped her down onto it. "Would you like some water?"

Lori felt the bite of hysteria just beneath the surface, and laughter pushed its way out. Not funny laughter, but laughter that held a crazed edge. "Water? What I want is a good, stiff drink. Too bad all we have is watered-down beer."

"I'll see what I can scare up." Rolf loped toward the house.

"Get hold of yourself." Karras sat down, facing her. "Give me your hands."

When she didn't reach for his outstretched hands, he laid them on either side of her face. "Breathe," he murmured. "Nice and slow. What happened today was destined to occur sooner or later. 'Tis good I was here. Magic isn't a bad thing, but it can be...surprising when you don't expect it."

"Surprising?" Lori snorted outrage. "Try shocking, disconcerting, alarming, bewildering—"

"Enough!" Karras's sharp tone interrupted her flow of words.

"Mom! Mother!" Amanda raced out of the house and

flung herself between Karras and Lori. "You leave her alone," she hissed at the wizard. "What have you done to her? She looks like hell." Amanda hugged her mother hard. Tears streamed down her face.

"Yes, dear. I know how scared you were," Lori crooned. As she stroked her daughter's hair, she wondered if Amanda could somehow sense that the mother she'd grown up with had changed. That a gateway had opened, and it would probably never quite close again.

Makes sense, her M.D.-trained brain insisted. *If I have this thing—likely she's got it too.*

"This will take some sorting out," she told her daughter, "but for now we're all still here. That's the important thing."

"Almost not," Amanda sobbed. "I...I felt things from the house. Eerie, horrid things. I was sure I'd never see you or Daddy again."

"That's what they want you to think," Ned said. He'd finally caught his breath somewhere between the house and the yard in front of the shop. "Infernals have many ways of conquering. Instilling hopelessness is one of their favorites."

Rolf came back from somewhere and handed Lori a mug. Dealing with Amanda's panicked emotions, she'd forgotten he was hunting for booze.

"Here's the last of the brandy."

"Thanks." Lori disentangled herself from Amanda and upended the cup. She wiped a few droplets off her chin. The liquor burned, but it numbed too. In a few minutes, she felt more herself. Rolf sat next to her. She laid a hand on his knee. "Did you get any brandy?"

He shook his head. "It's okay. You were way worse off

than me. I took a slug of beer. It's not much, but it'll do. And I wiped the worst of the blood off my face."

Stricken that she hadn't tended to his wound, Lori twisted to examine it. "You could use at least one stitch. Hang on I'll get my kit from the house."

Rolf held her in place. "I'll be fine."

Amanda wiped her cheeks with the backs of her hands. "Is anyone going to tell me what happened?"

Ned held out a hand to her. She grasped it, and he helped her to her feet. "I will," he said, and led her to a bench leaning against the barn.

Lori watched them go, worried he might drag her daughter somewhere out of sight. When they stopped in plain view, she relaxed, but not by much. Amanda was old enough to take care of herself, and Lori recognized she was focused on her daughter to avoid dissecting what happened in the barn. No point in putting it off further. She couldn't deal with something she didn't understand.

"Okay." She motioned wearily to Karras. "Talk. What the hell did I turn into in there? Am I channeling Medea or something?"

"Does this have anything to do with what happened yesterday?" Amanda asked. She'd gotten over her crying jag as she listened to Ned sketch out the bare bones details of their struggle in the shop.

Well, does it?

"I'm not sure," he said as truthfully as he could. "If this

were a more normal situation, I'd think not. After our defeat east of the mountains, it appears the Infernals are growing stronger faster than any of us anticipated." Ned cringed. He certainly knew what any wizard—except maybe Karras—would say about using the inclusive *us* to lump himself in with the rest of wizardom.

"What happened to Mother? She looked ten years older, and she had this…transparency. I could almost look right through her."

"Easy enough to explain." Ned gazed at her, trying to gauge how much truth she could tolerate. Either he told her. Or he didn't. There wasn't any middle ground.

"If it's so easy, then tell me." She hurried on. "I recognize the look on your face. You're trying to figure out some watered-down version. Don't. I can always tell when someone's lying to me."

I'll just bet you can.

"You would be able to. It's a wizard trait." He took a deep breath. "Your mother looked so depleted because her power caught her off guard."

"Huh? What power? What do you mean by wizard traits?" Amanda drew away from him. Her blue eyes grew large as pinwheels, and one hand grappled for her throat.

"Your mother has wizard blood." He paused. "You do too. It's why you can tell when people aren't telling you the truth." He considered mentioning her father, but decided against it. After all, what would he say? *So long as we're talking about it, your dad has magic too. I just don't know what kind.* Better to keep his mouth shut until he had a chance to talk with Karras.

Amanda appeared to accept the information. At least she didn't run shrieking toward the illusory safety of the house. When she met Ned's gaze, her expression was serious. "Mom was adopted. She doesn't know anything about her parents. It's always bothered her."

Thinking about his total lack of data about his parents, Ned felt mystified. "Why?"

"Maybe because she's a doctor, and they like to know things like that. There's lots of missing information about possible genetic glitches. I've heard her talking to Dad about it often enough." Amanda took a thoughtful breath. "I think it's why she chose medical research. Genetically-linked disorders were a big part of what she studied."

"What did your father do?" So long as Amanda was willing to talk, Ned thought he should get as much information as he could. Maybe it would help him untangle the mystery shrouding Rolf like a closely guarded secret.

"He was a petrochemical engineer."

Ned blushed for his ignorance. "What do they do?"

"He traveled all over the world looking for oil deposits and figuring out how to drill for them. After a while, he got worried we were draining the planet. Then he went to work for a green company that manipulated weather."

Hmmm...rocks and weather.

Something banged around in the back of Ned's mind, but he couldn't quite pin it down. "Did you know your grandparents?"

Amanda laughed bitterly. "Nope. Got short-changed all the way round in that department. The people who adopted Mom died when she was a teenager, and I think Dad was ashamed of his parents. Never would talk about them, even when Jon and I asked."

"You have more family than I do." Ned looked hard at her.

Her tanned skin developed a rosy tint. "I'll take your word for it," she murmured. "Guess that's a backhanded way of telling me not to feel so sorry for myself."

A goat *baahed*, and then another. "Think we ought to milk them?" Ned asked.

"Yeah. Never did get to it earlier. I'm sure they're miserable by now." She rose to her feet and brushed past him as she led the way into the barn.

Ned glanced toward the shop. Lori, Rolf, and Karras had their heads together, apparently deep in conversation. He doubted they'd even notice he and Amanda had left the rough-hewn bench. Another goat bleated—or maybe it was the same one—and he followed Amanda into the semi-dark barn. She'd settled next to one of the goats on a three-legged stool. From the looks of things, two more needed milking.

"Got another bucket and stool?"

She gestured toward a far corner where things were stacked in an empty stall. "You'll need to rinse the bucket. Use the pump. There's one just outside."

Ned gathered what he needed and settled in the double stall next to Amanda. "Tell me about your life before you came here."

Her magical laugh was infectious. "Not sure there's much to tell. I had friends, went to school, took ballet and piano lessons. We lived in a big house." A sigh whistled. "I used to complain about a bunch of things. Crap! I had no idea how lucky we were."

Milk spattered into the pail. Ned tugged rhythmically on the goat's udder until it was drained and then moved to the next goat. He wondered what to tell her if she asked about his life. He hated to admit he'd never had a single friend—unless Karras counted.

"Did you go to wizard school?"

Ned glommed onto her question. At least it was something he could answer. "Indeed I did." He snorted. "If I wouldn't have left the stronghold, I'd still be in classes."

"What kind of things did you study?" Her voice held genuine interest. "Was it language and math and history like I did?"

Ned thought about it. "Yes and no. I studied linguistics and wizard history and mathematics. But they also taught me war craft, mage craft, and about the various faces of evil."

She laughed again, but it didn't sound nearly as merry. "Sounds like you got a much better rounded education than me. I finished the last of what would have been high school here. Mom and Dad brought textbooks with us when we moved five years ago. I was only thirteen and in eighth grade."

"Maybe we can learn from each other." Ned tried to keep a wistful note from his voice. He wanted Amanda to see him as strong and capable.

"I hope so." She stood. "I'm done. How about you?"

He nodded and got to his feet, returning the stool to where he'd gotten it.

They both headed for the barn door at the same time.

Trying to avoid a collision, he stepped back the same time she did, and their bodies tangled together. Her intoxicating scent filled his nostrils. Cinnamon, lilies, and vanilla. Milk slopped over the pail dangling from his fingers. Ned set it on the packed dirt floor and reached to steady her. An electric shock traveled up his arm.

She leaned into him, their bodies almost touching, but not quite.

"Are you okay?" he asked. "Did I hurt you when I ran into you?"

Her gaze settled on his. "Not hurt, but maybe not okay, either."

He thought he read invitation in her eyes, but maybe he was fooling himself. After all, he didn't have much in the way of experience to draw on. "Did I hurt you?" He asked again, and then felt like an ass because she'd already answered him.

She shook her head and closed the final few inches between them. "Hold me. Please hold me."

A husky undercurrent in her voice swept reason away. Ned pulled her against him and twined his fingers in her unbound hair. When she turned her mouth upward, he kissed her, and his body heated instantaneously. Even if he had no idea what to do, it did. He cupped her head in his hands and pushed his tongue into her mouth. Trapped between their bodies, his cock surged against her warm belly, and he moved his hands downward to grip her ass, pulling her hard against him.

She opened her mouth under his, tasting of flowers and honey. Breath coming faster, he lost himself in her, reveling in the feel of her pressed against him—all warmth and curves, yet with sinewy muscle beneath. She curled her arms around him and splayed her hands across his back, holding tight. Her nipples peaked against his chest, and he cursed the layers of clothing between them.

"Ned!" Karras's stern voice in his mind shocked him, and Ned drew back.

Amanda reached up and tried to pull his mouth over hers again. Her clothing had come partially undone, displaying the tops of her breasts. Urgency boiled through him. He filled his hands with her breasts, rubbing her erect nipples and leaned forward to kiss her again. He had only the vaguest of concepts about what came next, but was confident he could figure it out.

"Ned!"

Long training and discipline took over. *"What?"* Ned wrapped his arms around Amanda, holding her just as close as he could, but he broke their kiss to converse with Karras. It must be important or the wizard wouldn't be bothering him. Not now.

"Celibacy may well be the price of your mage gift. Do not give it away until we find out."

Nooooooo.

Pushing Amanda gently away, Ned stumbled out of the barn.

She came after him. "What? Did I do something wrong?" Her lips were swollen from their kisses. Long, blonde hair hung about her like the finest spun silk. Tears glistened in her eyes. Her cheeks were flushed, and she pulled her top back into place.

She was the most beautiful, the most enticing creature in the entire world. His heart ached. If not having her was the cost of his magic, he didn't want it anymore. Frustrated beyond words, Ned punched a closed fist into the side of the barn, wincing from pain. He knew better than to devalue his power. It was all he had, but the price was steep. It had cost him everything, beginning with his mother.

"It's not you," he managed, finding it impossible to meet her gaze. "It's me. Karras... I..." He took an uneven breath as he pulled the tattered edges of himself together. The warm glow in his nether regions turned to a leaden throbbing from an erection that refused to subside.

He took one of her hands. "Part of my magic is mind speech. Karras, well, he figured out what we were doing. He warned me—"

"Warned you about me?" Fury twisted her beauty into something hard. "The old bastard doesn't even know me."

"No." Ned tightened his hand over hers. "This isn't about you. It's my magic. He told me it might be at risk if I... Well, if we...uh...did anything beyond kissing."

Her eyes went very round, and then a slow smile lit her features. She put her arms around him and laid her head in the crook between his neck and shoulder. "Not a problem. I wasn't going to do more than kiss you anyway. What sort of girl do you think I am?" Her laughter, bubbling against his skin, warmed him. Emboldened, he kissed her again.

Amazingly, she kissed him back.

"Ned." Karras used his out loud voice this time. "Get over here right now."

Reluctantly, he drew away from Amanda and rubbed a

thumb over her lower lip. "Maybe we can find some time later?"

"No doubt about it." She grinned and gave him a playful shove. "Better go see what Karras wants. I recognize that tone. God knows I've heard it enough from Mom and Dad."

WHAT'S WRONG WITH ME?

*L*ight leached out of the day and Lori lit candles, scattering them strategically so she wouldn't have to burn as many. She was running low, and it wasn't quite time to cull more wax from the hives. She worked in her familiar kitchen, preparing enough to feed all five of them. No matter how she tried to divert herself, it was impossible to ignore the smell of burning flesh from the funeral pyre the men had constructed to incinerate the dead.

Should have asked Karras what they're called.

She wasn't sure why it mattered, but an orderly part of her mind liked to catalogue things. She could put this right next to the undead under the heading *Supernatural Creatures.*

Damn. What could possibly come next? Sudden fury boiled up, and she hurled the spoon in her hand across the room. Gravy splattered as it hit the far wall. Fear followed in its wake.

Is the other part of me waking up? Crap. Fuck. Shit. Will it only be a matter of time before I lose myself entirely?

Lori shuddered. Karras had tried his best to allay the worst of her fears earlier, yet she'd never felt so out of control.

Rolf came through the back door. He eyed the gravy splotches running down the wall and quirked an eyebrow. "Dinner getting away from you?"

"It's not funny," she snapped.

"No," he agreed. "None of this is. If we can't laugh at ourselves—"

"Spare me. I'm not in the mood for a lecture."

He walked over to her, turned her to face him, and placed both hands on her shoulders. When she wouldn't meet his gaze, he tipped her chin so she had no choice. "You're fine at handing out the advice when it's me with the resident ghosts," he pointed out.

The sudden anger bled out of her, replaced by sorrow and worry. "What's going to become of us? You have your demons, and now mine are on the loose too." She ran a finger lightly over the cut on his face. "At least this is healing."

He tugged gently on her arm and led her to a chair. "Remember when we moved here, we thought we'd be dead inside of a year?" At her nod, he pulled out the chair next to hers and fell heavily into it. "Then, when Jon disappeared, we were certain we wouldn't be far behind."

"Yes, but—"

He held up a hand. "No, let me finish. Lor, we've been living on borrowed time ever since we moved here. If our time's running out, well, it's been longer than I thought we'd have."

"Amanda…"

"I know. It's not fair." He locked gazes with her. "All we can do is face whatever's coming and fight until we can't anymore." He hesitated. "It's why I didn't punch that young pup out when it was obvious he'd been doing things with Mandy." Gruffness lent an edge to his voice.

"I'm glad you didn't. Not sure why you don't like him."

"I hardly know him." Rolf's voice was still laced with irritation. "Mandy's pretty innocent. I don't like to see her taken advantage of."

The edges of Lori's mouth quivered. A reluctant grin split her face. "Yeah, she looked totally guiltless when she threw her arms around Ned and kissed him."

"Humph. Must have missed that part."

The wolves started howling. Lori redirected her gaze from Rolf to the nearest window. "What's got them so riled up? Last time they barked, we played host to those horrors in the barn."

Sudden light streamed through the window, much brighter than the wavery glow from the funeral pyre. She squeezed her tired eyes shut to rest them for a second.

Where's it coming from? The sun's going down.

The howling shifted to barks and snarls. Rolf leapt to his feet and grabbed his Winchester rifle off its rack near the back door before heading outside. She heard him swear, but at least he wasn't shooting at anything.

Lori bolted from her seat with her heart trying to beat its way out of her chest. Fear left a sour taste in her mouth. Was it more of those things coming back? Or perhaps some new iteration of ghoulish species since there had to be more than two of them.

The chill of early evening hit her like a wall after the heat of the kitchen. Reaching back inside, she grabbed a wool cloak and wrapped it around her. A distant corner of the yard was so brightly illuminated, she felt dumbfounded. They didn't have electricity, so how the fuck could all that light be happening? Rolf stood a few feet away, rifle stock held to his shoulder, sighting down the barrel.

She walked close and whispered near his ear. "What?"

"Don't know, but Karras and Ned don't look worried." He rolled his eyes. "Good thing. I'm about out of ammo. Haven't had time to haul out the reloading kit."

Neither wizard nor mage so much as glanced up from their work next to the funeral pyre. Karras's staff, propped against a wall of the shop, looked like a piece of inert wood once again.

"Where's Amanda?" Lori twisted to look over her shoulder.

"Asleep in the loft, last I checked." Rolf dropped the rifle to his side.

The brilliant light faded to a warm shimmer, and a glittering rectangle formed, glowing against the fading day. Two figures stepped through it. They were dressed similarly to Ned, mostly in stained, battered leather with high, lace-up boots. Cloaks tossed over everything made it impossible to determine their gender.

Ned wiped his hands on his pants, trotted to the newcomers, and bowed.

"You found the woman. Why did you not bring her to us and report in?" asked one of the strangers—a man, judging from his voice.

Lori found his tone high-handed and irritating. She rooted for Ned to tell him to piss up a rope.

"He didn't report back, Landarik, because he was with me." Karras strode over and placed himself between Ned and the other man. Sparks bounced between them as they faced off.

Lori rubbed her eyes, thinking she had to be mistaken about the sparks. Blatant audacity battled common sense. After a long moment, audacity won. She stomped over, hands on her hips. "Why'd you send him looking for me?"

The man—Landarik—turned to face her. His face was ageless. Blond hair, partially escaped from an intricate braiding pattern, hung about his face. Intense blue eyes augured into hers. Like Karras and Ned, he was tall, with broad shoulders tapering to slender hips.

Landarik moved his gaze from her to Karras, then back again. Eyes narrowing, he asked, "Which of us is she linked to?"

"You're talking about me like I'm a *thing*," Lori protested. Her stomach muscles tightened. The trepidation she'd felt approaching Landarik gave way to a rush of anger.

Karras shrugged, ignoring her. "Sorry. Couldn't figure it out."

Landarik snorted. "Sierna. Lend your magic to this problem."

The second figure detached itself from the shadowy place where the rectangle had disappeared. As she walked to where Landarik stood, the cowl covering her head slipped, revealing dark hair braided into many small sections. Her face had a high forehead, prominent cheekbones, and a timeless quality Lori guessed was unique to wizards. Her beauty radiated outward, pulsing like a beacon.

The woman extended her hands. Her deep, violet eyes sought Lori's and held them for a long moment.

Melodic laughter filled the silence stretching among them. "'Tis easy enough. This is Lira's daughter. Ha! Bet that supercilious bitch thought she got away with this one. Once it gets out, it'll take her down a peg or two."

"Who's Lira?" Lori felt mystified. "I was adopted. My mother's name was Carole."

"Your true mother was a wizard, child." Karras spoke gently. "We covered that ground earlier today."

Lori swallowed hard around a thick place blocking her throat. She'd heard Karras when they sat outside the barn, but his words hadn't truly registered. "Is...is she still alive?"

"Oh, very much," Ned chimed in.

"I heard that." Amanda materialized out of the gathering dusk. She moved next to Lori and threaded an arm around her mother's waist. "Means I have a grandmother. Not sure how I feel about it."

"That's only because you don't know her." Ned grimaced. In what light remained from the fading day, Lori saw him screw his mouth into a disgusted moue.

Amanda shot him a meaningful look and hugged her mother closer. "You're going to have to say more than that," she told Ned.

"No, he'll be holding his tongue," Karras broke in.

"Indeed," Landarik seconded, still staring at Lori, a speculative light in his blue eyes.

Lori shook her head to make her thoughts fall into some sort of order. It didn't work. They stampeded through her, displacing reason until she could scarcely breathe. At least the wizards' attention had shifted. They talked among themselves in a language she couldn't follow. Ned stood off to one side. He wore such a complex expression, Lori took the time to really study him. He stared fixedly at the wizards, so she hoped he wouldn't notice her scrutiny.

What she saw made her heart ache. Bitterness was reflected in his face, mixed with longing and hope. With sudden, heartbreaking clarity, she understood he'd spent his short years hoping for love and acceptance from his caregivers, and constantly coming up short. From what little she knew of Karras, she could see how a human—even one with magical ability—would always be lacking when viewed through wizard eyes.

Ned settled his dark eyes on her. "Don't," he said. "You don't understand." He turned and walked toward the house, back straight and shoulders squared.

Amanda started after him. "We'll figure Grannie out later," she called over her shoulder.

"Where do you think you're going?" Landarik's voice wasn't overly loud, but it stopped Ned in his tracks. Amanda caught up to him. She took his arm as he turned to face the wizard.

"He's coming with me to finish dinner." Amanda's blue eyes flashed. She placed herself between Ned and Landarik.

"I think not. He is returning with us. His place is with his unit. He had an assignment and now it is done. 'Tis why we came. To fetch him back and to examine yon woman." He pointed at Lori.

"She will return with us as well," Sierna announced. "To provide proof to the High Council."

"I'll do no such thing." Lori set her mouth in a hard line. "Maybe you can order Ned around, but I'm not leaving here."

Rolf moved to her side. He placed a protective arm around her shoulders. "No," he said clearly. "You are not taking my wife."

"You don't have a choice in the matter, human." Landarik, who hadn't been exactly cordial before, sounded positively hostile.

"Enough." Karras held up both hands. "More conversation is needed."

"Fuck conversation," Rolf said. "I'm done with all of you."

"Couldn't have said it better myself." Lori stared daggers at Landarik. "You can leave anytime. You're standing on my property, and my husband and I want you gone. Now."

I DON'T WANT to go back. By the goddess, I don't want to go back to being their whipping boy. Barely tolerated. Never quite good enough for anything but cannon fodder in their endless wars.

Ned gently detached himself from Amanda. He was loathe to return, but he didn't want them to take Mandy's mother away, either. "I'll go," he said resolutely and walked forward to face Landarik. "You're correct, my duty here has been discharged."

"More like it, *human mage*." Landarik's inflection left no doubt how he felt about Ned.

Helpless anger balled Ned's hands into fists, but he refused to grovel, no matter how much he wanted to stay.

"Now just a minute." Rolf let go of Lori and barreled forward. "I may not be overly fond of the young man, but I'll not stand by while someone disparages him in my presence. I was in the Army once, and you're a poor excuse for—"

"Amanda mentioned dinner," Karras broke in. "Is there enough to feed all of us?"

"No," Rolf said succinctly.

"Even if we had food to spare," Lori tossed out, "I wouldn't waste it on the likes of you." Face screwed up like she'd tasted something sour, she turned and stomped toward the house, grabbing Amanda's arm as she passed.

"Do I need to stay?" Rolf touched Ned's shoulder.

"No, sir. I'll be fine if you want to go with your wife and daughter."

Fine enough. I've had to put up with these bastards my entire life.

"I'm as close as a shout." Rolf squeezed Ned's shoulder before following after his family. Watching him, Ned understood he'd give just about anything to have come from a family like this one. Where the people actually cared about one another.

Raising his gaze to meet Landarik's, Ned said, "They were kind to me. Even though they didn't know me. Despite the fact they didn't trust me. Still they fed me and offered me shelter. It's far more than you would have done in their place."

"Your point?"

"Leave the woman here. The only reason you want to drag her back to the stronghold is to humiliate Lira and get her in trouble. I will testify to having seen her spawn, and if my word isn't good enough, Hreth can raise Karras through the stones or the pool. Besides, the two of you have laid eyes on Lira's shame." Ned sucked in an anxious breath, surprised one of the wizards hadn't told him to shut up.

"Lira's not the only reason," Sierna murmured. "Though goddess knows I'd love to see her squirm for once."

"What other?" Ned spun to face her.

"The woman needs to entrain her power. Likely her daughter as well, though we haven't discussed her yet— mostly because we didn't know about her until quite recently. Right now, both are fair prey for the Infernals. From what our informants told us, the woman's son is captive and has been for years. 'Tis possible, nay likely, he's been turned."

"I can work with both women here," Karras said. "No need to remove them from their loved ones. They'll work harder if they feel safe."

Ned had his doubts. From what he'd seen of Lori, she struck him as an independent thinker. If she weren't interested in learning about magic, that would be the end of things. Maybe if she saw it as a way to rescue her son, she'd be more cooperative, though.

Amanda might be more open to lessons. He opened his mouth, but shut it with a snap, hesitant to forward an opinion when there were so many unknowns. And so many wizards who'd be quick to spit on his ideas.

"What?" Landarik skewered him with chilly eyes.

Ned shook his head.

"You can either tell us, or we can read your mind," Sierna pointed out.

Ned glared at the three wizards and slapped a ward about himself. Karras burrowed through it easily and laid a hand on his arm. "We'd be interested in your thoughts on this matter." Though his tone was friendly, the words were more command than invitation.

"Three things," Ned said stiffly. "The first is Lori will be more likely to work with us if she believes it will bring her son back. The second is Amanda may well want to learn about her magic—without the bunch of you bludgeoning her with it."

"The third?" Sierna added her violet gaze to Landarik's blue one.

"There is something...different about Rolf. I've been trying to figure it out." Ned's voice ran down. He was afraid the wizards would bray with laughter if he told them what conclusion he'd drawn.

"Yes." Now it was Karras who looked intently at him. "I've been trying to puzzle my way through that mystery as well. Whenever I get close, something diverts me. 'Tis almost like someone doesn't want me to know."

"Surely not the man." Landarik snorted derisively. "He's naught but a dull-witted lout."

"Not at all." Familiar anger surged through Ned. "He

built everything here and managed to keep his family alive through brutal winters."

"His moods change the weather," Karras said softly.

"You must be mistaken." Sierna shook her well-formed head. "Your assessment is scarcely possible."

"I know what I've observed." Karras tightened his hand on Ned's arm. "Tell us your thoughts, lad. I'd like to hear them."

Color rushed to Ned's face. In its own way, Karras's kindness was as hard to take as Landarik's disdain. "I... uh...went through all the different races in the *Book of Spells*—"

"Where'd you get one of those?" Landarik broke in, sounding furious.

"I gave it to him." Karras turned to face the other wizard. "If you don't mind, Landarik, be quiet long enough to let him finish."

Muttering under his breath, Landarik stepped back a pace or two. "Go on," he said, though his tone didn't match his words.

"Uh...like I was saying..." Ned's guts twisted with nervousness. They'd laugh at him, and it would be more than he could bear. "I went through all the possibilities in the book, and the only one that might conceivably fit is...is Earth Mage." Ned squeezed his eyes shut waiting for Karras's pity and Landarik's scorn. Silence rode heavy, and Ned opened his eyes to get a look at the expressions on everyone's faces.

Karras looked thoughtful. "Yes," he said. "I pondered that one as well."

"Except there hasn't been an Earth Mage on Earth for at least a thousand years," Sierna pointed out.

"Exactly." Landarik sounded smug. "Where would one of them have come from?"

"How should I know?" Ned felt defensive.

"There are at least a few possible answers." Karras spread his hands before him and glanced at Ned. "You can drop the wards, lad. No one here is going to attack you. Save them for the Infernals."

Embarrassed, Ned withdrew the magic powering his shield. It was disconcerting Karras had reached through it as though it weren't even there.

"Rolf—or his Earth Mage parent—might have come from one of the other worlds," Karras went on.

"Ceres or Cybele may have spirited him here to help save Earth." A note of awe lit Sierna's voice.

"We need to get a closer look at the fellow." Landarik's entire demeanor shifted, likely in response to the other two wizards' comments.

Ned made a rude sound, midway between a snort and a grunt. "You managed to alienate the lot of them pretty effectively. How are you going to go about it?"

"I shall just go inside the house and—"

"You'd be better served if you knocked first," Karras said drily.

Sierna's laughter trilled. "'Tis true we have little enough in the way of manners." She linked arms with Landarik. "Lead on. I shall attempt to use my charm to cover your lack thereof."

Landarik looked so wretchedly uncomfortable, Ned

nearly laughed. The battle lord hissed something into Sierna's ear, but she just grinned and butted him with her hip.

"Do not flaunt yourself at me here." Landarik wrenched himself away.

Karras clapped his hands together. "Stop it. Both of you. We have more serious matters at hand than your love affair."

"B-but," Landarik sputtered. "We're not—"

"Oh? I'll remember that the next time you get your cock out and wave it about." The acidic undernote in Sierna's voice could have etched granite.

Ned's mouth gaped open, but he snapped it shut and studied the ground near his boots, trying to get his mind around Landarik fucking anyone. Sierna was beautiful. Surely she could have her choice of lovers. Why wouldn't she pick someone nicer to share her bed?

"The house." Karras pointed. "Now."

TEMPERS RUN HIGH

*L*andarik thudded his fist against the front door of Rolf and Lori's humble cabin. When no one responded, he knocked again. Standing off to one side, Ned snickered to himself. He would have been surprised if any of the Haraldssens answered the door. After all, they had enough magic to know who was outside. Even absent magic, they could figure it out.

The rustle of footsteps ruined the internal bet he'd made with himself. Amanda pulled the door open. When she saw Landarik, she slammed it in his face.

"By the goddess's teats," the wizard swore, "I've had about as much of this abuse as I'm willing to take." He snaked his hand out and grasped the doorknob.

You can dish it out, but you don't like it one bit when it's tossed in your direction.

"Rather than storming in there and upsetting them further, how about if I go inside and try to talk with them. At least they're not angry with me," Ned suggested, keeping his tone silkily smooth.

"The lad has a point." Karras's normally sardonic inflection was notably absent.

Without waiting for the three wizards to chew the point to death, Ned slipped around the house and pulled the back door open. "It's me," he called so as not to alarm anyone. Identifying himself felt particularly important if Rolf really was an Earth Mage.

Though Ned didn't recall everything he'd learned about the ancient race, what he did remember was daunting. They had a direct link to one of the earth goddesses, either Ceres or Cybele. Earth Mages worked as tools of a particular goddess, doing her bidding. When he'd been very small, Ceres had visited the wizard stronghold. From his hiding place under one of the beds, Ned watched the wizards running this way and that, clearly unnerved by her presence.

"I'm so glad you're in here with us and not out there with *them*." Amanda met him in the pantry running between the back door and the kitchen. "My God, they're perfectly awful. How could you stand to live with them? So patronizing and holier-than-thou."

"Amanda, stop," her mother called. "You don't know, so you can't judge."

"It's all right, ma'am." Ned followed Amanda and inclined his head toward Lori, who worked busily at the woodstove. "I've gotten used to wizards. How they are doesn't bother me much anymore."

"It's still not right," Amanda persisted. At a pointed

glance from her father, she quieted and linked an arm through Ned's. "Come sit. Supper's nearly ready."

"Not that any of us are very hungry," Rolf muttered, "but it will be good to have a hot meal. It's been a long day."

Lori pushed past, holding a tureen between two folded towels. "Soup's on," she said. "Grab a glass and get yourself some beer if you want."

Ned slurped at his soup and put butter on his pine nut flour bread. He wasn't quite certain where to begin. It wasn't likely the wizards would be welcome in this house no matter what he said. Finally, he looked at Lori.

She glanced up from her meal. "Yes? Can I get you something else?"

"Oh no, ma'am. I can get whatever I need. I...um...well—"

"Whatever it is, son, just spit it out," Rolf said. "Sometimes it's easiest that way."

Nodding, Ned laid his spoon down and took a slug of beer. "The wizards want to talk with you."

"We know," Lori said, her tone curt. "We, however, do not choose to talk with them."

"They've altered their plans about taking you with them." Ned decided not to mention they'd intended to drag Amanda along too.

"Doesn't change a thing. The fact they were even considering it tells me they have no respect for anyone who isn't like them."

Truer words were never spoken.

"The compromise is for Karras to teach you about your magic, and Amanda too, if she's interested."

Amanda quirked a brow at him. "That might be—"

"Quiet, Mandy," Lori snapped. "We don't want to learn about it."

A mulish look entered Lori's blue-green eyes. Ned felt proud of her independent streak and frightened for her at the same time.

"It might help you get your son back."

Lori looked hard at him. Ned stared right back. It wouldn't do to have her think he was concealing anything.

"Okay," she conceded after a long pause. "That might be a reason to consider changing my mind." Without missing a beat, she said, "You know my mother. Tell me about her."

"She's a sanctimonious bitch. Whoops." Ned clamped a hand over his mouth. "Uh, sorry. That was really disrespectful. She's one of the warrior caste, and female warriors are always hard-edged and intolerant. Plus, she's daughter to Hreth, seer to the wizards. He always gave her everything she wanted."

Lori laughed, but it held a bitterness that tugged at Ned's heart. "She's spoiled and self-indulgent. Sort of like the crew out there?" Lori waved a hand toward the windows.

"Worse."

"We can do without meeting her then." Amanda sounded a lot like her mother.

Ned took a deep breath. "You may not have a choice." He launched into a brief description of wizards and their lost children.

"You say she'll show up so she can murder me before my long life attracts undue attention?" Lori repeated incredulously. "Attention from whom? That strategy may have been valid before the world imploded, but certainly not now."

As Ned thought about it, he agreed with her. "There's something else," he added reluctantly. "It's possible she may come to you, not to kill you but because she has no other children. You're her only heir, insofar as we know."

"Isn't that just great." Lori jumped up. She paced the length of the small room. "Christ, I'm trapped, and there's nowhere to run."

The front door banged open, slamming against the wall. Rolf lurched to his feet, grabbed the Winchester from its rack, and planted himself in the kitchen doorway with the gun in firing position.

Landarik walked in from the front hall but stopped at the far side of the room. He raised his hands, palms outward. "Do not shoot, Earth Mage. We mean you no harm. Yon youngster was supposed to smooth the way for us to converse with you." He cast a spurious smile Ned's way.

Ned ignored him.

"We have no interest in talking with you and even less having you in our home." Rolf's measured tones were firm. "So you can just turn around, gin up that thing you came through, and get the hell out of here. Oh yes, the *youngster* in question will be staying with us. I wouldn't send a dog I didn't like with you."

Landarik's jaw tightened. Ned understood the wizard was struggling against calling power to vaporize Rolf where he stood. *Wonder if he could?* Ned had a niggling hunch the goddess would protect her own.

The two men faced off against one another, with

Landarik's ice blue gaze locked onto Rolf's slightly darker one.

Karras pushed past Landarik. "Stand down," he hissed. "Both of you. We have an enemy, and 'tisn't within these walls. Not yet, anyway."

"It's how they conquer us." Sierna slithered past Landarik. Now that he knew what to look for, Ned thought she pushed a lot more of her body into him than she really had to. "Infernals sow dissention and turn us against one another to weaken us internally."

"Can't you all just leave?" Annoyance shot from Lori's gaze. "We were fine without you."

"Were you?" After an uncharacteristically long silence, Landarik found his voice again. "How fine could you possibly be? Your son is missing. Your daughter was nearly taken by Infernals. You have power simmering so close to the surface, it will burst if you don't learn to control it."

He swung to face Rolf. "And you. I didn't believe him when the human mage suggested it, but you hold the goddess within you."

"What the fuck are you talking about?" Rolf growled. An uncomfortable look washed across his gaunt features.

"Put the gun down. Sit and talk with us," Karras urged. His tone sounded a shade too smooth, and Ned heard compulsion beneath the surface of the words. It worked because Rolf clicked the gun's safety, hung the old Winchester back on the wall, and took his seat. After a moment's hesitation, Lori sat too.

Switching sides of the table, Amanda positioned herself next to Ned. "This should be interesting," she whispered.

The three wizards arranged themselves in empty spots around the table, dragging an extra chair over in the process. Landarik looked longingly at the soup tureen, but Sierna shook her head very slightly. *"Do nothing to rock this boat,"* she said. *"'Tis tippy enough."*

Ned glanced from one wizard face to the next. He could almost hear Karras's thoughts churn. Before his old mentor could say anything, though, Lori spoke. "Ned tells me if I learn about the wizardry you all think I have, it might help get Jon back."

A look passed between Landarik and Sierna. Ned remembered Sierna's conjecture about Jon being assimilated by Infernals—if he weren't already dead. He wondered if the wizards would be honest, and then laughed bitterly to himself. They'd say whatever they needed to secure cooperation. He'd seen it happen often enough. Why should tonight be any different?

"'Tis a possibility." Sierna sounded like she was choosing her words with care. She met Lori's worried gaze. *"I too, am a mother. So though it pains me, I must tell you 'tis likely your son is either dead or taken."* She paused. *"Our understanding is he's been gone for years."*

Ned's mouth fell open. Sierna had told the truth. He didn't understand why, but she had.

"What do you mean taken?" Color drained from Lori's face.

"When Infernals keep captives for years, they turn them to their own use," Karras answered. "Or try to."

"In truth, we have no idea what we'll find, assuming we

can even locate your son. He was young when he left you. His age would make him more vulnerable," Sierna added.

"If they harmed Jon and we get him back, is there a way to save him?" Lori's voice held anguish. Her hands were clasped together in front of her so hard the knuckles turned white.

No one answered. Not with words. The look in three sets of wizard eyes said it all.

Karras cleared his throat and shifted his attention toward Rolf. "Have you noticed your moods influence the weather?"

"What are you talking about, man?" Rolf sputtered. "Don't be absurd."

"You're lying," Karras said gently. "Don't bother denying it. I can tell."

Rolf pushed to his feet. Color suffused his bearded cheeks. "Go to fucking hell. You can all leave. Right now. No one accuses me of dishonesty in my own home." He pointed toward the door. "Get out. Now. The lot of you fuckers."

Lightning split the night sky outside the kitchen windows. Thunder followed quickly on its heels. Karras cocked his head to one side. "Yes," he muttered. "Exactly what I mean. This is just like the other night when your anger brought a storm."

"Here's proof. You *are* linked to the goddess." Landarik bowed slightly from where he sat. "'Tis an honor, not something to be shunned."

Rolf's eyes rolled wildly. He clutched his head between both hands. "Get out," he moaned. "Get out."

Lori was by his side in an instant. "Lie down," she urged. "I'll get you something for your headache. Go on up to the loft before it gets worse. Don't worry. I'll make sure the wizards are well and truly gone from here."

Rolf jerked away from her, his eyes so haunted he looked like a man dogged by demons as he turned and ran through the pantry. The back door crashed against its stops. Rolf's footsteps echoed on the wooden steps before the packed dirt of the yard muffled them.

"I'll go after him." Ned leapt to his feet and raced after Rolf.

"I'll come with you," Karras called.

"No, stay there. He doesn't trust you," Ned shouted over his shoulder. "If I need anything, I'll let you know."

Once outside, he sent his mage senses spinning in a full circle. Rolf's energy thrummed like a live thing, easy to find. "I could track him even without my gift," Ned muttered under his breath. He ran toward the creek, following the sound of Rolf's heavy footsteps hurtling through thick undergrowth.

"Stay away. I figure you mean well, but leave me alone." Desolation underscored Rolf's words, damage so deep it made Ned's heart hurt. He knew how it felt to have despair take up residence in his soul.

"All right, I won't come any closer. I just want to talk with you." Ned kept his distance. No point in having Rolf run miles from the cabin.

A nearby cry told Ned the wolves were close. Good. Maybe he could bend their animal energy to his benefit. He mimicked a howl and was gratified when an answering howl came almost immediately. Branches snapped, and Nikki broke into the clearing, his tail pluming. The wolf's breath steamed in the frigid night air.

A pair of amber eyes met his gaze. Two more wolves—Ned dredged his brain for their names and came up with Kua and Naia—crowded close. Karras's wolf wasn't with them. Cold noses nudged him. Ned buried his hands in thick, matted fur and linked to their strength. He sent out a calming spell but soon withdrew it. These wolves were used to people. Their voices in his mind demanded food and love.

"She comes." Kua, who'd been luxuriating under Ned's stroking, straightened.

"Who?"

"Mistress of all life." Nikki too, stood at attention. His rumpled fur looked smoother and fuller in moonlight streaming through the aspen trees.

A glow formed a few feet away, pushing the darkness aside. At first, Ned thought one of the wizards had come anyway, but then realized the energy was different. He tossed up a ward and was shocked when it shattered around him. Fear jumped his heart into a stuttering beat. The wolves didn't look scared, but it didn't pacify him. What the hell was out there? The coruscation brightened until Ned had to look away.

"You will help me." The voice echoed all around Ned. Multi-toned, it took compliance for granted.

Nikki turned and bowed his shaggy head toward the glow. *"We would help if we could."*

"I know you would. Noble beasts. When I have need of you, I will call."

Nikki faded into the shadows, his panting mute

testimony to how intimidated he felt. The other wolves followed their alpha.

Sudden understanding shot through Ned. He scrambled upright from where he'd hunkered among the wolves. "Y-you must be the goddess l-linked to Rolf," he stammered and bowed low.

Laughter came at him from all sides. "Perceptive of you. You've got it mixed-up, though. He is bound to me. Pah! Stupid human. He fights me at every turn. You will tell him to open himself to me. He is mine. He must do my bidding. If he does not, I shall destroy what is left of his mind."

Ned heard Rolf muttering to himself. He pled with *the bitch in his head* to leave him alone. Ned turned to Ceres—or perhaps it was Cybele, his thoughts a jumble. "Do your other Earth Mages recognize you?"

"From birth."

"Why is Rolf different?" Ned didn't want to irritate the goddess, yet he needed to understand if he was to have a prayer of breaking through Rolf's wall of denial.

A long sigh sent what felt like spring breezes to ruffle Ned's hair. "Because the circumstances of his conception were unusual."

After a long silence, Ned gathered his courage. "I have to know more."

"Gutsy one, aren't you?" The glow faded enough for Ned to see a tall female form clad in flowing golden robes. Rings flashed from her fingers, and a golden torc circled her neck. Dark hair long enough to sweep the ground swirled about her. Silvery eyes met his, and she parted her full lips in an almost feral smile. "You're a pretty thing," she crooned. "If I had a bit more time—" She snapped her fingers. "I do not. Come close, little manling. I shall tell you secrets."

Her scent intoxicated him, made him as hard as Amanda had, but in a way that made him feel vaguely dirty. Between her raw sexuality and his unslaked desire from earlier, it was all Ned could do to concentrate on her words.

Questions spilled through his mind. When he opened his mouth, she shook her head. "Now is the time for you to listen. I am Cybele..." Minutes passed—or maybe hours. Ned lost track of time in the goddess's presence. Finally, she gave him a gentle push in Rolf's direction. "You have what you need. Tonight you are my instrument. I will remain close, yet not so near as to frighten my Earth Mage." She paused a beat. "I don't want to destroy his mind. Not really, but I shall if it is the only path left to me."

Feeling like he'd awakened from a long sleep, Ned shook himself all over. Once he could form thoughts again, he was surprised Karras hadn't come out to check on him. He stepped cautiously closer to where Rolf sat, his back against a thick evergreen bole. Ned stopped about twenty feet away. "I have a story to tell you," he began softly, weaving compulsion into his words.

"I don't want to hear it."

"Oh, but I think you do. It concerns your birthright. A sacred gift lives within you. Let me tell you about it." He hesitated. "If you refuse to hear me, the goddess will destroy you."

Rolf's head snapped up, and he curled his lips into a snarl. "She damned near already has." He blew out a ragged sounding breath. "Fine. I give up—for now. Let's hear what you have to say."

"Your father was an Earth Mage. He fell in love with your mother while she was wed to another, but the other man was a drunk and abusive..."

Not Karras, but Landarik, came near the spelled circle Ned had drawn about Rolf and himself. He interrupted his tale and turned to address the wizard, but Cybele said, "Leave him to me."

By the time he was finally done Ned felt like an empty gourd. He tottered with fatigue. Cybele had filled him, and he'd emptied her wisdom into the velvet of an otherwise silent night. He rubbed his tired eyes, waiting.

When Rolf finally responded, his voice sounded rusty, as if he hadn't used it in centuries. He coughed and cleared his throat, beginning again. "Thank you." The simple dignity in the words warmed Ned. "If it's all the same to you, please leave us alone now."

Ned glanced toward where he'd last seen Cybele. She was no longer visible to him, but he heard her voice deep in his mind. *"Go, manling. You have done well. Your task here is complete."*

WILL I STILL HAVE A HUSBAND?

*L*ori pounced on Ned the second he pulled the front door open, her red-rimmed eyes stark testimony to her pain, her expression edgy. "Well? Who's out there? When will Rolf be back?" she demanded and dragged Ned toward the living room.

When he glanced around the room, everyone's faces could have curdled milk. After a quick peek upward, Landarik found something very interesting to look at on the floor. Ned wondered what Cybele had done to him.

"I'm not sure how long Rolf will be gone." Ned spread his hands apologetically. "The goddess Cybele is out there with him. I did as she instructed and then left."

"What instructions? What exactly did she—?" Lori persisted.

Ned shook his head and held up a hand to halt her flow of words. "That's for Rolf to tell you—along with Cybele. Goddess sendings are one of the mysteries." He opened his mouth to say more, and realized he couldn't. Cybele's message had been for Rolf and Rolf alone.

"But he's my husband." Her voice took on a shrill note. "I have a right to know."

Because he didn't want to cause her more pain than she already had, Ned said, "Yes, you do, but it doesn't change things."

"What's going to happen?" Lori clung to Ned's arm. "They," she looked pointedly at the wizards, "wouldn't tell me anything."

Ned met Karras's gaze, and the wizard spoke into his mind. *"Careful, lad. None of us knows much about Earth Mages. Least of all you."*

Ned transferred his attention to Lori. "What exactly do you want to know?" Her fingers felt like pincers. Ned loosened her grip. He was trying to buy time and figured she knew it.

She drew her brows together into a worried line. A tear rolled down one cheek, but she brushed it away. "Will Rolf still be my husband when he comes back into this house?" She hesitated. "Worse, is there a chance whatever's out there will just snap him up and I'll never see him again? Even that arrogant bastard," she pointed right at Landarik, "looked like he'd met his match when he slunk back in here with his tail between his legs."

Landarik's face reddened, but he didn't contradict her.

Thinking about Cybele's frank sexual interest, Ned felt heat rise in his face. Rolf was a very attractive man. Ned had no idea what Cybele might do with him. He walked Lori to a chair, but she shook her head. "I don't want to sit."

"I'm sorry, ma'am, but I can't guess what the goddess has in mind." A corner of his mouth turned downward. "I have a hard enough time figuring out wizards, and I grew up with them."

Something registered in Ned's exhausted mind. Amanda. Where was she? He scanned the small room again, thinking perhaps he'd missed her in a dim corner.

"Upstairs asleep," Karras said, reading his thoughts with ease. "Which is not a bad idea. You're dead on your feet."

Nodding, Ned turned toward the front door intent on returning to the tree where he'd slept before. He had his hand on the knob when Lori said, "There are extra beds in the loft. Take one. Just not too near my daughter, please."

WHEN HE OPENED HIS EYES, sunlight streamed through a skylight carved into the steeply pitched roof. Still feeling like someone had tossed him in front of a carriage and all four horses ran him over, Ned groaned.

"I wondered when you were going to get up, sleepyhead." Amanda's soft voice was like a balm.

Ned turned so he could see her. Amanda's blonde hair was sleep tousled. Only her head was visible under a thick pile of blankets. At first he thought she was sleeping on the floor, but when he jockeyed himself up on an elbow, he saw she lay on a low cot pushed under a window cut from under the eaves. The loft was one large room. A curtained alcove sat off to one side. Presumably, Rolf and Lori slept there.

Trunks lined the walls, likely full of clothing judging from what was draped over them.

Last night rushed back to him. "Have you seen your mother or father this morning?"

She shook her head. "No, but I heard Mom crying a little bit ago. She never came upstairs last night."

Not good.

"We should get moving." Ned started to toss the blankets back, but remembered he wore only his smallclothes. Glancing about, he saw his clothing strewn across the wooden floor. He'd been so tired, he didn't even remember undressing. "I need to gather my things," he said. "Could you shut your eyes or go downstairs or something?"

"What if I want to stay?"

The response from his body was instantaneous. Desire raced through him like high voltage magic. "Probably not a good idea," he managed, pulling the covers up under his chin. His newly erect cock throbbed hotly against his belly. He wanted to stroke himself, relieve the ache in his balls. Instead, he gritted his teeth together and tried to think of something besides Amanda and the tempting allure of her lush body.

She slithered from under the bedclothes and crossed the loft to him in just a few steps. Breasts, hips, belly, and a mat of golden hair between her legs were clearly visible beneath a threadbare nightshirt that ended at the top of her thighs.

His mouth went dry when she perched on the edge of his bed and reached a hand to touch his face. "Are we all going to die? Because if we are, I don't particularly want to die a virgin. All those reasons Mom and Dad drummed into me about saving myself went out the window once we moved here." She burrowed a hand under the blankets and caressed his chest and shoulder, sending shivers all along his body. Angling her head, she settled her mouth over his.

Her kiss was sweet and tender and laced with sexual innocence. For a few precious moments, he wrapped a hand around her neck, held her to him, and kissed her back. She tasted wonderful. He wanted to pull her down next to him more than anything in the world. She was beautiful, and willing, and who knew when they'd get another chance? With the last of his ability to reason, he broke away.

"I...you... Blast it, we can't." Aware of the pitched battle between his body and his brain, Ned let go of her neck and moved back from her touch. "Besides," he said with a lopsided smile, "how would I explain it to your mother?"

Then there's the small matter of my magic, which might be at risk...

After a hesitation, she smiled back. "I suppose you're right, but I'm tired of always doing what's proper. There are lots of things we can do that shouldn't harm your magic." Her smile grew impish. "I've been thinking about them." She tugged back the bedclothes and lay next to him, fitting her body to his.

Ned's token resistance evaporated like dragon's fire in a stiff wind, and he groaned low in his throat before pulling her into his arms and crushing his mouth down on hers.

She opened herself to his kiss and tangled her tongue with his. He cupped one of her breasts and teased the nipple, delighted by how it hardened beneath his fingertips. She repositioned herself so she straddled one of his legs and the heat from her core seared him as she writhed against his thigh.

Unsure how to please her, he moved his hand experimentally from her breast to between her legs. Tearing his mouth from hers, he struggled to form words with a tongue that felt thick and uncooperative. "You'll have to help me. I've never…"

"Me either. But I know what I like, and I bet you do too. Here." She placed her hand over his and showed him the motion she wanted. Hard, little circles around the nubbin at the very front of her woman's parts.

"Like this?" He mimicked her motion.

"Exactly." She sounded breathless when she wrapped her hand around his erect cock and started moving it up and down.

Breath clotted in his throat. He'd never imagined someone else's touch could feel so much better than his own. He slithered lower and closed his mouth over her breast, still keeping his hand between her legs. Her hips bucked beneath his touch and her breathing quickened.

"Faster," she gasped, followed by, "Yes, oh God, yes. Keep touching me. I'll come again if you do." She squirmed beneath his ministrations, and pure, unshaped magic streamed from her in multihued waves of light.

She quickened her stroking up and down his erection. Ned's balls snugged against his body just before semen jetted from him in long, lazy waves that shook him from the tips of his toes to the top of his head. She thrust against his hand, moaning softly, while he drifted down from the most intense experience in his life.

He let go of her breast. "Do you need more?" he asked, wanting to share the intense pleasure she'd given him.

"It's perfect. You're perfect. Just a little more. Almost." Her words had a catch in them, and her face and chest were splotched with a lovely rose color.

As he rubbed, her nubbin slicked with even more moisture, and she trembled beneath his touch. Her responsiveness made him feel invincible. He tried a different touch pattern on her engorged flesh. She wrapped her arms around him and held on as her body vibrated with release. Watching her while she came made him feel like a god. Her neck corded with passion, and her lovely lips were parted. Her nipples formed stiff peaks, and the color in her face deepened.

For long moments afterward, he cradled her against him, luxuriating in the feel of her body against his. When he finally let go and brushed his lips over hers, he balanced on an elbow looking down at her. "You're so beautiful. Gods, but you're stunning. Thank you for that."

She smiled crookedly. "Thank you. We're still technically virgins, but at least we managed a small incursion into forbidden territory."

Heat flooded his chest and face. "I'll do my best to figure out if celibacy is the price of my magic. Until Karras blasted me with that, it never occurred to me." He chewed his lower lip. "Lots of different magics here. Wizards don't know much about mine, and no one knows anything about your father's."

Her smile faded, replaced by a serious expression. "I care about you, Ned. A lot. And it's not because you're the first guy my age who's happened along. It's way deeper than that."

He matched her mood. "I care about you too, Amanda. And I shall look forward to us getting to know one another ever so much better."

She giggled. "You sound so stiff and formal sometimes."

He shrugged. "Can't help it. We're both products of who raised us. For you, it was humans. For me, wizards."

She extricated herself from his arms. Pulling one of several obviously hand-loomed blankets off a nearby shelf, she wrapped it around herself and sat on the edge of the bed. "That truly was amazing for me too, but we have to focus on big picture stuff." She made a wry face. "*Big picture stuff* is one of Dad's sayings. Anyway, first Jon's gone. Then I'm almost, well, dead. Now it looks like Dad isn't coming back—"

"What makes you think so?"

"Why else would Mom be crying?"

Ned could think of lots of reasons, including Rolf telling Lori he'd been unfaithful to her. Cybele had been downright seductive with him, and he was just a half-grown kid. Rolf was a mature man who'd know exactly what to do if a woman threw herself at him.

Goddess's breath! I can't tell her that.

"Let's go downstairs," he suggested again. "So we can find out about your father." Amanda kept her eyes on him while he got into his garments. He found himself staring at her rather than dressing, and dragged his gaze away. A village maid or two had been intriguing, but nothing like what he felt toward the lissome creature not twenty feet away. She was eager for him too. What happened between them proved it.

"I don't want to, but I'll give you some privacy. If I stay while you're dressing, we may never make it downstairs." His voice sounded gruff, and he felt flustered as he climbed down the ladder. Although he'd just come, his cock was hard again, curved against his belly.

"Music to my ears," floated after him. Even the sound of her voice sent chills cascading up and down his back.

Could I be falling in love?

Don't be ridiculous. I barely know her.

But he knew the important parts. She had a bright, shining soul, and it called to him louder than any Siren song.

Lori sat by herself at the kitchen table clutching a cup of tea between her hands. It appeared she'd never stopped crying. If anything, her eyes were redder and more swollen than the night before. Ned wondered where the wizards had sequestered themselves. Questing outward with his mage senses, he decided they'd left. Maybe not far, but distant enough he couldn't discern them.

He nodded good morning at Lori, but she sat like a statue, with no indication she even recognized his existence. Ned felt awkward. He didn't know how he could comfort her. Wizards didn't behave like this. They led with their heads, not their hearts.

"Is there anything I can do to help?" he asked, but she didn't answer.

Feeling useless, Ned headed toward the kitchen to forage something left over from the previous night. He was just focusing magic to warm some soup and biscuits when Amanda came in through the pantry, her cheeks aglow. He hadn't seen her leave the house and figured she must have used the front door.

"Brrrr, chilly out this morning. Getting used to cold water was probably the hardest thing about leaving civilization."

"Why don't you heat it?"

She looked at him. Her clear blue eyes caught the morning sun shining through the kitchen windows. "There's a hot spring back behind the house. If I don't want a full soak, though, it's the pump or nothing."

Ned explained how she could focus Earth and Fire magic to heat the pump water once it was in a basin. Amanda had just requested clarification on some of what he said when Rolf strode into the house. His eyes glistened with an inner fire, and he looked positively numinous. Like one of the gods. Relief hammered Ned. He'd been feeling guilty about whatever role he might have played in eroding Rolf and Lori's long relationship.

Lori must have sensed Rolf's presence. When Ned looked up, she stood under the archway between the kitchen and the dining room, her heart in her eyes. Pleading, but proud too. Somehow, Ned knew she wouldn't beg.

Rolf crossed the space between them in a twinkling and crushed her to him. "Beloved," he murmured. "Beloved of my soul."

"Come on." Ned gestured to Amanda. "Grab some food, and let's give them time alone. I can teach you how to heat water outside just as well as in here."

~

LORI THREADED her arms around her husband and kissed him over and over, her body heating under their fervent embrace. She'd been certain he wouldn't come back, except maybe to tell her goodbye. Otherwise, why would those damned wizards have been so close-mouthed about the *thing* wooing him outside?

Finally, needing information more than kisses, she broke away. Leaning back, she looked up and met his gaze. "You're not leaving me?"

"Never." The smile she'd almost forgotten played about his lips, making a dimple that winked at her. "I'm not losing my mind, either."

"Should I ask what happened?"

"I learned a lot about myself," he said, his forehead creasing into a frown. "Come sit by me. I'll give you the short version. Then maybe we can sleep. Doesn't look like you had any, either."

She shook her head. "I didn't. Would you like some tea?"

"Sure, Lor. That would be wonderful."

Armed with steaming mugs and the last of the previous night's biscuits spread with butter and wild blackberry jam, she found Rolf on the front porch. Leaning their backs against the wall of the house, they sat in the morning sun.

"...appears Ma took lovers from time to time. I told you she was Irish, but never the rest. I always thought she was a Selkie." He laughed softly. "She loved the water so. Cybele told me she was really one of the Sidhe. The father—my father—she'd never tell me about was an Earth Mage." Rolf held up a hand. "Don't ask me too many questions about what it means because I'm not sure yet myself. All in all though, it's an improvement over the drunken Irish brute I assumed was my dad.

"From what Cybele says, Father always meant to return to indoctrinate me. By the time he showed up, guess I was long gone to college. According to the goddess, something magical bonded him and Ma. The second time he came to her, they ran off together to an enchanted land. Cybele was put out because she had to fetch him back. It's been years, and she remembers it like it was yesterday."

"How long were they in fairyland?" Amazed she could still smile after the night she'd spent, Lori took a sip of mint tea.

"Don't know. I think they measure time differently than we do." He shrugged. "In any event, after chastising Dad and sending him off somewhere, the goddess remembered me and hunted us down. She started doing what she did with her other Earth Mages, and I assumed I was going nuts. We got everything squared away, though."

A sudden flare of suspicion chilled her. Lori knew she wasn't going to like sharing Rolf, especially not with a goddess. "How so?"

"She came to terms with me not knowing shit about the things I'm supposed to be able to do. On my side, I promised to at least try." His expression turned serious. "I always wondered why I knew the location of petroleum deposits without checking the maps. Every once in a while one of the guys would catch me and make a snide remark. I always kept a map folded in my pocket or briefcase. Kind of like a cheap prop I could drag out with a flourish."

Lori took a thoughtful breath. She spoke around a mouthful of buttered biscuit. "This explains a couple of things."

"Like what? Better make it simple, Doctor. I'm pretty tired."

"Well, you have one type of magic, and it appears I have another. It could explain our strong attraction to one another, and why you never had any other women, or me any other men. When I was afraid that immortal witch was going to make off with you, it felt like my life was over. I started to go outside to confront her, scratch her eyes out if need be, but the damned wizards dragged me back."

Rolf pulled her against him. "I feel the same way about you. We're part of one another, you and me." His voice was muffled in her hair.

"Awk, I'm getting jam all over you." She pulled the hand holding her biscuit out from between them. "Butter too."

"Doesn't matter." Blue eyes sparkled at her.

"What do you think about us being linked because of two types of magic? And if your mom was a Sidhe, how'd she get linked to a drunk? Why didn't she just vaporize him with magic?" Lori licked butter and jam off her fingers.

"In terms of Mom, she mucked around in some wizard-driven spell and had to do penance. It stripped a lot of her power. I honestly don't know about your theory regarding the two types of magic. Maybe you could ask Karras, since it looks like we'll be seeing more of him."

"He's okay." Lori nodded slowly. "Those two other

wizards, though. Meh! I don't care if we never see them again. Did you notice how rudely they treated poor Ned?"

Rolf snorted. "Poor Ned, who's all but bedded our daughter?"

Giggling, Lori punched him in the arm.

"So long as you're in an abusive mood," he grinned at her, "what about the mother you've never met? Even the wizards roll their eyes when her name comes up."

"Don't know." She shook her head. "I'm too tired to go there." Lori's eyes felt sandpapery and heavy. Before she could catch herself, they closed of their own accord. "Maybe we could catch a catnap. I can't think any more right now."

"Um-hmm. Did anyone milk the goats or let the sow out? It's a nice enough day, we could even let the horses graze a bit since we never took them back to the lower meadow."

"Maybe Mandy and Ned could take care of those things."

Rolf found her lips with his. After a kiss, which told her more eloquently than any words he was hers and hers alone, he nuzzled her neck. "I'll go find the kids and give them the chore list. Then I'll join you upstairs. Don't start without me."

It was an old joke between them, and it made her laugh. "The only thing I might do is fall asleep."

"Never fear. I excel at waking the dead." He took her hand and laid it over a very erect cock before getting to his feet.

"Wait," she protested. "Bring that back here."

"The loft, woman. I'll be there soon."

~

KARRAS SAT at the table in his cabin with Sierna. Landarik paced from one wall to its opposite, and back again. Shyla nipped at him when he got too close to her tail. "Worthless cur," Landarik snapped.

"Just because Cybele told you the truth about a few things is no reason to take your ill temper out on my wolf." Karras's patience wore thin. He'd thought a conversation about strategy might best be accomplished away from the Haraldssen home, but so far all they'd done was carp at one another.

"Ned's place is with his regiment," Landarik insisted, shifting gears.

"Why?" Getting to his feet, Karras was aware how tired he was—and how old. "It isn't like the lad has any affinity for the military. You—or someone like you—stuffed him there in hopes he'd get himself killed."

Landarik turned an unattractive shade of red, his pale skin blotchy. "So what if we did? It's not like he's one of us."

"Stop!" Karras stepped in front of the other wizard and made his dark eyes hard as stone. "Did you hear what you just said?"

"Well, he isn't one of us. Do you have a problem with the truth?" Supercilious blue eyes blazed into Karras's dark ones.

"Karras is right," Sierna said from her place at the table. Head resting on an upraised hand, she bit her lower lip. "I hate to admit it, but we—none of us—treated the boy fairly, starting with when we chased his mother out of the stronghold. We took away the only one who ever loved him and replaced her love with scorn and contempt. No matter what Ned did, it was never good enough. Not for any of us."

"You're going to start making it up to him now?" Landarik inquired caustically. "We have enough problems with the Infernals. He's one pathetic human. Not even a terribly competent one. I fail to understand what all the fuss is about."

"Since he's so incompetent, let him remain here." Karras recognized an opening and jumped on it. "Surely you won't miss him."

"He made a commitment when he accepted the warrior tattoos."

"At least give him a choice," Sierna murmured. "He said he was willing to return with us yesterday."

"Yes." Karras's tone was acidic. "He understands the concept of duty, or he would have told all of you to go to hell long since."

"There's something growing between him and the girl." Sierna reached across the table for the kettle and poured more water over her tea leaves. "If we force him to leave, we may be subverting Aphrodite."

"Oh, so now I'm standing in the way of true love?"

"You wouldn't recognize it if you tripped over it," Sierna sniped.

Landarik pushed past Karras and slammed a fist into the wall. "Fine. I give up. Let us talk of something else." Cradling reddened knuckles with his other hand, he glared at the other two wizards.

"Now that the matter of Ned is settled, there are, indeed, other topics to cover." Karras broke off a hunk from a round of bread sitting on a nearby counter. He sat heavily in his favorite reading chair and looked at Landarik. "Oh, do sit. None of us likes to lose, least of all you. Try to put it aside. I would speak of how we can best protect Rolf and Lori and how we might find their son. Or at least determine if he's dead—or beyond salvage."

"They do need protection. The Infernals have them in their sights." Sierna pulled her chair closer to Karras. Reaching with nimble fingers, she filched some of his bread.

"I'll stay as close as I can," Karras went on. "Ned will help me, but I need at least one more wizard here since I must sleep sometime. Lori is vulnerable until she learns something about her magic. Her daughter too."

"What do you know of Lori's abilities?" Sierna leaned closer, clearly curious.

Karras frowned and blew out an exasperated breath. "Not much. She expends much of her power keeping me out of her head. 'Tis likely an unconscious reflex. I'm certain she's used it all her life to keep others from getting too close."

"There's also the Earth Mage problem. I've culled through my memory ever since Cybele showed up, but I'll be damned if I can remember aught about them." Landarik hunkered between the other two wizards and rocked back on his heels.

Karras was grateful the battle lord was getting over his pique. In the dim reaches of his memory, he recalled Landarik had banished his only son to a distant world for a minor episode of disrespect.

Karras nodded agreement. "Yes, I'd give much for access to the stronghold library—without taking the time to travel to the Old Country. It must be a thousand years since any of us have seen one like Rolf."

Landarik spat on the floor. "I tried to ask Cybele. You know how well *that* went."

"No," Karras looked pointedly at him, "we actually don't."

One corner of Landarik's mouth twisted downward. "She told me I was a young incompetent who couldn't remember my lessons. Said it wasn't her job to remind me of them. It was like she expected me to remember everything I've ever learned about every single type of magic-wielder."

Karras thought the goddess had treated Landarik much as the wizard treated Ned, but kept his counsel. No point getting Landarik riled up again.

"I wonder," Sierna murmured, "just what Amanda—and this missing Jon—will be able to do. Magic combined is often stronger than any of the strains alone." Sitting straighter, she snapped her fingers. "I've got it," she exclaimed. "Landarik and I will return tomorrow. We shall tell the Council about Lira and recommend she be ordered here to help you."

Karras sighed. He was less than thrilled by Sierna's suggestion. Lira was so high-handed, she made Landarik look like a piker. Daughter of one of the three wizards comprising the High Council, she'd been pampered and spoiled since birth. Yet, she was Lori's mother, so such an assignment made sense. After all, it was a parent's responsibility to look after their young, even those they'd just as soon forget they ever had.

"Lira's not going to accede. At least not easily," Karras muttered.

Sierna snorted. "Likely not. 'Tis easy enough to ignore a mistake you'll only have to kill later." She paused for a beat, her lips pursed in thought. "We really ought to rescind that requirement concerning our lost children. No point in destroying them now that scarcely any humans remain to notice anything. I'll make a point of bringing it up before the High Council."

"I'm not so certain Lira will fight this," Landarik chimed in. "When knowledge of her illegitimate child becomes public, her shame might make her welcome an excuse to flee."

Sierna snorted. "Are you suggesting we can be a tad judgmental? Never mind our tendency toward gossip."

"If the shoe fits..." Landarik smirked.

"Give it a rest you two." Karras felt like yelling, but he modulated his voice and added a smidgeon of compulsion to his words. "Mayhap Lira will become more manageable in a week or so. With a bit of time, the worst of her anger may blow itself out."

Landarik laughed. "Oh, you think so? She's worse than I am."

"At least you admit it." Sierna poked him hard. Landarik ended up on his rump on the floor, falling on Shyla, who snapped at him.

"Sorry, sorry." Landarik smoothed the silvery fur with a calloused hand until Shyla bared her teeth. "Your wolf never has liked me," he muttered and pulled his hand back.

"Because she sees your true character," Sierna simpered.

"Enough. Both of you. Ned can help me until Lira shows up." Catching Landarik's disbelieving glance, Karras added,

"You've never appreciated the lad. He has far more of an affinity for trees and animals than we do."

"*Yes.*" Shyla's greenish gaze blazed at Landarik. "*I like the human far better than you.*" With a tail swish to punctuate her words, she moved to the far side of the room.

"Goddess's breath! In the last few hours I've been criticized by a goddess and a wolf." Landarik grunted his annoyance through clenched teeth. "Time to go back to the war. At least my troops appreciate me."

I wouldn't be so certain.

Karras had been expecting Landarik to meet with an unexplained accident in battle for years. That it hadn't happened yet remained one of the mysteries.

LOVE BECKONS

$\mathcal{N}$ed couldn't recall a time he'd felt quite this happy. When Karras told him he needn't return to the war on the other side of the mountains, Ned jumped at the opportunity to remain with the Haraldssens. A week passed when he lost himself in prosaic tasks like caring for animals and helping Rolf ready the cabin for the winter to come. The wizards had castes where some were warriors, some farriers, some agriculturalists, some archivists, and so on. To find an entire universe of skills between Rolf and Lori amazed him. It also reassured him he could actually live on his own. Subjected to wizard brainwashing since birth, Ned assumed he'd be a lost soul outside the structure provided by one of the wizards' several strongholds. To find it wasn't true delighted him.

The best part, though, was Amanda. They spent hours talking, and more hours cuddling. Ned asked Karras about the need to maintain his celibacy. Not in so many words. He sort of talked around the point because it embarrassed him to come right out with it.

Karras just shook his head. "I don't know, lad. Till we do, you will not jeopardize your magic."

"How can we find out?" Ned persisted, but Karras hadn't answered.

Maybe it's for the best, Ned thought as he helped Rolf tack weathered plastic sheeting over windows in the cabin, barn and shop. He'd come to respect the tall, blond man. Rolf didn't talk much, but he'd been very much to the point regarding Amanda, telling Ned to keep his hands off her. Ned wondered guiltily what Rolf would think about all the hugs and kisses he and Amanda shared. Never mind the proficiency they'd developed pleasuring one another during stolen moments.

They couldn't do much at night because of the tight sleeping arrangements in the cabin's loft, but he and Amanda managed to stroke each other to orgasm several times each day. So much so, he'd come more in the last week than in the previous year. He loved her fingers on him, and they'd graduated to using their mouths too. He ached to find out how it would actually feel to immerse his cock inside the scorching heat of her body, but trusted Karras's advice enough to hold off.

One of the pieces of plastic disintegrated when Ned attempted to tack it in place. It had happened before. He'd tried focusing magic to mend the material, but it didn't work the same as it did with cloth—probably because plastic wasn't a natural substance.

"It's okay." Rolf handed him another sheet. "I'm surprised it's lasted this long. Should have brought more with us. I'm going to need to come up with something different for next year."

"Looks like you did pretty well figuring out what you'd need."

Rolf laughed. "I studied a well-documented prototype. American pioneers."

Ned scratched his head. "Afraid I only studied wizard history."

Cocking his head to one side, Rolf looked at him. "That's a damned shame. We have books. Lots of them. You could read about the human side of your ancestry."

"I suppose they're in English?" At Rolf's nod, Ned went on. "I can read Elvish, wizard script, Greek, and Latin. Though I speak English, my reading skills could be better."

"All the more reason to read." Rolf hesitated. "Maybe you could help me with Greek and Latin since Cybele left me things to look at. I took both in school, but it was a long time ago." Pounding a last tack into place, Rolf rubbed his hands together, presumably to warm them. It was cold enough, Ned had to channel magic to keep his fingers from freezing. "In exchange, I could help you with English," Rolf offered.

Ned nodded at him. "Sounds like a deal, sir."

"Stop calling me sir."

"Are you certain, sir, uh, Mister Haraldssen?"

A snort, followed by, "Just Rolf will do," brought a smile to Ned's lips. He couldn't recall smiling quite so much, ever. His facial muscles felt a bit odd from all the stretching.

Ned sensed familiar energy. It created a subtle

displacement in the air, and he knew Karras would be there soon. Sure enough, a wizard materialized a few feet away. Except it wasn't Karras.

Shocked, Ned fell back a few feet, hands raised in case he needed to call magic in a hurry. A swirl of long red hair and black robes swooshed out of a traveling portal. Blue-green eyes shot darts at the world in general as Lira surveyed the scene. Her face would have been beautiful, if it weren't drawn into a snarl. She clutched one of the ancient Dyerwood staffs, rich with runic carvings, in a long-fingered hand.

Goddess help us, where'd she get one of the nine sacred staffs?

"My lady." Ned bowed low in Lira's direction and steeled himself for her infamous temper. He didn't have to wait long.

"You!" She raised the staff menacingly, and Ned threw wards up. "Ha. Those puny things wouldn't keep an acolyte out. Why aren't you with your unit?" Her mouth twitched with derision. "Finally deserted, did you? Never fear, I'll see you back with Landarik in a trice."

"I have his permission to be here."

"Likely story." She screwed up her face as if she'd smelled something horrid and moved her head from side to side. "What a pig sty this is. Oh look, there's even a pig." She pointed to the sow in her outside pen, surrounded by growing piglets.

"Lori's mother?" Rolf moved to stand next to Ned, his face a study in amazement—and anger.

"Uh-huh." Ned considered using mind speech to call Karras, but decided he probably didn't need to. Even miles away at his cabin up canyon, the wizard would surely sense Lira's potent energy.

"Why are you all standing about like dolts? Isn't anyone going to welcome me?" Lira sneered.

"That would be just about enough out of you." Rolf strode toward her. "Either find some manners or go back to where you came from."

They were the same height. Ned watched as sparks flew between the two of them. Storm clouds gathered in response to Rolf's mood. They closed quickly, blotting out the weak, late autumn sun.

"You dare to speak thus to me?" Lira curled her lips with derision.

"Funny, I could say the same thing to you. This is my house, and these are my lands. I will not tolerate disrespect toward myself or my guests."

Lori came around the corner of the house, a gathering basket looped over one arm. It was filled with some of the last of the garden's bounty. "I heard shouting..." Her words faded as she took in their new arrival.

"What's all the ruckus?" Amanda called from the front porch.

"You may as well come on over," Lori said. "It would appear your grandmother has arrived."

Amanda covered the fifty feet quickly. She stopped when Rolf shook his head. "Close enough, Mandy. This one's about as friendly as a pit viper."

"You forgot to comb your hair," Lira snapped, her eyes leveled on Amanda.

"Well, *Grannie.*" Amanda's sarcastic inflection was unmistakable. "Nice to meet you too—I think." She stared frankly at the wizard.

Where was Karras? Ned shifted from foot to foot. Somehow he didn't see either Rolf or Lori inviting Lira in for tea. He was certain the wizard wasn't about to back down, either.

"You must have been expecting me, since none of you are surprised by my arrival. Where are my quarters?" Lira's glance strayed from one to the other before settling on Lori. "Daughter, I expected a more fitting welcome."

"My apologies, your highness." Lori stepped forward, splotches of color high on both cheeks. "We failed to prepare adequately for your arrival. Given our lapse in judgment and manners—which aren't likely to improve—why don't you go back to where you came from?"

Bravo, Ned cheered, wishing he'd had the moxie to stand up to the wizards. The expression on Lira's face was priceless. *You can dish it out,* he thought, *but you can't take it. Just like Landarik.*

"Because she can't." Karras's form winked into existence on the heels of his words. He must have been close because he didn't come through a portal. "She was sent here as punishment."

"Have them send her somewhere else," Lori said, balled fists on her hips and fire flaring from her eyes.

"What a bully idea," Rolf seconded. "We have enough problems without her."

"I'm not used to hearing myself characterized as a *problem.*" Lira's tone was haughty. "My quarters?"

"There aren't any, *Grannie*."

"Stop calling me that."

"You'd probably think even less of the other things I'd like to call you."

Ned draped an arm around Amanda. Laying a finger over his lips, he shook his head. "It's not wise to bait her," he whispered into Amanda's ear.

"I have a cabin not far from here." Karras took Lira's arm and led her off to one side.

"So?" She shook him off.

"You can stay there when you're not guarding this family from Infernals."

"I told Father I wasn't interested in guarding humans—"

"I'm guessing he told you what you wanted was irrelevant." Karras snapped the words out.

"How could you possibly know?" Lira croaked. Something very much like fear flickered across her ageless face.

"Because I know Hreth. We were boys together. You really are behaving very badly. You don't want me to raise him through my scrying pool—or the stones—to give him a report. Or do you?"

An almost imperceptible headshake.

"Good. Shall we begin anew? Tell your daughter you're pleased to make her acquaintance."

"Oh, stop." Lori tossed her hands in a disgusted gesture. "I'm not particularly pleased to meet her. She dumped me when I was a baby. Why on earth would I give a rat's ass about a perfect stranger who happened to give birth to me?"

She stomped toward the house. "Come on, Amanda. Let's get something going for dinner."

It was all Ned could do to maintain a neutral expression. He wanted to laugh in Lira's face and ask how it felt to be on the receiving end of ridicule and rejection. Instead, he turned back to the plastic, plucked a sheet off the pile, and walked to the far side of the barn, hammer in hand.

The wolves charged out of the nearby forest. Shyla had joined the other three. They dragged a freshly killed doe between them. Ned heard Lira grunt in disgust, "Ewww..." He peeked around the side of the barn and watched the wizard back away from the wolves.

How odd. Surely she's not afraid of them.

Many wizards weren't particularly attuned to animals, but Lira's reaction was odd enough, even Karras seemed puzzled.

"They're just wolves. Talk with them." Karras bent to ruffle Shyla's thick winter coat.

"I'd rather not." Lira drew closer to Karras. "Landarik said one of them bit him—twice."

"He exaggerated," Karras said sternly.

"I don't care." Lira folded her arms across her chest and turned away.

Shaking his head, Ned returned to his work. Rolf soon joined him.

Dinner had been over for a while. Rolf, Lori, Amanda, and Ned sat around the table avoiding any conversation that included Lira's name. When the men came in for the evening meal, Lori told them Lira was off limits—in every way. Including she wasn't allowed to set foot in the house, even if she apologized for her earlier behavior. After thinking things through for several hours, Lori figured there weren't enough words in the English language to apologize for walking away from your own child.

Her adoptive mom and dad had been wonderful. Lori couldn't have asked for better parents. They'd loved and cared for her right up until they died in an avalanche on a high-altitude mountaineering expedition when she was thirteen. Young and grieving, she'd gone to live with her mother's straight-laced maiden aunt. The transition wasn't an easy one, but Lori never wasted time feeling sorry for herself. She wasn't about to start now.

Ned looked at Rolf. "Say, maybe you could show me some of those history books you told me about earlier."

"Good idea." Rolf pushed to his feet. "Do you need help clearing things?" he asked Lori.

"No, we're good, Dad." Amanda smiled at him. "Mom and I will join you once we're done."

A knock on the front door startled Lori. She shot a worried glance at her husband.

"Not many possibilities," he said. "I'll go see." Pulling the Winchester off the wall, and clicking off the safety, Rolf headed for the door. "Don't worry," he called over his shoulder, "the bad guys never knock."

"Then why do you have the gun?" Lori countered.

"Insurance."

Lori didn't realize how nervous she was until pain and

the salty taste of blood told her she was biting too hard on her lower lip. She gripped her hands together in her lap. Karras's voice didn't help, until it became apparent he'd arrived alone. The tight place in her chest uncoiled, and she inhaled raggedly. Despite her brave words about Lira, the woman aroused a welter of conflicting emotions.

The little-girl part of Lori wanted to throw herself into the female wizard's arms and demand to be loved. Another more grown-up part wanted to slap her until her supercilious expression dissolved, leaving her naked and vulnerable.

Karras walked slowly into the room. He looked at the remains of their dinner still on the table. "May I?" he asked, gesturing toward the food.

Lori nodded and got out of her chair to find him a clean plate. She handed it to him, furled her brows, and asked, "Well?"

"I told her not to come." Settling into a chair with his plate, Karras shoveled food into his mouth. He ate so ravenously, Lori wondered if he was out of food at his house. From the stocks she'd seen there, it hardly seemed possible, but she decided not to bother him with any more questions until he was finished.

Rolf and Amanda cleared things off the table. On one of his trips, Rolf detoured into the front room. Returning, he dropped a thick book in front of Ned. "The history book," he explained. "One of them, anyway."

"Thanks." Ned opened the leather-bound volume and bent his head to survey its contents.

Karras laid his fork aside. "Wonderful! Thank you. I

didn't want to take time to prepare anything at my own house." He drew his thick, gray eyebrows together. "No easy way to say this, but there's something...wrong with Lira. It may be as simple as her shame at being found out. Or it may run far deeper. I spent time conversing with her father." Karras blew out a frazzled-sounding breath. "Hreth admitted to being rough with Lira. I have no idea exactly what he meant, since neither of them would give me any details."

"I don't care what happened to her. She's not welcome here," Lori blurted.

Karras eyed her sadly. "I understand why you'd feel that way, but I'm asking you to reconsider. You haven't lived as one of us. You don't understand our laws, nor our customs. Having children out of wedlock with another wizard can be cause for excommunication. To breed outside our race is a serious crime, one always punished by exile—sometimes even by death.

"I did discover that your father was a human mage. Lira wouldn't divulge his name to either Hreth or me. Or tell us whether his magic was compromised afterward." The wizard looked meaningfully at Ned.

"I always knew there had to be more like me," Ned murmured. "After my mother fled—or was banished—the wizards ignored me whenever I asked about my father." He caught Karras's dark gaze. "Do you suppose Lori's father might be related to me?"

"'Tis unlikely and not the topic at hand."

"Why won't you tell the boy about his father?" Rolf tossed a conciliatory smile at the wizard. "I can understand why he'd want to know."

"Because I don't know myself. Not for certain. There's a guild of human mages. I intended to introduce the lad there when he was a bit older. They don't have the same strictures as us. Ned's father would surely make himself known if the lad asked directly."

Ned straightened in his chair. "Why wouldn't I be old enough now?"

"You're barely past childhood." The wizard shot an indulgent glance his way. "I don't recall exactly, but you can't be even twenty-two yet."

"Twenty-two!" Rolf glanced at Lori. "We thought he was somewhere around eighteen, like Amanda."

Karras waved a dismissive hand. "Fifteen, twenty, thirty... What difference does it make? The lad is young. All of you will live very long lives. Hundreds of years. A few one way or the other are meaningless."

"I was old enough to muster into the Army," Ned pointed out.

"If I'd been there, I would have had something to say about that." Karras clacked his jaw shut and stood. "Time for me to be going. Hreth terminated Lira's ability to use our traveling portals as soon as she arrived here by blocking her access. I should check on her all the same, though."

He laid a hand on Lori's shoulder. "We shall begin your lessons in earnest tomorrow. I may bring Lira with me."

"Don't—" Lori began before her conscience tripped her up. She wasn't doing any better in the temper department than her mother. Shame filled her, making her cheeks burn. Lori rose and faced Karras. She squared her shoulders before meeting his eyes. "If you think it's what needs to happen, go ahead. I'll find a way to come to terms with it."

"I knew you would." The wizard beamed at her. "Thank you. We have larger problems than the disgruntled daughter of one of our leaders. I shall attempt to get her to understand that *again*, once I return home."

DARK GODS OUT FOR BLOOD

"**I** don't wish to see her any more than she wants to see me," Lira screamed at Karras. "Leave me to my own devices, old man. I shall serve my time here in my own way." She raised her hands to call power, and he wondered if she was about to strike him. At the last minute, she spun and stormed out of the cabin, slamming the door behind her.

"She needs to do without a few meals. It might make her remember what it is to be humble," Shyla commented. The wolf crawled out from under the table where she'd taken refuge when the argument escalated.

Karras snorted. Frustration scoured his nerves till they felt stretched over hot coals. He'd been alternately cajoling, reasoning with, or yelling at Lira for hours—ever since they'd awakened that morning. He understood why Hreth had punished her. Personally, he thought a good flogging might help, followed by a public display of whip marks on her back and buttocks.

"Karras," sounded through his mind-link to Ned. Something in the lad's tone, even projected over distance, alarmed him.

"What?"

"Infernals. You must come. Lori... Amanda..."

"How many? What kind?"

Ned didn't answer. Karras checked the mind-link. Severed. He didn't waste any time. Racing outside, he spied Lira sulking next to the barn. Clutched in one hand, her staff glowed an angry red. Annoyance made his skin crawl. He raised a hand, drew power, and sent a bolt crashing into her.

"How dare you?" She spun to face him, staff raised, and rubbed at a reddening spot on her face.

"'Tis treason—and an affront to your heritage—to point the Dyerwood staff at me," he hissed. "We must fight. Pull your sorry self together. The Haraldssens are under attack."

Karras chanted. A glowing, rectangular portal formed. He considered their destination. He needed to bring them out close to Rolf and Lori's, but not so near they'd walk into a trap.

Shyla trotted up. *"Trouble?"*

"Yes, little one. Run find your family. Warn them, but take care. I don't know what stands against us."

The wolf took off, a silver streak against the midday light. Speaking a word to hold his spell, Karras hustled back to his cabin. He grabbed his wizard's staff, slammed the door, and warded his home against intruders. It wouldn't keep much out, but at least it would slow them down.

"Ready?"

Lira hadn't moved.

Karras girded himself to hurt her again and then thought better of it. Instead he spoke to her formally in their wizard tongue. "Lira. You are a warrior of our clan. This means you will fight to the death if necessary whenever called upon to defend the innocent. I, Karras, outrank you. I order you to accompany me and do your level best against the Infernals. Should you refuse me, you shall be called outcast for the remainder of your days."

"I already am," she said. Sorrow and defiance battled for ascendency on her face. Tears tracked down her flawless cheeks.

"Did you truly think no one would ever find out?" he asked, struggling to find compassion. "Lira, we live almost forever. 'Tis a very long time to hide something of this magnitude."

"I don't know what I thought," she muttered. "I should have aborted the child, but I couldn't force myself to do so."

"I offer you an opportunity to redeem yourself."

Lira squared her shoulders. "I accept." Expression grim, she sprinted to his side, staff in hand. "I'm through wallowing in shame. You're right, Karras. I owe my daughter and her family an apology." She grimaced. "Though 'tis painful to admit, I owe my daughter far more than that."

"Let us hope 'tisn't too late for you to deliver your message." He yanked Lira into the portal he'd drawn. Karras visualized a large oak tree about a quarter mile from the Haraldssen's and entered the Ways.

In the few minutes before the portal disgorged them, a

transformation took place in Lira. Her eyes reflected rigid determination to make reparation for her sins. Karras knew she'd put her long training in self-discipline and war craft to good use.

"Your father would be proud of you," he murmured as he sealed off their portal. "'Tis why he sent you to me—to give you an opportunity to think on what you've done and make amends. Now, help me figure out what manner of being we fight."

Eyes closed, arms outstretched with her staff in one hand, Lira joined her power with his.

"Wirricow. Many of them." She spat the words, her lips curled back in distaste. "I sense a goddess too. How can it be?"

"Rolf is an Earth Mage. The goddess protects him, though I doubt Cybele would lift a finger for his family."

"Goddess's breath. An Earth Mage." Shock registered on Lira's face. Eyes wide, eyebrows raised, she said, "You have to tell me more, but not just now. Look at my staff. I don't think I've ever seen it quite this bright."

"You're right about the Wirricow," Karras growled. Try as he might, he couldn't detect Rolf, Lori, or Amanda. He thought of trying to raise Ned, but didn't want to compromise the lad. Demons could intercept mind speech.

"Karras..." Ned's sending was weak.

"Yes, lad."

"It's a trap. The house..." A bolt of lightning cut off further words. A staunch wind blew up out of nowhere, making the tree branches sough.

"What'd he say?" Lira asked. "I heard your name, but not the rest."

Karras shook his head. Worry for the lad filled him.

"Mayhap I underestimated the boy if he's still trying to help." Lira gazed at the thick forest surrounding them. She raised her staff. It glowed bright white: a beacon against the darkness they faced.

"Mayhap you did. Come, we shan't be much assistance all the way back here."

"Wherever this storm came from, it provides good cover. I'm right behind you."

Brilliant light fell across their path. "Well." A dry voice stopped Karras dead. "It is about time *someone* showed up."

"My lady." Karras bowed low. In recognition of the goddess's presence, he laid his staff at her feet. "At your service."

After a pause, Lira followed suit and placed her staff in front of the goddess.

"You do not bow easily to me?" Menace twined through the silken tones.

"I was surprised and slow to react. I worship you, Cybele." Lira bent almost double, her forehead near the ground. "Command me, my lady."

"I plan to. Come. I need the two of you to draw the spell of the unmaking while I open a rent in the Earth to swallow the demon spawn. Guard your magic. This version of the casting won't be familiar to you. It requires many days, and you'll be naught but dead weight if you expend too much power too soon."

Karras wanted to ask her about Ned, or Lori and

Amanda, but judged now wasn't the time. Cybele's strategy was sound. Even if he hadn't agreed with her, it was unwise to argue with any deity. She was one of the most ancient, famous for her tempers and for retribution that fell upon those stupid enough to cross her.

His staff levitated, and then clunked to the ground next to him. Astonishment thrummed through Karras. Lira's staff flew through the air too. She caught hers handily.

They hurried forward. The clearing between the house and barn came into view, and Karras's mouth went dry. He was suddenly thankful for Cybele and any help she chose to give them. More than a hundred black-furred demons milled about the yard twirling clubs and maces. With blazing green eyes and snaggle teeth, they were hideous to look upon. Standing three feet high, they were swarthy and broad with heavily muscled arms and legs. A cross between goblins and apes, Wirricow were another of the Infernals' genetic experiments.

His wizard's staff pulsated in his hand.

The vermin had dragged one of the horses out of the barn. Mercifully, it was dead. Karras sent up a hasty prayer it hadn't suffered. Entrails splashed about the yard, and the Wirricow feasted on bloody horsemeat. Though he wasn't easily frightened, Karras's guts constricted. Lira's energy vibrated next to him, and he felt grateful for her youth and strength.

"Ready?" Cybele breathed into his mind.

He nodded.

"It begins." Cybele turned to a pillar of blinding light, and

the air melted around her. Colors splashed across the carnage.

Knowing the spell, Karras and Lira pulled power from the Earth and mixed in air currents. Though they tried to be unobtrusive to gain an edge, the demons noticed them almost immediately. Pulling magic as if from an endless source, the abominations stormed toward them.

Caught up in the goddess's spell, time flashed past. For every demon they killed, more poured through the hole leading to Hell. Hours turned to days. Karras felt his grasp on his power slip from time to time, but if Lira and he tag-teamed their joined power, one shored up the other.

He'd burned up damn near every trick in his arsenal to keep fighting when the yard rolled in slow waves, and he knew they'd almost won. "Finally." The word tore out of him.

"Finally, indeed," Lira spat back. "Cybele's ability may be endless, but ours isn't."

A fissure opened with a wrenching, tearing noise and spread into a crater. Some of the Wirricow fell through. They screeched imprecations and caught at the edges of the rapidly shifting earth with their sharp claws.

Karras dug deep and ramped up the energy pouring through his part of the unmaking spell. He was close to tapped out, but pushed harder anyway. Hesitation would mean death for him and Lira. Goddess only knew how the others were doing. What had Ned meant about the house being a trap?

"Karras." Lira panted. "More."

Mind speech took magic. Apparently, Lira's well was running dry too. Power flowed straight and sure from her hands in multicolored arcs. Her staff glowed so brightly, it was hard to look right at it.

He couldn't siphon off even so much as a stray thought. The spell required all his attention, and then some. Linking a hand to one of hers, he felt a slight increase in their magic. "Yessssss. Take that you goddess-forsaken spawn," he shrieked. A ball of raw energy burst between a clump of Wirricow and drove them into the pit.

Cybele added suction to her vortex. Karras felt life spill from first one demon, then the next, as they were dragged into the ever-widening hole. Some were still alive. The smell of their terror rose into the air, acrid and rotten. The crater spread rapidly from house to barn. One after the other, Wirricow fell prey to its hungry maw.

"Two more." Lira could barely talk. It looked like the energy from her staff was the only thing keeping her on her feet.

He knew how she felt. He wondered if he'd have enough power left to keep himself upright after this was over, or if he too, would get sucked into Cybele's hole.

Finally, they were done. The earth closed as quickly as it had opened and with far less fanfare. Blinking stupidly, Karras stared at the yard. It looked like nothing had happened. Even the horse was gone. He staggered and fell against Lira. She reached a hand to steady him. Sparks flew from their staffs when they clanked together.

"We must locate everyone. Days have passed." Lira started toward the house.

Something nagged at the edges of Karras's mind. What

was it? Lira was nearly to the porch. Memory crashed into him like an out-of-control wave. "Noooooo..." he screamed.

She turned slowly. "Have you lost your mind?" Red hair hung about her face. Dirt smudges marred every inch of exposed flesh. A jagged cut ran from eyebrow to chin. Karras wondered what had caused it.

"Ned." Shuffling forward, Karras caught up to Lira and made a grab for her arm. "He told me the house was a trap. We just got one gateway closed. We do not want to open another."

"If Lori and the rest aren't inside, then where are they? Goddess's teats but I'm tired." She wiped a grimy hand across her face, leaving more black streaks.

"I hope Ned and Mandy are safe in the forest." Rolf strode out of his shop with one arm firmly around Lori. Annoyance shot from him in hard, pulsing waves, and his jaw was set in a furious line.

Cybele materialized out of the ether and narrowed her eyes. The goddess didn't look much better than Lira. Her robes were torn, with long burned places.

Rolf glanced at Karras. "Sorry I wasn't more help, but she," he gestured toward Cybele, "stuffed me in the root cellar along with the canned goods, and hog-tied me with something invisible to boot. I had to threaten her before she found Lori and tucked her in next to me."

"Ungrateful wretch." Cybele shot him a look. "You could have found another wife—"

"I don't think so." Lori focused a death-gaze on the goddess.

With lightning speed, Rolf twisted to face Cybele. "If you

ever say anything like that again, I will bar you from my mind just like I did before. Even if you drive me mad, you will never again have access to me. Lori is part of me. Don't you ever forget it."

Karras felt the timbre and pitch of the goddess's ire rise like a hot wind. "We need to find the others," he said firmly. "Everything else can wait."

"COME ON, Mandy. We have to keep moving. It's not safe here." Ned tugged on her hand clasped firmly in his. He and Amanda were still in the forest, but ranging ever farther from the house as Rolf had instructed right after the yard filled with Wirricow.

A sudden storm rolled in, complete with thunder and lightning. On its heels, the sky lit with brilliant light in the direction of Rolf and Lori's cabin. The stink of magic scoured the air, burning his lungs.

"Where would we go?" Her voice was thin, scared.

"We can travel the same way the wizards do, using their portal system. You couldn't do it by yourself, but I can instruct the Ways to accept you."

"Okay, I guess." She closed her teeth over her lower lip and held tighter to his hand. "Going back's not an option, not after what crawled into the yard. You said the house isn't safe, either."

"It's not. Wirricow laid a trap there. I felt it just before your dad told me to keep you safe."

A muted rustling drew his attention, and Shyla broke

into the clearing, flanked by the Haraldssen's three wolves. If the wolves had been Infernals, he and Amanda would have been in deep shit.

Shyla relayed Karras's instructions about staying well away from the Wirricow, and Ned considered their options. None of them were good. The safest bet was taking their chances on the other side of the mountains. For all he knew, an entire Infernal host lay between them and Mono Lake. He thought about going higher, but didn't want to be trapped between a glacier and the crest of the Sierras. If it had just been him, Ned would have chosen to fight, but he had Amanda to think about.

The house was booby-trapped, probably right into an Infernal's lair. He'd cloaked himself in invisibility and watched Wirricow lay their insidious webs. At least he'd warned Karras. He wanted to tell him he was taking care of Amanda, but dark magic severed their mind link, and he didn't want to risk another spell.

Ned summoned a portal, waiting while it formed. "Come on." He pulled Amanda through the gateway, sealed it, and painted runes in the still air to make certain the Ways didn't jettison Amanda.

Uncharacteristically silent, she leaned into him. When he drew her tight against him, she was trembling. "Ssht. It'll be all right." He stroked her silky hair and invoked a calming spell to soothe her. No wonder she was rattled. Everything was all so new. She might hold a unique combination of magics, but she'd never leveraged any of them.

The trip was over quickly, and darkness from the Ways cleared as they stumbled out the gateway at the other end.

Amanda blinked, looking about her. "Where are we? This used to be a city. Which one?"

"San Francisco, if I calculated correctly. There are wizards here. They should shelter us until it's safe to go back."

At least I hope they will.

A tear rolled down her cheek. "Mom and Dad. They'll think we're dead."

Ned swallowed hard. Rolf and Lori might assume something like that when they couldn't locate them. "We need to find the wizards," he said. "They have ways to reach Karras over distances."

"Can't you?"

He shook his head.

"I'm scared. What if I want to go back?" She pulled away from him, her blue eyes troubled. "I know you did what you thought best, but maybe we should have talked about it first—"

"Back to where, pretty lady?" A swarthy little man, dressed in a collection of stinking rags sidled up to them. Matted dark hair straggled under a filthy bandana. "You're a ripe young thing. How's about if you come with me?" Black eyes flashed lecherously. Ned nearly dismissed the fellow as just one more vagabond, detritus from what was left of civilization, when he caught a whiff of magic.

Ned threw wards up and tried to drape them over Amanda, but he wasn't quick enough. While he pulled power to fuel his defenses, the intruder sheathed Amanda in a fiery circle. Worse, the man dropped his protective disguise, and Ned saw him for what he was, one of the Infernals' Chosen: a Dareli.

Fear thickened his throat. In an out-and-out contest of magics, he'd lose. Not just lose, he'd be annihilated.

No! I can't think that way.

He'd come across a Dareli once before, leading a charge that should have been the end of him, but the damned thing had a thousand lives. When he asked Landarik, the wizard grimaced and told him Dareli were nearly impossible to kill, almost as hard as their immortal masters.

Ned forced his panicked brain to think. Was there some link between this and the wave of Wirricow they'd just escaped? There almost had to be.

Amanda screamed. She reached for him through the fire, but it pushed her back.

Ned's heart shredded. He tried to dive through the flames, but the demon's power defeated him again and again. His distress and Amanda's terror amused the Dareli. He obviously liked toying with them.

Fury clenched Ned's guts into a burning knot. He wanted to kill the thing, but couldn't get close enough to land a single blow. The Dareli understood the source of Ned's power and subverted it effortlessly.

"Had enough?" The demon laughed and redirected a trail of fire. It raked agony over one of Ned's arms. "Because I have." Raising heavily muscled, apelike arms, the Dareli chanted words so ancient and so wicked, they immobilized Ned where he crouched, cradling his wounded arm.

The circle of flames imploded with Amanda inside, making a thunderous, booming sound. Ned shrieked his fury and powerlessness to the skies, and then did it again. Pain rocked him. Liquid dribbled from both ears after his eardrums ruptured. Sick at heart, he kicked himself for leaving the Eastern Sierra.

Ned stared at the smoke-filled air. Amanda was gone. He couldn't believe how fast it happened. Or how irresponsible he'd been.

Forcing his shell-shocked brain to think, he sent his mage senses outward, but cautiously. No point in drawing another of the demon spawn. Even stretching his magic to its limits, he couldn't find a hint of Amanda. She was as absent as if she'd been whisked to another universe.

Ned shook his head. There must be something compelling about the wizard-Earth Mage mix. It drew Infernals like a lodestone. Otherwise, why would they have converged on Rolf and Lori? More to the point, how else could they have located him and Amanda so fast?

The distant rattle of gunfire told him it wasn't wise to stay in the open. He'd thought to hole up in the wizards' underground quarters atop Edgehill Mountain. When he hatched the plan in the forest near Amanda's house, it felt logical. A good deal of the city was under water. The battle had moved inland once the sea began to rise. San Francisco had felt so safe...

He ducked into the doorway of a burned-out Victorian and summoned a portal. About to jump into the Ways and run back to Karras, he stopped himself. This was where Amanda had disappeared. He had to locate wizards here to help him. Karras was too far away. By the time he found him —if he even could—Amanda's trail would be much too cold.

Taking a shaky breath, Ned peered out of his hiding place to pinpoint his location. It was only about a five-minute walk to his original destination. He drew magic to cloak his presence and cursed himself for a fool. He should have drawn invisibility about himself and Mandy before they exited the Ways. He hadn't. Now it was too late.

She'd trusted him. Ned shut his eyes against self-recriminations bludgeoning his soul and ran hard for the wizards. He hoped he'd find someone who knew him and who might try to help.

"Who am I kidding?" he moaned. "They all hate me. They'll laugh in my face. When I tell them Amanda is part Earth Mage, they'll dismiss me as mad."

Ned jumped over gaping holes in the sidewalk. Power cables still spit occasional flames since the hydroelectric generators weren't entirely dead. He skirted rubble heap after rubble heap, dislodging rats feeding on rotting corpses. A pack of feral dogs barred his way, snarling at him. He used mind speech to calm them, but it took longer than he would have liked. Even though they let him pass, he felt their antipathy, and jumped out of the way just as a mangy black cur made a lunge for his Achilles tendon.

The caved-in stairway leading to the basement the wizards had commandeered finally came into view. Ned double-checked his landmarks. Yes, it was the right one. He sent magic ahead of him into the darkness. Finding only rats, he plunged downward and called his mage light into being.

Its warm, blue glow mocked him. Amanda. What was

the Dareli doing to her? Had he taken her where his execrable buddies tortured animals for pleasure?

Muttering a spell to open the hidden door, Ned fell through into a circle of very surprised faces. Then he remembered to drop the invisibility cloaking him.

"Oh—" A female wizard he didn't know rolled dark green eyes. "It's the pesky human mage. Aren't you supposed to be with Landarik?"

"Yes. No. Please, please, I need help."

"Help getting back to the war, you mean?" A male wizard rose to his feet. Dark eyes shot a challenge at Ned.

An unseen puppeteer cut the strings keeping him upright, and Ned crumpled to the floor. To his horror, sobs rose. He tried desperately to choke them back. Wizards *never* cried, not once they were past the age of five or so.

"For the love of the goddess," the male wizard sneered. "You're a disgrace to those who raised you. Sleep it off, human. Then we'll talk."

Before Ned could protest, blackness descended, trapping him in unconsciousness.

NED TAKES A STAND

*L*ori cried her daughter's name again. She was hoarse from screaming, but Amanda didn't answer. Ned was missing too. At first, she thought they'd made themselves a love nest somewhere. That possibility faded, along with what remained of the day.

Hatchet-faced, Rolf stalked through the woods beside her. From time to time, he railed against Cybele, exhorting the goddess to, "Find my daughter, goddammit."

"Christ! I hope the wizards know something. I had no idea how many days we were stuck in the root cellar until Karras told us." Lori clutched her husband's arm. "Maybe Mandy and Ned went to ground somewhere. He was in the Army. He should have known how to take care of her."

"I can't believe the lad would do something stupid." Karras materialized out of the air with Lira by his side.

Lori curled her lip into a sneer. Of all people, she did *not* want to see Lira just now.

"I am sorry for your loss, Daughter." Lira held out a hand.

Lori stared at her mother. Acid bit deep into her stomach lining, the burning almost unbearable. "How could you possibly know the pain of losing a child? Oh, that's right. I'd almost forgotten. You abandoned yours."

Lira drew back as if she'd been slapped. She sucked in what looked like a steadying breath. "You're right to be angry with me," she said simply. "If our places were reversed, I'd feel the same way."

Lori turned her face away. "I don't have the energy to deal with you right now. If you want to help, find my child."

"They're not here," Karras said. "It must mean Ned took her somewhere. I know he used the Ways. I sensed traces of her energy as well."

"The what?" Rolf stopped dead, skewering Karras with a hard look.

"Do you want the long explanation or the short one?"

"Short will do."

"The way we travel from place to place, using magic."

"Can you figure out where they went?" Lori was surprised she was still capable of conversation. What she wanted to do was curl up in a ball and howl.

"No—"

"Maybe," Lira interrupted him. "If we blend the masculine and feminine halves of the seeking spell."

"Not wise. It could blow up in our faces. 'Tis why we no longer teach it to acolytes."

Lori shivered. "I need to go back into the house to get more clothes."

"You can't." Lira spoke briskly.

Lori thought about asking *why not*, but didn't want to give her bitch of a mother the satisfaction of any conversation. Turning, she stalked toward the clearing.

Footsteps sounded behind her. Lira grabbed her arm. "Wirricow spelled it. You cannot go within until Karras and I have neutralized the binding."

"How could you possibly know?" Lori met her mother's gaze for the first time. A shock ran through her. Lira's eyes were the same unusual blue-green as her own.

"The human mage warned Karras."

Eyes narrowed, Lori asked, "Just how well do any of you know Ned? It's convenient he showed up here about the time those monsters took Mandy. Now he's gone—and her with him. If it's only his word about the house, I'll take my chances."

Lira shook her head. "Ned has always been trustworthy. If he was working for the Infernals, we would have known years ago. I sensed something odd emanating from your cabin, probably because I got right up next to it before Karras called me off. Good thing he did. The working is subtle. As tired as I am, I might've sloughed off the oddness without his warning."

"Humph." Lori held her mother's gaze and searched for truth. She found it behind the smudged beauty of the woman standing next to her. "It still feels oddly coincidental, but you believe what you just told me."

Lira's mouth twisted downward. "Yes, Daughter. I do." She exhaled sharply, sounding uncomfortable. "None of us liked having the human mage around. Believe me. If we could have ferreted out a reason—any reason—to throw him out of our ranks, we would have done so. Our knights refused to oversee him in battle, which is why he reported to Landarik or another battle lord."

Lori recalled Landarik's attitude. Reluctantly, she found herself forced to agree with Lira's assessment.

Rolf and Karras caught them up. "Follow me." Karras laid a hand on Lira's arm. "We must find and fix what's amiss with the house, and then we can determine what to do next."

"Forget the house," Lori said, afraid further delay would signal her daughter's death knell. "Let's work on finding Amanda."

"We have to close off the portal Wirricow linked to your house," Karras explained. "To leave it is akin to inviting them back."

"They're all dead," Lori said. Her next words came hard, not wanting to leave the safety of her throat. She forced them out anyway. "Amanda will be too, if we don't hurry. Too long's already passed as it is."

"While your fears for your daughter are well taken, the Infernals are scarcely all dead," Lira said acidly. "There are always more."

Lori felt stupid—and naïve. Her face heated in embarrassment.

On a completely different wavelength, Rolf snapped, "Blasted goddess! She's been harassing the hell out of me." He shook his head briskly and rubbed his temples. "I wish she'd go back to wherever she was before she showed up here."

"What does she want?" Lira sounded interested.

"Don't know."

"Quiet your thoughts, man." Karras spoke harshly. "She may know something about your daughter that could help us."

"Oh." A subdued note crept into Rolf's voice, and he looked cowed, his head bent in embarrassment. "Of course you're right. So much has happened these past few days, I'm not thinking straight."

They reached the back of the cabin. Lori made a grab for one of Rolf's hands. "Let's see who's left in the barn. I hope Noah was the only casualty, but we ought to find out."

"Are you sure you want to?" Rolf tipped her chin up until their gazes met. "I can go. You could just sit for a bit until after the wizards do whatever it is they've got in mind. Besides, I need to let Cybele into my head. She likes it better when I'm alone."

"Really?" Lori modulated sarcasm out of her voice. She didn't like the sound of that, but thought better of protesting. "You do whatever with the goddess. I'll go to the barn. Meet me there when you're done. We need to be ready to help the wizards once they decide what to do about Amanda."

"Don't get your hopes up, Lori. It's not likely they'll take us along."

"They'll take me. Whether they want to or not." Turning on her heel, she stalked toward the barn.

"Some of the animals might be dead," he called after her. "You could still wait for me."

"I used to cut up cadavers," she shot over her shoulder.

"This can't be much worse." Reaching the barn door, she pulled it open and realized how wrong she was.

NED REGAINED consciousness battling nausea and a blinding headache. Wizard voices rose and fell around him, and he cracked one eye open, but held still to see what they had to say about him. Would they even consider helping?

"Now that we're back to this problem, I tell you he deserted." The male wizard, red hair tied back with a leather thong, slapped his hands together. He apparently thought human mages were famous for jumping ship.

"Only reason he'd have been so upset," the female wizard concurred. She shoved her blonde braids behind muscular shoulders.

"I did not desert." Ned struggled to his feet. His head spun, and his stomach threatened to rebel. Bile stung his throat, but he swallowed it back.

"Hah! Awake are you?" the female wizard looked askance at him. "I'm Breanna. We thought you'd never come around."

Shit, aw shit!

"How long did your sleep spell last?" Ned could barely get the words out.

The male wizard shrugged. "Days. We didn't mean to knock you out for so long, but we had to leave and wanted to ensure you'd still be here when we returned."

Sucking in a despairing breath, Ned told them

everything—including his fears Amanda must surely be dead by now. When scoffs and jeers gave way to questions, he began to feel hopeful they just might help him.

Time was a problem, and it wasn't on his side. They'd already lost days, and his explanation to the wizards ate up another hour. With it all, they had yet to hash out a plan. So much time had elapsed since Amanda, his Amanda, had been taken, whatever help the wizards provided would probably come too late.

Regardless, the wizards argued over what to do about Ned and his dilemma for still more hours. Ned chafed at the delay. Every wasted moment made the difference between Amanda being alive—or not. Knowing she had to be slipping away, maybe to somewhere they'd never be able to reach her, galvanized Ned into wanting to do *something*. Anything but pace back and forth in this underground room where there wasn't enough air.

He battled fury at the wizards for knocking him out, but nothing he could do would change any of it. And if he gave voice to his anger, they might not help him at all.

"Boy!"

Ned's head snapped up. Had he been so lost in his own misery he'd missed something important? "Sorry, sir. What?"

The red-haired wizard, Kühl, shot him a disgusted look. "You said this was important. The least you could do is pay attention."

"I said I was sorry."

"We've decided to go after this Amanda. Not because of

you, but because of her wizard and Earth Mage blood. We cannot let her remain in dark hands."

"Your task is to locate Landarik," Breanna told him, her green eyes snapping with impatience. She looked amped up —and scared. "We travel to the Infernals' lands. We must have assistance. Tell Landarik to follow us with at least two companies. If he could raise a full regiment, it would be even better."

Panic hammered against his chest like a weighted broadsword. "B-but this is my fault. I should go with you. If anyone becomes the sacrifice for this mission, it should be me."

"While we agree with you conceptually," Kühl growled, "none of us knows if you are capable of traveling to the Infernals' dimension. We must pass through a difficult force field. The electromagnetics have proven fatal to humans— even occasionally to one of us."

"We understand the necessity of haste," Breanna broke in. "Your best use is to find reinforcements for us."

Ned knew what he was supposed to do. Bow and say *yes sir*, or *yes ma'am*. He flinched under the unwavering eyes of the nine wizards watching him. Nine against the Infernal hordes was a suicide mission. They truly needed Landarik or another battle lord just like him.

Ned bobbed his head forward in what he hoped looked like acquiescence. He choked out, "I understand and I will obey," through clenched jaws and held out both hands beseechingly. "I love her," he blurted, surprised to hear himself say the words. "Try to save her. I shall blame myself to the end of my days if she dies."

Breanna laid a hand on his shoulder. The harsh planes of her face softened for the briefest of moments. "We knew afore you told us. Your heart shines through your eyes. None of us, save Hreth, can foretell the future. You gambled to try to keep the girl safe. Right now, it appears you may have lost, but do not give up hope, youngster. We know not what we shall find."

Nodding agreement, Kühl added, "If the goddess is with us, we may locate the girl's missing brother as well. If nothing else, we can put him out of his misery if darkness has entered his soul." Kühl paused a beat. "Find Landarik as fast as you can, and once you do light a fire under him."

Ned cast an incredulous glance Kühl's way. "What makes you think he'll do anything I suggest?"

"He'd better," Breanna cut in. "Time runs differently in the dark ones' lands. Goddess only knows how long we'll have been there before he shows up with reinforcements."

Swallowing hard, Ned asked, "What does that mean about how long Amada's been held prisoner?"

"I wish I had an answer for you, lad, but I just don't know," Breanna replied.

Hot tears pricked behind Ned's lids. He didn't trust himself to speak. Kindness from the wizards was always so unexpected, it jostled his emotions. He latched onto the task at hand, shakily called up a portal, and jumped into the Ways. Questions tumbled through his mind as he tried to remember what he knew about any of the Infernals' worlds. Few wizards had ever ventured there and returned alive to tell about it. Those who did had conflicting stories.

Karras once told him people found their worst

nightmares in the Infernals' lands. The very air dragged primal fears to the surface and gave them corporeal form. Something like cold, broken glass scraped down his spine so viciously, Ned reached back, certain he'd find blood. When only the smooth surface of his skin met probing fingertips, apprehension filled him.

I can't think about this now. Maybe Landarik will let me come with him.

He readied himself to exit even before the Ways stopped pulsating. He remembered to drag shadows about him. No point in getting killed before he could find Landarik. Smoke and the acrid stench of discharged weapons burned his nose and throat as soon as he stepped out of the traveling portal. Everything was either gray or burning. The only things to hide behind were stacks of asphalt, concrete, or shattered lumber.

Ned started to use mind speech to call Landarik. *No,* an inner voice screamed. It forced him to remember mind speech was frowned on in battle—unless there weren't any other options. Shaken such a simple thing almost got away from him, he hunkered down, pulled off his rucksack, and found the communications device he'd stashed in a pocket. A thought staggered him. Kühl assumed he'd know where to find Landarik. Last Ned knew, the temperamental commander had withdrawn. Or had he? Ned remembered the battle lord telling him at least one company was in full retreat.

With shaking fingers, Ned positioned the mouthpiece. "Landarik?" he called softly. No answer came, so he tried again.

Wishing he had the wizards' facility with speaking stones—and they'd trust him with one—Ned was just getting ready to draw another portal to take him back to his home stronghold in the Old Country when he heard, "You? What are you doing here? When I gave you permission to—"

"Yes, yes," Ned broke in. Normally, he would never have interrupted a wizard, not if he wanted to avoid a solid ear cuffing, but he was frantic. Time kept ticking by. Time meant Amanda's life. He didn't want to relay sensitive information over the air. Goddess knew who might be listening. "I-I have a message from Kühl. I must give it to you in person."

"Walk twenty paces to your left. I'll find you."

Even though he expected it, Ned was surprised at the strength with which Landarik's arm snaked out and dragged him into the ruins of some kind of store. A *Target* logo flashed past. He crunched over broken glass as he trotted after the wizard. Bloated corpses littered the aisles like macabre merchandise.

"This should do."

Ned looked around. They were in a bathroom. Doors had been ripped off the stalls. Piles of feces sat in most of the toilets. The stench was thick, and he swallowed back bile.

Landarik stared at him, hollow-eyed. "This better be good," he muttered.

Ned made it to the part about gathering a couple of companies when Landarik's jaw dropped.

"Where does Kühl think I can raise those kinds of numbers? Doesn't he understand we're losing this war? I can't believe he expects me to divert troops from something important to run straight into the Infernals' hands for a single girl. This is folly. I will *not* commit my troops to a fool's errand."

Ned balled his hands into fists. Acid scorched the back of his throat. Sick and desperate, he swallowed it down. Landarik *had* to help. Kühl outranked him. To refuse meant treason—and serious sanctions. Landarik could lose his commission and his social standing in wizard society. Pointing that out—or begging and pleading—wouldn't change the wizard's mind, so he just said, "If you don't send more wizards, then those who went after Amanda will die."

"It would serve them right." Landarik spat on the floor. Blood streaked his phlegm.

Ned wondered where the battle lord was injured. He drew himself up so he could meet Landarik's cold, blue gaze dead on. "I promised I'd find help for their mission. I will honor my commitment to Kühl. If you won't help, I'll travel to the stronghold where I was raised and ask the Council to send aid."

"I suppose you'll tell them I refused?" Landarik sounded so hostile, Ned was nonplussed. The wizards weren't usually this openly antagonistic toward him. Nasty and patronizing, sure, but Landarik sounded like he wanted to kill him.

"Ah, no. Of course not. I shan't tell them we've spoken at all." Ned lied automatically, smoothing things over with the smallest of spells. He'd never trusted Landarik. Now something fey danced behind his eyes. If the battle lord saw him as a threat—and he'd almost have to—anything was possible. Ned couldn't help Kühl—or Amanda—if he was imprisoned.

Or dead.

"Like hell you wouldn't." The wizard spoke low, almost like he'd forgotten Ned was there. "If you didn't tell the Council, Kühl certainly would—if he got back from Darehôl."

"You dare say *that* name aloud?" Ned was so shocked, he was almost beyond words. No one spoke the name of the Infernals' realms. It had been bad enough trying to tell Kühl about the Dareli. Glancing at Landarik, he froze. The wizard stared hard at him. Ned felt like something about to be crushed and disposed of without recourse.

"No offense, I'm sure." Ned backed slowly away, his gaze glued to Landarik's face. "Sorry to have bothered you. If you need my help here, just tell me where you want me. You're right, of course. This rescue probably wasn't one of Kühl's best ideas."

Once his back is turned, I'll be gone.

"Nice try. I saw you with the girl. You're entranced by her." Landarik started to laugh. His dark mirth turned into a coughing fit. He bent over double, hacking blood onto the filthy floor. Ned turned and ran, pulling invisibility about him like a winding sheet.

Landarik's energy quested after him. He'd spent enough time under the wizard to know how he thought. He'd expect Ned to put distance between them.

So, I need to do something different.

A pack of feral dogs snarled over human bones in a corner of the store, Ned sprinted for them, sending a calming spell ahead. He scattered his energy among the dogs, taking care to project enough of himself outside the spell to fool the wizard. He'd perfected this trick years before when he wanted to be left alone in the stronghold. What began as an experiment had turned into a way to escape from the wizards' prying eyes and barbed tongues.

Landarik passed within twenty feet of him. He staggered as he ran.

Timing was critical. The wizard's energy was pushed out in front of him, searching. Hopefully, he wouldn't notice the burst of magic when Ned called a portal. Fear made it hard to breathe. Landarik would backtrack if he didn't find him soon.

"It's now or never," Ned mumbled. Hands trembling, he cast a spell to take him into the Ways. He jumped through, congratulating himself on a move well played, when Landarik's fingers scrabbled at the edge of the portal. Ned pulled a knife from his belt. He stabbed Landarik's hands repeatedly until the wizard, cursing and threatening, finally let go.

"Goddess's breath. What have I done?" The portal snapped shut on Landarik's curses. Hunkering into a crouch, Ned wrapped his arms about himself. Attacking a wizard was grounds for torture, exile or, depending on the circumstances, death. Landarik would tell one story, he another. It would get sorted out, but by the time it did, Kühl, Breanna, the wizards with them—and Amanda—would certainly be dead.

He wasn't surprised when he stepped out of his portal into the stronghold keep and two warrior wizards circled him with chains.

"Please, I must speak to Hreth. It's a matter of survival for Kühl, Breanna, and the seven wizards with them."

The gendarmes just laughed. They dragged him to the dungeons, locked him in, and left.

THE BACK SIDE OF HELL

"Jesus fucking Christ!" Lori played her gaze over a scene right out of the way she'd always imagined Hell might look. Her empty stomach roiled. Blinking hard she pulled herself together. The barn, her cozy barn where she'd milked goats, gathered eggs, and curried horses ran slick with blood and guts. The sow growled from her corner. Four sets of piglet legs revealed where the babies had taken refuge behind their mother's bulk. The other four probably added to the red slime beneath her feet. An outraged squawk from the lean-to told her at least one chicken had survived. Two goats looked crazed with fear. They *haahed* the minute Lori opened the door. The other one, and her kid, lay on their sides, dead eyes staring.

A strangled-sounding neigh pulled her toward Nellie. The mare dripped blood. Her eyes rolled frantically. Lori shut her own eyes to steady herself. The living animals needed her. A few deep breaths and her horror receded enough to allow her to do something besides gawk.

She pumped water into a bucket from the spigot outside the barn door. Grabbing a couple of cloths, she let herself into Nellie's stall and wiped the mare down. She spoke softly to the animal and sent soothing thoughts into her equine mind. Maybe because she was open to it, she heard the horse, much as she heard the wolves. In fits and starts, Nellie told her Noah died protecting her. He'd thrown himself in front of her in the stall they shared.

Nellie loved Noah. They'd been together since they were yearlings. Now he was gone. Her keening sorrow pierced Lori's heart. She tried to lead the mare out of the barn, thinking clean air and getting her hooves out of bloody muck might help. Nellie resisted. Blood was the only thing left of Noah. She wasn't ready to leave quite yet. Lori left her to herself and quieted the other animals.

The horse, her soft gray winter coat visible again, had just acquiesced about going outside to join the sow, piglets, and goats, when Rolf appeared. Lori didn't notice him until she heard, "Christ on a crutch. This is horrible."

"Yes, it is. Here." She clipped a lead rope to the halter she'd slipped over Nellie's head. "Let's get her outside with some feed and fresh water."

DAWN STREAKED the sky with pale pink. Lori emptied the last bucket of blood-tinged water far enough from the house so predators wouldn't show up on their doorstep. The wolves had come during the night and scavenged the animal parts Rolf couldn't smoke or salt.

By the time she got back, Rolf had returned from butchering the dead animals and was buttoning up the barn. She wove her arms around his waist and said, "We lost half the piglets, one goat, the kid, two chickens, and a horse. I suppose it could have been worse."

"Lori," he spoke in measured tones, "there's no way to replace our animals. Losing *any* of them challenges our survival."

She wasn't sure she wanted to survive if both her children were lost, but it was too hard to talk about. What came out of her mouth was, "Wonder if the sheep are safe?"

"We can check on them later. Let's see if the wizards are through with the house."

An exhausted-looking Karras sat on their front steps, staff clutched between his hands.

"What'd you find?" Even though she'd asked, Lori wasn't certain she wanted to know.

"A pathway straight to one of the dark lands with roots so deep it was all Lira and I could do to sever them. We used her staff to conjure an arcane cleansing ritual. That's why it smells burnt in there."

Moving past him, she found Lira in the kitchen. A grease spot discolored one cheek. Lori saw the container of pine nut flour out. "Flatbread," the wizard said shortly, "We all need to eat." Her staff lay on the table. Drawn by its intricate carving, Lori reached out to run her hands over it. "Stop! You mustn't touch it." Lira continued rolling out dough.

"How'd you even know I was looking at it? Your back is turned."

Lira laughed grimly. "I'm linked to its magic."

"What would have happened if I touched it?"

"You'd be dead."

Sorry I asked. Guess there are lots of answers I'd rather not have.

"Does Karras's staff work the same way?"

"No. Mine is special." Lira moved to the table. She ran floury fingers the length of her staff and spoke a few words in the wizards' language. "There." She motioned to Lori. "It can't hurt you now. If I'd been thinking I would have taken care of that before I laid it down."

More dead than alive, Lori gathered butter, preserves, and tea leaves. After she ran into Rolf for the third time, she shooed him onto the porch to wait with Karras. She and Lira worked in silence. It wasn't exactly companionable, but it wasn't as uncomfortable as it might've been, either. It didn't take long before the bread and tea were ready.

With everyone scattered around the front porch like refugees, Lori ate hungrily. She had to sleep before she could do much else, but pushed it aside for now. "What about Amanda?" she asked, still worried sick about her daughter.

"We discussed her while we closed off the conduit." Lira shot a meaningful glance at Karras.

"I must talk with Ned." Karras drained off half his tea. "He holds the answer to this riddle. I know it in my bones. While Lira worked, I raised Landarik through the stones."

"And?" Rolf, who'd been even more silent than usual

since whatever transpired between him and Cybele, trained his blue gaze on the wizard.

"He told a curious tale. Said Ned attacked him. I know there's more to it. Has to be." The wizard settled his mouth into a gruff line.

"I talked with Father," Lira broke in. "He said Ned is in prison in our home stronghold. Under guard, and considered dangerous."

"I knew it." Lori clenched a fist and slammed it down on her leg. "Slimy son of a bitch—"

"You're being hasty." Karras's dark gaze bored into her. "I don't believe for a moment that a lad I practically raised has grown a second head. Landarik is another matter. He never cared for Ned. Goddess's kirtle. He hates most other wizards, and he's totally intolerant of humans. If he could find an opportunity to discredit the lad, he'd jump on it with both feet."

Lira nodded her agreement. Color high in her face, she said, "Karras speaks true. Landarik and I were, uh, close at one time." She snorted. "The goddess did me a favor when his roving eye settled on Sierna."

"Can I go to where Ned is?" Rolf jumped to his feet and paced from one end of the porch to the other, then back again.

"I'm going." Karras pushed heavily upright, shaking out a foot, which must have fallen asleep. "I plan to leave as soon as I finish eating. 'Tis hard to manipulate magic as drained as I am." He looked at Lira. "What do you think? Can an Earth Mage use the Ways?"

She shrugged. "I don't know." Shifting her aqua gaze to Rolf, she asked, "Why do you want to go?"

Rolf cocked his head to one side and frowned. "I'm not sure I can answer you. Cybele told me I need to pay more attention to my inner voice—whatever the hell that means. Now that she has my attention, she talks in riddles most of the time."

"Instinct," Karras murmured. "It often serves as a guide. Damn! Should have gotten the *Book of Spells* from Ned. It would tell me if you can travel as we do."

Rolf shrugged. "Do you want me to ask Cybele? Maybe she has her own ways of getting from Point A to Point B."

Lori knew her husband well enough to understand he was fascinated with any magic if it might open the gates of their self-imposed exile. They'd been stuck in the Eastern Sierra since right after moving there.

"Good idea," Karras agreed. "Do it now. I must leave afore some wizard kangaroo court decrees death for my lad."

Not waiting to be asked twice, Rolf melted into the woods between the cabin and the creek.

Death?

Karras's casual statement shook Lori to her core. She'd thought of wizards as high-handed and standoffish, but she'd also seen them as highly socialized. Knowing they plotted to kill their adversaries like something out of Medieval Europe—or Nazi Germany—put a big crimp in her emerging ideology.

"Oh, yes." Lira looked oddly at her, apparently having read her thoughts. "We kill. 'Tis part of the last test afore we're vetted as warriors."

"I suppose it's understandable for warriors," Lori said uncertainly. "How about everyone else?"

"Most everyone, except those few with religious objections, must kill to prove loyalty to their clan." She scowled. "We've had enough turncoats over the years, so we test practically everyone. Why would you believe us to be so different from yourselves? We have infighting, and disagreements often lead to treachery."

Lori looked hard at her mother. "Is your life in danger now that your people know about me?"

Lira laughed mirthlessly. "Were it not for the fact that my father is one of the High Council, I would have been banished. Had my, uh, fall from grace been discovered when it happened, I would have been forced to abort my child and probably been sterilized."

Oh my, they play hardball in wizard-land.

"Who was my father?" Lori quirked a curious brow. She hadn't meant to blurt it out, but she was so tired, it was impossible to keep thoughts from spilling out of her mouth.

Karras raised an interested eyebrow. "Yes, we'd all like to know."

"Once the men leave, you and I can talk more." A soft smile played about Lira's mouth.

Rolf clumped back up the porch steps. "I heard that." He looked at Lira. "You must have known what Cybele would tell me."

"No, I didn't, but I assumed she'd have her own ways to assist her Earth Mages. I really need to read up on them. Should have asked Father when I talked with him earlier. He knows everything."

Karras, who'd been leaning on the porch railing, raised a hand and sketched a rectangle in the air. "I'm leaving. Are you coming with me?"

"Yes." Rolf stepped to his side. "Cybele says the journey won't kill me, but it will be uncomfortable. I can do uncomfortable."

Karras rolled his eyes. "If you give me too much trouble, I may thump you over the head."

"So long as I get there and Ned tells us where my daughter is, I don't care."

Lori watched her husband disappear. It was the oddest thing. He and Karras just stepped through what looked like a doorway in the air—and vanished.

"Could I do that?" Lori eyed her mother.

"Certainly. Far more easily than your mate I suspect."

"We didn't get off to the best start." Lori extended a hand to Lira, who clasped it after the briefest of hesitations.

"No, Daughter. We did not. I'm sorry for my part."

Lori felt a small smile tug the edges of her mouth. "Me too." She dropped her gaze, suddenly shy. "Could you teach me how to use one of those disappearing doorways?"

"After we've both had some rest."

Lori nodded. Her eyes really did have to close soon. Too tired for subtlety, she prodded, "My father?"

"A human mage from your country. I met him right after completing my warrior training. I was young and drunk on my own power. He had hair like yours and eyes like the summer grasses. He played a lute, and I used to lie in his arms while he sang to me."

"I-is he still alive?"

Lira shrugged. "I don't know." Taking a deep breath and blowing it out, she went on. "I never told him about the child we made."

He doesn't know about me.

With sudden clarity, Lori understood his name didn't matter.

"His name is meaningless," Lira concurred, "except to my people, who would hunt him down and kill him. Enough for today. Get some rest. I'll wake you if aught happens."

LESS THAN HUMAN

Amanda screamed just before the cat-o-nine tails slashed into her back again. And then she screamed again. At first, fueled by anger, she'd fought her captors. The extent of their brutal retribution shocked the rebellion out of her. Now she didn't even meet their alien eyes.

She'd lain unconscious for brief, welcome periods when the pain was so bad she couldn't stand it. Longing for something, anything, to dull the horror of what the vile creature with sharp claws and breath like a charnel pit was doing to her, she willed herself to faint. For a minute, she thought it would work, and then the lash landed again. Pain, bright as teardrops, spread across her bare shoulders obliterating everything else.

"I hate you." Christ! She shouldn't have said that. Fear punched her in the guts, and she fought the restraints holding her in place.

"Just warming you up," the thing snarled in heavily accented English. Teeth bared in a parody of a grin, it placed itself between her and where she was chained to the wall. The thing leered at her with amber eyes. Matted fur-like hair covered its body, growing thicker on its head. The gray-black stuff was greasy, and it stank. An obscenely long phallus hung between its hind legs; sometimes it grew longer and thicker, but at least the abomination hadn't tried to rape her—yet.

Her tormentors stood more than six feet tall with heavy muscles and broad shoulders. While she'd seen them sink to all fours, they appeared to prefer standing upright. Both hands and feet sported long, curved reddish claws. She'd stopped trying to figure out what manner of being they were days ago.

The whip whistled. Steeling herself for the next blow, Amanda squeezed her eyes shut. Something about the multi-headed torture instrument made a sound like nothing else as it moved through the thick, sticky air of...wherever she was.

It was so hard to breathe when she first arrived, she panicked. Then someone in long, dark robes had placed his mouth over her nose and blown air into it. Her lungs burned like mad, but at least they worked again.

I'd have been better off if they let me die, she thought with soul-crushing finality.

The expected blow didn't come. She pried her eyes open and glanced at her jailer. Another like him had padded noiselessly up to the small enclosure outside her cell. The two ape-men, heads together, conversed in the odd combination of clacks and whistles she assumed was their language. Amanda straightened. She pulled against leather thongs binding her wrists to metal rings set high in the stone walls surrounding them. One ankle was shackled to a stake in the ground. She hoped they'd let her go back to her cell. They'd left her chained to the wall before. It took longer each time to get feeling back into her fingers.

She wished she had her mother's medical knowledge. At least then she'd understand what was going wrong in her body.

Pah. I don't need to be a doctor to know I'm starving to death. I have infections where the filthy metal has rubbed my flesh down to bone.

"Done for today, my pet." The creature strode away, chattering to the newcomer.

"You forgot something," she called after him, wondering where her sudden burst of courage came from.

"What?"

It trotted back, amazingly light-footed for something so large. It bent close, and she turned her head away from the stench. It reminded her of meat so rotten it fell off the bones.

"C-could you cut me down...please? My hands are numb."

"She said *please*." The thing chortled, followed by a complex series of clacks. The other one laughed too. Sidling over, it scraped the already-raw skin on her nipples with its teeth. Saliva dripped from a slack-jawed mouth as the thing slurped at her. To her immense relief, it finally reached for her wrists. Long, shiny claws hooked into the knots and made short work of the leather bindings.

The full weight of her body made her knees buckle. Amanda reached for the wall so she wouldn't fall into her own filth, puddled below where she'd been tortured. Knowing at an intuitive level she'd be lost if she let go of her dignity, she managed to stagger the few steps to the door of her cell. As soon as she passed the lintel, the heavy door, made of some sort of greenish metal she'd never seen before, clanged shut.

Grateful for the reprieve, she sat gingerly on the raised slats of her bed. Its gray-green tubular extensions were actually living vines with short tempers. She'd poked at them soon after her arrival. Apparently annoyed, they'd exuded a fluid that melted some of the skin off her fingers. She'd been excruciatingly careful since then.

"You leave me alone," she patted the vines, "and I'll do the same." She felt brain damaged talking to her bed. Sadness welled. She was more alone than ever before in her short life. If she hadn't been so fearful and argumentative with Ned when they first arrived in San Francisco, he might've ferried them to safety. The awful man had come out of nowhere, his fire cutting deep into her flesh.

The look in Ned's eyes when he tried his damnedest to rescue her made her heart ache. Young and inexperienced as she was, Amanda was almost certain she was in love.

She hadn't had much opportunity to learn about love—she'd only been thirteen when her family moved to the Eastern Sierra—but what flowed between her and Ned felt like the real thing. A small smile formed when she thought about holding him and kissing him and their brief forays into sexual experimentation. He was as naïve as she, but they'd managed anyway. They'd had wonderful, long conversations too, getting to know one another. Dear God but she missed him—and her parents.

None of this matters. I'll never see him or anyone else ever again. I'll be here until I die.

Sinking into an abyss of self-pity, Amanda lay down, wrapped her arms around herself, and muttered childhood prayers. Sleep, blessed sleep where she didn't have to think anymore, finally came.

HER CELL DOOR thudded against the earth and stone walls of her prison, and the noise jarred her to wakefulness. A scared-looking woman came in, holding a cracked plate with something piled on it. She handed the plate to Amanda and pantomimed eating. Next she dragged a dirty jug over and left it within reach.

Amanda pushed herself to a sitting position and looked at the hag with gray hair chopped off at shoulder level. Rheumy blue eyes stared back. "Who are you?"

The woman opened her mouth and pointed. Someone had cut out her tongue. Perhaps reacting to the horror reflected in Amanda's eyes, she crab-walked to the door, casting anxious glances over one shoulder.

Amanda set the plate down and jumped to her feet. She winced as pain from a hundred sore muscles ripped through her. "I don't care if you can't talk. Please just stay and keep me company."

Shaking her head, the woman threw a piteous glance at Amanda, then turned and ran a few steps.

Wondering if this was the chance she'd been waiting for —after all, the door was open—Amanda moved as fast as her aching muscles allowed. She'd not quite made the door before the woman returned. Shaking her head and waggling one begrimed finger in Amanda's face, she mouthed the word *no* clearly enough. The next words might have been *not yet*. Amanda's heart was a little lighter when the door slammed in her face.

She looked curiously at the contents of the plate. This was the first food they'd given her. She wasn't sure how much time had passed since she was taken prisoner, but at least three or four days, judging from the cycles of darkness and light. Once they' took her outside at night, and she'd been rattled to see three moons. Two right next to one another and a third on the other side of the sky.

Her stomach clenched. It didn't care where it was. It also didn't give a good goddamn if what was on the plate was poison. It wanted feeding. Deciding it would be a mistake to look too closely at the plate's contents, Amanda poured a little water from the jug over her fingers to try to clean them before plunging them into the gelatinous mass. It tasted bad, but not so bad she couldn't choke it down.

Something wriggled on her tongue. She forced her mind away from the possibility she was eating worms or lizards or bugs. Amanda chewed and swallowed over and over until she emptied the dish. For a while she didn't know if her meal would stay down. She paced the length of her cell, back and forth, until she was certain she wouldn't puke. Then she took a cautious swallow of the brackish water.

When she sat on her bunk again, she thought about her brother, Jon. Was he here somewhere? If so, did he know she'd been captured? He disappeared so long ago, it was more likely he was dead.

What had the woman who'd brought her food meant about *not yet*? Or had she said those words at all? Contemplating the possibility of escape, Amanda felt stymied. Even if she managed to break out of her cell, how on earth would she find her way home? She had almost no memory of how she'd gotten here. Only a smothered sensation that had worsened until blind panic overwhelmed her. She'd blacked out, coming back to herself in this prison with the man in robes ministering to her. At least he was human. Or he *looked* human, anyway. Not at all like the ape things.

The unusual sensation of food in her belly made her tired. Praying to a god she'd forgotten about since childhood, Amanda let sleep reclaim her.

FALSE ACCUSATIONS

*N*ed paced in his cell. He wasn't worried about himself, but Amanda's life was slipping away like sand in an hourglass. For all he knew, she was already dead. The thought drove him mad. Pain shot up his leg, and he grimaced. The wizards had been rough when they chucked him into the dungeon. He was pretty sure he'd sprained an ankle. Ned rubbed gingerly at the outer part of his right leg under his boot. A swollen spot made him wince, but it wasn't important.

He turned his mind to the problem at hand. He needed to escape. But how? Even if he could get free, he had no idea how to travel to the Infernals' lands. It wasn't one of the things wizards taught their own acolytes, much less someone like him.

He used mind speech to call for help. His voice bounced back, reverberating in his head. He tried sliding into the Ways and was rewarded with a shock so severe his vision blurred and he saw stars. The stones of the prison must be warded, a fact he'd forgotten—if he ever knew it in the first place.

Eyes snapping open, he remembered the *Book of Spells*. The wizards had left him his backpack. With their typical arrogance, they probably assumed he didn't have enough magic to spell his way out of his cell, regardless of which tools were at his disposal. A bitter smile creased his face. The wizards always underestimated him, a tendency he'd nurtured since it meant they left him alone.

Or maybe they hadn't taken his rucksack *because* of the book. It found ways of sticking with him. Ever since Karras gifted it to him, it made sure he never left it behind. For all Ned knew, the book might've made the entire backpack invisible to wizard scrutiny. Only about ten of the books existed. They took years to write, penned by hand and sealed by magic. He was fairly certain Karras was the only wizard who knew he had one of the special spell books. Then he remembered mentioning it in front of Landarik and Sierna.

One more nail in my coffin when they drag me in front of the High Council.

Retiring to his bed, comprised of wooden slats attached to damp stone walls, he picked up his backpack and reached inside. The leather-bound tome almost leapt into his hand as if it wanted him to search through it. His bleak depression and weariness lifted somewhat. Ned asked the book for specific answers before opening it at random. Karras had suggested that strategy, and Ned used it when he couldn't think of anything else. It wasn't like the book was indexed.

He needed to know two things. Was there a way out of the wizards' prison? Once out, how could he find Amanda?

He was reading, half-asleep over the book, when the cell's door rattled against its frame. Shoving the tome behind him, Ned tried to send his magic outward to see who was coming. It crashed back on him.

"Stubborn one, aren't you?" Marena, one of the few female guards, set down the bowl she was holding just inside the door. "Every time you try to focus a stream of your pathetic human magic, we make bets about how long it will take you to try again." Braying laughter filled the small space. "I lost this time."

She drew a flask out of her dark robes and tossed it in his direction. "Here. 'Tis a sleeping draught, not poison. One of the healers remembers you as a child and took pity on your plight." With a swirl of robes, she was gone.

Ned shuffled to the bowl. Mush over a square of cornbread. At least they weren't trying to starve him. *Yeah, it might be hard to explain to Hreth and Karras.* He ate with his fingers and continued his hunt through the *Book of Spells.* He was concentrating so deeply, he'd uncorked the flask and raised it to his lips when the book sent something like a shock through him.

He recoiled, confused. Understanding came in a rush. *Not* a good idea. He needed to leave this place. Not sleep. Maybe the flask had been spelled. Lucky for him, the book's magic was stronger.

Shaken by how close he'd come to drinking the contents of the carafe, Ned stood, walked to the privy bucket in the corner, and upended the flask's contents. He pissed on top of it for good measure and then returned to the book.

He licked the last of the mush from his fingers and drew in an excited breath. Anticipation zinged through him. His magic *was* different from the wizards'. Even they'd told him as much—apparently without fully appreciating what it meant. Energized, Ned read about an incantation to scatter his energy in ways they wouldn't recognize. His pulse raced. He could summon a different sort of portal. One that would drop him out of the wizards' clutches as easily as he'd fallen into them.

In the little time since he'd been imprisoned, Ned had identified a pattern to the guards' comings and goings. They'd just served him dinner—topped off by a sleeping potion. It should mean a break of several hours when no one looked in on him.

"All right," he muttered. "I know how to get out of here. Now how do I find Amanda?"

It took longer, but the answer showed up—replete with warnings. He could travel—maybe—to an Infernals' lair, but returning would be dicey. Perhaps impossible. Some sort of frequency differential created a barrier between Earth and the worlds the Infernals called home. It was more pronounced coming toward Earth in hopes it would keep Infernals out. Ned read the few pages again and tried to cull more meaning out of them.

Nothing came.

Okay. I know how to draw a portal to get me out of here, and I know how to get to an Infernal world—hopefully the right one if

I follow Amanda's energy. The only thing missing is I may not be able to return.

He felt wretchedly unprepared for what he was about to undertake. Despite a plethora of misgivings, Ned wasn't willing to waste any more time. He stood, slipped the book back into his rucksack, and secured the pack to his body. Pulling his cloak over everything, he emptied his mind and chanted softly. Heart in his throat, he expected his cell door to bang open. It didn't. His confidence in what he was attempting edged up a notch or two.

Darkness swirled, but he stood ready. When the traveling portal closed around his body, Ned gasped. It fit snugly, like well-worn riding gloves. This was nothing like the portals he was used to where he could stand or sit or even lie down. With an entreaty to the goddess to watch over him and Amanda, Ned prayed his spell would run straight and true, like the best of arrows. He refused to go back. Either he'd done things right, or the woman he loved would die.

He was in the portal for a long time. Panic set in a time or two. He tried to reassure himself it took much longer to travel to another world than anywhere he'd ever been. It was uncomfortably hot in his pod. The air felt stale—like there wasn't enough of it. He tried to reduce his oxygen consumption by taking shallow breaths.

All of a sudden something shifted. The cocoon surrounding him wasn't there anymore, and he fell end-over-end, arms wind milling. The air turned much worse. He grabbed at some branches as they flashed past. They broke his fall—barely.

Ned landed with a spine-cracking crunch. He tried to throw a protective ward about himself until he could get his bearings, but he couldn't breathe. Gasping like a hooked fish, he forced himself to calm down. He'd gotten the wind knocked out of him, which didn't help, but the air in this world was thin. So thin, he wondered if it would kill him. He envisioned the air molecules and wove them together with magic. Things got marginally better, so he added power to his spell. After a time, he molded a mantle of air around himself.

Past his immediate fear of suffocation, Ned took a moment to look around. A colorless country stretched as far as he could see. Everything looked dead. Bushes, trees, even the grasses. Huge boulders littered the landscape. The terrain gained elevation toward distant mountains, their heights streaked with dirty snow. He sent out a trickle of magic, but found no birds or animals. Not close by anyway.

He contemplated calling for Kühl and Breanna. Someone should tell them about Landarik. What if they'd been captured and calling them led to his own undoing?

Ned stared at the barren land. Someone must live here, but who—and where? He reached for Amanda with his soul. After all his trouble, was she even here? Heart tangled in his casting, Ned felt the faintest of *pings*.

She is *here and she's alive.*

Exultant he hadn't arrived too late, Ned struck out in the direction his magic indicated. He tried to draw invisibility about himself, but it was hard juggling enough air to breathe with keeping shadows next to his body. He had to have air, so the shadow overlay wasn't as elegant as he would have liked. He hadn't gone a hundred paces when he heard distant hoof beats. Ducking behind a boulder, he peered out cautiously. A herd of horse-sized six-legged animals with wicked-looking silvery horns thundered past. They were mostly black, with a few brown ones in the mix. Like unicorns, but with extra legs.

Ned couldn't understand why his mage senses hadn't picked them up. He reached out again with his magic, but withdrew it immediately when the lead beast's head whipped about. It trumpeted irritation, and its tongue snaked out, seeking the source of the power it had felt. Sweat slicked Ned's palms. Even though they were close, he couldn't sense the animals with his magic, but it appeared they could detect his power if he directed it toward them.

This world has different rules. I'd better learn them damned fast if I'm going to stay alive.

Karras kept an arm around Rolf so he wouldn't fall on his face. He was grateful to be out of the Ways. Their journey had been hideous. Rolf fought him at every turn. Something about the traveling pathways made the Earth Mage panic. Karras noticed something was wrong almost immediately, but things hadn't truly disintegrated until well into their journey. Rolf was a big man. Managing him in the confined space of the Ways while hostile and combative wasn't easy.

Karras had finally flattened him with magic, and Rolf was just now coming around.

"Sorry." Rolf pulled away from the wizard. He stumbled

but kept his feet under him. His demeanor radiated determination.

Karras opened his mouth, and then shut it with a clack. He'd been about to reprimand Rolf, much as he would a young wizard. Instead, he muttered, "Good you can walk on your own again. This way. Hurry."

He led them upward along a deserted trail high in the Carpathian Alps. Never heavily populated, this part of Earth was nearly as devoid of humans as the Eastern Sierra. He was gratified to hear Rolf's steps pound along behind him.

"I really meant it about being sorry," Rolf said. "I-I don't know quite why, but I had this overwhelming sensation if I didn't get out of that damnable tunnel, I'd die."

Looking over his shoulder, Karras replied, "It doesn't matter. We're here now. We shall figure out something different next time."

"I should hope so since I need to get back to Lori, or go with you after my daughter."

I'm not taking you on a journey to another world. It'd probably kill us both.

Karras unclenched his jaw. "We're almost to the stronghold. Once we get there, don't talk unless someone asks you a direct question. Do you understand?"

"Uh-huh. Why?"

"Wizards don't care for humans. The more invisible you are, the better." Karras turned and skewered Rolf with what he hoped was a stern expression. "Idle chatter may get you thrown into a cell alongside Ned."

Rolf drew his brows together; anger flashed from his

blue eyes. "They can't imprison me. I haven't broken any laws."

Karras sighed. "You don't understand. Your world—the world of men—is dead. Wizards have always made their own rules, and they're nothing like yours. Hold up. We're here."

Karras set his fingers into indentations in a rock face. A tone sounded. He sang a harmonizing note. Another tone, followed by another note. With a scraping like rusty metal, a door-sized section of rock moved inward.

"Hurry," he hissed. "They think I'm by myself. We don't want them to look too close or slam the door in your face. They would, if given a choice."

Karras looked down several long corridors hacked out of the interior of the mountain and let out a tightly held breath. Torches in wall sconces set at intervals provided flickering light. So far, so good. They were alone. If the goddess was with him, mayhap they could get all the way to Hreth or Liefes without being detected.

They moved along at a good clip, but his luck ran out when they reached the second level. He sensed a group approaching. Trying to hide Rolf to avoid explanations, Karras shoved him through a door and right into the arms of one of the battle lords.

Vymil, clad in a light hauberk over leathers, scowled. Even his tattoos vibrated with outrage. Shiny black hair was caught up in an intricate warrior braiding pattern. Vambraces graced both arms, and a broadsword was lashed across his back. "How in the name of the goddess did you get in here?" He closed one ham-sized hand over Rolf's shoulder. "What manner of being are you? I had thought you human, but the energy is wrong."

"I brought him." Squaring his shoulders, Karras drew himself up. Vymil still towered over him by several inches.

The battle lord's clear, green eyes moved from Rolf to Karras. "Why would you do such a thing?" The question was laced with scorn.

"We have business with the High Council. Let us pass."

Vymil looked at Karras through narrowed eyes. "If your business were honorable, you wouldn't have been trying to conceal this piece of garbage."

"I resent your implication." Rolf twisted from under Vymil's grasp, his eyes blazing with outrage. He raised hands, balled into fists, to fighting level.

Karras groaned inwardly. If he'd known how much trouble the Earth Mage was going to be, he'd never have brought him. "I instructed you to keep your mouth shut," he snarled at Rolf, but he kept his gaze glued on Vymil. Karras readied himself to call magic. While the battle lord was younger and stronger, Karras believed he might prevail in a contest of mage power so long as it didn't include swords.

"If this is how your friends treat you," Rolf went on, apparently oblivious to Karras's earlier command. "I'd hate to come across a wizard enemy."

No longer watching Karras, Vymil cocked his head to one side. "We have few wizard enemies. We almost always stand together. 'Tisn't like it is with humans where you can't wait to war with one another. We warned you." He lowered his face so it was even with Rolf's. "You didn't listen. What you have out there," he gestured widely with both hands, "is exactly what you deserve. A dying planet. Problem is you ruined it for the rest of us too."

Rolf's jaw tightened. Squaring his shoulders, he met Vymil's gaze. "You're right. I can't speak for others, but I did what I could. When it became obvious my efforts were trivial against the enormity we faced, I took my family to a place I hoped they'd be safe." He turned his head and spat onto the wooden floor. "Bah! Nowhere is safe. My son was taken—Karras says by some dark overlord. Now my daughter is gone too. We need help. It's why we're here. If you won't welcome us, we'll look elsewhere."

The battle lord shifted his attention to Karras "What is he?" The battle lord pointed toward Rolf. "I'm betting you know, what with all the time you spent in the library afore you deserted us."

"I did not *desert* you." Karras bristled.

Vymil shrugged to the accompaniment of jangling metal. "Semantics. Nor did you answer my question."

"Earth Mage—and Sidhe."

Vymil frowned, deepening the lines across his forehead and around his eyes. "Refresh my memory, wizard. Not about the Sidhe, but the other."

Karras gave a short bark of a laugh. "I fear I must return to the library afore I can honor your request. He's favored by Cybele. She's commandeered his aid to repair some of the damage done to Earth. That's all I know at present."

"If this is the reason for your long-overdue return to the stronghold, why the need for secrecy?"

"To avoid lengthy conversations, just like the one we're having." Karras snorted. "We're not the most trusting race."

"With good reason." Apparently over his ill temper, Vymil asked, "Would you like an escort?"

Shaking his head, Karras said, "Thanks, but no. I'm going to do what I should have done in the first place. Use magic to shield us from prying eyes." He hooked a hand over Rolf's arm and pulled hard. "Follow me."

"Last time I did that, we ended up embroiled in a conversation we don't have time for."

Karras didn't dignify Rolf's comment with a reply; he just kept moving.

Liefes met them just inside the door of the Council Chambers. Karras was grateful there'd been no more unexpected stops along the way. He swept his gaze about the room, inlaid with quartz and marble tiling, and relaxed fractionally. The simple elegance of the High Council's meeting room always soothed him.

"Vymil found me," Liefes said, his moss green eyes serious. Long, blond braids almost brushed the floor, cascading about robes such a pale shade of green they appeared white. A carved golden medallion, symbol of his office, hung from his neck. "My guess is thy visit has something to do with Ned's imprisonment, though I did not share my hunch with the battle lord."

"It does," Rolf blurted. "He and my daughter were together. She's missing, and we think Ned may know where she is. My son was kidnapped too," he rushed on, ignoring Karras's jabs in his side. "It happened years ago. We never did find him. Amanda is our last child. Please, won't you help us find her?"

Karras rolled his eyes. "I'm sorry," he said to Liefes with a small bow. "I told yon human not to speak unless spoken to. So far he's completely disregarded my commands—ah, wishes."

"We're in a hurry," Rolf said solemnly. "My daughter may be dying. I can't wait for you to go through your wizard rigmarole."

A faint smile lit Liefes's gaunt features. "Humans are hasty," he said to Karras, "because they live such a short time. Despite that one," he pointed at Rolf, "not being exactly human, it appears he inherited many of their worst traits."

Rolf opened his mouth. Before he could say anything, Karras broke in. "May we talk with Ned? It would only be for a few minutes. You're welcome to be present."

Liefes nodded. "Certainly. Walk with me."

Karras asked for clarification regarding Landarik's charges against Ned. When Liefes was done talking, Karras said, "It appears you have Landarik's side of things. Has anyone asked Ned what happened?"

"No. We will, but no one has done so yet."

Because Ned isn't a wizard.

"I imagine the lad is frightened. He knows he has few friends here."

"Thou hast always taken up for him."

"Must be my affinity for underdogs."

The stairs leading to the dungeons lay just ahead. The staircase was narrow and winding, wide enough for only one person at a time. Liefes moved in front of Karras. Reaching the bottom, he strode to a heavy, oaken door with metal reinforcements running across it. He spoke a single word and laid his long-fingered hand over a panel next to the door. It sprang open.

The wizard fell back a pace. "This is hardly possible," he muttered.

Karras ran past. He gazed at a cell holding vestiges of Ned's energy, but no Ned. Turning on Liefes, he snarled, "You let them murder him, didn't you? Without so much as a trial."

"I did not." Liefes held up both hands, palms outward. "Use the truth spell if thou dost not believe me."

Probing, Karras found truth in Liefes's words. "What the hell happened here? I can still smell magic. Not ours, but not dark castings, either."

Liefes shook his head. "I have no idea. Beyond enchantment and reason, the boy has escaped."

"Beyond our enchantments," Karras agreed, aware how tired he was—and how frightened for his acolyte. "Mayhap Ned finally came into his own brand of power."

Rolf grabbed Karras's arm. "I don't care what kind of magic the boy's dabbling with. It appears any hope of finding my daughter disappeared right along with him. What are we going to do now?"

JOURNEY TO ANOTHER WORLD

Ned walked for what was left of the day. The herd of six-legged unicorn things had moved on quickly. Used to relying on his magic, rather than his eyes, Ned kept reminding himself to scan the places where open country posed a threat. Though offering more in the way of concealment, the boulder fields presented their own set of problems. Large snakes curled on the sunny side of many rocks. He gave them a wide berth since he had no idea whether they were poisonous. About the only animals that looked familiar were the rats. Except he couldn't talk with them like he could back home. He tried, but like the other beasts, they appeared not to hear him.

He sweated profusely. Thirst dogged him after the first couple hours. Ned would have sat out the sun's transit across the sky if not for the urgency of locating Amanda. Heedless that it might lead the dark gods right to him, he sent out magic from time to time, tracking her. To his dismay, her life force waned, but very slowly. Panicked, he willed himself to hurry. Dusk finally fell, and three moons rose over the barren land. The temperature plummeted. Wet through from perspiration, Ned shivered. He picked up his pace and hoped the heat from his body would dry his clothing.

Water.

He needed to find some soon. Surely the animals drank somewhere. If he could just talk with them, they'd tell him. Or maybe they wouldn't here. He scented the air, hoping for the cool, clean tang of water. When that didn't work, he switched strategies and probed for something that smelled different. Not dry and dusty like the rocks and heat-parched dirt.

A cracking noise sounded to his right. Not sure what he'd heard, Ned slowed. Even though he didn't think it would do any good, he sent power spinning outward. No point in walking right into something that wanted to make a meal of him. Par for the course on this world, his magic bounced back at him without so much as a scrap of information. Wary, he continued on.

He heard splashing before he saw anything and groaned. He'd finally found water, but something was in it. He'd have to wait for whatever it was to leave. He couldn't wait long. Amanda weakened with every moment. She needed him.

He wondered what had happened to Kühl and Breanna and the other wizards. It was risky enough sending out magic to keep tabs on Amanda. He was hesitant to roust the wizards until he had no other choice.

Tense moments later, he decided he had to take his chances and reveal himself to whatever stood between him and filling his water skins. Maybe it was friendly—or at least not actively hostile.

Ned slipped between two boulders. Twice as tall as him, they formed a gateway, eerie in greenish moonlight. Just beyond sat a pool of blackness. A pale-colored bird with at least a six-foot wingspan swam in circles. It skimmed the water's surface with its wings extended. Watching silently from the shadows, Ned understood it was trolling for fish. The beautiful bird, with a long, graceful beak, was the comeliest thing he'd seen since his arrival. He relaxed a little. Surely something so lovely would share the pool with him.

He sent out the tiniest tendril of magic, just to see if the bird would notice. It let out a horrendous squawk, spun around using its wings for balance, and headed straight toward him. Its wide-open mouth revealed two rows of razor-sharp teeth.

If he took time to think, he'd be dead. Ned sent a killing blow right at the bird's heart. The thing kept coming. Then it was on him. Unexpectedly sharp feathers batted his head. Teeth tore the skin on his face. Forgoing magic—it wasn't working, anyway—Ned grasped the thing by its sinuous neck and squeezed as hard as he could. Its spinal column snapped, and the body went limp in his hands.

Panting with effort, Ned tossed it aside. He had to hurry before any more animals showed up. From here on, he'd assume everything he met wanted him dead. Ned fell on his belly. He lowered his mouth to the water and took an experimental sip. It had a brackish, sour taste, but he had to drink. If the water in this wretched place killed him, he hoped it took its time.

He drank until he couldn't drink any more. Pulling off his pack, he got three water skins and dragged them through the pool, staying near the surface. Water was usually cleanest where the sun had a chance to sterilize it. He focused a thread of magic, intent on healing the worst of his injuries from the bird attack, then decided he couldn't afford the time. His face and neck stung, but he'd tend to them later.

He considered taking the bird along to cook. After he hefted it, he kicked it to the side. It must have weighed thirty pounds. If he had time to gut and dress it, he could cut its weight by half, but he needed to get to Amanda. There'd be opportunities to hunt once he rescued her. Since his magic wouldn't kill things, he'd find other ways. Wondering why he was bothering, Ned said a hasty prayer to the goddess for the bird's soul and left the rocky shore in a hurry.

He traveled through what felt like an unnaturally long night. He wished he knew more about this world—like why his magic worked for some things, but not others.

Amanda was definitely closer. Her life force drew him like a beacon. A thought stopped him in his tracks. *If my magic won't work to kill the animals here, how will I wrest her away from whatever's guarding her?*

He started walking again. Rescue was a nice fantasy, but he couldn't do it alone. He needed help. Hell, even Kühl had the sense to request reinforcements. Maybe it would be better to see if he could find Kühl now, before he got much closer to Amanda.

Ned crossed a moonlit patch of open dirt, feeling naked and exposed. He took a deep, steadying breath, got ready to reinforce his invisibility spell, and focused a beam of magic outward with Kühl's name on it.

"*Landarik?*" came back almost immediately.

"*No, it's me,*" Ned sent. Then he felt stupid and added, "*Ned.*"

"*Where's Landarik?*"

"*Not coming.*"

A resigned sigh rang inside Ned's head. "*Wait where you are. We'll find you. No more mind speech.*"

They must have been close. Within minutes, eight shadowy forms closed about him.

"I thought you were nine—" Ned began.

"We lost one to something that looked like a cute little lizard." Breanna spoke softly. "Turned out its bite contained fast-acting poison."

"Never mind." Kühl stepped right next to Ned and hissed into his ear. "Tell me why Landarik isn't here." After Ned finished speaking, the wizard swore softly. "That bastard."

"So, 'tis just us," Breanna said, accompanied by murmurs from the others.

"Have you found her?" Ned asked. With Kühl's question answered, Ned figured he was entitled to know at least this much.

"Aye," one of the other wizards replied. "She lives."

"Under heavy guard," another added.

"Does your magic work in this place?" Ned looked at their small troop, hope fading from his heart.

"Parts of it," Breanna replied. "We're still experimenting."

"We made a camp not far from where Amanda's imprisoned. 'Tis shielded with magic. At least so far we've escaped notice." Kühl took Ned's arm. "Follow us. In terms of using magic here, avoid weaving fire into anything. And if you use air in your spells, there's less to breathe..."

Ned listened intently to what Kühl could tell him about Darehôl and how to maximize his magic.

Kühl turned to face him, curiosity stamped on his fine-boned features. "How'd you find your way here?"

Ned swallowed hard. Nothing for it but the truth. "When I got to the stronghold, they threw me in the dungeons on Landarik's word—"

"Yet, you came anyway." Kühl's voice reflected grudging respect.

Ned sketched in how he'd escaped, leaving the details involving the *Book of Spells* a bit murky. Before they could question him, he hurried to add, "I came for Amanda and because someone had to warn you. Do you think there's a way back for me if we can manage to free Amanda? I've been worried about it."

The wizard stopped moving long enough to stare at him. "Apologies, human mage. You're braver than I gave you credit for."

"I love Amanda. It was my fault she was captured." Ned hesitated. He'd learned not to press his luck with wizards, but he was desperate. "Can I get back?" he repeated.

"I don't know. It appears your traveling pod worked as well as our portal system—at least in this direction. Mayhap you could share the way of your working, so I can determine if it will lend itself to our brand of magic."

"Your magic won't help me get back. Once I escaped, I'm sure the other wizards barred me from the portals."

Kühl shot him a weary glance and interrupted. "You can use our portal system. I'll see to it, and I'll vouch for you once we return."

Ned recognized the conversation was over. Despite Kühl's assurances, he expected the wizards' portal system would probably kill him as soon as he got close enough to a stronghold for the sentries to sense his energy. Once the wizards discovered he was gone, they'd have keyed the portal frequencies to annihilate him if he so much as opened a gateway.

The sun rose above the edge of the world in a blaze of orange that stung his eyes. They stepped through what looked like the side of a boulder. Ned felt the sizzle of magic and knew it for illusion. It looked exactly like the thousands of other boulders littering this place, which was no doubt why the wizards had escaped notice.

"You look dead on your feet, lad," Breanna said kindly. "Have a biscuit and get an hour's worth of rest. Nothing we can do just now anyway. The two morning guards will have her in the yard for her daily session with their whips. After the noon hour, there's only one guard, which increases our odds of success."

"How long have you been here?" he asked. Surely, they'd only arrived a few hours before him.

"Better than two days," Kühl replied. "Remember, time runs differently here."

Ned blanched as Breanna's comment about whips sank in. He swayed and felt the wizard grab his arm. "They're torturing her?" he choked out. It was difficult to meet Breanna's eyes.

She looked hard at him. "Of course they are. It's what's done with prisoners. Goddess's breath. We torture our prisoners to break their spirits and ensure cooperation. What did you expect?"

Well, what did I expect?

"I hoped we'd be able to get her out of there before she was harmed." Ned cringed. He sounded hopelessly naïve, even to himself. "You're right. I need rest." Stumbling away from Breanna, he took off his pack and tossed it to one side where it wouldn't be in the way.

Ned lay down in the dirt next to it and shoved it under his head for a pillow. He thought sleep would be elusive, but he barely felt someone press a square of hardtack into his hand before his eyes closed.

KARRAS FUMED and shook Rolf's hand off his arm. He was positive Liefes told him the truth about Ned. Traces of the boy's energy proved he'd been in the cell, and not very long ago. Karras snapped his fingers and muttered, "Of course." He left the cell and walked the few feet to the command station, where Liefes was questioning the guards. Touching the other wizard briefly on the shoulder he asked, "Could you get me one of the books?"

"Which books?" The high wizard sounded confused. He looked around from a terse discussion with one of the guards. Ned was their only prisoner. The two wizards who'd guarded him knelt before Liefes, declaring they'd noticed nothing. Nothing at all. Karras believed them. Lies had a particular stink conspicuously absent from the underground chamber.

"Never mind," Karras replied. "I'll find one myself." Hauling on Rolf's arm, he said, "Come on."

"Where are we going?"

"To the library. Ned found some sort of magic in the *Book of Spells*. It allowed him to get out of here, so he could go after Amanda. I'm guessing he told Landarik where Amanda is. Ned probably requested aid from the military. Landarik turned him down. They had some sort of major disagreement, so we need to question Landarik too."

Karras reached the steps, but turned back to project his voice toward Liefes. "I assume Landarik is here." At Liefes's nod, he continued. "Have someone place the spell of truth-telling upon him. Then ask him where Amanda Haraldssen is. Once you have the answer, find me in the library. I'll be in the attic where the ancient tomes are kept."

"Certainly. Let us hope Vymil didn't get to him first. Those battle lords tend to stick together." Pushing past Karras, Liefes took the steps two at a time. Partway up, he vanished.

"I wish I could work magic," Rolf murmured. "Admittedly, it's a bit unnerving, but still..."

"Mayhap you can." Karras led them at a brisk trot up several flights of stairs, then down another long, curving stone corridor. Wizard strongholds were almost always carved into mountainsides, and usually damp. Karras felt every one of his thousand plus years in his bones as they rattled down the passageway. "We don't have time right now to test you for latent ability. Later, once we have this problem with your daughter well in hand, I'll research those like you."

"I can read too," Rolf retorted acidly. "You could give me something to look at while you're hunting for information in the *Book of Spells*."

"I know where to find a *Book of Spells*," the wizard replied. "Finding something relevant about Earth Mages will take time."

"Maybe I can check the card catalogue."

Karras laughed. He couldn't help it. The raucous tone silenced Rolf.

Something to remember next time I want to shut him up.

"Take those stairs." He pointed. "All the way to the top."

They were both panting by the time they reached the top of the two-hundredth flight. Karras spoke a word. The wall to their left opened onto an enormous room lined from floor-to-ceiling with books and scrolls. Light filtered in from cutouts high in the walls. Iridescent dust motes danced in the air, lending a fairylike air to the generous space.

Karras barked a word to seal the door in place. He floated upward, plucked a volume from a high shelf, and settled at one of several large trestle tables.

"Mind if I look around?"

"Go ahead." Karras was already deep into the *Book of Spells*. "Just don't talk to me. This book shows different things to different readers, and I need to simulate Ned's energy to discover what he found. For that, I need to concentrate."

It didn't take as long as he feared to find what he sought. Karras marveled as he truly looked at a book he'd taught acolytes out of for hundreds of years while forcing the human mage section to reveal itself. He was reading intently when the library door flew open, banging against a bookcase.

Liefes and Hreth marched in, Landarik between them. Hreth had the same floor-length blond braids and pale green robes as Liefes. "Thou wert right, Karras," Liefes snarled.

Karras stared, shock running through him. The expression on Hreth's face was thunderous. Karras had never seen him this angry—even with Lira. Liefes gripped Landarik's arm so hard, blood welled where nails dug into his arm.

"Well?" Karras looked from one to the other.

This must be worse than I imagined.

"There is truth here. 'Tis far from attractive." Hreth spoke in a whispery voice. He gave Landarik a sharp kick. The battle lord shot a sullen glare at his captor, and Hreth slapped him. "Behave like a wizard, now thou art caught. Thou art an embarrassment to us all."

This time it was Liefes who kicked Landarik. He let go of the wizard's arm long enough to haul off and let his boot fall across Landarik's shin. "Open thy mouth." Liefes spat the words. "This wickedness is of thy making."

Landarik focused his gaze on the floor. When he finally spoke, it was in a jerky monotone. "Ned moved the girl to San Francisco. He thought it would be safe since we're not fighting there. One of the Dareli accosted them and took her. Ned found Kühl. He and his band of warriors went to the Infernals' lands to rescue the girl. Ned asked me for help at Kühl's behest." Landarik fell silent.

"Never mind the rest. I see it in your filthy mind." Fury boiled in Karras's guts. "You refused him. Then you got scared the boy would come here and tell someone what you'd done. Kühl outranks you. You rejected a direct order from a superior officer, which constitutes treason."

"We understand." Liefes spat. "He will be executed as soon as we leave here."

"Executed?" Rolf, who'd been mercifully silent, bolted to his feet. A strangled sound crept into his voice. "I want to find my daughter, but—"

"Do not concern thyself with this. 'Tis none of thy affair," Hreth said.

Something about his tone silenced Rolf. No one ever talked back to the high wizards.

"We're sending the regiment Kühl requested," Liefes added. "They're mustering in the courtyard now."

"I'll accompany them." Karras got to his feet, and then he looked at Rolf and groaned. What to do with him?

"I'm going with you." Rolf looked Karras stubbornly in the eye.

"It *is* his daughter," Hreth pointed out.

"He cannot travel—" Karras began.

"Try a short-acting sleeping draught," Liefes suggested.

Landarik's form wavered. "I did not give thee permission to leave," Hreth gritted out. He began to chant, and the battle lord's form solidified. "We must get him to justice afore he defeats our binding." The blind seer's milk-glass eyes reflected fury—and pain. "To have him loose in the world—any world—would be an affront to all wizardry."

"Good hunting." Liefes set his mouth in a hard line.

"Bring yon Earth Mage back when this is over. The Infernals are fixated on capturing his children. I would know more about him to figure out why." He drew a hand downward. All three vanished.

Karras sighed. He closed the cover of the *Book of Spells* and got to his feet. "Let's go. We must stop by the armory afore we leave. Fortunately, you're close to Landarik's size. His armor should fit you."

"I'm not sure I want to be weighted down with armor."

"'Tisn't a choice. You heard Liefes. The Infernals want Earth Mage blood. What they plan to do with it is uncertain. You will be in grave danger, and I won't be able to watch over you every moment. I could create a spell to make you invisible, but you'd have to stay in one spot."

Karras directed a speculative glance Rolf's way. "Would you obey me?"

"Probably not." Rolf looked sheepish—but determined. "I know I'm not what you're used to dealing with, but I'm not accustomed to taking orders. I've been an adult for a long time. You treat me like I was a brain-damaged ten-year-old."

No, just a brash, hasty human.

"It might be different if we had an opportunity to teach you to entrain some of the magic you have. Even if you only had access to the Sidhe side of things—and the other part were human—you'd be able to make yourself invisible and do many other things as well. There's not time for you to learn an entirely new set of skills before the battle that's coming, though." Karras took a measured breath. "I don't want to be the one who tells that wife of yours you died when my back was turned for an instant."

Color stained Rolf's face above his bearded cheeks. "Touché." He swept one arm downward with a flourish. "Lead on. I just hope the blasted armor isn't too heavy. I remember reading about it being hot too…"

Karras tuned out the last of Rolf's complaints. He was surprised the man wasn't more grateful. Wizards mostly did what they were told. By contrast, Rolf seemed to pride himself on being an independent thinker. Despite Hreth's and Liefes's exhortations, Karras didn't have to take the Earth Mage anywhere. If he left him in the stronghold, the wizards would just have to live with it.

Chuckling to himself, Karras knew it wouldn't take too many of Rolf's handy suggestions or *yes, buts* for the aforementioned wizards to whisk him back to his wife's side.

BIRD IN A GILDED CAGE

manda woke to light spilling through a small window high on the wall of her cell. She was amazed she'd slept so long. Her tormentors usually had her up and out at dawn. It was far more uncomfortable to be mostly-naked in the chill early morning than under the intense midday sunlight. The two whatever-they-weres seemed to feed off her misery. The more pain she suffered, the better they liked it. This was the first morning they'd left her alone, and she didn't understand why. Surely they hadn't tired of whipping her. Or raking their claws down her naked skin. Or— Amanda tossed her head from side to side to clear the images flooding her mind.

She heaved herself to a sitting position, groaning. Every muscle in her body ached. Despite eating yesterday, she was hungry—and thirsty. An unpleasant thought hit her like an out-of-control train. Maybe today was the day they planned to kill her. After all, they'd fed her for the first time yesterday. They weren't flogging her today. Wrapping her arms around herself, she sought comfort in the meager warmth of her body.

Ned's face floated before her. She was glad he wasn't here. This place was so ghastly, she couldn't find words to describe it—like something out of her worst nightmare, ratcheted up a million times. The bogie men under the bed were real. They'd laid hands on her and hurt her, and they could come back at any moment. She shuddered. How would they kill her? Would it be long and painful?

A pitiful moan rose from her throat. Amanda bit the inside of her mouth to stifle it.

"Stop it," she said, hoping for solace in the sound of her own voice. It sounded a lot like her mother's, which helped. Lori was one tough cookie. She'd made it through medical school when not very many women went, and she'd excelled in medical research, a male-dominated field. She'd figured out what to do once they moved away from the remains of civilization too—raising animals and coaxing plants to grow at eight thousand feet. Her mother would tell her she didn't have time to feel sorry for herself. She should pull out all the stops to discover a way out of her prison.

Have I given up? Is that what's wrong?

She remembered her father saying attitude was everything. A tear floated down one cheek. Her parents would be disappointed in her. This was the first time in her life she'd been challenged, and it only took a handful of days to turn her into a gibbering ball of mush.

"Pull yourself together, Amanda." She made her voice as commanding as she could. Maybe if she truly believed she had choices, she'd do better finding the key to her freedom. One of the books her father had brought with them was *Man's Search for Meaning* by Viktor Frankl.

"If he could find a reason to live in Auschwitz, I can find a reason to survive here," she muttered, thoroughly ashamed of herself.

Getting to her feet, she forced herself to walk the length of her cell, then back again. Her body screamed in protest, but she kept moving. She'd spent nearly every moment when she wasn't being tortured curled into a ball on the bunk made of deadly vines. Not anymore. She swung her arms back and forth to ramp up the intensity of her exercise.

The door opened abruptly. She turned toward it, placed her hands on her hips, and took in the tongueless hag from yesterday with more food and water. Amanda accepted the dish and flask from her and hunted for shards of humanity behind the woman's tired eyes. "Can you talk to me?" she whispered.

A definite headshake. Fear rolled off the woman in waves.

"I know you can't talk with your mouth, but we could draw letters." To illustrate, Amanda laid the food and water aside. She knelt and formed the word *help* in the dirt floor.

Please, please let her be able to read and write English.

The woman peered back over one shoulder, maybe to assure herself no one was there. Kneeling with surprising agility in one so old, she wrote, *no help here,* her blue eyes round with apprehension. Once she was sure Amanda had read the words, she scraped her palm across the dirt to obliterate them. Scrambling to her feet, she turned and fled through the open door.

Amanda waited for her to come back, to lock her in again. Long minutes passed. Food forgotten, she walked tentatively to the door and gazed out into the walled enclosure around her cell. She was alone. She'd feared the open cell door was some sort of trap that would spring shut the moment she poked her head outside.

Excited and hopeful, she raced into the yard and made a full transit of the stone wall. Made of overlapping stones mortared together, it stood about ten feet tall. A gate bisected it at one end. It was locked. She examined the stones, set a bare foot on one, and tried to climb. The pattern wasn't consistent, though. The stones stuck out enough for a little bit, then lay flush with one another. After falling to the ground a third time, she bit back tears of pain and frustration.

While getting to her feet to try again, the gate creaked open. Her first instinct was to cower, but she forced herself to stand straight. She'd meet whatever was coming head on, goddammit.

The robed man who'd helped her breathe stood before her. The gate gaped open behind him. She judged the odds of making a dash for freedom. They weren't good. No doubt why the gate was still open.

Amanda settled her gaze on her captor, and it remained there, almost against her will. He was one of the most beautiful men she'd ever seen. Tall like her father, his bearing was regal, almost kinglike. He looked like the heroes in her childhood fairytale books. Long, dark hair fell about him to waist level. He wore black robes with a jaunty red sash holding everything together. Intelligent dark eyes set in a fine-boned face took her measure.

Amanda decided she had nothing to gain by remaining silent. "You're not the one who brought me here. What do you want with me?"

The man smiled, revealing very white teeth in his clean-shaven face. "Observant of you. The man who delivered you to me is one of my servants."

Not observant at all. He was short and squat, like a toad.

The man laughed. Almost like he could read her mind.

She opened her mouth, but he waved her to silence. "Of course I know what's in your mind. You could cloak your thoughts, but you have no idea how to do so. A criminal waste of power. Both you and your brother. At least I've taken the time to teach him. Something those precious parents of yours couldn't be bothered with."

Skin tightened along the sides of Amanda's face as her eyes widened. "Jon. You have Jon here. Where is he? Can I see him? We thought he was dead—"

"Enough." Though the man hadn't moved, he exuded danger. "I like my women silent unless I've asked them something. Can you remember?"

"I can, but why should I?"

"Because if you don't obey, I'll hurt you. Like this."

The man flicked an idle finger. Pain, bright and searing,

rolled over her and took her breath away. She bit her lip so she wouldn't cry out.

He smiled again. "Good. Good. We haven't totally quenched your spirit. A woman who knows how to be silent, yet retains some gumption is an almost irresistible combination." He rubbed his hands together.

"I'm not your woman," she managed through clenched teeth. "I love someone else."

"Who said anything about love?" Coarse, ribald laughter filled the yard.

Suddenly he didn't look beautiful anymore. She saw the truth of what he was. Someone who'd destroy her for less than perfect obedience to his every whim. But he had Jon. She needed to hang on long enough to try to help her brother. Heat rose upward from her chest, staining her face crimson. This was hard. So hard. A sophisticated game where she hadn't been told all the rules.

The man narrowed his eyes. "You're coming with me. You need to bathe. You're filthy and you smell."

If he wants me clean, maybe he's not going to kill me after all.

Remembering he could read her thoughts, she clamped down on them.

"Come, little bird. I'm not going to kill you—not today anyway. Perhaps not at all if you please me."

"What does that mean?"

"I think you know. You're a bright girl."

Sick knowledge moved through her like a thief, robbing her of hope. "What if I said I'd rather go back to my cell?" she asked defiantly and raised her chin.

"Not an option. Move." He pointed through the open gate. "Just in case you're considering running, my minions are everywhere. You wouldn't get ten yards before they mowed you down." His disconcerting smile settled on her again. "Besides, you wish to be reunited with your brother, do you not?"

"Y-yes." Her legs trembled so hard, she wondered if they'd carry her through the gate. He was wickedness incarnate. Like the fallen angels they tried to shove down her throat in barely-remembered Sunday school lessons.

He clasped his hands together and rested his chin on them. His dark, hypnotic gaze bored into her until she felt stripped of dignity. "We have the beginnings of a deal," he said at last. "I have something you want, and you have something I may want. We shall see how strong the blood runs in you."

A lazy grin spread across his face. "My name is Tantalus. Nice to meet you at last, Amanda Haraldssen. What is the expression? Your brother sends his best."

The parody of civility was almost her undoing. It took everything she had to march past him and out the gate.

NED DREAMED about Amanda and a tall, dark stranger in wizard's robes walking side-by-side. The man had an arresting face with high cheekbones, a sculpted jawline, and intense, dark eyes. He kept one arm draped casually about Amanda's shoulders. From time to time, he bent and spoke into her ear. They looked like lovers. Ned's stomach lurched. He tried to force himself awake, but the dream world held him close.

Amanda and the man came to a stone building. It looked like it might've been a stronghold or castle in its better days. Made of dirt-colored stones, its walls rose in an unbroken line beyond Ned's field of vision. Barred windows dotted the central tower at intervals, and a portcullis gate creaked slowly upward. The man placed a proprietary hand on Amanda's bottom, propelling her forward. She didn't pull away, or spin to slap him.

Did she forget me already?

Anguish filled his heart. Something rocked him. He batted it away. He had to keep watching. To see what Amanda was going to do with the man. Whatever it was shook him again. "Noooooo..." he moaned. "Leave me alone."

"Ned." Breanna's firm hand kneaded his shoulder. "You were crying out in your sleep. You must hold silence, or our illusion won't protect us."

"S-sorry," he mumbled, the tug of the dream still strong in him.

"'Tis time you were up anyway. We march shortly."

"Is there a castle nearby? With a tower?" Ned clambered to his feet and rubbed sleep from his eyes.

She gave him an odd look. "Yes, but how would you know? We found you in the opposite direction."

"I dreamed it just now, and about a man who looks like a wizard. He has Amanda."

Breanna nodded. "Aye. Tantalus."

Ned's eyes flew open. The last vestiges of drowsiness fell away like rotten petals on a week-old rose. "He's here? I thought he was imprisoned in Tartarus."

She snorted. "He's been ruler of the Infernals' world for millennia. Ever since he killed his son and tried to feed him to the other gods for dinner."

Ned struggled to recall his lessons. "The other gods jailed him—"

"He got loose. I saw him on one of our reconnaissance trips. It has to be Tantalus. No one but him has such unearthly beauty." Breanna shook her head, perhaps to rid herself of an unwelcome image. "That one could lure women to their doom."

Ned thought of Amanda, so young and so innocent. If it was a struggle for Breanna to resist Tantalus and his charms, what hope could there be for his Mandy? He swallowed back fury mixed with a deep uneasiness.

"I saw them clearly. I wonder... Is there a mirror I could use to scry? Or a pool?"

"You know such magics?" Breanna raised a disbelieving brow.

Ned shrugged. "If I could see them in my dreams, I should be able to channel the same energy while I'm awake. It appears I had a true vision. Let's see if I can summon it back."

Kühl came up behind them. He dragged a shiny piece of metal out of a pocket. A signaling mirror. Ned reached eagerly for it.

Taking a couple of deep breaths to steady himself, Ned focused his magic. The vision returned. Amanda sat naked in a large bathtub. A fat old woman with matted gray hair helped her wash. Ned scanned the room and zeroed in on Tantalus. The dark god stared intently at Amanda, lust stamped on his patrician features.

Bile rose in Ned's throat, but he ignored his roiling stomach and clutched the shard of metal so hard it cut him. Tantalus shifted his gaze from Amanda and glowered at Ned. Cold fingers of fear marched across his spirit, but Ned held the vision.

He can't see me. There's no way.

Another figure entered the room. Ned gasped. It was a masculine version of Amanda—and a dead ringer for Rolf. "I'll be damned," he muttered. "Must be the brother." Mercifully, Tantalus moved his intimidating gaze to the newcomer.

"What?" Kühl stood beside him in staring into the metal. "Tell me. I can't see a goddess-blasted thing."

"Wait." Motioning for Kühl to give him a few more seconds, Ned watched as Amanda reached for Jon. A welcoming smile lit her face. Jon's eyes flicked to Tantalus, who nodded encouragement. With an enigmatic smile on a face eerily like Rolf's, Jon strode forward, planted a kiss right on Amanda's lips and curled a hand around one of her breasts.

Ned heaved the bit of metal away. Fury buffeted him, and he clenched his hands into fists. "That answers one question." He stifled a growl. "Or two, really. Amanda's brother is here. It looks like Tantalus co-opted him on as an acolyte..." He sketched in the details of his dream, adding what he'd just seen in his vision. Moving to where he'd chucked the mirror, he picked it up and held it out to Kühl.

Breath hissed from the wizard's mouth. He looked at Ned and said, "Keep it. You can use it to tell us things. None of the rest of us has your particular gift."

"Thanks." Ned wiped bloody fingers on his pants and regarded Breanna and two other wizards who'd come close. "What do any of you know about Earth Mages?" No one said anything. Shoulders shrugged. Heads shook as the wizards looked back and forth at one another.

Guess there's no help for it.

Ned reached for his backpack. It was an instantaneous decision—and a risky one—after years of keeping the book's presence mostly hidden from the wizards. Dragging out the *Book of Spells*, he pressed it into Kühl's hands. "Here. The answers you need are probably in there somewhere."

"Where in the goddess's name did you get one of our books?" A wizard Ned didn't know with long red hair stepped closer. He sounded decidedly unfriendly.

"He must have stolen it," another wizard muttered, also closing in.

"Karras gave it to me. Go ahead, weave a spell. You'll see I speak true." Ned met their hostile gazes directly. "Besides," he hurried on, "the book has a mind of its own. If it didn't want to stay with me, it would have found a way to leave long since."

Kühl handled the book reverently. Muttering an incantation, he opened it at random and read aloud.

Earth Mage skills: Excavation, finding metal and mineral

deposits, tending oceanic creatures, calling wind, calling storms, encouraging crops to grow, finding water, creating balanced ecosystems...

"Enough," Kühl muttered. "Let's see where they came from. Mayhap 'twill shed light on the source of their power." He paged backward, scanning the closely written lines. "Aha! Here it is."

Cybele and Ceres had need of others to help them keep the Earth and oceans fruitful when the other gods refused manual labor. After long deliberation regarding the advisability of such a plan, each goddess lay with a mortal. Their offspring—part divine, part human—became Earth Mages. Close to immortal, they are bound to the goddess who birthed them. Or the goddess linked to their lineage for those who came later. Because the first two were successful, the goddesses created ten more...

"Tantalus is divine," Ned interrupted, too wound up to worry about being rude. "Wasn't he the son of Zeus or something? Don't you see? It's why he wants Amanda. To create immortal, divine children. What better way to get them?"

"Jupiter," Kühl corrected. "He was the son of Jupiter. I do believe you're right. It does not, however, explain why he kept the brother all these years, but I'm sure we shall find out. Come. If they are otherwise occupied with bathing and...other pursuits, we may have the element of surprise on our side. Ned will use the mirror to look ahead and tell us what we face."

Ned reached for the book.

Kühl clutched it close and began to turn away. The wizard jumped. A curious expression blossomed on his face, and he dropped the book into Ned's waiting hands. "It shocked me when I hesitated." A corner of his mouth turned down wryly. "I guess it was trying to tell me it belongs to you."

"Yes, it lets me know when it wants something too." Ned tucked the book away and shouldered his pack. The temperature was almost too warm for his cloak, but it helped contain his invisibility spell, so he draped it over his shoulders and secured the clasp.

Ned would have preferred to wait until dark, but it wasn't his choice. The small group crept from behind the illusory rock, and Kühl instructed them to spread out. They'd be less noticeable individually. Ned let his third eye guide him as he balanced invisibility with maintaining enough air to breathe. It was one of the tricks Kühl shared, which made magic more manageable in this world. Though it taxed him, Ned kept a trickle of power focused on the mirror.

They'd covered half a mile or so when Ned saw the tower and the keep. Still quite distant, it was unmistakably the same one in his vision. Checking the mirror, he saw Amanda emerge from the tub. She reached for a towel hanging from a nearby hook, but Jon slapped her hand away. In her first show of spirit since Ned spied her in his dream, she curled her mouth into a sneer. Shoving past Jon, she lunged for the towel.

The scene in the mirror changed. Gray-black, apelike creatures running on their hind legs spewed from the castle. Ned screamed a warning. They'd been seen, so silence wasn't important. Neither was the mirror. He tucked it away, raised his hands, and called magic, concentrating it so he'd be ready. He couldn't marshal enough power to breathe, stay invisible, and fight, so he dropped the illusion making it look like he wasn't there.

The things spotted him. They threw rocks as they ran, uttering chilling, unearthly cries. The projectiles traveled surprisingly far. Ned forced himself to wait, heart pounding against his ribs. He'd been in a lot of battles. His magic would be more lethal once the enemy moved closer.

Kühl's voice sounded in his head. Ned knew it was meant for all of them. The battle lord planned to use mind speech since they were so few. After the enemy became aware of them, communication was more important than stealth.

"I count twenty. Each of us must kill two. Which will leave two for Breanna and me to finish off. Starting with our right flank..." The battle lord rattled off directions. Ned's assigned targets closed. His body shook with the effort of containing magic. He worried he'd burst before he got a chance to discharge the power rushing through him. It was heady in an odd sort of way and, for the first time, he understood the allure of battle.

"Now."

Taking careful aim, Ned unleashed killing blows and prayed they'd be more effective than when he targeted the bird in the pool. His magic flew straight and true. Thank the goddess, his targets fell. He scanned the clearing to see how the others fared.

Goddess's breath! More of the things were attacking from behind. Kühl had been so focused on the frontal attack and the castle, no one guarded their rear flank.

"Behind us. Look sharp," he cried.

Ned pulled power and attacked until he thought he'd drop from the effort. During a brief lull in the fight, he saw least fifty of the ape-men lying dead in a rough circle around them. Three wizards were dead or dying. Ned tried to drag one of the bodies out of harm's way. Kühl's panting voice in his mind told him to save his energy for killing.

The battle high dissipated. Horror at the carnage hammered him, but Ned pushed it away.

Don't think. Just kill.

Finally, nothing moved beyond five wizards and Ned. He stumbled to one of the fallen wizards and started to hoist the body over a shoulder.

"Leave him." Kühl materialized beside him, his dark eyes filled with sorrow—and anger. The wizard looked exhausted. His red hair, escaped from its braids, straggled about a soot-smeared face. "We must get out of here afore Tantalus sends any more Infernals. We are too few and too depleted to mount any sort of response."

The wizard limped away. Assuming Kühl had already spoken to everyone else, Ned sucked in what he could of the thin air and tried to rebuild the illusion to render him invisible.

As he hunted for enough energy to drag his weary body back to camp, he thought about Amanda for the first time since the battle began. His heart sank. They truly were too few to storm Tantalus's castle now. In truth, they'd been too few before the last three deaths. Though they'd dealt out far more damage than they sustained, who knew what other abominations Tantalus had on tap to send against them?

Maybe there'd be some way for Kühl to go after

reinforcements. Ned couldn't since the wizards at the stronghold had probably thrown a death sentence over him for escaping from his cell. Besides, unless the *Book of Spells* held new information, Ned wasn't certain he could get back at all.

I CAN TOO LEARN MAGIC

"Okay." Lori panted, eyeing her mother. "I can get in and out of the damned portals. Now can we go after Karras and Rolf? They've been gone for days. I want to find my daughter."

Lira exhaled, the breath whistling through her teeth eloquent testimony to her frustration. "I suppose I could try to raise Father through the stones. Again."

"You already did. He didn't answer."

"There may be some sort of problem at the stronghold. He is seer to our people. When he goes into his vision states, he's often unavailable for long periods."

"All the more reason for us to go," Lori insisted. She kicked at the dirt with a booted foot, dislodging a crust of newly fallen snow. "If we're going to leave, we have to go now. If we wait, winter will be here, and the animals will die without someone to tend them. As it is, we'll have to get one of Karras's kids to suckle my goats before we can go."

"Which means we'll have to bring all his goats down here. Or move yours there."

Lori considered which would be easier. Maybe Lira was warming to the idea of them leaving. After all, she'd taught her to open a portal, visualize a destination, and travel there. Lira couldn't travel under her own steam until her father lifted some sort of spell he'd cast, but that didn't mean they couldn't use Lori's newly awakened magic.

"Well." She elbowed her mother. "Let's get going."

It took them hours to get everything situated. It was easier to move the goats to Karras's since he still had pasture that wasn't eaten down to nothing. They left Nellie there as well. When Lori asked the mare, she said she wanted to go with the goats. It would be too sad for her to stay in the barn where she'd lost Noah, with only the sow for company.

Lira tried twice more to activate the round, white, speaking stones wizards used to communicate over distances, but no one answered her. Dusk was closing fast when Lori pulled the door shut, slipped an old backpack over her shoulders with extra warm clothes and a bit of food, and bid farewell to the wolves.

"It's your job to guard the sow and her children. The chickens too. Look in on the sheep up canyon in their pen, and the goats and Nellie at Karras's. I expect to find all of them here when I return."

Nikki solemnly licked her chin. *"We will do our best,"* he assured her.

Mouth suddenly dry, Lori felt anxious about what they were about to do. Using the Ways to travel a few miles from home was quite different from traveling halfway around the world.

"Having second thoughts?" Lira inquired.

"Of course. It doesn't mean we're not going."

A smile played about Lira's usually serious mouth. "Even though I didn't raise you, you got a healthy jot of my spirit from somewhere."

Lori sketched a portal in the air as her mother had taught her. It glowed pale lavender, and she stepped through.

Lira joined her, placing hands on either side of her head. "I will send you a mental image of where we're going. You must employ it exactly as I send it, or we may not come out in the right place."

Nodding, Lori closed her eyes. A sensation of falling created mild vertigo. Yet it wasn't any different from her earlier experiences in the Ways. Time passed. Lira must have sensed when her concentration wavered because she strengthened their mental bonding when Lori needed it most. She felt deceleration far sooner than she expected, but didn't want to risk breaking her concentration to think about it.

"We're here." Lira's voice sounded sharp. "Draw a gateway."

"Right." Lori felt like she'd been sleepwalking. A disconnect inserted itself between her brain and her body. It took almost more energy than she had to summon magic and sketch a portal. "Crap! I can't get it to come."

Lira tried to help, but the partially-formed portal sizzled

ominously where she touched it. "Goddess be damned," she ground out, sounding furious. "Let's see if we can do it this way."

Lira moved her hands from Lori's head to her shoulders. Energy, dazzling in its intensity, shot through her. It reminded her of the extent of Lira's power and how much there was yet to learn. The color of her gateway brightened immediately. More important, it finished forming. Lori peeled the door down and stepped shakily through into what looked like a medieval courtyard. "Thank you for the help." She smiled at her mother. "Why am I so tired?"

"Because you took us thousands of miles on a neophyte's magic."

The flagstone square was deserted. Lori glanced curiously at debris scattered among the stones. It looked like a lot of people had left in a hurry.

"Daughter." Lira's voice was stern. "You forgot something."

The portal was still open. Saying the words to close it, Lori shook her head briskly. "My mind's all jumbled, like I've been asleep for centuries."

"Not surprising. Follow me." Staff grasped in one hand, Lira took off at a very brisk walk. Lori trailed after her but soon broke into a trot to keep up. They passed under an archway and into a long, torch-lit corridor.

"What happened back there?" Lori gestured over her shoulder.

"Troops left for somewhere. Not long ago from the feel of things."

After many twists and turns and more than a few stairs, Lira tapped peremptorily on a door. When nothing happened, she knocked louder.

"Who are we waiting for?"

"Ssht." Lira whispered. "I'm listening." After a moment, she said, "Father isn't here. Come. He must be in the Council Chamber."

Though she didn't have time to examine anything closely, Lori tried to look at some of the murals and sculptures lining the walls. A small fortune in artwork graced the wizards' stronghold. She wondered how many such places the wizards kept and if all of them were this large and lavishly appointed.

Turning hard left, she followed her mother through a pair of heavy doors. Elaborately carved wood, they could have graced an old-fashioned church. The room beyond radiated an elegant simplicity. Quartz and marble glittered in sunlight filtering through high cutouts. Wainscoting decorated the walls. Three men sat at a long table. All had floor-length blond hair braided and set with jewels. They wore pale green robes. One had golden rings set with stones on almost every finger.

"Daughter. How is it thou art here? Why hast thou disobeyed me?" One of the men stood. His eyes, staring straight ahead, looked like pale milk glass. Lori assumed he was blind.

"It wasn't her fault." Lori stepped forward and kept her gaze on her hands twined together in front of her. "I'm Rolf's wife—the one who came with Karras a few days ago. I was so worried about my daughter, I talked Lira into showing me the way here, so we could find out what happened." She glanced up to see three sets of incredulous eyes trained on her. Lori stared back. "What?" she asked. "Do two of you speak another language? If you do, tell me what it is. There's a good chance I could translate what I just said."

"Even other wizards wait for an invitation to speak before the three of our High Council," Lira said softly. "'Tis unheard of for a stranger to offer unsolicited commentary."

Feeling like an idiot and well out of her depth, Lori looked at each of the wizards in turn. "I'm sorry. I don't know your customs, but I still need help finding my daughter. Will you provide it, or do I have to look elsewhere?" Lori glanced at her mother in time to see Lira wince.

The wizard with deep green eyes laughed, but without much warmth. "Funny, thy husband said almost exactly those same words. I am Liefes, human woman. Or mayhap not entirely human. 'Tis certainly apparent whose daughter thou art. Lira is known for her sharp tongue and overbearing ways."

Bright color stained Lira's fair skin. She bowed her head and kept the angle of her gaze glued to the floor.

"Thou hast not answered me." Hreth walked to Lira.

The wizard laid her staff on the floor at her father's feet and curtsied. "Apologies, Father. I tried to reach you many times through the stones. Days passed with no word from Karras. My..."

She inhaled sharply and then looked right into Hreth's blind eyes. "My daughter thought we should come here to see what had transpired. I happened to agree with her. You'd told me Ned was imprisoned, accused of sedition by Landarik, but we had no idea what happened after that." Lira paused a beat. "Though I knew it wouldn't please you, I taught my daughter how to manipulate the Ways, so we could travel. If you need more hands to follow those who just left from the courtyard, mine are sworn to our defense."

"Had thou been here, thou couldst have gone to the Infernals' world with the company," the third wizard said. Turning bright blue eyes on Lori, he bobbed his head in a quarter bow. "I am Dagget."

"I could still follow them if Father would lift the spell forbidding me the Ways," Lira pointed out.

"Not without me." Lori stepped to her mother's side. "I couldn't stand being left here to wait." She looked at the wizards. "I'm a doctor. If there are wounded, I could help."

"We have our own healers." Liefes didn't sound nearly as friendly as Dagget. "Besides, our physiology isn't quite the same as a human's."

"I'm certain I could find some way to be useful," Lori persisted.

"Father?" Lira held out her hands.

After a pause so long Lori was certain he'd refuse, Hreth took Lira's hands in his, barked a few words, and kissed her forehead. "There are things thou shouldst know afore leaving," he said.

Lori opened her mouth.

Liefes glared at her. "Not another word out of thee, if thou wouldst hold onto thy tongue."

Outrage flooded her. No one spoke to her in such a patronizing manner. No one. "How dare you—" she began.

"We have different customs," Lira inserted hastily. Picking up her staff, she guided Lori to a seat at the marble-topped table. "Bear in mind they can read your thoughts."

"Thou came in search of information," Hreth said, his voice carefully neutral. "I suggest thou maintain silence so we may tell thee what has occurred."

"I'm listening." Lori straightened in her chair.

"Silence," Daggett thundered.

Lori pressed her lips together. So far, she wasn't impressed with the wizard half of her heritage, but she cleared her mind and focused on the smooth, shiny tabletop. After a pause, Hreth began talking.

"In a bold and desperate move, Ned escaped from our dungeons..."

AMANDA FELT ILL. Her stomach twisted into a hard knot, but she refused to let her discomfiture show. She'd been so happy to see her brother. Shock and outrage set in when he touched her like a lover. What the hell had happened to him? She looked around the room Tantalus had tossed her into. Though a big step up from her cell, Amanda wasn't fooled. She was little more than a bird in a gilded cage. Her captor even called her *little bird* in the yard outside her cell.

He'd told her to pick what she wanted to wear from an armoire leaning against one wall. She grabbed the first thing she saw, a deep purple robe with a teal sash. The fabric felt like fine silk, but she was flayed and raw from all the whippings. Anything rubbing against her skin was torture.

She worried about what would happen next. The way things were heading, Jon was as likely to rape her as Tantalus. Bile gathered in the back of her throat, scoring it with liquid fire. She swallowed with effort and forced herself to focus. She needed to make good use of the time to herself before Jon or Tantalus returned.

Amanda made a transit of the room. It was large, with a fireplace at one end and a canopy bed at the other. Carved wooden paneling lined the walls. Examining the carvings, she blushed. The art portrayed such blatant sexuality, she averted her eyes. She felt she'd trespassed on something intensely private, and it made her skin crawl with dread.

A large window looked out on a balcony at least two floors down. She tested the mechanism, surprised when it opened easily. She leaned out, letting the warm, afternoon breeze play through her wet hair. She was supposed to comb it out. Tantalus wasn't fond of curls. He told her as much when she picked the robe to wear. Amanda leaned out farther. Would a fall kill her? Death was a better alternative than rape—especially at the hands of her brother.

I wonder if I could... She eyed the thirty foot drop.

It wouldn't take much. A single heave and she'd be airborne.

Can't think about this. I just have to do it.

She dragged one foot over the sill. Tears formed in her eyes. She begged her parents and Ned to forgive her. The door to her room glided open.

She had to act *now* or the opportunity would be lost. Amanda took a deep breath and threw her body outward. To her horror, cold surrounded her. She bounced back into the room and hit the floor with a *thunk*.

"None of that." Jon's voice sounded just like Rolf's. "Jesus Christ, Mandy. We waited a long time for your arrival. We couldn't take you before you were eighteen and three months. It's an ancient law. Being one of the gods, Tantalus is bound by their strictures."

Looking up from where she'd fallen, Amanda trained her gaze on Jon. "If you ever loved me, let me go. There's nothing for me here." She scrambled to her feet and made another rush for the open window. She hit the floor harder this time. So hard, the wind got knocked out of her.

"I told you. None of that." Jon's voice rang with annoyance.

"Mother and Father would be so ashamed of you," she managed when she could talk again.

A grin, so much like Rolf's it broke her heart, spread across his face. "You have no way of knowing."

"The hell I don't," she hissed.

He ignored her statement. "Are you going to try to kill yourself again? Because if you are, I can have the window sealed. I assured Tantalus you'd behave. It's why you're here and not in the filthy pen outside."

"Gee, thank you." The acid in her voice could have burned holes through metal.

He knelt next to her on the floor and caressed the side of her face. She bit down hard on his thumb. Temper sparked from his eyes, and he slapped her. Rolling to one side, she dug her nails into his arm.

He grunted. "So you like it rough, do you? Guess you

grew up, little sister." He pinned both of her hands above her head, holding her to the floor easily.

"Not particularly." She pulled away, stunned when he let her go. Amanda scrambled to her feet, keeping her gaze on him. "What happened to you? You used to take care of me. Once upon a time you were kind and sweet."

He stood too. Something flickered behind his eyes—a weary resignation. Maybe memories danced just beneath the surface of conscious thought. It was hard to tell. Taking a huge chance, she walked toward him and took one of his hands in hers. "Jon. It's me, Mandy."

He snatched his hand back. "My life is here. I had no life before this."

Is that what Tantalus did? Brainwashed him?

"You did. You used to live with Mom and Dad and me in the big blue colonial on Phoenix Avenue in Fair Oaks. You were going to go to Stanford. They accepted you when you were just a junior in high school. Remember how excited you were? You wanted to be a doctor just like Mom. Because of all the shortages and the riots, Mom and Dad moved us to the little cabin not far from where Mammoth Lakes used to be."

He's listening. Keep talking.

"Quiet. It is enough. In fact, 'tis probably too much."

Tantalus's cultured voice stopped her cold. She moved her gaze from Jon and saw the mage—or whatever he was—standing in the open doorway. Jon hadn't closed the door. It wouldn't have mattered if he had. She doubted any sort of lock could keep Tantalus out of the rooms in his own keep.

"Why?" She narrowed her eyes at her captor. "He's my

flesh and blood. I love him. Whatever you've done to pervert him can be undone. I know it can."

"You don't understand." The tone was silk, but steel sat just beneath its surface. "I expect you to become like him. Not the other way round."

I'll just bet you do.

"She'll behave," Jon said, meeting Tantalus's dark stare. "I was just, ah, indulging her. When I came in here, she was trying to jump out the window."

"Really." Tantalus's ancient, humorless gaze bored into her. "Why?"

She squared her shoulders. "Because I'd rather be dead than let you touch me again."

Something savage flashed from his eyes. It jabbed her, trying to make her back down, but she held her ground.

"I really do have things under control." Jon smiled weakly at Tantalus. "If you could just let us have a bit more time alone, I'm certain I can bring her around."

Tantalus looked from one to the other through speculative eyes. Amanda was grateful when his gaze left her and augured into Jon. After a long hesitation, Tantalus swept his long hair back over his shoulders and inclined his head. "Be sure you call me *before* things get out of hand again. I don't want my latest acquisition damaged before I get my investment back."

So I'm an acquisition. Yeah, right. Bite me.

Concealing her rage, Amanda watched Tantalus turn and walk out of the room. Gracefully swaying robes displayed his broad shoulders to advantage. For a moment, she wondered how she could possibly be angry with such a beautiful man. Then she recognized he wove a spell. Lacking weapons to fight against it, she tried to ignore his magic, but it was impossible. Hoping movement would break the hold the god had on her, Amanda strode to the door, shut it, and turned the key.

Jon's soft laughter made her spin to look at him. "Really? You think a lock will keep him out?"

Amanda sidled next to her brother. "No, I locked it to make myself feel better. If you and I work together," she whispered, "maybe we can come up with something to defeat him."

"It's hopeless," he whispered back. "I tried lots of things after I ended up here. None of them worked. The only way he won't hurt you is if you do exactly what he wants. I could show you scars—I have lots of them."

Jon closed his arms around her. "If he's watching," he said into her ear, "this may fake him out. Or not. I've found it's best not to underestimate him." He pressed his body against hers and kissed her.

I can play along, but it may not fool Tantalus unless he believes everyone is as besotted with sex as the models in those wall carvings.

Twining her arms around Jon's neck, Amanda looked at him and said, "Come lay next to me. Like those games we played when we were kids."

Shock registered in his eyes, and then quick understanding shone from his face. "Sure, Sis. It's been a long time."

Snuggled under the covers, she murmured low, "Hopefully, even he won't be able to see through bedclothes. We can talk so long as he thinks we're, ah, well…"

"Uh-huh." He pulled her against him and told her in fits and starts what had happened since he'd been captured. "He never really wanted me," Jon whispered low. "Only my blood to see if you'd be a good mate for him. He wants an immortal child just like him. I convinced him I was worth more alive when I began tending the lab in the basement. Never go down there, Mandy. He creates terrible things. I think he used my blood to make some of them.

"The nights were the worst, though. While he forced me to pleasure him, he made me tell him about you over and over. Everything I could remember. When I couldn't think of anything else, he'd whip me…"

"MY TURN, YOU LITTLE LETCHLINGS." Tantalus's sweetly spoken words woke her. She'd fallen asleep in Jon's arms, secure in the knowledge he was still the brother she'd loved since she was born. "Or you could move over, and I could join in."

"Sure, Tantalus," Jon said sleepily. "The more the merrier, as you always say."

"Except we've rarely had such a delectable morsel to share."

Amanda looked up to see Tantalus's robe puddle about him on the polished wooden floorboards. She started to turn away, but his body was so striking, she couldn't tear her gaze from his well-muscled arms, flat stomach, and long, graceful legs. A fine sprinkling of dark hair circled copper-colored nipples. His cock rose, long, thick, and without shame from its mat of dark curls at the apex of his legs. Noticing her eyes on him, he curved a hand around himself and stroked his erection suggestively.

The hunger Ned had kindled during their stolen embraces ignited so brightly it startled her.

BITTER RETREAT

Ned sat with his back propped against a boulder. He, Breanna, and the three remaining wizards —spaced well apart from one another—poured what little energy they had left into the illusion keeping their camp invisible. Kühl had caught a few moments rest before sketching a portal and leaving. They needed help, and the only way to get it was to travel to one of the strongholds. No one knew how long he'd be gone. Time ran differently in each world, so it was possible it might be as little as a turn of the glass, or as long as a day or more.

A sudden jolt of magic made Ned jump to his feet, his hands extended. *Yeah, like I could summon so much as a castle rat, as beat as I am.* The air shimmered. Breanna materialized next to him, her hands in battle position too.

"What is it?" she raised an eyebrow, but not by much.

"Damned if I know. It has a wizardish feel."

"Not entirely," she snapped. "Don't drop your guard until we see what comes through, and Ned—"

"Yes?"

"If you don't recognize whoever—or whatever—it is, aim to kill."

"Agreed. We're too tired to do this twice."

The air turned bluish, then bronze. Finally, a wavery portal formed. An acrid taste filled Ned's mouth. Too much adrenaline. Part of him wanted to blast the wretched portal right out of the air and be done with it. If it were a wizard's spell, the wizard in question should have been out long since.

A white-faced, hard-jawed Lira stepped through, Dyerwood staff in hand. She pulled a very bedraggled Lori behind her. "A fine welcome," she barked at Ned and Breanna. "After all the trouble it took me to get here. Fuck! This place is *not* easy to find." She hooked a finger at Lori who'd collapsed into the dirt, her eyes rolling back in her head and lips turning blue. "Help her."

"She probably can't breathe. I had the same problem when I first got here. It took some experimentation before I figured out how to concentrate the oxygen molecules." Ned knelt next to Lori. He spoke urgently into her ear. In moments, her color shifted from mildly blue to rosy, and she opened her eyes.

"Jesus fucking Christ! I thought I was going to suffocate." She looked up at Lira. "Why didn't she have this problem?" Lori asked, still panting.

"Oh, she did," Ned assured her. "Likely, she solved it without even thinking about it. Wizards often travel to other worlds. The air is rarely like it is on Earth, so they've learned to compensate rather quickly."

"Where's Amanda?" Lori clutched Ned's arm. "We traveled all the way to the wizard home in Eastern Europe to talk with you, only to find you'd escaped."

"She's here. We're trying to figure out how to rescue her."

"What do you mean *figure out*?" Lori's voice was shrill, and she grabbed Ned's upper arm. "What are the roadblocks? Why are you just lying around?"

Ned uncurled her fingers from his arm. "We're doing all we can. It may not seem like much but—"

Lira poked Breanna in the chest with an index finger. "Where are the others? A company of several hundred wizards left well before we did to come to your aid."

"Stop it." Breanna shot an annoyed look at Lira before stepping out of range of her finger. "You can be incredibly rude, even for one of us." She hesitated, frowning. "'Tis good news indeed if reinforcements are on the way, but we haven't seen them. Our location is rendered invisible. 'Tis the only reason any of us are still alive. How is it you managed to come out within the circle of our spell?"

"We had this." Lori held up a glove. "Fortunately, Ned left some things in his cell. Lira said we should bring something to act as a homing device."

"Smart." Breanna clapped Lira on the back. "Too bad the others didn't think of it."

Ned rocked back on his heels and stood. "Do you want me to hunt them down?"

"It should be one of us," Breanna said. Draping an arm around Ned, she added, "Nothing against you. You've helped us beyond measure, but you know how the battle lords are."

I certainly do.

Memory of the last conversation he'd had with Landarik sent chills cascading down Ned's spine.

"I don't have the energy to do much more than sit until I figure out how to automate the oxygen concentration around me." Lori wheezed. She still sounded very short of breath.

"I'll go," Lira said. Turning to Ned, she added, "Help my daughter. She won't be able to protect herself from Infernals if she can't breathe."

"Rolf should still be with Karras," Lori reminded Lira. "Bring him back with you."

Nodding curtly, the wizard vanished.

Ned settled next to Lori. He'd barely begun to show her how to focus her magic so she'd have some left to address things beyond staying alive when Lira returned. "They're not here," she said, looking rattled. "I found many things outside this protective circle, but no wizards." She eyed Breanna. "Tantalus is here, is he not?"

The other wizard nodded.

"Have you seen him?" Lira persisted.

Another nod.

"Is he the one who has my granddaughter?"

Breanna turned away. "Aye, and he's as irresistible as he ever was," she said so softly Ned strained to hear.

"Goddess be damned," Lira swore. "That charm-slinging bastard nearly had me a few hundred years back. I didn't know who he was, or I would have run like hell. He wakened things in me no one has before or since. I hate to admit it, but I still dream about him occasionally."

A horrified expression spread over Lori's face. It mirrored the distress coursing through Ned. "Just who is this person who has my daughter?" she asked in a strangled voice.

"You've heard of the Sirens?" Ned asked.

"Christ! So this is like a male version, dealing out seduction and death?" Scrambling to her feet, Lori paced a few feet one way, then back again, hands clasped behind her back. Ned watched carefully, but her breathing appeared less labored.

He couldn't make himself answer Lori's question. If he did, it would make Amanda's abduction too real to bear. As it was, he chafed at their inactivity. The conversation highlighted why they had to get Amanda out of there—and damned fast. Before the dark god, masquerading as a Lothario, had his way with her.

Lira, Breanna, and the other three wizards stood in a circle, hands touching. Ned knew they were talking. The wizards' silent way of communicating worked far more privately than mind speech, so long as they stayed in physical contact. He hoped they were working to solve the problem of the missing company. Another few hundred wizards would make a huge difference. It might be enough to storm Tantalus's citadel, rescue Amanda, and decide if her brother was worth saving.

From what little he'd seen, he'd prefer to run Jon through with a sharp saber and be done with it, but it wasn't his decision.

He glanced at Lori. She looked so forlorn, he decided

against telling her both her children were half a league distant. Her anxiety about Amanda was almost palpable. No point in doubling her angst.

"How's the breathing?" He walked over to where she stood next to a dead tree.

"Better. Why is everything here dead?" She patted the tree's trunk. "Or is it just this little sector of this world?"

"No, it's everywhere. Nearly all the plants are withered. A variety of animals live here, though—all of them hostile so far." He thought about the bird he'd strangled and shivered despite the heat of the day.

"What's killing the plant life?"

"The Infernals spread poison wherever they settle. It chokes the will to live out of everything they can't corrupt."

Lori's expression grew even more uneasy, and the lines in her face deepened. It was obvious she hadn't much liked his answer. "What is this place? It has an odd feel to it. Really creepy, like the old Lon Chaney movies. While you're at it, where are we? Some other planet?"

"It's one of the Infernals' worlds. The main one I think, but I'm not sure. It's not so much another planet, as in solar systems, but another world. Think parallel universe rather than space travel. Some of the Infernals, like Tantalus, are rejects from the gods. Others are the result of experiments. Over millennia, followers of the Dark Arts created some true abominations. Though we've only fought one so far, I assume many others also reside here."

Ned paused to think what else Lori might want to know. "Tantalus was imprisoned on a world called Tartarus. The other gods considered him dangerous enough they tried to limit the damage he could do."

"I remember him from mythology." Lori's voice held a flat, dead sound. "He was the one who killed his own child and made a stew of him or something."

Good she already knows. I didn't want to be the one to tell her.

The wizards broke from their circle. "I'll leave again to hunt for the others," Lira announced. "Mayhap they too, are concealed."

"If she cannot find aught," Breanna chimed in, "she'll return and wait for Kühl with the rest of us. We won't leave this spot until he's back."

"Can't we do anything besides wait?" Lori's expression, the defeated set of her shoulders, and her blue-green eyes all reflected torment.

"Not without more of us," Lira replied. "If we throw our lives away in misplaced heroism, your daughter—my granddaughter—will have no chance at all."

KARRAS WAS LIVID—HIS fury fueled by a pervasive helplessness. This was the third world they'd visited. And yet another dead end. Someone—or something—had to be subverting their mission. Steeling himself for a distasteful project, Karras sorted through the ranks of wizards to determine if the sabotage had an internal source.

He found it hard to concentrate, though, with Rolf nattering away at him like an annoying insect. Rolf had been far better traveling this time. No doubt because one of the wizard healers dosed him with an herbal concoction before they left. A sentient Rolf was a chatty Rolf.

Immersed in his own problems, Karras grew increasingly exasperated that he'd brought the Earth Mage along. Taking a brief break from his mental scavenger hunt for wizard traitors, he tried to come up with a way to ship Rolf back to Earth.

"You're not listening to me." Rolf clapped a hand around the upper part of Karras's arm and stepped in front of him. Every time he moved, his armor clanked, setting Karras's nerves further on edge.

"Do not touch me," the wizard gritted out through clenched teeth. "How many times do I have to remind you?"

"If you'd pay attention when I tell you something, I wouldn't have to." Rolf's tone was mild, but his blue eyes glinted like ice chips.

Looks like he's not having a much better time than me.

Karras sucked in a frustrated breath, met Rolf's gaze, and snapped, "Fine. What?"

"It's Cybele. She says she'll help." Rolf quirked an eyebrow. "She said a whole lot of other things too. They don't bear repeating. Basically, she doesn't want my life jeopardized by wizard blundering, so she will guide us to where both my children are. Some fallen god named Tantalus has them."

Karras sucked in a startled breath. That wasn't good news at all, but he'd be damned if he'd lay his fears out in front of Rolf. The less the Earth Mage knew the better. He was hard enough to manage without a gritty description of the depth of the dark god's depravity. Besides, if Cybele wanted to enlighten her Earth Mage, she could.

"What?" Rolf stared at Karras through narrowed eyes.

Karras snorted to cover his discomfiture about Tantalus. "Nothing. It's great Cybele's offering to help, but a bit self-serving. She wants your children the same way she wants you."

"So what? At least we might get there before Jon and Amanda both die."

Karras offered Rolf points for accuracy and spread his hands wide, flexing tense fingers. "Tell the goddess we'd be grateful for her help."

"I heard your words." A silvery voice floated around them. If Karras looked obliquely through his third eye, he could just make out Cybele's form behind a numinous curtain.

Wizards standing nearby looked up, shock stamped on their faces. The ones nearest the goddess bowed low.

"Tantalus guards his world well." A fluty laugh, reminiscent of temple bells, filled the wooded glade where Karras stood with the others. "Unfortunately for him, all the energy he's spewed forth gave away his position. Stupid of him. Mayhap he's forgotten his fellow gods have been hunting him for millennia—ever since he charmed his way out of Tartarus. When we're done, there'll be nothing left of him or the world he's in the process of killing."

"You promised to wait until my family is safely gone from there," Rolf reminded her.

"I did," Cybele concurred. "Don't take too long, though.

If it appears we may lose our quarry, we won't hesitate, regardless of the collateral damage."

"Jon and Amanda could help you," Rolf pleaded. "They're part Earth Mage too."

"Their blood is diluted. Of course I want them, but bringing Tantalus to justice is more important. You waste time in senseless argument. The coordinates for the Ways are seven degrees north-northwest by thirty-two degrees east. Wait through three turns of the glass. Be precise, or you'll miss the Infernals' world—again."

Karras clapped his hands sharply. "You heard her," he cried. "Spread the directions down the lines. Everyone into portals. We shall regroup at our destination."

FLIPPING the glass for the third time, Karras watched it closely. He hadn't cared for Cybele's statement that she and the other gods would blow Tantalus's world to smithereens no matter who currently inhabited it. He believed her, though. The gods were egocentric. They saw other races as not just inferior, but inconsequential. Likely because they'd ruled all the worlds long before they had to share them with anyone else.

"Do you really think she'll wipe all of us out?" Rolf broke into Karras's musings.

"If it means the difference between the gods recapturing Tantalus or not, then yes, I do," Karras replied. "Help me watch the sand in this glass. We must slow at just the right time."

"Is where we're headed in some other solar system? I've been trying to figure out if it could be in ours, and decided it was impossible."

"'Tis another world, sharing many things with our own. You know how Cybele appeared earlier, behind the gossamer curtain?" When Rolf nodded, Karras went on. "'Tis similar with the different worlds. They coexist with our own on a different plane, but in the same universe."

"Like parallel worlds in science fiction."

Karras smiled. "Exactly. Don't tell anyone, but I've read some human authors. Their fiction isn't so fictional after all."

"The sand." Rolf pointed.

Karras looked at it closely. He needed precision, but wasn't certain just how soon before the grains ran out to start the deceleration sequence. When he could hold a picture in his mind of a destination, the problem took care of itself. He had no idea which world they'd find Tantalus on, so he didn't have imagery to project into the Ways. All they'd had when they left the stronghold was a sketchy idea, drawn from Hreth's scrying.

Karras remembered too late he should have brought something of Ned's along.

He started the incantation to slow their travel, eyed the sand, and aborted it. He tried to tell the Ways to hurtle them along faster to make up for his error, but gave it up for wasted effort. He'd just have to wait a touch longer.

Sweat beaded his brow despite the chill air in the Ways. His hands felt clammy. It would be a miracle if even a tenth of the wizards made it to their destination. A healthy jot of luck was the only thing standing between success and failure. He'd never liked to rely on providence. It was far too unpredictable.

"The sand's nearly run through." Rolf sounded panicked.

Sucking in a centering breath, Karras instructed the Ways they were at their destination. Before he could let himself think what might happen if they arrived in the middle of the vacuum cementing various worlds together, he drew a portal. "Get behind me," he hissed at Rolf. "Hold your breath until I tell you 'tis safe to do otherwise."

He caught a glimpse of the Earth Mage's face, pale, but determined. Praying Cybele hadn't sold them out, Karras peeled back a corner of his portal and peered out onto a landscape peppered with dying trees and house-sized boulders. He hadn't known just how rattled he was until he saw they were safe on yet another world. It almost didn't matter at this point if it was the right one or not.

"We're here," he said tightly. "Come out so I can seal the portal."

Rolf stepped through, his armor clattering. He clutched his throat and gasped, "There's not enough air here. I-I can't breathe."

Damn it! Nothing but trouble.

"There isn't as much oxygen," Karras infused a calm he was far from feeling into his voice, "but there's enough. Imagine the air thickening about you."

Rolf slowly turned blue. Karras was just about to step in so Cybele's charge didn't die. If that happened, they may as well all go home because the gods had slated this place— assuming it was the right one—for certain destruction.

"I-it's okay," Rolf stammered. "I mean, I'm okay. I'm

getting the hang of it. I can't stop concentrating, though. The air sort of slithers away if I'm not pulling it toward me all the time." He yanked his helmet and hauberk over his head and dropped them on the ground.

"What are you doing?"

"Too heavy," Rolf panted.

"Put them back on. Now. We don't know what we'll find here." Karras softened his tone. "You have to pay attention at the moment, but it'll get easier to breathe. In fact," he clapped Rolf on the back, making an effort to sound encouraging, "you'll be surprised how soon it becomes automatic." Karras retrieved the items and handed them to Rolf, who grimaced before donning them.

A portal opened off to one side, and then another. Wizards in battle regalia—mostly light armor with stun guns and short swords—poured out of dozens of portals, two and three at a time. Karras started to believe things might be all right after all, when a flock of grayish-white dinosaur-like birds with huge wingspans and long, sharp beaks dive-bombed them.

The welcoming committee, courtesy of Tantalus.

Karras snapped off a sarcastic salute at their unseen host and focused his magic. Balls of deadly energy flew from his hands and his staff. He screamed at Rolf, "Warn the others, so they aren't annihilated leaving their portals. Look sharp. It means the difference between life and death."

Peering upward, Karras saw so many predators they blotted out the light. A hundred times more than there'd been moments before darkened the sky, flying in groups of threes and fours.

Goddess's tits! Tantalus plans to kill us where we stand. If we waste all our energy here, we'll never even get close to Amanda or Jon.

Lira strode across the clearing from out of nowhere, pulling power as she came and directing it skyward. Her staff blazed blue-white. Karras wondered where she'd come from, and then understood she must have shown up with Lori on her own. Even such a minor alteration in his concentration nearly lost him an eye.

Lira sent a blast of energy that killed the bird threatening him. Greenish blood and feathers drifted down.

Karras smiled grimly. He chucked lethal bolts of energy at six new birds attacking from a different direction. Lira had always been a hell of a warrior, gutsy and intimidating. He was glad to have her by his side.

"So you finally got here," she snapped, breathing hard. "Do you know who has my granddaughter?" The stench of ozone filled the air. One of the birds fell to the ground, spraying everyone within range with its blood.

"Tantalus." Karras found it hard to kill, keep an eye on new arrivals, make sure Rolf didn't do anything stupid, and maintain enough oxygen to support everything. A bird screeched past. He ducked, but not soon enough. It raked his head with ugly, curved talons. Blood flowed down his face in a steady stream. Cursing, he wiped it away and diverted a trickle of magic to seal off the wound. He could clean it later.

"Got him," Lira shouted. Another bird crashed to the ground. She glanced upward. Karras happened to be looking right at her, or he wouldn't have seen fear flicker behind her eyes.

SEDUCTION GONE BAD

Almost falling out the other side of the bed in her haste to put some distance between herself and Tantalus, Amanda pulled her robe close about her. "I, ah, need the facilities. Are they near where I had my bath?"

Tantalus caught up with her easily during her headlong dash for the door. He slid an arm underneath her robe. Where he touched her, her skin crawled and turned to simmering liquid heat at the same time.

"Go prepare yourself," he said, shoving her toward the door. "Your brother will entertain me while we wait for you. Don't worry, little bird, before this day is done you'll want me more than you've ever wanted anything in your short life. You'll beg me to bed you." He laughed wickedly and moved his hand down the curve of her bottom, giving it a squeeze. "If you ask nicely, I might just grant your wish."

She took as much time as she thought she could get away with closeted in the windowless bathroom right across from the bedchamber. Unfortunately, *that* door was wide open, making it impossible for her to slip away down the broad, marble-inlaid hall. Desperation battled despair. She banged her fists against the bathroom wall, muffling the sound with a thick towel.

The disgusting truth was she wanted him. Any woman would. He was like the serpent in the Garden of Eden: irresistible and hopelessly seductive. He'd won Jon over. Her brother had told her about it toward the end of their discussion earlier. She knew he was ashamed. Yet he too, was mesmerized by Tantalus.

He's gotten everything he's ever wanted for thousands of years. How am I going to stand against him?

When no answers came, Amanda prayed to every god she could think of to make her strong enough that her body wouldn't betray her. Riddled with doubts, she pushed the door to the bathroom open so hard it clanged against the wall. Head high, she marched into the bedroom. Jon and Tantalus were locked in a shockingly intimate embrace, grappling with one another's cocks while they kissed.

This is my chance.

Wheeling as silently as she could on her bare feet, she pelted down the hall. Before she even made the stairs, she ran into an invisible barrier so hard it knocked her backward onto her ass. Yelping with pain, she grabbed her nose. It sounded like a gunshot went off in her brain when she hit the wall she couldn't see. Pain arced through her face. She tasted blood, choked on it as it ran down her throat, and lurched upright.

"Not quite the blood I hoped we'd spill, but the day is

young." Chuckling softly, Tantalus took her arm and led her back down the hall, stopping just shy of the bedroom door. "You misjudge me, my dear. Did you truly think I'd leave you an escape route?"

When she didn't answer, he shook her hard enough to rattle her teeth. It sent shock waves through her face, and she stifled a cry.

"I don't know what I thought," she answered dully.

"Would you like me to fix that pretty face of yours?"

She hesitated, but not long enough for him to shake her again. "Sure. Mostly I'd like it to stop hurting."

"Easy enough," he purred. "Turn toward me."

When she did, she saw he was still naked. She swallowed hard, fighting against the hot tide the sight of his body roused in her. It was like she was two people. The Amanda she knew, and the one he was able to manipulate as easily as a card shark pulled aces out of his sleeve.

He laid one hand on either side of her head, thumbs crossed over the bridge of her nose and began to sing. Her resolve crumbled, laid waste by his clear, pure tenor. After a few moments, the pain in her face receded. Blood stopped dripping down her chin and throat.

"There." He cocked his head to one side, assessing his work. "I don't think there should even be much in the way of bruising." His hands still cradled her head. It took too much energy to ignore their soothing warmth. To her horror, Amanda found herself relaxing into those hands.

"Better," he cooed. Moving his hands downward, he caressed her neck before touching her shoulders and drawing his hands down her arms. When he got to her hands, he grasped them and gave a little tug. "Shall we?"

Unable to tear her gaze from his body, she nodded, not trusting herself to speak. She feared she'd tell him how unutterably beautiful he was and how hungry she was for him. Disgusted with herself, she tried to hold a picture of Ned front and center, but she could barely remember exactly what he looked like.

Tantalus stopped, skewering her with his gaze. "I will be the only man in your mind. Never forget that." With barely a pause, he went on. "Lucky for you that relationship was never consummated. If it had been, I'd have had no use for you alive. Your blood might still have been useful, though."

He smiled as if talking about killing her was the most prosaic of conversational topics and ushered her toward the bed.

Trapped in a silken web, stuck in its sticky strands, Amanda let Tantalus lead her forward.

"Hey, Sis." Jon smiled at her from where he sat cross-legged on top of the bed. "I was getting worried about the two of you."

She couldn't bear to look at him for very long because he reminded her of her old life. Of Mother and Father and Ned. Of everything lost to her. She mumbled something indistinct as she tried to control her emotions. Heat from Tantalus's body pressing against her side was like an insidious mantra. It battered against what little resolve she had left.

"You had your time with her." Tantalus laid a hand on Jon's shoulder. "Why don't you leave us alone for a bit?"

"Are you sure?" Jon trained guileless blue eyes on Tantalus.

"Quite sure. Don't be greedy, now." Tantalus's dark gaze bored into Jon. "Reactivate the barrier once you're through it."

"Of course." Jon inclined his head.

Amanda heard her brother leave, footsteps padding away down the hall. She'd never felt quite so alone. Or so conflicted. Her body screamed for Tantalus. Her mind recoiled in revulsion.

She felt him come round behind her. Hands pulled at her robe where it draped over her shoulders. "Let me look at you." The hands pulled harder. She clutched the fabric close, wishing the floor would open and swallow her. Anything to get away from where she was.

"Have it your way—for now. I always get what I want eventually." He sent a string of kisses up her neck. "I enjoy a challenge. Now, come lie on the bed."

"I-I'd just as soon not—" she began.

His hand snaked out. He slapped her so hard her head snapped back on her neck. Stars danced in front of her eyes.

"The bed."

Horrified by how little pain it took to make her fold, Amanda wrapped her robe as close to her body as she could and crept under the bedclothes. She made herself small, so close to one side of the bed it was a struggle not to fall off the edge.

Pulling the covers away, he said, "We won't need these. It's warm enough in here, and we shall make our own heat. Ah, sweetling, you're so young and so lovely."

He started with her toes. He kneaded her feet with his hands, drawing his nails softly down her soles from time to time. His skin was electric with promise where it connected with hers. When he moved to her ankles and calves, Amanda felt herself weaken. What he was doing felt so good, she moaned softly.

"Yes," he said, his breath warm and provocative against her inner thighs. "It's a good beginning. After all, you could scarcely have a better teacher in these arts than myself."

What a conceited ass.

"Guess I'm luckier than I thought." She tried to smile and catch his gaze. Maybe if she played to his elevated opinion of himself, she could buy enough time to quench the flames burning their way through her.

She soon found herself reaching for him, though. Waiting impatiently for where he would touch her next. Or even better, kiss her. He teased her, trying to get her to ask him for more. The words were there, just on the tip of her tongue. Another spate of kisses like the last bunch, and she'd be lost.

"More like it." He tipped her chin up with a finger. "Open your eyes. See me for what I truly am."

Warmth gleamed from his dark eyes—and reassurance. He cared about her, loved her, worshipped her. She'd never want for anything. He would see to it. She wondered if she were the hundredth lover he'd had, or the thousandth. A distant part of her brain shouted a warning that he was beguiling her with some sort of magical spell.

Then she just didn't care. He sensed the shift in her, because he moved close and covered her mouth with his. He tasted wonderful, spicy and exotic. His kisses stoked the flames turning her insides to molten heat, and she wrapped her arms around him.

When she came back to herself, the light in the room slanted differently. Time had passed. Maybe hours. Shame licked at her. She wanted to run away, to cry for her blatant fall from grace, but he was watching her like a very satisfied cat. She tried to shut off her thoughts, to hold onto some shred of pride.

It was hopeless.

"Most maidens feel as you do once they are maidens no longer." His deep voice rumbled against the silence of the room. "The child will be a comfort to you."

"Child?" She clutched wildly at her belly. "What child?"

He laughed. "Why the one we just made."

"D-doesn't it take more than once?"

"It was more than once. Where were you?" His laughter deepened her humiliation. She wanted to hide.

"You didn't answer my question." The words flew out of her mouth before she could stop them. Cowering away, she shut her eyes, expecting another slap. It never came.

"Surely you're not afraid of me." The voice was silky smooth, the tone suggestive of injured innocence. "The answer to your question is it often takes more than once for mortals, but I'm a god. I decide the fate of my seed."

She shook her head. Even if she found a way out of this hellhole, she could never face her parents again—or Ned.

Tears threatened. She felt them behind her lids, hot and bitter. It required enormous effort to keep them contained.

"Come, little bird. Back to my arms. We're far from done with one another." He opened his arms, but then a frown creased his perfect forehead. "It cannot be." He bared his teeth in a snarl. "No one has found me for millennia."

He sprang from the bed, lithe as a panther. Scooping up his robe, he secured it around himself. "You will remain here. If you need aught, tug the bell pull there." He pointed at a length of green velvet fabric she hadn't noticed before, hanging from a corner of the room. "One of the servants will attend you if there are any left. I may well need all of them to fight. You'll be allowed this room and everything off the hall between here and the barrier."

"What's happened? Where are you going?"

His warm demeanor fell away. His other face, the one with cruel edges took its place. "You do not question me. Not now. Not ever."

"Sorry." She looked down. He'd used her, played her like a favorite instrument, but now the show was over. She felt unbelievably young—and stupid. Even if she got lucky, and whatever threat was out there managed to annihilate him, she was still stuck with his child. Or was she?

Maybe Mother could fix it somehow. If I ever see her again.

"You'll learn. Let us hope it happens quickly." He stalked from the room.

Amanda paced the length of the bedchamber and back again. She winced. She was sore in places that had never hurt before. When she thought about how she'd asked—no, make that begged—Tantalus to do things to her, the tears she'd held back earlier broke through. Sinking to the floor, she dropped her head into her hands and wept for her lost innocence and the sham her life had become. Just because he could waken lust in her didn't mean a thing. She was an animal, programmed to reproduce like every other creature.

The knowledge steadied her, but it didn't excuse her weakness. Amanda shook her head, scattering her tears. She'd never stood a chance—not against a god who'd been mowing his way through women like a scythe through grass for thousands of years.

She crawled onto the bed, thinking she may as well try to rest since she didn't have any other options. Jon pushed the door open. Amanda lurched to her feet and raced to his side. Her heart pounded. Her mouth was dry. It frightened her how much she wanted someone to ride to their rescue and kill Tantalus. She'd never hated anyone enough before to want them dead.

"He didn't want me to keep you company, but I convinced him you'd be worried and scared all by yourself." Jon hesitated. "He was as rattled as I've ever seen him. I still had to do some tall talking to get him to agree to let me stay with you. I played the *important to keep the mother of your heir happy card*, and he finally bought it."

"Eeewww. I do not want to be the mother of that bastard's heir."

"Not much choice. It's a done deal. Even I can sense your pregnancy." He hugged her hard. "Shit, Mancy. I'm sorry. I'd have done damn near anything to save you from that." Shame marched across his features, and he looked away. "I still remember how I felt after the first time he had it off with me. He broke me, and we both knew it. I enjoyed what he did to me, and hated myself for it."

She knew exactly what he meant, but wasn't ready to talk about it. Not yet, and maybe not ever. Her humiliation was too fresh to pick the scabs off it, so she changed the subject. "Do you know what's going on?"

"I think so." A genuine smile spread across his face. "Part of it anyway. It could be very good news for us."

Hope flared so bright it hurt. "Tell me everything. Is there anything we can do to get ourselves out of here?"

DEAD BIRDS LITTERED THE GROUND. Their blood slicked everything, making even small rocks treacherous. Karras had stumbled so many times his robe was streaked with green gore. Though he tried to conserve his strength, exhaustion was nearly as insidious an enemy as the birds. If he closed his eyes for even a moment, he'd fall asleep. Clutching his staff, he leaned on it.

He glanced at Lira. A long, jagged cut ran down her face. It was easy to see because the rest of her skin was black with grit and dirt. Hair hung in her face. She shoved it out of the way just before killing two more birds.

All but about twenty of the three hundred wizards who'd left the stronghold had arrived. It was little shy of miraculous, given the hair-trigger calculations required to follow Cybele's directions.

He thought about the goddess and winced, expecting an explosion, which would annihilate them all. That it hadn't come yet meant Tantalus must still be somewhere on this world, and the other gods weren't expecting him to flee.

Makes sense, Tantalus always was an arrogant bastard.

A slight break in the steady stream of birds opened the possibility of a staged withdrawal. They needed to regroup and connect with the few wizards already here. He wanted to move Rolf somewhere safe. The Earth Mage stubbornly resisted Karras's orders to sequester himself in a cave between two boulders. Karras had checked it out thoroughly and deemed it safe. Yet, almost every time he scanned the wizard troops, Rolf trotted among them offering advice and support, his armor flashing in the sun as he strode back and forth. Frustration simmered, but Karras pushed it aside. He didn't have the energy to waste. Rolf meant well, but his disregard for his own safety was one more thing to worry about.

Gathering the battle lords, Karras floated his idea in between drawing on increasingly slim reserves to keep killing the flying death machines. Goddess's teats. Where were they all coming from? What was even more disturbing was they couldn't be the only type of Infernal here.

"We are agreed," Raen, a battle lord with dark braids and ice blue eyes, nodded decisively. "Get Lira. She knows where Breanna and Kühl are."

Karras was almost to her side when four of the birds converged on her. He pulled power and one of them fell. The falling body alerted Lira, who looked dazed. With a blood-curdling cry, she shot another. Karras aimed for the third. He thought he hit it, but it kept flying. Lira brought down the fourth, but the one he'd missed came straight at her. It was too late to take it out with magic. He didn't have time to gin up enough power to kill a sand flea, much less a bird that weighed two stone. By the time he got to Lira, she was grappling with the bird in hand-to-hand combat. Its beak was buried in her neck. Blood spurted, coating everything. Her staff thumped helplessly by her side, trying to get to the bird.

Karras wondered why she hadn't used it.

Fury gave him just enough of a boost to wrap his hands around the Infernal's neck. He strangled it, pressing until vertebrae broke for good measure. Tossing the carcass aside, he knelt next to Lira and placed a hand over the wound in her neck. If he couldn't staunch the blood—and damned quickly—she'd die.

He called Raen, risking mind speech to ask for protection from the Infernals, while he did what he could to patch Lira together. She lay unconscious. Did it mean she had other injuries he wasn't aware of? He worked feverishly. Karras did *not* want to have to tell Hreth he'd failed to save his daughter's life. Lira was his only child.

Karras had never been much of a healer. His skills lay on the battlefield and in the classroom. From a rusty part of his brain, he visualized what was damaged in Lira's neck. The bird had punctured either the carotid artery or the jugular vein. Magic flowed weakly from his weary hands. He urged the vessels to knit together enough to keep blood in her body.

As he worked, her eyes fluttered open. "You?" A ghost of a smile crossed her face. "I need a healer."

"Agreed, but you have me. Lira, are you hurt anywhere else?"

She nodded. "My stomach. One of those damned vultures drove its beak into me hours ago. Probably infected."

She kept fighting with a gut wound...

Awed by her courage, he bent and kissed her brow. "You should have said something."

Lira launched into a halting explanation. She snaked out a hand and curled it around her staff. Her color improved almost immediately. "Dropped it when that goddess-blasted bird tangled its talons in my hair. Good to have it back."

"Hush. Let me work. Unlike one of our healers, I must concentrate on what I'm doing, but I think I'm nearly done." Borrowing materials from his own body, he finished closing the hole in her neck, after making certain the vessel beneath would hold. "We need to find Kühl and Breanna. You must tell me where they are. Once we get there, I'll find you a real healer."

"Keep your hands on me. I'll show you. T-too weak to talk much."

"Understood." He surveyed his work, satisfied his patch job would hold. "There. I'm done. Raen, come close. Lira will show us where Breanna and Kühl are."

The battle lord hovered nearby. He and several other wizards had formed a circle around Karras, Lira, and the impromptu field hospital. The birds were slowing, but with unerring instinct, the ones still in the sky targeted the wounded wizard and Karras as he battled to save her life.

Raen joined his hand to Karras's. Glancing up, Karras asked, "Did you get Lira's image?"

"Yes. I'll send it down the line."

"Thanks for standing guard over us."

"You would have done the same for me."

Karras knew it was true. He placed his arms around Lira and pulled her to him. She'd lapsed into unconsciousness again. He chanted, using what felt like the last of his power to move them to safer ground.

NO GOOD DEED

Ned faced off against a very annoyed Kühl. The stern-faced battle lord had returned with orders to return to the stronghold.

"The Council sent troops. We must wait for them."

Kühl shook his head. "No. We will wait for Lira to return since 'tisn't right to strand one of our own in this Infernal-infested world. Then we shall depart."

"What about the company? They're coming. I know they are." Desperation raced along Ned's nerve endings. He was *not* leaving Amanda here. Even if it meant he had to figure out a way to rescue her all by himself.

Don't be stupid. If better than half a dozen wizards couldn't manage it, what hope is there for me?

Kühl pounded a fist into his open palm. "Do you not think I argued similarly? The Council believes we have expended enough of our strength on this quest. After all, 'tis only a single human life—or mayhap two at the outside—

balanced against three hundred wizard warriors. Dagget fears the Dareli got wind of our plans and sabotaged the company. He's worried they're lost somewhere in the Ways."

Lori walked over to where they were standing. "Surely you're not thinking of leaving here without my daughter?"

"Who are you?" Kühl glared at her, narrowing his eyes. "Never mind. A wizard half-breed." He shifted his dark gaze to Ned. "Where'd she come from?"

"I came with Lira." Ned knew Lori well enough to see anger just below the surface. "My mother."

"Well, that explains the half-breed part." Kühl screwed his face into a disgusted grimace. "Go away. I need to finish my conversation with the human mage."

"You can't talk to me like that," Lori sputtered, moving a step closer to Kühl.

"I just did. Now go." He made shooing motions with both hands. "Before I hurt you."

"Oh, and your threats of abuse are supposed to intimidate me?" Spots of color bloomed high on her cheeks, and Lori balled her hands into fists. "Well, let me tell you something, buddy—"

Ned readied himself to play peacemaker. He opened his mouth to say something conciliatory when magic crackled about them. Instantly on alert, he blew out a tense breath once he recognized wizardry behind the shimmers in the stale air.

Kühl, his attention drawn away from Lori, apparently came to the same conclusion. As battle-stained wizards stepped out of hastily drawn portals, a smile lit his gaunt features. "Thank the goddess," he muttered. "They found their way here." He shot Lori a pointed glance. "Stay out of the way if you don't want to be mistaken for the enemy and killed by accident." Sauntering off, he greeted the newly arriving wizards with a word or a clap on the back.

Ned took Lori's arm and spoke low. "This means Rolf is here somewhere. If I see him, I'll tell him to find you over by where you were sitting." He pointed to the spot on the ground where her backpack lay.

She nodded. "Thank you. Christ on a crutch, are all wizards so rude? He was worse than Liefes—or Landarik."

You have no idea...

Ned sucked in a breath. "They don't like humans very much. They think even less of those like you." Lori wanted to talk. He saw it in her eyes, but he shook his head. "I need to find Karras—if he's here. I'll check on you in a bit."

Thank the goddess indeed, Ned thought, sprinting after Kühl. This meant they'd have a prayer of rescuing Amanda. Maybe even her brother—if he weren't irretrievably damaged by evil. Heart in his throat, he counted to make sure the company was intact.

"Karras!" Ned caught sight of the familiar form as he stepped out of a portal cradling a wounded wizard in his arms. Coming closer, he saw it was Lira.

"I need a healer." Karras's face was drawn. His robes were torn and smeared with grime and ichor. His dark eyes shone true, though, and Ned was ever-so-glad to see him. He'd have to fess up about Landarik and how he escaped, but figured it could wait.

"Lori's right over there. You can lay Lira next to her. She's a doctor. Maybe she can do something while we're trying to scare up one of our own."

"Walk with me, lad."

Ned held out his arms. "I can carry her."

Once the burden had shifted, Karras straightened. "Thanks. I'm as dead on my feet as I've ever been. My magic needs time to recover. Ned—"

He turned toward Karras, Lira warm and heavy against him.

His old mentor smiled. "Landarik told the truth—with a little prodding. The High Council executed him. You have nothing to fear upon your return."

"Really? They killed him?" Ned's heart soared. He would have hugged Karras but for Lira in his arms. "Let me lay her down." Ned covered the distance to Lori in a few steps. He felt like he was flying. For once justice had truly been served. A wizard who'd tried to harm him had actually paid for his crimes.

At the hands of other wizards.

He was so elated, he could scarcely believe what Karras told him. The best part was he could use the wizard Ways to travel; they wouldn't be warded against his energy. A broad grin split his face.

I can leave here after all and take Amanda with me.

"What's this?" Lori looked up at him and the bundle in his arms.

"You're a doctor, right?" Ned laid Lira down, taking care not to jostle her. Karras walked up beside them.

"It's Mother!" Lori exclaimed and made a grab for Lira's wrist. "Pulse is steady," she muttered and moved her practiced hands up and down Lira's body, assessing damage.

"The worst problem was a puncture wound in her neck," Karras explained. "I may have fixed it. Not sure. She says there's another in her stomach."

Lori didn't answer. She was clearly in her element, doing something she understood. Ned wondered if they'd need a wizard healer after all, but decided to send one over anyway. Lori probably depended on things they couldn't supply: western medicines, antiseptics, and bandage materials. If the healer was in a generous mood, they might teach Lori how to focus her magic to take the place of the accoutrements of modern medicine.

"Can you tell me what happened?" Ned grasped Karras's arm. "With Landarik, I mean."

"Certainly, lad. Not just now, though. I fear our time in this world will be short. I must find Kühl and the other battle lords to craft a strategy."

Rolf strode past to the accompaniment of rattling metal. Karras lunged for him. "Lori is over there." He gestured. "Stay near her until this is over."

Watching the one-sided exchange, Ned surmised the Earth Mage hadn't been particularly compliant. "I'm sure he'll stay by his wife's side," Ned murmured next to Karras's ear. "Gave you some troubles, did he?"

The wizard shrugged. "It doesn't matter. Come with me, lad. You may well have a role to play in what comes next."

"As soon as I find a healer."

Karras sighed. He rubbed his forehead with begrimed fingers. "Good thing you remembered. Hope I have a few minutes to revive myself afore we're in the thick of things again."

NED WAS PLENTY SCARED. Karras's prediction he might play a role turned out to be way too true for his taste. The consensus had been Ned would have a far better chance of sneaking into the keep than any of the wizards, because his magic had a different feel to it. Tantalus was gearing up for a wizard invasion, since wizards showed up to battle his birds. He might not be as alert to someone like Ned, particularly if Ned cloaked himself.

He watched as the wizards assembled in neat battle lines ringing the castle and its tower. Only ten of the original company were missing once everyone straggled in, so they had close to three hundred warriors.

It just might be enough.

Once the wizards were well engaged in battle, Ned was supposed to find a way into the castle. His communications device had been altered to operate despite the odd energy in this world. Kühl and the other battle lords made it clear mind speech was off the table. Once Ned either had Amanda safely away, or was hopelessly snarled in something he couldn't get out of, he was to call Karras with the communicator and the wizards would act accordingly.

Sounds simple enough.

He attempted to calm himself. If he couldn't get better control of his fear, Ned risked capture. Fright had a certain stink about it that magic couldn't mask. Instructing himself to breathe, he walked in tight circles to loosen his muscles.

The wizards had tolerated him in warrior classes. Probably because they saw war as an easy way to rid themselves of him. Death on the battlefield was honorable. He rolled his eyes. It didn't matter why they'd trained him. Or that their motives were far from altruistic. He was grateful for all those classroom hours now and culled centering exercises out of his brain's archives. Latching onto them, he began a series of slow, cadenced movements that would bring enough inner peace to allow him to rescue his love.

Harsh cawing shattered his concentration. The birds Karras described approached in hordes out of a sky that had been empty moments before. Thousands of wings made an ominous droning sound so loud it hurt his ears. Listening to Karras, Ned suspected they were the same as the one he'd battled at the pool. Seeing them, he knew he was correct, and damned lucky there'd been only one in the water that night since they appeared to travel in flocks.

Or maybe that was Tantalus's doing.

The ground around the castle rippled. A wrenching, tearing sound vied with wing beats for which was loudest. Ned could have sworn he heard the dirt crying out in horror at being used for such a purpose. Sudden holes in the castle yard disgorged ape-men like those who'd quashed their first attempt to rescue Amanda. They looked even more ominous than before, with their matted fur, upright stance, and menacing eyes. Once on their feet, they formed a line and charged the wizards. From what Ned could see, they didn't possess any magic. Instead, they used cudgels and maces to slam against any wizard they got close enough to touch. Magic was a clear advantage—even on this uncooperative world—since the wizards could kill from many paces away.

Shouts, shrieks, and screams escalated. Fire from the wizards' castings filled the air with smoke and soot. It didn't take long for the characteristic smell of war to permeate things. Shit from split entrails, blood, and vomit mixed into a disgusting mélange, one Ned had smelled so many times he ignored it.

He was just gauging his chances of slipping past the carnage when another group of ape-men emerged from the ground, followed by yet one more. Each group formed a new row, providing backup for the ones ahead of them.

Cannon fodder. Tantalus doesn't give a good bloody fuck how many die defending him.

Ned scanned the castle walls, looking for the god who'd taken Amanda. It was almost like his thoughts drew the dark god because a door opened midway up the tower. Ned's eyes widened. The most alluring man he'd ever seen stepped onto a balcony and looked about. Seeing him in dreams and visions hadn't done him justice. A self-satisfied smile formed on his perfect features.

Tantalus raised a hand skyward. Ned saw his mouth move, but couldn't hear the command over the din of battle. Following the line of the god's upraised hand, Ned gasped. His jaw dropped. Monsters with the heads of women on birds' bodies jockeyed for airspace with the dinosaur-like birds. Wicked-looking red talons curved from unnaturally long front legs.

Pulling shadows more firmly about him, Ned's heart stuttered in his chest. Harpies. Soul stealers. The wizards had wasted much conversation speculating which of the other Infernals Tantalus had at his beck and call. Harpies hadn't even entered the discussion.

The clash of battle rang about him. Blood smell, hot and coppery, overpowered the reek of shit for once. Still watching Tantalus—mostly because it was hard to tear his gaze away—Ned saw him raise the other hand. At first he thought the god was calling more Harpies, and then the things flying from the east took form. Terror threatened to annihilate him. Sour-smelling sweat dripped down his sides. His throat thickened, making it hard to swallow.

Griffons, with their eagle heads and lion bodies, drifted lazily down on thickly feathered wings. Fire spewed when they opened their mouths. The already fetid air grew heavy with the odors of sulfur and dead things. Ned took shallow breaths, panting through his mouth so he wouldn't smell the charnel stench of rotting flesh. One glance at the wizard lines told him they were taking heavy casualties.

Ned gathered himself. He had to move now, or the wizards would all die, along with his only chance of saving Amanda. He considered the gaping holes in the ground. Since he couldn't believe the ape-men lived in the ground, he figured the fissures led to tunnels opening somewhere underneath the castle. An underground route into the fortress held a certain appeal, especially since the portcullis gate was directly below where Tantalus stood commanding his troops.

Nothing had come out of the holes since the Harpies and

Griffons appeared. Ned hoped it meant there weren't any more ape-men waiting below.

Go now. Right now. Everyone will die while I think this to death—including me.

He moved toward the rear of the castle, out of sight of Tantalus. Even though he thought the other Infernals probably couldn't see through the magic that kept him hidden, he wasn't confident his disguise would hold up to scrutiny by a god.

He picked the closest hole, waited until he had a clear shot at it, and ran, catapulting into the opening. He sent his mage senses spinning outward just long enough to determine the tunnel was empty. Cutting off the flow immediately to reduce the risk of discovery, Ned crept forward. He placed a hand against one wall to make sure he was moving toward the castle. Numerous side tunnels confused him, yet he couldn't risk his mage light. He was effectively blind, but if he moved in a straight line, he had to come to the right place—he hoped.

He'd judged himself about a hundred twenty paces from the fortress when he entered the tunnel. Counting his steps carefully, he was pleased when he came to thick stones that had to be the foundational structure for the castle. Thanking the goddess for his luck so far, he passed under a low archway he felt with his hands, but couldn't see. Daylight flickered ahead. Disconcerted by the sudden illumination, he flattened himself against a wall.

Ned sent out another flash of magic. It reassured him he was still alone. Emboldened, he hurried forward. The passageway widened into a circular underground chamber.

Light filtered in through cutouts high on the walls. Understanding slammed into him, and Ned's heart plummeted into his boots. He was under the fortress all right, in some sort of pen. Probably living quarters for the ape-men. It stank from urine and piles of excrement littering the dirt floor. The walls loomed tall and straight. From what he could see, even if he could levitate upward twenty feet it wouldn't help. Deep gouges in the walls spoke eloquently of escape attempts on the part of the creatures.

A sudden burst of compassion for the beasts, which were likely the result of genetic exploitation, filled him. Ned recognized it for the indulgence it was. The ape-men might not like Tantalus, but they didn't care for him, either. Or the wizards they were busy destroying. Soulless things, they'd probably been created to kill mindlessly. To wipe out anything standing in front of them.

Amanda.

He had to get to her. Did he dare chance using his magic just enough to move himself to a higher floor in the keep?

Ned wasted several moments considering options. He could retrace his steps and try to find another way inside. Or he could take advantage of already being right beneath the castle. Now that he wasn't surrounded by tons of earth, sounds from the battle reached him through the same cutouts admitting light. The high-pitched squeals had to be Harpies. He'd heard about their battle cry. The author of the book he'd read described it as so blood-curdling, you'd never sleep easy again.

It decided him. He'd take his chances inside the castle. If he went back out, a Harpy or Griffon might pick him off before he found another way in. He had to drop the invisibility illusion to free up enough magic to travel. No way around exposing himself for a brief time. He decided to aim for the first floor. He didn't want to end up on the same level as Tantalus.

Please, he prayed to anyone who might be listening, *let his attention be elsewhere.*

Ned visualized where he hoped the main floor of the castle was. He considered the kitchens, but they usually had cooks and such. If possible, he wanted to avoid anyone at all seeing him. When traveling such a short distance, he didn't need to use the Ways or a portal system, which was a boon. The less magic expended, the less his chance of discovery. Mouth dry as ashes, he forced himself to move before his slender courage failed entirely.

Because he pulled his power back the second he no longer needed it, Ned landed in an ignominious heap in the center of a round room. Stifling a grunt, he leapt to his feet and made a dash for long curtains hanging on either side of several big windows. Safely behind a length of very dusty, red velvet drapery material, he resurrected the illusion to make his energy invisible to casual eyes.

Expecting to be plucked off at any moment, his heart settled back into an almost normal beat when several minutes ticked by, and Tantalus didn't storm down the stairs. Ned crept from behind the curtain. Two doors—in addition to the one leading outside—opened off what had to be the entry hall. He tried both. One was locked. The other turned. As silently as possible, Ned cracked it and peered in. The kitchens. They were empty. He eased the door shut and eyed a circular staircase. If he got very lucky, he could make it to the next floor fast enough he wouldn't meet Tantalus coming down.

Steps boomed on the risers. Ned scuttled behind his curtain. His heart hammered against his ribs. He tried to not even breathe. Any sound, even the slightest respiration, might give him away. A door clanged open. Ned assumed it had to be the kitchen because cultured tones demanded food for his special ones. "The poor hearties are fighting as if their very souls depend on it. We must have nourishment for them."

Who the hell is he talking to? There's no one in there.

A diabolical laugh scattered ice shards through the room. A few lodged in Ned's soul. He wondered if he'd ever be able to get warm again. He stuffed a hand in his mouth to still teeth wanting to chatter and understood the true meaning of fear. What the wizards had dished out over the years paled as a mere annoyance.

The kitchen door banged shut, followed by a pause so long Ned was certain Tantalus knew he was there. He couldn't even ready himself to fight because drawing any magic would create shifts in the air currents. A voice deep in his mind urged him to forgo this foolishness. To show himself and have done with things. The compulsion was so strong, Ned almost gave in to it until he understood the voice in his head wasn't his. He bit his lip so hard it hurt.

Tantalus was on a fishing expedition, hunting for any wizard brave enough to have stormed his castle. If the god knew where he was, Ned was sure he would have dragged him out by his hair, gutted him, and moved on.

At last, the great front door of the keep creaked open. It had to be the main door because he heard metal bolts being drawn back. Footsteps marched outside. The door slammed shut.

Ned didn't wait. With panic riding on his back like a crazed monkey, he flew from behind the curtain and up the stairs. A hasty search of the second floor revealed several empty rooms arranged off a central hall. Unlike the first floor, the large circular entry way had been traded for living space. Mounting the stairs again, Ned reached the third floor. Partway down the hall he ran headlong into something he couldn't see.

Careful not to touch it again, in case it was some sort of spelled trap, he reached a tendril of power outward and saw an invisible barrier held in place with magic. Amanda had to be on the other side. Otherwise why squander power to construct such a device. Maybe the god had inexhaustible resources, but Ned didn't think so.

Since he didn't want to disturb the obstacle, there was only one way around it. Dropping his shielding, he pulled magic to move to the other side, up and over the obstruction. Invisible again, and pleased he'd managed to circumnavigate the barrier without so much as a flutter in its filaments, Ned tried the nearest door. An old, toothless hag stared back at him, cowering. Of course she couldn't see him. For all she knew, her door opened all by itself. It didn't require magic to tell him she wasn't a threat. He pulled the door silently shut. The next one led to a tub room. He blinked when recognition slapped him hard. This was where he'd seen Amanda in his vision.

Almost running, he pulled open the door at the end of the hall. He dropped his protective illusion as soon as he saw Amanda sitting on the bed with her brother. Her eyes widened when she saw him, and then tears spilled over and streamed down her cheeks. He motioned her and Jon to silence and closed the door quietly.

Crossing the distance to her in three long steps, Ned crushed Amanda to him. Love rushed out of him so violently he thought bells should be pealing and flower petals fluttering down. For the briefest of moments she returned his embrace, her body rocking against his as she sobbed. He was shocked when she pulled away shaking her head. She wore the saddest expression. Like hope had died, leaving nothing in its stead.

What was wrong? What had the monstrous dark god done to his love? Baffled, Ned didn't have time to sort things out.

Jon rose and extended a hand. He mouthed thank you.

Ned didn't have time to sort that problem out either, so clasped Jon's hand briefly and then strode to the window. Thank the goddess it was big enough to accommodate an escape. He didn't want to risk retracing the route he'd used to get into the castle. Not with Tantalus on the prowl.

Casting his gaze toward Jon, Ned wondered about him. The one and only time he'd seen Amanda's brother, he'd been taking unseemly liberties with her. Without using magic, though, Ned couldn't test Jon's integrity.

A Harpy zinged past the window. Fortunately, she wasn't paying any attention to him. Why should she? Insofar as she knew, her enemy lived on the ground wearing wizard's robes or battle leathers. Throwing his body to the side, Ned moved away from the glass. He'd done pretty well so far. No point in taking chances.

He keyed his earpiece and called Karras. While he waited for the wizard to answer, Ned focused a thin stream of magic to shield the conversation from prying ears. The headsets helped to some extent, but they might not be enough to outwit Tantalus.

ESCAPE CARRIES A PRICE

*N*ed waited, but Karras didn't answer. He called three times before he switched to Kühl's frequency. The wizards had set up four fallback positions in case some of them were killed. He couldn't imagine life without Karras. Ned told himself his old mentor must be under attack and too busy to heed his call.

He didn't realize how tense he was until Kühl's harsh voice came through his earpiece. Glancing down, he noticed red blotches on both his hands from gripping them together so tightly.

"Can you get her out of there?" the wizard asked without preamble.

Ned was going to ask about Karras, but something in Kühl's tone discouraged anything beyond essential communication. "Not sure. The brother is here too."

"Has he been corrupted?"

"I don't know."

"Find out and call me back." The connection hummed. Kühl had disconnected.

Sick helplessness filled Ned. He wanted to scream at the wizard to wait. He had questions. Like was it safe to use magic? How was the battle going? Could they use the window for an escape route, or would he have to find something else?

Knowing he'd get nothing more from Kühl until the wizard received the answer he'd requested, Ned moved quickly. Drawing a bit more magic, he extended the conversation-muting spell to include the three of them, then gestured to Jon and Amanda to come close enough so they could whisper back and forth.

"What's wrong?" Amanda asked, tension twisting the beauty out of her face. "Jon and I have been peeking out the window. Can't any of those wizards get us out of here?"

"Probably, but there's a question I have to address first—about your brother."

She flinched at his honesty, but nodded understanding.

Ned shifted his attention to Jon. "I need to see to what extent Tantalus has corrupted you."

Gazing back through clear blue eyes so like Amanda's it was unsettling, Jon said, "Go ahead."

Ned worried about using even more magic. It acted like a lodestone. At some point, no matter what Tantalus was doing, he'd surely notice. "Can I touch you? It takes less magic than doing this from a distance."

"Do whatever you need to."

Laying a hand on either side of Jon's head, Ned projected himself into his mind. What he found was fascinating—and troubling. Clearly Tantalus had visited many times. His signature scored many of Jon's thoughts, yet he retained a certain innocence in spite of his time with the god.

Wishing he'd found a more definitive answer, Ned withdrew. He pulled his magic back and muted it. "Do you wish to return to your family?" In spite of his reluctance to use magic, Ned sent the truth spell to eddy between them.

The eagerness in Jon's eyes was so poignant, it had to be real. Even though he said nothing, truth vibrated between them. Dispersing his spell, Ned keyed the earpiece again.

"Well?"

"No, he hasn't been contaminated—at least not beyond salvage. There is evidence he's been tested, but he retains his own mind."

A long, tense breath came through the microphone. "Let me know when you're clear of the castle."

"Wait."

"What? We're sore pressed here." Indeed, the sounds of battle rang through. Screams rumbled on top of one another. It sounded like people—or things—were dying. Ned hoped it was Infernals.

"Can we use the window to leave?"

"Use your eyes, boy. Does it look like you could use a window? There are Harpies and Griffons all over the damned place. We haven't made a dent in the birds. Think we killed all the ape-things."

"Karras?"

"I don't know. No one's seen him for the past turn of the glass or so. We've lost at least fifty wizards. He may be one of them."

Ned started to ask if he could risk magic, but the connection died. He swallowed hard. No help from the wizards. He'd have to take his best shot. His heart constricted, and he hoped to hell his *best shot* would be good enough.

He looked at Jon and Amanda. "We're going to travel via a portal to leave here. It's the only way I can think of where we won't risk immediate discovery."

"The downside?" Jon's level gaze caught Ned somewhere in the solar plexus. Amanda's brother would settle for nothing less than absolute truth.

"The more magic I deploy, the bigger the chance Tantalus will notice I'm here. So far, I've been lucky. Also, he's looking for wizard magic. What I have feels different. Unless he was looking for it, he'd not necessarily notice it."

"It will take a big honking jolt of magic to move the three of us out of here," Jon muttered. "I'd help, but Tantalus would recognize my power immediately."

"I hadn't even considered you helping, but you about summed it up. Plus, it's not something I can do fast. I have to draw a portal, and then we have to get inside and leave. The whole process takes several minutes. There's no way to hurry it up."

While Ned and Jon talked, Amanda slithered to the wall with the window. Stooping, eyes at sill level, she peered out before crawling back to where they sat. She shook her head. "We'd never make it out the window unseen. Not unless we were invisible. Maybe not even then."

"I can make us invisible one at a time, but that would draw magic too, and take far longer than the portal." Ned hesitated. "I was incredibly fortunate getting in here. I don't think we *could* leave by the same route, even if we wanted to."

"Guess you've settled things," Jon said grimly. "Get the portal thing cooking. We haven't seen Tantalus since the fighting started. It would be very like the old bastard to show up to reassure us he's winning."

"I'm going to draw a door in the air. When I motion to you, jump through. No matter what's happening, don't hesitate. I'll come last, since the portal will close once I'm in it."

Ned worked as fast as he could. Jon's statement about Tantalus showing up was unnerving. Like all his magic in this perverted world, it took longer than he expected for the portal to materialize. He'd just motioned Amanda through when the door to the bedchamber flew open.

"Like hell you will," Tantalus cried, his handsome face distorted by fury. He extended his hands and power shot from them. The portal wavered, but didn't wink out.

"Go. I never expected to leave here alive." A white-faced Jon shoved Ned after Amanda. "Mandy, tell Mom and Dad I never stopped loving or missing them."

As soon as Ned moved inside, the gateway closed of its own accord. His last glimpse of Jon before it slammed shut was him screaming as Tantalus bent his fingers back, breaking them one by one.

The god laughed, apparently drunk on Jon's pain.

Nearly overcome with sorrow and guilt, Ned sealed the portal. He called up an image of the hidden place the wizards had gathered—where he hoped Rolf and Lori still were—and drew in a ragged breath. He blew it out, hoping to steady himself.

"I'm sorry," he said. "So sorry..." Jon flashed through his mind. Ned would live with an image of the man's agony for the rest of his life.

Misery flared from Amanda's eyes. She looked as if she were holding on by a thread. "Not your fault." Her voice held a flat, dead note. "It's amazing any of us got out of there."

"We're not out yet." Something tore at the magic holding them in the Ways. Ned poured energy into his casting until his hands cramped from channeling so much power.

In spite of Amanda's words, he felt he'd failed. He still had to face Rolf and Lori—and tell them he'd found both their children. The deceleration presaging arrival began. It came so fast, Ned worried Tantalus did something to the Ways to make it dump them right back in the bedroom they'd just left. He stepped in front of Amanda, getting ready to drape them in invisibility. "Stay behind me," he instructed and peeled open the door with an unsteady hand.

Were they still in the damned castle? Pushing past fear, he readied himself to fight. It didn't matter how much power he pulled now. He could use all the magic he wanted. Tantalus already knew about him. Ned forced himself to look out, ready for just about anything, including finding Jon's mangled body, broken and bloody.

"It's the wizard encampment." Breath streamed from between his teeth. Ned was so relieved he didn't have to go head-to-head with Tantalus, he almost couldn't stand it. At least one part of his mission was accomplished—sort of.

Stepping out onto a deserted stretch of dirt littered with

battle regalia and the odd hastily erected supply tent, Ned extended a hand to Amanda and said, "Your parents are here. At least they were when I left."

"I-I'm so ashamed of myself," she murmured, ignoring his hand and following him out of the portal. "I don't know if I can face them. It's hard enough facing you. I should be the one left there, not Jon."

Ned sealed his gateway immediately. No point in leaving a way for Tantalus to follow them. He ran after Amanda, who'd walked away, and placed his hands on her shoulders to make her stop and listen to him. "No matter what happened to you in there," he jerked his chin toward the castle, "it wasn't your fault."

"You wouldn't say that if you knew—" She pulled away from his touch.

Rolf loped up. "Mandy! Aw, Jesus Christ! You're safe!" His heart was in his face, which worked with emotion. He folded his daughter tightly into his arms and met Ned's gaze over the top of her head. "Thank you."

Ned couldn't meet Rolf's forthright blue gaze, so like his son's. "I failed you," he mumbled. "Jon was there. It was only because of your son's quick thinking and courage that Amanda and I escaped."

"It wasn't Ned's fault, Daddy." Amanda's voice was muffled against Rolf's shoulder. "He was really brave. Jon too. H-he said to tell you he loves you and Mom. That he never stopped missing you. You would have been proud of him."

Pain rippled across Rolf's bearded face, and he shut his eyes. When he opened them, tears glistened. "I'm sure I would have. Hell, I *am* proud—of all of you." His gaze sought Ned's. "Come on. Lori's tending Lira. She'll want to lay eyes on you and thank you." Keeping an arm around Amanda's shoulders, Rolf guided her back the way he'd come.

"Sir," Ned said to Rolf's retreating form.

"We can talk once we get to my wife."

"We'll have to talk later, sir. I'm going back to the battle. It's not going terribly well. They need every magic-wielder they can get."

Letting go of Amanda, Rolf turned to face Ned. "I understand. If I knew more about how to fight with magic, I'd be there right next to you. Karras was right. I'm nothing but an impediment. I even took off that blasted armor. Couldn't stand it a moment longer. If you think of anything I can do, any way I could be of help—"

"Is Lira well enough to return to the field?"

"No, but I'm coming with you anyway." Limping up to him, she laid a hand on Ned's arm. "I underestimated you, human mage. Badly, it appears." She leaned heavily on her staff.

Scuffling footsteps sounded. Lori and a wizard wearing healer's robes raced up to them. Lori's eyes widened at the sight of her daughter, and then brimmed with sudden tears. "Amanda! Oh my God. Amanda! I'm so glad to see you." She threaded her arms around her daughter while silent tears coursed down her cheeks.

Lori glared at Lira over Amanda's shoulder, and loosened their hug. "You should be lying down. You're not well enough—"

"Silence! This conversation is over." Lira's old, imperious

ways fell about her like a well-used shawl. "Not a word out of you, either." She addressed the healer before the wizard even opened her mouth. "My people are dying out there. I sense it. The least I can do is try to help. I'm well enough."

Ned longed to give Amanda one last hug, but she was ensconced in her mother's arms. Besides, she didn't want to hug him. She'd been clear enough about it in the castle. Maybe the heartbreakingly beautiful god, wicked though he was, had stolen her affections. Heart aching, Ned pushed his pain aside. It would only be a distraction on the battlefield. He locked gazes with Lira. "If you're sure," he said, "we need to go."

"I'm certain. We should walk so we know what we're getting into."

A dour smile played about his face. After his nerve-wracking escape from the castle, the last thing he wanted was another pass through the Ways. "A woman after my own heart. Shall we?" He extended an arm. Switching her staff to the other hand, Lira took it. She leaned on him, but not as much as he thought she might, considering the gravity of her injuries.

KARRAS OPENED HIS EYES. Disoriented, he couldn't comprehend why it was dark, but then he understood. He lay buried under both wizard and Infernal bodies. It took a bit, but he was able to reconstruct what happened.

He'd feinted to one side, barely escaping a Harpy's lethal claws. They stole your essence by hooking you. Once they had hold, they drew your soul out through your mouth. Karras shuddered. It had been an extremely close call. What saved him was one of the ape-men falling on top of him. The Harpy left him alone then, apparently going in search of more accessible prey.

Before he could crawl out from under the ape-man, something else joined the pile. A falling cudgel hit him in the head and knocked him out. Karras dunned himself for not wearing a helm like the younger class of warriors.

He tried to move but an ungodly amount of weight pinned him in place. Pain shot through one leg like bright fire, making his heart race. Karras sent a dribble of magic downward and assessed his injuries.

Smaller bone in my lower leg is broken. Other than that, I believe I'm fine. Thank the goddess.

Another effort to move convinced Karras he needed magic. He didn't have enough strength to muscle his way from under hundreds of pounds of flesh. Something jabbed his side. His staff. Karras smiled grimly. He'd need it if he could ever extricate himself from under the bodies.

Stewing in his own problems, Karras felt ashamed when Ned crossed his mind. Had the lad called for him? What had he thought when Karras didn't answer? He scrunched his head to one side and determined his communications device was still in place. He pressed his head sideways into the dirt to activate the button, but it didn't work since the switch sat inside his ear. He tried wriggling an arm upward. Then the other. Neither budged.

Karras forced his body to relax. He listened carefully. If he heard someone close by maybe he could use his voice to summon aid. Mind speech would allow the enemy to pinpoint his position with shocking accuracy. Given how helpless he was, that wasn't a good idea.

Try as he might, he couldn't hear a thing. The roar of Griffon fire trumped everything. They sounded like small dragons. Karras twisted his mouth into a wry smile. Nothing combustible grew around the castle. Not even any dead trees. It must have come as a blow to the Griffons, with their love of fire.

A Harpy's shriek tore through the air. He didn't realize how much he'd hoped all of *them* were dead until he heard it. Listening even harder, he made out wizard voices, but they were far away. Too far to get their attention with everything else going on.

No help for it.

Magic would give his position away, but he couldn't remain where he was. Probably no one would even notice him since so much power was zinging through the air. He thought he ought to try to mend his useless leg first, but decided against it. The leg had to be straight, or it wouldn't heal properly.

Something else heavy fell on the pile of bodies above him. It hurt when the weight shift jostled his leg, but a bit of light filtered through after everything settled. He was half on his side, half on his back. His neck was about the only thing he could move. He spied a fist-sized rock. If he could press the communications device into it, he might be able to activate the switch. Sweating and straining, Karras struggled to move the couple of centimeters he needed. After two failed tries, he was able to turn his head and press the earpiece gently against the rock. The electronics were delicate. If he wasn't careful, they'd shatter.

He thought he'd never heard a sound quite so welcome as the static bursting forth. Karras didn't hesitate. "Ned?"

"Karras!" Something that sounded like a muted sob followed his name.

"Yes, lad. I'm buried under a whole bunch of things. Leg's broken. Get someone to help you dig me out."

"I'm with Lira. We'll find you."

She survived. Good.

"I'm sending a burst of magic. It'll tell you where I am."

After a long pause, Ned said, "We didn't get it. Try again."

Karras thought it odd Ned and Lira hadn't sensed his energy. Each wizard's magic was unique. Then he understood. So much magic—wizard and Infernal—cluttered things. His weak signal would be almost impossible to detect. Maybe it might help if he told Ned where he was when he'd fallen.

"I'm southeast of the castle. About sixty paces from the wall, if I remember correctly. Did you get the girl?"

"Yes."

"Her brother?"

"No. It's a long story—"

"Which is not important right now," Lira interrupted, having apparently keyed her device to their frequency. "We'll come closer."

"Yes, closer," Ned echoed. "I'll let you know when we're near and you can try again. Duck, Lira! Damnable Griffon almost nailed us."

Karras grinned. Ned hadn't taken the time to disconnect.

The lad was a treasure. He'd known it from the time the boy was small. Wriggling, he sent threads of magic to keep blood circulating in his crushed extremities. He was glad Amanda was safe. He hadn't held out much hope for her brother. As Karras settled in to wait for rescue, he wondered why Ned sounded so upset about someone who'd been corrupted by Tantalus. The lad possessed a strongly practical side, and misplaced concern wasn't like him.

BACK IN THE LINE OF FIRE

Smoke burned Ned's lungs. The air was full of it. The worst part of battles was always the smell. While he'd ignored it earlier, it had grown particularly bad. A noxious brew of vomit, shit from split entrails, and blood permeated everything. The Infernals had their own stink. Harpies smelled like something from an untended crypt and Griffons like burning garbage.

Locating Karras was easy. Getting him out proved much harder. It took both him and Lira to pull bodies off the wizard. Infernals closed in, and they had to focus all their magic on defense. They'd just cleared one group of dinosaur-birds when two Griffons moved in. Ned shot a despairing glance at the piled bodies still standing between Karras and freedom.

He readied himself to ask Kühl for help when Lira said, "This isn't working. I'll summon magic to move the last bodies. Keep us safe."

Ned swallowed hard. He focused a killing blow, and one of the Griffons exploded. The other veered away. Ned's mouth was so dry, it felt like it was lined with sand. He looked around them. The nearest wizards were fifty paces away fighting for their lives. No help from that quarter. Fire shot from a Griffon's sharp-toothed mouth. A wizard wearing battle leathers went up like a torch, screaming in agony. Thinking it might help, Ned spun a curtain about Lira. It wouldn't make her totally invisible, but it might at least slow the enemy down.

"Hurry," he hissed.

"Got him," Lira crowed.

Ned shifted the angle of his gaze for the briefest of seconds, relieved to see Karras's gray head emerge from the pile of bodies. Something tore his sleeve. Pain followed, racing through his arm like shards of glass gone wild. He spun to find himself face to face with a Harpy. She radiated beauty in an eerie sort of way, with long, wispy red hair and the greenest eyes he'd ever seen. Lush, red lips curved in a scimitar of a smile. He tried to draw away, to shake her off his arm, but he couldn't move. Fear scuttled down his spine, turning his guts to water.

"Human mage," she purred. "'Tis long since I have seen one such as you. What a charming addition you will be to my collection."

The Harpy's head exploded, spattering Ned with gore. He tried to wipe blood and bone chips out of his eyes, but his arm wouldn't obey.

Karras tottered unsteadily to his feet, in spite of his broken leg, and hobbled over to Ned, using his staff as a crutch. "Cover us," he shouted at Lira and grabbed Ned's wounded arm.

Magic flowed into his body as Karras chanted urgently. The curious paralysis that had kept him staring at the Harpy dissipated. In moments Ned felt whole again.

He wanted to hug the wizard, but they had to move him to a safe place. He was helpless with his leg broken. "Thank you," he said. "Do you want to go back to camp?"

Karras shook his head. "Look about you, lad. We're losing. All our magic is needed. What sort of warrior would I be if I hid to save myself?"

"Your leg," Lira protested. Her staff blazed fire at a Griffon. It cartwheeled out of the sky. She jumped to one side, so it wouldn't hit her.

"You of all wizards have no room to chide me. You're here despite wounds that aren't yet healed." Karras gazed from side to side. "Settle me over there." He pointed. "The bodies make a defensible wall. You two can fight from here. If we spread out, we won't be at cross-purposes."

Movement drew Ned's gaze to the tower balcony. Tantalus stood upon it, his arms raised. Jolts of power shimmered outward from his hands, turning the air a bluish color. A Harpy fluttered on either side of him. A Griffon fawned at his feet, like a misshapen dog.

Ned followed the bolts of energy. The god was shoring up the Infernal host—and doing a damned good job from the looks of things. At least he wasn't summoning more of them. Hope flared in Ned, a welcome counterpoint to the piles of dead. Maybe there weren't any more to call.

Fiddling with his communicator, Karras called Kühl. Ned

switched frequencies so he could listen. "We must retreat," Karras said. "Ned got the girl out. Our reason for being here no longer exists. If we tarry too long, Cybele and the other gods will lay waste to this world."

Goddess blast it!

Ned slapped his forehead with an open palm. He and Lira had hightailed it back to the battle, but neither of them had the presence of mind to tell a battle lord they could leave. He'd been weary almost beyond reckoning, and Lira was wounded. Jaw clenched, Ned wondered how many lives had been lost because of his oversight and stupidity.

"They'll just follow us," Kühl replied dully. "This will be our last battle, Karras. I know it in my bones."

"Enough. I am senior here. Determine who remains. Call back when you have the information."

Sounds like Kühl's instructions to me.

Two of the dinosaur birds dive-bombed them. Power flew from Ned's hands, and the birds exploded midair. Feathers and guts showered down around them.

The radio crackled. "We are two hundred twenty-three."

"Not as bad as I feared. We will execute a staged retreat."

"At last you are ready to leave?" Cybele's unmistakable voice reverberated around them.

"Hold up," Karras told Kühl, the excitement in his voice unmistakable. "We may yet win this day."

Ned looked around, but didn't see the goddess. A blistering flash of insight catapulted through him. She'd been here all the time. If the wizards chose to keep fighting, Cybele would have let them all die before she and the other gods moved in to finish off the Infernals.

We mean nothing to them.

"Yes, we're ready to leave," Karras said. "Your assistance would be much appreciated."

Ned swallowed a smirk. Karras hadn't said a word about her lack of help thus far. He was being diplomatic in hopes she'd help them at all.

Soft chortling filled his ears. "See what you think about this, wizard."

A host of shadows charged from the sky. As they drew near, Ned saw they were robed in brilliant colors, wearing diadems set with obscenely large stones and carrying gold and silver scepters.

Tantalus saw them too. Against their splendor, his beauty looked cheap and tawdry. Lowering his hands from shoulder level, he held them out like a supplicant. A welcoming smile split his face as if he were greeting long-lost relatives.

Well, I suppose it's who they are. His kinfolk.

Ned licked dry lips. He hoped the other gods would tear Tantalus to shreds.

The Harpies and Griffon next to Tantalus took flight. They shattered into bloody chunks as soon as they were airborne. Ned scooted to one side to escape being hit by parts from the falling Griffon. Four of the gods seized their errant brother and yanked him from his spot on the balcony. As quickly as they'd descended, they rose back into the sky, Tantalus suspended among them.

"I'm going back in there," Ned told Karras, gesturing toward the castle.

"Whatever for, lad? 'Tis past time for us to leave. The gods will destroy this world as soon as they get clear of it."

The Infernals apparently shared Karras's opinion. Harpies, Griffons, and dinosaur-birds flew from the clearing like all the dogs of Hell chased after them. The sound of their combined wing beats was deafening.

"Jon is in there," Ned said, already running toward the castle. "If he's still alive, we're taking him with us."

Lira caught up to him, keeping pace by his side. "Two can search faster," she said, panting slightly. Calling over her shoulder to Karras she cried, "Get a portal ready. Send one of the wizards back for those left in camp."

Through his communications device, Ned heard Karras tell Kühl to send two wizards to get Rolf, Lori, Amanda, and the wizard healer and to be quick about it.

He and Lira arrived at the barred castle gates. Lira blasted the portcullis with a bolt of magic from her staff. Ned jumped back. A piece of wood hit him in the forehead, burying itself. He yanked it out and funneled a thread of magic to staunch the blood while he bounded up the stone stairs to the entry hall. Ned didn't hesitate. He mounted the spiral staircase.

"Last I was in here, Jon and Amanda were on the third floor."

"You search high, I'll take the lower levels," Lira said, the tatters of her clothing flapping around her.

Ned ran through the upper floor rooms, wiping blood still trickling down his forehead, so it wouldn't drip into his eyes. The hag lay dead on the floor of her small chamber. The other rooms were empty. Coming back down, he checked the second floor rooms. All empty as well. He was headed for the kitchens when Lira's voice floated up. "Found him."

Ned pounded down the last of the interior stairs, but didn't see Lira.

"Where are you?"

"In some sort of dungeon. There's not a direct route. I sensed a lower level and used magic to find it." She hesitated. "There's a horrible laboratory down here. I located Jon in a cage. Once I got him out, I killed everything else. Even Infernals shouldn't suffer in such a fashion."

Ned knew she must be near the ape-men's pens. Drawing power, he visualized the lower space and transported himself there. Lira faced away from him. Past her was a doorway leading to a blood-choked chamber. Cages of different sizes were stacked on shelves and each other. At least fifty of them. Ned reached out with his magic.

"I told you everything in there is dead." Lira sounded as close to panicked as he'd ever heard her. "Get over here. We need to move."

Racing to her side, he saw the body in her arms and stopped cold. His mouth fell open in horror. "Merciful goddess. Is he still alive?"

"Barely."

Jon's face was bruised beyond recognition. Blood streaked his blond hair. His fingers were bent at unnatural angles, but he was breathing, moaning in fact.

"'Tis a kindness he's unconscious," Lira muttered. "I pray Tantalus will suffer far worse than this. Come." She was already moving down one of the tunnels. "Get my staff. I deactivated it, so it won't hurt you. This pathway should lead us back to Karras."

"It does. Here, Lira. Let me take him. I'm stronger." She shifted the burden into his arms, took her staff, and raised a mage light. They retraced Ned's steps from earlier in the day, moving as fast as they could. It seemed years had passed since he last traversed the underground route.

An ominous rumbling met their ears as they climbed out of the tunnel. Hurtling into the yard in front of the castle, they sprinted to Karras. The ground shook. Black smoke filled the air.

"Hurry," the wizard screamed as he held the portal door open. "We're the last. Everyone else is safely away."

Ned jumped through with Jon in his arms. Lira came right behind him. Spinning, she helped Karras balance. He stepped through the gateway, leaning on his staff, and yelped when he weighted his foot. Sweat beaded his forehead. His face was pasty. The door shut. Barking the command to seal the portal, Karras slid to the ground. "We are returning to the stronghold," he said, his voice laced with pain. "If I pass out, the two of you can hold our course steady."

THEY ACCELERATED TO TRAVELING SPEED. Jon thrashed about where he lay unconscious. Blood sprayed, along with saliva. He twisted his head in one direction then another. His already-battered head made an eerie thumping sound when it banged against the floor of the Ways. Watching the young man, with a face so like his father's, Karras remembered

Rolf's problems in the Ways with painful clarity. He'd stunned Rolf to make him manageable, but Jon's condition was so precarious, Karras was afraid if he deepened the lad's unconscious state it would kill him.

"What's wrong with him?" Ned asked, ducking to avoid one of Jon's flailing fists. "This seems worse than even his injuries would account for."

"Something to do with Earth Mage blood," Karras replied. He tried a light calming spell, but it didn't slow Jon's thrashing one whit. Next he reached into Jon's mind, intent on seeing if there wasn't some other way. Not liking what he found, he withdrew. Every time Karras moved, his leg felt like hot knives sliced into it. He thought about asking Lira to do something, but healing wasn't exactly her forte either. He'd made it this far. He could hold out for a healer back at the stronghold.

One of Jon's feet landed a direct hit to Karras's injured leg. He cursed. It had been misplaced heroism on Ned's part to rescue someone who'd spent so long with the dark god, but they were stuck with him. It wasn't like they could jettison Jon into the Ways.

Almost like he'd read Karras's thoughts, Ned mumbled, "Sorry. I looked into his mind. Though I wasn't certain, it appeared he was more than Tantalus's puppet."

"You acted honorably," Lira assured him. "If we can just get him home, we'll turn him over to our healers. They'll judge if he can be salvaged."

"I fear this will be a long trip." Karras moved beyond the range of Jon's limbs and sighed heavily. He directed a touch more magic into his calming spell. For a moment, Jon stilled, and Karras dared hope he'd found a compromise to keep all of them comfortable. If they could get Jon under control, maybe Lira could take a crack at stabilizing his leg.

"Whatever you did appears to be working—" Ned began when Jon's eyes snapped open. Fury belched from them the second they landed on Ned.

"You." He pointed a shaky finger at Ned. "We were fine until you came. He even found Mandy for me. Then you had to go fuck everything up with your fine words. Eieeeeee—"

Blood bubbled from the corners of his mouth. Jon's body bowed in agony, and he drummed his heels against the tubular floor of the Ways. "Hurts," he moaned. "Everything hurts." Something shifted in his blue eyes. When he looked at Ned again, he said, "Sorry. I'm sorry. I don't know why I said those things." Another heartrending shriek tore out of him.

Lira went to him, her normally sharp blue-green eyes soft with compassion. Laying hands on either side of his head, she crooned a tuneless song. Karras felt her magic and yanked his own back. Too much would almost certainly kill the lad in his present state. From the looks of things, he could easily die on his own without any intervention from them.

Lira met Karras's gaze. "His organs are punctured. Liver and spleen I think. 'Tis where the blood is coming from. I can try to repair them and put the ribs back into place."

"Go ahead. He'll die if we do nothing."

"He might die anyway," she cautioned. "I must have him quiet to work on him, but the sleep spell may well be enough to send him back to the goddess."

Silence stretched through the cylindrical space. The gentle rocking distinctive to the Ways might've been soothing, but Karras's nerves were stretched to the breaking point. His brief sojourn into Jon's thoughts had left him feeling dirty. Tantalus's contamination was thorough. It permeated the young Earth Mage's mind. Why hadn't Ned sensed it and left well enough alone?

Rocking back on her heels, Lira wiped a hand across her face. It left streaks in the dirt crusting her cheeks. "I've done all I can." She frowned at Karras. Matted red hair hung in her eyes. "Do you think I should leave him asleep?"

Karras sent magic snaking into Jon. His heartbeat was disturbingly slow, and he was barely breathing. "Mayhap 'tis for the best," he said. "If you withdraw your spell and he begins battering himself about again, he'll undo whatever healing you've managed."

"At least your assessment matches mine." Dropping her head into her hands, Lira rubbed her face with fingers as dirty as the rest of her. "Goddess be damned but I'm tired. I fear this day will never end."

Mayhap it won't, Karras thought sourly. He rethought asking Lira to help with his leg. She looked exhausted and maintaining Jon would take all her concentration for the remainder of their journey.

"Do you know why Earth Mages have trouble with the Ways?" Ned asked, his voice sounding rusty.

He tried to clear his throat, but all that came out was a gurgling sound. He'd long since polished off the water skins he'd filled at the pool where he killed the bird. "Does anyone have any water?"

Ned had been silent so long, Karras almost forgot he was there. Shaking his head, he said, "No, lad, on both counts. No water, and I know precious little about Earth Mages. Hreth was going to research them. I expect he'll have answers once we get back."

Jon moaned. Cursing, Lira turned her attention back to him. "More trouble than you're worth, hybrid trash."

"Watch your tongue. Your daughter is of mixed race, and this young man is your grandson," Karras reminded her sternly.

Even under the dirt, Karras saw color rise from the open neck of Lira's robe. "Ach, don't pay any attention to me. I'm so worn out, I don't know what I'm saying."

"He's trying to talk." Ned moved closer to Jon. Bending, he placed his ear close to Jon's lips. When he straightened, he looked devastated.

"What?" Karras laid a hand on Ned's arm. "I didn't bother to listen because it's all I can do to manage the pain in my leg and keep us on course."

"There's a baby," Ned choked out. "At least he says there is."

"He's delirious." Lira laughed grimly. "Look about you. There's no baby here."

Ned shook his head. "Not here. Amanda is pregnant. I know he's babbling and out of his mind, but Jon thinks Tantalus will return in the babe once it's born."

"Not if Cybele has anything to say about it," Karras grunted.

"Yes," Lira chimed in. "By now, Tantalus is surely chained back in Tartarus."

"Aren't they going to kill him?" Ned narrowed his eyes with disbelief. "Surely, after all this," he spread his arms, "the gods will kill him."

"They don't do away with their own, lad," Karras murmured. "I'm not sure they could, even if they wanted to. They merely punish them through all eternity."

SOME THINGS NEVER CHANGE

The jerkiness of deceleration woke Ned from an uneasy doze. He'd been dreaming about Amanda giving birth to a miniature version of Tantalus. Stomach sour and mouth so dry he wondered if he could find enough water in the universe to soothe its raw tissues, he sought the energy to pull himself together. Despite Karras's earlier reassurances, a part of him still worried the wizards would clap him in leg irons and throw him back in the cell he'd escaped from the minute the portal doors opened. This time, they'd make sure to chain him to iron eyebolts in the walls.

"Goddess's breath. We're finally here." Lira stood, raised her arms above her head, and stretched. Face etched with tension, she looked so vulnerable Ned did a double take. The Lira he knew was tough, bitchy, and indestructible. The woman standing shakily waiting for the portal to open didn't look like any of those things.

"It would appear we are." Karras tried to rise. A sharp cry escaped him, and he sank back down. Knowing the bone ends in the wizard's leg must have rubbed against one another, Ned moved to Karras's side.

"I'll help you." Ned bent, got both arms around the wizard's chest, and hauled him to his feet. It took all his waning strength. Karras was solid and mostly dead weight.

Ned sent magic toward Jon and found life barely treading the surface like butterfly wings.

"Yes." Lira inclined her head. "Against all odds, he still lives. You help Karras. I'll see that the young Earth Mage gets to our healers."

A slight shudder indicated they'd arrived. Karras gave the command to open the gateway. "Hope I did this right," he muttered. "It could mean all our deaths if I miscalculated. None of us has enough energy left to fight Infernals—or even renegade humans."

Ned thought about something Kühl told him. "Why wasn't this trip more difficult for me? Kühl said something about frequency shifts. Getting to the Infernals' world and back wasn't any harder than going anywhere else. Just longer."

"He didn't want to be bothered to take you," Lira said. A flatness in her voice held the ring of truth.

"He lied?" Betrayal left an acrid taste in Ned's mouth.

I should be used to wizards treating me like leftover dragon shit by now.

"Yes, lad, wizards do lie, and they still won't like you very well." Karras blew out a pain-laced breath. "Prejudices die hard. There will be some who want to see you hanged for escaping—" He held up a hand, apparently in response to something in Ned's expression. "The Council will stand behind you. You have nothing to fear, but don't expect a hero's welcome, either." He peered at Ned. "See a healer for that gash in your forehead."

Karras peeled back the portal doorway to reveal the stone courtyard outside the Carpathian stronghold. "Goddess be praised. We're truly home. Help me out, lad."

Ned closed off the portal once Lira was out. She set Jon's body on the inlaid flagstones. The deep blue of the sky and a cloud-shrouded sun suggested midday. It didn't take long before a bustling gaggle of wizard healers converged on them, blue robes swirling as they clucked over Karras, Lira, and Jon. Ned wasn't sure if Karras or Lira had summoned them, or if unseen sentries made certain help would arrive. After all, two well-respected wizards had returned, obviously damaged from battle.

Other portals opened, disgorging battle-weary wizards. For reasons unbeknownst to Ned, some wizards had picked a less direct route back to the stronghold. Perhaps they had other places they needed to stop first.

Regardless of their arrival time, everyone had somewhere to go. No one so much as looked at him. Healers didn't bother with his wound. Standing off to the side, Ned wasn't surprised when everyone just left him there. Karras was right. He still didn't count because he wasn't a wizard.

Good enough to die for them in combat. Not good enough to care about.

Saddened—and annoyed—by how much the wizards' bigotry still rankled, Ned limped to a water spigot. He knelt on the stones, pumped the handle a few times and put his face under the icy flow. His leather breeches were soaked through from knee to ankle before he finished drinking. So were his boots. He thought about food, but didn't want to go as far as the kitchens. Someone had left one of the stronghold doors ajar. Good thing, since he was damned if he could remember the incantation to open them. Staggering with weariness, he dragged his body into the long hall and over to a raised bench. He fell asleep before all his limbs straightened themselves out.

His own shivering woke him. Night had fallen and the temperature in the stone hallway dropped by a good twenty degrees. Ned wondered if his old garret room was unoccupied. It was likely since no wizard worth anything would deign to occupy such a humble space. Slinking through the stronghold like a thief in the night, he stopped by the back of the kitchens and scrounged some stale bread, a hunk of cheese, and watered-down wine out of a pantry. Thus armed, he climbed the winding staircase to the small attic room where he'd spent much of his boyhood.

The door was locked. Feeling unaccountably lucky—after all, he'd gotten this far without seeing anyone—he spoke the spell that had once opened the door to his erstwhile room. After a pause as if the door were considering who might want in, it sprang open much to Ned's relief. He had no idea where else to settle if this didn't work. Kicking the stout wooden panel shut behind him, Ned dropped his food on the bed. He stripped off his still wet breeches and boots and pulled a soft, well-patched woolen robe out of the clothes chest.

He dropped the rest of his filthy clothes on the floor before snugging the robe close about himself. The reek of his body was thick in his nostrils, but he didn't care. Ned settled on the narrow bed. With his back leaning against the wall, he stuffed food into his mouth like he'd never eaten before. He knew he should have gotten more partway through his meal, but shrugged. It didn't matter.

Nothing mattered except Amanda, and she was lost to him. The minute her image entered his mind, he knew he'd avoided thinking about her because it hurt so much. He loved her. She loved another. A man whose child she carried. When he visualized her in Tantalus's arms, Ned could barely stand it. He recalled how she looked when she was being kissed, her eyes closed, a spot of color high on each cheek. To his horror, a tear tracked down one cheek. He wiped it away. He was a warrior, and they didn't cry. Not over something as trivial as a love affair gone wrong.

She was my soul mate. My chosen one.

Don't be stupid. She's the first girl I knew well enough to get close to. Don't make more of this than it is.

Ned wondered if the wizards would send him back to the war if he asked nicely. Deciding it was likely, he hatched out a plan. Come morning, he'd stop by the war desk, get his orders, and sneak out of the stronghold. If his luck held, he wouldn't have to see Amanda again.

"It's for the best," he muttered. "I'll sleep. Have another meal. Clean up. Then I'll be gone. If I see her, it'll tear the scabs off my heart all over again."

He drained the last of the wine and used a begrimed fingertip to clear the final crumbs of bread and cheese off the bedclothes. His stomach begged for one more trip to the kitchen, but Ned pulled a blanket over himself and fell into a dreamless sleep.

"THERE YOU ARE, LAD." Karras's hearty voice and a hand on his shoulder woke him.

"Mmph. Go away." Ned burrowed deeper into the blanket.

"Time to get up," Karras insisted. "Whew! I can smell you from here. You need a good bath and some clean clothes. The Council would speak with you."

Ned's eyes flew open. He pushed away from Karras's hand. "Council? I don't want to talk with them. I'm leaving. Going back to the war. Just needed a bit of rest first—"

"Enough." Karras's stern voice was back. Ned had heard his mentor's firm voice plenty, correcting him when he was younger. "You can't refuse the Council. What are you thinking? Now get up and come with me to the baths. I have fresh clothing for you down there."

Ned swung his legs over the side of the bed. He pulled the patched, woolen robe he ended up sleeping in more firmly around himself. Between standing and walking to the door, every muscle in his body complained. He bit back a groan. Ned needed a diversion from pain. Wondering what the Council had in mind for him didn't help. Maybe they were going to punish him for his escape after all.

He glanced at Karras. "They fixed your leg."

The wizard nodded. "Yes, they did. 'Twas a clean break. Hurry up. It'll take time to clear the snarls out of what's left of your braids." He frowned. "You never did get that gash in your forehead tended to."

"You're right. I didn't."

Karras ran fingertips over the wound, and Ned felt the zing of magic.

Sorrow filled him, making a place beneath his breastbone ache. Amanda had braided his hair. Right before the Wirricow attack... Ned sucked in a ragged breath and followed Karras down several flights to the bath chamber. With a warrior's discipline, he cleared his mind—of everything.

Long, wet hair hung straight down his back. Ned cinched a deep green robe about himself and wished for his familiar battle leathers. He slid his feet into soft leather house boots. "Why the finery?" he asked. "Leathers have always been good enough for me before."

"The Council asked me to attire you properly."

He wanted to ask Karras more, but the wizard was already out the door and climbing the stairs to the upper hall and Council Chamber. When they got there, Karras set fingers into the indentations to open the door. It slid back. He turned and gripped Ned's arm. "In you go."

Ned took two paces inside the door, keeping his gaze downcast. He'd learned long ago not to look directly at the wizards unless invited to do so. It just gave them one more reason to criticize him.

"Come." Hreth's breathy voice ordered.

Ned took a few more steps, keeping his hands clasped behind him and his eyes trained on the floor.

"What in the goddess's name have you done to him? He's afraid to look at you." An unfamiliar voice sounded shocked —and annoyed.

Ned wanted to look up. To see who'd spoken in his defense, but long years of obedience bound him.

Liefes cleared his throat and said, "Thou may look at us. Please. Approach the table and take a seat."

They're inviting me to sit?

Curiosity consumed him. Ned raised his eyes from the floor. Hreth, Liefes, and Dagget were in their usual places on the side of the long table facing the door. Someone he didn't recognize sat with his back to him. Unbound dark hair was cut to shoulder length. The stranger wore earth-toned leathers and a black boot was thrust casually out to one side.

Karras took Ned's arm and led him to an empty chair at the head of the table. Fear knotted Ned's guts. What was going on? After brief glances at the Council members, Ned took the indicated seat and schooled himself to wait for the banishment he was certain would happen next. Or the execution. After all, they'd made sure he was clean and well dressed. A perfect sacrifice to the goddess.

"I am Sören." The stranger got to his feet, walked close, and extended a hand to Ned.

"Ned. Pleased to meet you," he mumbled, scrambling to stand and take the proffered hand.

He tried to pull his hand back, but Sören held on. "I'm your father," he said. "Had I known about you, I would have come far sooner. The wizards have made some progress with your magic, but you need other human mages to fully develop your power."

Ned's heart sped up. His gaze shifted to Karras. He suspected another of the unfunny jokes the wizards had played on him over the years. It would be very like them to raise his hopes, only to dash them on jagged rocks. "Can this be true?"

Karras nodded. "Hreth was busy while we were gone." He exchanged glances with the blind seer, who saw more clearly than those with normal sight. "Do you wish to tell the tale," Karras asked Hreth, "or would you like me to?"

"I will. Look at me, Ned. I want thee to see what I tell thee is true. I wouldn't be offended if thou were to weave the truth spell betwixt us."

"I'm sure it won't be necessary," Ned said a little stiffly.

"Art thou certain?" It felt like Hreth looked right through him and scanned his soul. "We've not dealt fairly with thee, nor given thee cause to trust us."

Because he didn't know what to say, and wasn't sure what might come out of his mouth driven by years of bottled anger, Ned just nodded. It didn't matter Hreth was blind, the seer would recognize Ned's assent.

"Since thy mother refused to tell us anything—again—I went to the human mages' seer. He and I have worked together in the past. I described thy mother and he asked his men. It didn't take long afore Sören stepped forth—"

"I'm grateful to have a son," Sören interrupted, still clinging to Ned's hand despite several efforts on Ned's part to free himself. "I'm here to take you home."

Shocked someone dared to speak over Hreth, Ned waited for the wizard to strike Sören. It didn't happen.

"The other thing my meeting with the mages' seer brought to light," Hreth went on like nothing had happened, "is the necessity of all magic-wielders working together."

Dagget cleared his throat. "Yes, we've discussed things thoroughly and decided we have become a bit too insular over the years. Once we had good reasons—"

"But not anymore," Liefes finished for him.

"Karras told us of thy bravery in rescuing both Earth Mages from Tantalus's castle," Hreth said, smiling.

"Indeed and we have something for thee," Liefes said.

"Since thou art already standing, if thou wouldst step to this side of the table—" Dagget too, sported an unholy grin. Ned couldn't recall ever seeing any of them do anything but frown sternly at him.

"Go on." Sören released Ned's hand, pride shining from his dark eyes, and returned to his seat. Encouraged, Ned took the time to really look at him and saw well-sculpted cheekbones, soft dark hair set with jewels, and a beard spilling partway down his chest. He wore snug-fitting leathers with something like ribbon decorations over one breast. A short sword hung in a sheath from his waist.

Ned walked around the table and stood behind Hreth. The blind seer got to his feet, as did Liefes and Dagget.

Turning, they formed a circle around him. Hreth fished a shiny, golden disk from somewhere in his voluminous robes.

"This medal is awarded for extreme bravery in combat. Thou rescued both Earth Mage children, returning to the Infernals' lair a second time at grave risk to thyself." Hreth pointed to a likeness of Mercury on one side of the disk. "The god of war will bring thee luck in battle." He tapped an imprint of Ceres on the other. "The goddess of the Earth will remind thee of thy responsibility to keep Infernals from damaging her."

Ned knew what the medal looked like. There had been fewer than fifty awarded in all the years the wizards kept records of such things. One had never been given to a non-wizard. He'd read about the heroes who received them.

"I-I can't take your medal," he stammered, his face heating. "Why, I'm nothing like Tamta or Brön. Besides," he choked out, "Lira was just as brave as me."

A shadow crossed Hreth's face. "She had sins to pay for. Her slate is finally clean. This is not about my daughter. 'Tis about thee." He slipped the medal, suspended on a golden chain, over Ned's head.

Ned felt the metal warm where it sat against his skin. "I... I don't know what to say."

"You might try thank you." Karras's dry voice came from where he sat next to Sören.

"Thank you," Ned said. Joy filled him. His throat tightened, and he had a hell of a time swallowing around thickening at the back of it. Was it possible he'd truly have a family now? The wizards had finally accepted him as one of their own. If that weren't enough, he had a father to boot.

"Thou art now one of our Knights," Hreth said solemnly. "Should thou choose to continue to fight alongside us, it will be an honor to place thy first command under thee."

Ned's face split into a broad grin. He considered pinching himself. This had to be a dream.

"First, he must spend time among his own kind," Sören said. Something in his tone sounded like he was reminding the wizards of an agreement.

"Yes, of course. We haven't forgotten. Sit down, lad," Karras instructed. "Sören has at least one piece of news I believe you will welcome."

His father's eyes followed Ned as he walked back around the long table. "I understand from yon wizard," Sören gestured at Karras, "there is some question about celibacy and magic. You need have no fears in that regard. If human mages required celibacy for our magic, we would have died out centuries ago. 'Twas a wizard myth, wound up in their own discomfort around the topic."

Ned's face got even hotter. He pulled his chair out and sat. "It doesn't matter anymore. I suppose it's good to know, in case... Well, in case the issue ever comes up again."

He felt Karras's sharp gaze home in on him. "I thought you were in love with Amanda Haraldssen."

Ned winced. This was *not* a conversation he wanted to have with his father and the High Council listening in on what was said. "I believe she loves another—" he murmured.

"You've jumped to conclusions," Karras broke in. "There are some people who have been waiting—and rather impatiently, I might add—to talk with you. We," he made an inclusive gesture with his hands, "told them they had to wait until the first matter of business was concluded."

"Which it has been," a still-smiling Hreth said.

Chanting an incantation, Liefes opened his arms wide. A corner of the large room Ned hadn't even noticed shimmered. As wispy darkness fell away, Rolf, Lori, Jon, and Amanda rushed forward.

"Thanks for at least letting us hear." Rolf clapped Hreth on the back and sprinted past him, making a beeline for Ned. Used to the wizards' understated emotional expression, Ned was shocked when the big, bearlike man jerked him out of his chair and folded him into an embrace.

Tears ran unabashed down Rolf's bearded face. "You saved my children," he said over and over again. "How can I ever thank you?"

Lori was there too, her arms around both of them. She pushed her husband aside. "My turn," she declared and clasped Ned against her. "We're forever in your debt. Once we could have repaid you with something to make your life easier, but now all we can offer is our home. It's yours whenever you want to visit." Her eyes, so like Lira's, shone with unshed tears.

"If the two of you are done hogging him." Jon limped over. "I'd like a turn."

Ned reached for his hand, but stopped. "Bet they still hurt." He smiled crookedly at Jon.

"Yeah, but not so much. Mom could borrow a page from those wizard healers."

"Thanks for the vote of confidence." Lori cuffed him, but Ned could tell they were teasing each other. The old ache he'd always had for a family of his own surfaced, but he ignored it.

I do have a family. He reminded himself of Sören—and the wizards. *I just have to get to know them.*

"I'll keep it simple," Jon said, laying a hand gently on Ned's shoulder. "You saved my life, man. Rescued me from a monster who'd gone a long way toward convincing me he was my best friend. Thank you for risking yourself for me. I'll never forget what you did. Never."

"Don't be too hard on yourself." Ned met Jon's gaze. "Tantalus snared you with spells. I felt them in your mind, but a lot of your true spirit remained too. Somehow, you kept that bastard out of the important places." Ned grimaced. "I'll have to admit I wasn't so sure during our trip back. I'm glad you found a way past the darkness."

"It wasn't clear which direction things were going to go," Lori said somberly. "The wizard healers are truly amazing—and very fast." Her gaze moved from Hreth to Liefes to Dagget and settled on Karras. "They purged Jon's mind of the madness I saw in his eyes when he first returned. I still can't believe that was only a few short hours ago."

Rolf nodded. "Words feel inadequate, but thank you from the very depths of my heart. I never believed I'd see my son again—or my daughter."

During everything, Amanda had hung back. Ned saw her out of the corner of one eye. When it was apparent she was just as uncomfortable as him, he gathered courage from an internal reservoir he didn't know he possessed. After all, he'd been about to sneak off like a criminal to avoid having to talk with her at all.

"Excuse me." Ned extricated himself from the other Haraldssens.

Coming around the table, he thanked each of the High Council in turn. When he stopped next to Karras, his old mentor surprised him by coming to his feet and scooping him into a hug. "I've wanted to reassure you of my caring since you were a child," he admitted sheepishly. "'Tis hard for us. We hold our feelings close."

Ned hugged him back, a tidal wave of emotion running through him. "You gave me a reason to keep going when I was very small—and helped me believe in myself."

Once Karras let him go, Ned walked to Sören's side. "I'm looking forward to getting to know you," he said.

"The pleasure will be all mine." Sören's smile warmed Ned's heart. "Now go sort things out with your lady."

Ned strode toward Amanda. Enough joy tumbled through him, he felt equal to whatever their conversation might bring. "Would you like to talk?" When she nodded without exactly meeting his gaze, he said, "Come on then," and led her out of the Council Chamber.

Because he didn't know where else to take her, Ned guided Amanda to his room. It was the only place in the stronghold that truly felt like his. Once he closed the door, though, he wondered if maybe something with more chairs —and no bed—might've been more appropriate.

"If you'd rather, I could take you to the library—" he began, but she waved him to silence.

"This is fine. I have some things to say. It doesn't much matter where I say them." She settled herself on the wooden clothes chest.

Silence fell between them and grew uncomfortably long. At last, she trained her sea-blue gaze on him. "Like Jon, maybe it would be better if I kept this simple. I'm not going to offer any excuses for what I did with Tantalus. Yes, he probably ensorcelled me, but the unpleasant truth is when he hurt me, I caved so fast I was disgusted with myself." She swallowed hard. "I am pregnant. The wizard healers confirmed it. They also refused to destroy the child. I guess they see it as murder."

Once she'd begun talking, Amanda's words raced out almost faster than she had breath to support them. Ned wanted to go to her, to draw her close, but he held back.

"I went to Mother. She said she didn't have the instruments to get rid of the baby. So it looks like I'm fresh out of choices. At least until it's born. According to Cybele, the gods want it. I don't know quite how I feel about turning it over to them. Don't suppose it matters, though. The wizard with those unnerving green eyes—"

"Hreth."

She nodded. "Yeah, him. Anyway, he said when the goddess arrives to demand the child, I have to give it to her. Christ! It sounds like something out of Rapunzel or Rumplestiltskin." Laughing uneasily, she said in a stage whisper, "Give me your firstborn, human."

"What about us?" Asking so directly was a huge chance, but Ned couldn't wait any longer.

"What about us?" she countered, her gaze never leaving his. "Could you possibly still want me after what I've done?" Not giving him a chance to say anything, she hurried on, "I wouldn't blame you if you told me to have a nice life. So please, just be truthful. You don't have to sugarcoat anything for me."

Ned was off the bed in a flash. He crossed the small space to her in a single step. Kneeling before her, he pulled her into his arms. "I love you, Amanda. By the goddess, I love you. Tantalus doesn't matter, and if the gods don't come to collect his child, I'll love it like my own."

The rest of his words were lost as he kissed her.

When she wound her arms around his neck and kissed him back, Ned's heart spilled over. He'd never felt such joy. Tenderness filled him, and he cradled her in his arms. "We'll make this work," he whispered when he could talk again.

"Yes." She beamed, all the love in the world shining from her eyes. "We will." Rising to her feet, she extended both arms. Once he stood in front of her, holding her tight against his body, she kissed him again until they were both breathless. He nuzzled her neck, his hands roaming down her curves. Heat kindled every nerve, creating exquisite waves of longing.

He knew exactly what she'd feel like next to him without all those layers of cloth in between. Ned nudged her toward the bed. He'd waited so long, even another few moments were too much.

She wriggled against him and moved back enough to talk. "The wizards say we have to get married first. Cybele said it too."

Ned laughed. "Yes, the wizards would see it that way." He sucked in an unsteady breath. "They're probably right."

"Come on." Amanda disentangled her arms from around

his neck and grabbed one of his hands. "Let's tell Mom and Dad—and Jon. I know they're worried about me."

"I suppose they would have been angry—"

She laid a hand over his lips and shook her head at the question mirrored in his eyes. "They wouldn't have blamed you if, well, if things didn't work out between us. No matter what, you'll always be a hero in their eyes."

Me. A hero?

Heat rose from the open neck of his robe. He felt his face turn crimson at the unexpected compliment.

"You'll always be my hero too. You would have been, no matter what. You saved my life. And you went back for Jon." She stroked the side of his face tenderly. "I love you."

"I love you too." A thought struck him. "I must ask your father before we wed. We need his blessings."

She laughed. The warm, musical sound struck a chord in his soul. "I don't think you have much to worry about. Let's go."

He guided Amanda—his Amanda, really and truly his now—down the narrow staircase. A warm glow radiated from his midsection.

Maybe I'm finally done with apologizing for not being born a wizard.

The thought made him laugh.

"What?" Amanda stopped on a landing, turned, and looked curiously at him.

"Nothing. I think too much. Right after we reassure your parents—and I ask your father's permission—let's find out how soon Hreth can consecrate our vows."

She wove her arms around him. He hugged her close

and covered her mouth with his, reveling in the wonder of her in his arms.

Rolf's deep laughter and footsteps on the stairs interrupted their kiss. "Welcome to the family, son." He held out a hand, muttered, "Oh, to hell with it," and gathered Ned and Amanda into his arms.

EPILOGUE – SOMETIMES DREAMS COME TRUE

Three Weeks Later

"Tell us again how you vanquished Tantalus," a drunken voice shouted from a corner of the courtyard.

Ned snorted and narrowly avoided rolling his eyes. The shift from virtually no attention unless a wizard was finding fault, to so much attention he could barely find time to himself was unnerving. He hadn't *vanquished* Tantalus. Far from it. He still remembered the fear that nearly annihilated him as he hid behind the velvet curtains in the keep's entry hall.

Ned sorted through crafting an appropriate response to the unseen speaker, but Sören and a group of human mages moved toward the direction the voice had come from, and Ned breathed a little easier. He didn't really want to relive the span of time in the Infernals' world again He'd told the story numerous times, and it never got any easier. Parts still made his skin crawl.

In the few weeks since his return from Darehôl, he'd spent hours with his father. The interconnected warrens that made up the mage stronghold weren't terribly distant from the wizards' home base in the Carpathian Alps. Once he understood the roots of his particular brand of magic, blending it into his current strategies added to his ability in subtle but significant ways, without the enormous output of energy he'd feared would be required.

He'd even gotten to spend time with his mother. She'd been tentative around him, but it was clear she was thrilled to her bones by how well his life turned out. The wizards hadn't quite apologized to her, but they'd offered her old job back. After mulling it over for a few days, she accepted, taking up her previous spot as head seamstress. The stronghold where she'd taken refuge was sorry to lose her, and Ned suspected she was sorry to leave. After all, they'd taken her in when she had nowhere else to go.

Karras made his way through the milling crowd and caught Ned's upper arm. He'd fully recovered from his broken leg, and an unnatural grin spread across his face. "About ready, lad?"

"Are you kidding?" Ned did roll his eyes then. "I've been ready for this since before Amanda was kidnapped.

"I'm happy for you." Karras squeezed his arm. "'Tis time to get moving, though. You'll want to be at the altar to greet your bride-to-be."

Ned followed Karras into the stronghold. The wedding would be in one of the great halls, a place he'd never seen since it was reserved for visiting dignitaries. His silken robe, deep blue embroidered with gold runes, brushed against his skin as he walked. His feet were bare to symbolize the human mages' linkage to Earth's power and bounty.

As wizards and mages had designed a wedding ceremony to join their bloodlines formally for the first time, one of the arguments revolved around which traditions would be included. Ned stayed out of it because emotions ran high. Fortunately Cybele stayed out of it too, or they'd probably still be hashing out the details.

The wizards wanted a traditional ceremony with all their trappings; so had the mages. As emissary for the wizards, Lira bent just enough to avoid a full-blown conflict. She told him later that it didn't matter much if she pissed off the wizards. Many of them would never forgive her for giving birth to a mixed race child. Her primary concern was designing something elegant and meaningful for her grandchild.

After walking down numerous hallways and the odd set of stairs, Karras paused before twelve-foot-high carved doors, twin to the ones shielding the wizards' High Council chambers. He sang a note, paused, and sang another. The doors snicked open. Ned peered in and stopped cold with one foot extended over the threshold.

"This can't be for me—for us," he amended. "It's amazing." He gazed at long trestle tables festooned with colored ribbons and sprinkles of gold dust that gave everything a sparkly, fairytale effect. Fresh cut flowers sat in vases on every table and were woven into a bower at the front of the room. Goddess only knew where they'd come from this time of year, but they smelled of spring and hope and growing things.

Hreth, Rolf, and Sören stood on the far side of the bower.

Sören beckoned to him, but Ned couldn't force himself forward. He grappled with trusting all this splendor was for him and Amanda.

Karras gave Ned a push, underscored by a hint of magic. At least it got him moving. He made his way to his appointed spot facing Hreth and the other two men. Several wizards and mages, holding a variety of musical instruments, moved to a raised dais behind the bower. After tuning up, they began to play a song so haunting and evocative, Ned suspected they'd woven magic in with their strings and flutes.

He hadn't seen Amanda for the last three days. That part of things was wizard custom. Lira teased him that it was a woman's last chance to change her mind and inferred the other women in the stronghold would do their damnedest to dissuade her from getting married. When he asked why, she shrugged and muttered something about it being a fine, old custom and not to be questioned.

People gradually filled the hall. Hundreds of them. Sören was highly placed in mage society, so many of the guests were his doing, but far from all. Lori and his mother walked shoulder to shoulder to seats in the front row. Both women wore long simple gowns in a creamy color. It was the first time he'd seen Lori in anything other than breeches. Ned was intrigued that his and Amanda's fathers had roles to play in the wedding ceremony, while their mothers were relegated to spectator status.

Jon made his way to where his mother was and joined her. He'd taken to wearing battle leathers and seemed well on the way to putting his years with Tantalus behind him. He'd told Ned he was practicing up to join the wizard army.

The pacing of the music shifted and Ned stood tall, waiting for his first glimpse of Amanda. When she walked through the door, he couldn't tear his gaze away. Her blonde hair hung in loose curls to her waist. A gold circlet around her head held her tresses away from her face. She wore a long ivory gown set with colored gems, pearls, and feathers arranged in runic patterns. Her arms were bare and filled with flowers. He couldn't see her feet beneath her skirts, but assumed they were bare like his to maximize her connection with her Earth Mage roots.

His heart swelled, and his throat grew thick with love for the woman walking toward him. She was beautiful in every way that mattered. He still couldn't quite believe she was joining her life to his. Suddenly he understood why wizard women made a huge deal out of the three-day ban on seeing their intended prior to the ceremony. Wizard weddings were permanent. Divorce wasn't an option—ever.

Amanda drew close and raised her sky-blue gaze to meet his. He smiled encouragingly and held out his hands to her. She closed the last few feet between them and mouthed *I love you.* Taking her place by his side, she placed the flowers in a golden vase on a small table near Hreth.

"Today is truly a joyous occasion," Hreth began in the wizards' tongue, followed closely by the English words.

By the time the wizard got through welcoming everyone, Ned wanted to shake him. At this rate, he and Amanda would never be married.

"We'll only do this once," she said into his mind with her newly-acquired mind speech ability. *"Enjoy it."*

"You're wise as well as beautiful." He beamed at her.

Hreth shot a pointed glance at both of them, and Ned settled in to wait through the ceremony they'd practiced a few days before. Sören said the words to give him to his bride, followed by Rolf doing the same thing to bind Amanda to him. They shared nectar from three different flowers.

"Are you both certain?" Hreth eyed them sharply. "Once I join your blood, this cannot be undone."

"I'm certain," Ned replied.

"As am I," Amanda said in a clear, ringing voice.

Ned chafed. He wanted to draw her into his arms, but he couldn't. Not yet. He held out his right hand, Amanda her left. Hreth chanted until cuts opened in both their wrists. When their blood dripped onto the floor, he held their wrists together, continuing his incantation.

Ned felt the jolt when Amanda's sprit entered his heart, his mind, his soul. A breathy sigh from her told him she felt it too.

Hreth hit a high note and held it. The slits in their flesh mended as if they'd never been there, and Hreth ended his chant abruptly. He smiled warmly. "'Tis done. You are wed."

Ned was a little slow on the uptake, but Amanda faced him and turned her mouth up for a kiss. He wove his arms around her and pulled her against him. Dear goddess, she felt amazing. She hugged him hard, her hands splayed across his back.

"I love you so much," he murmured near her ear.

"Then kiss me, silly. You know. Kiss the bride and all that."

He thought about telling her it was a human custom—one which might shock the wizards in attendance. But he wanted to feel her mouth against his more than anything. He angled his head and met her mouth with his. Maybe it was Hreth's blood binding, but she felt different when he kissed her, like she'd always been part of him, and would be forever more.

He lost himself in the kiss, never wanting to let go of her, but someone tapped his shoulder, and someone else jostled his arm. Finally, he raised his mouth from Amanda's and gave in to social pressure from a plethora of guests, who wanted to toast them and wish them well.

All we have to do is get through the wedding dinner, then we'll get to be alone.

Ned could hardly wait. They'd done plenty of hugging and kissing and stroking and teasing, but now they were wed, and he was finally free to make love to her like he'd done so many times in his dreams.

When Rolf and Jon pumped his hand and slugged his shoulder, followed by Sören and Karras, he hooked a hand beneath Amanda's elbow and led her to the front table where they could receive their guests. The sooner they did what they were supposed to, the sooner he could bring her home. While she'd been preparing for their wedding, he'd readied a surprise of his own.

～

AMANDA LEANED into him as they made their way out of the hall where their reception was held, amid ribald catcalls and lewd suggestions, mostly from the human mages. Between dinner, multiple toasts, and wizards and mages outdoing one another to be friendly—after centuries of animosity—hours had passed.

When they came to the main passageway, she stopped and tugged on his arm. "It's that way." She pointed. "We're going to your room here, aren't we?"

"Goddess's teats, I thought we'd never get out of there." He sidestepped her question and kissed her lightly.

"Me too. Not that I don't appreciate everyone's kindness to us." A troubled look creased the smooth line of her forehead. "I still don't feel very worthy—"

"Ssht!" He laid two fingers over her mouth. "None of that. To answer your question, we're not going to my room here in the stronghold."

"Where are we going? We've waited so long, I'd be content to drag you behind that mural panel over there." Her musical laughter filled him with such joy it almost scared him.

"I figured we deserved a real home, not just a garret under the stronghold's eaves where I spent my boyhood. Sören offered us a place of our own, and I accepted."

Amanda opened her mouth, but before she could say anything, he hurried on. "I know we probably should have discussed it, but I wanted to surprise you. We can come back here every day so you can be with your mom and dad—"

She waved him to silence. "They'll be going home soon. And taking Jon with them. He changed his mind about the wizard army. Or maybe Cybele changed it for him. Anyway, he and Dad will be doing some work for the goddess, and Mom misses our place in the Sierras. Plus, the animals need for someone to be there."

"What about training her magic?"

"Karras and Lira will see to her lessons in expanding the wizard part of her magic. Not sure anyone's talked about how to leverage the human mage aspect she got from her father. Guess there're plans for me too, but not until I'm done being pregnant."

Ned reminded himself that Amanda and Jon had wizard, human mage, earth mage, and Sidhe blood, a hell of a potent mix.

"I could help develop your human mage power now that I understand it better, but we'll have all our lives to talk about magic. Want to see our new home?" He sucked in an anxious breath. "If you don't like it, we can select a different place. We had three to pick from."

Her smile melted his heart. "I'll love it because you choose for us. How shall we get there?"

"Like this." He wrapped her in his arms and summoned the spell to take them the short distance to the human mages' haven.

The rounded walls of the cozy space he'd selected formed around them. It was modest, just two rooms, but at least it would be theirs. Much like the wizards, the mages provided communal meals and had a shared bathing room. Low slung couches lined two walls, and large, colorful pillows scattered about the polished wooden floor. A long table sat in front of one of the couches, with two smaller ones at either end. A table and chairs suitable for reading or eating were tucked into one corner. Light filtered in from windows on one side of the room. The other side was built into a steep hillside.

"What do you think?" Ned watched her closely, seeking clues.

A huge smile crinkled the corners of her eyes and moved to her mouth. "It's wonderful!" She spun in place, holding her arms out from her sides. The full skirts of her dress rose with the motion of her body.

"Come see the best part. We'd have gotten tired of that narrow little cot in my old room." He spanned her waist with his hands, stopping her mid-spin, and led her to an open doorway. Beyond lay their bedroom and a soft, double mattress, replete with pillows and a patchwork comforter in a wedding ring pattern.

"Lira and your mom and my mom made the quilt for us. You should have heard Lira's choice words about how sore her fingers were from being stuck. She's far more used to wielding her staff than a needle."

Amanda's smile faded, and she faced him. "Thank you for believing in me."

"It wasn't hard. I never stopped."

"Well I did, but you pulled me out of the pit my thoughts turned into after that monster—"

Ned shook his head. "He doesn't belong here. This place is for us. You and me."

"I agree." Her expression turned solemn. "About you and me. Are you sure? Hreth asked you, but I'm asking you too. My body will change soon. I'll get big and ungainly—"

"I'll always love you, Amanda. If the pregnancy is hard, just ask for what you need. I'll do everything I can to support you. Maybe if it's not too bad an experience, someday we'll have children of our own. Come here." His voice roughened with needing her.

"I'm already here." A gentle smile curved her lips, and she looked like the most beautiful woman in the entire world.

"Then turn around. I want to undress you."

"I thought you'd never ask." She looked away, her long lashes sweeping her cheeks. "I guess I figured we'd fall into each other's arms the second we got away from the others. When we didn't—"

"You were afraid I didn't want you. Never think that way, beloved. I want you so much it scares me." He worked the tiny buttons running down her back loose. Once they were undone enough, he slipped the dress off her shoulders, and it pooled around her on the floor. Next he undid the blue satin ribbons holding her chemise together in the back.

When it was on the floor too, she stepped out of both garments and turned to face him. He'd seen her naked before, but never tired of the curves of her body. Broad shoulders with sculpted muscles gave way to full breasts with strawberry circles for nipples. Her narrow waist flared into slender hips, and a tangle of tight, golden curls guarded the entrance to her woman's parts.

"This is beautiful." She traced the gold embroidery on his robe. "But what's beneath is even better." Untying the sash holding his robe in place, she pushed the silken garment aside, and he shrugged it off. His chest ached with wanting her, and his cock swelled, jutting out from his body. When she undid the laces and his smallclothes dropped to the floor, he held out his arms, and she came into them.

He sought her mouth with his, kissing her with an urgency that swept everything else in the world away. Their tongues met, withdrew, and met again. She wound her arms around him, and ran sharp nails down his back. The rasp of their breathing filled the room, and he scooped her into his arms and tumbled them onto the bed.

He sank his hands into her glorious hair and drank her in. "You're the most beautiful woman. There's nothing about you I don't love—from the freckles across your cheeks, to your lips, to the way you get a little line between your eyebrows when you're thinking hard about something."

"You're quite the rock god yourself."

"Huh? That would be earth mages, not human mages."

"It's just an expression. It means you're incredible. I could look at you forever and never get tired of the view."

His heart warmed, and he scooped the quilt aside so they lay on fine linen sheets. Now that they had all the time in the world, he wanted the first time they made love to be perfect. Every other time they'd been together had been quick grappling as they muffled their moans of delight, rushing to orgasm as fast as they could get there.

Running his hands down her body, he filled them with her breasts and rolled her nipples until they grew long and hard beneath his touch. She arched her back with delight and leaned into his touch, reaching to curve a hand around his ridged flesh.

"Tell me what you want." He gazed at her, loving the warming tone of her skin as she grew more excited.

"We've done everything else and then some. I want you inside me."

His breath hitched. "Are you sure you don't want me to make you come first? In case I don't last very long."

Love shone from her eyes, capturing him in its net. "No matter what happens, we'll figure it out." She let go of him long enough to swing a leg out of the way and position him between hers. Wrapping her legs around his waist, she opened herself for him and squirmed to get as close as she could.

He knelt over her and seated himself at the entrance to her body. Rubbing her nubbin with the small circles she loved, he pushed gently inside, a little bit at a time. Sensation threatened to swamp him. The scorching, silken heat of her settled around him in the most exquisite feeling he'd ever experienced.

He encased himself fully inside her body, an inch at a time. His balls tightened, and he stopped moving until the imminence of a climax backed off a notch.

He teased her nipples with the hand that wasn't rubbing the seat of her pleasure and felt her tighten around his cock. He upped the ante, wanting to watch her come while he was buried deep inside her. She thrashed beneath his touch just before she dissolved around him in a pool of molten heat.

The rhythmic contractions around his shaft almost pushed him over the edge. Almost, but he hung on by a ragged thread, focused on how lovely she was, with rosy splotches coloring her chest and face. Heat lust shone from her eyes, and she opened her arms, reaching for him. He lowered himself atop her and crushed his mouth down on hers.

Amanda threaded her arms around him and ran teasing fingertips down his back. Ned groaned. His body developed a mind of its own, and he withdrew partway before plunging back inside the heat of her. She gripped his hips, encouraging him, and ground her pubes against him. Time stuttered to a halt as he plumbed her body. After the first few strokes, when he feared he'd lose control, he funneled bits of magic into his arousal that held him dancing along the edges of ecstasy.

Shrieking and laughing, she came again, the points of her breasts like fine agates pressing against his chest. And then she was pushing him over and straddling him. Her breasts bounced as she rode him, and her hair trailed over them creating a soft curtain.

When the ache in his balls became too much to bear, he stopped riding herd on the climax that wanted out. With a guttural cry he barely recognized as his voice, he exploded, jet after jet of white heat pumping into her. His heart beat so hard, he was surprised it didn't jump from his chest. Love for the woman in his arms ran through him until his heart cracked wide open and spilled over.

"That was amazing. Perfect," she gasped, as out of breath as he was.

He gathered her into his arms and turned them on their sides, making certain not to dislodge his cock from her body. "Better than perfect," he murmured. "I'll love you until the end of my days, Amanda, and then some."

"We'll love each other," she said, her voice vibrating with emotion. "It doesn't get any better than that."

Ned smoothed her tangled hair back from her face. This was the beginning of their life together, a beginning filled with hope and promise. He made a silent vow to be worthy of her, to always cherish her, and to make sure she knew how important she was to him by telling her so often she got sick of hearing it.

Her full mouth curved into a soft smile. "I'll never tell you to shut up when you're plying me with compliments."

"How did you know what I was thinking?"

"I was eavesdropping on your thoughts just then. It's much easier than it used to be."

"Likely a byproduct of Hreth's binding. And a good one. I've nothing to hide from you."

"Nor me from you. I'll do everything in my power to make sure we have the best of lives together." A thoughtful expression crossed her face. "I've watched Mom and Dad. They've had problems, but they talk things through until they solve them—no matter how long it takes."

"We will too, Mandy." He cuddled her close, and love swelled within him. Outside of Karras, he'd never had a family, and an almost feral protectiveness surged. He'd make certain nothing harmed Amanda ever. Or any of her kin.

"We'll take care of each other." She cradled his face in her hand.

He kissed the tip of her nose. "And we'll do such a good job, everything else will sort itself out."

Her body turned warm and fluid around him, and he

kissed her. The night was far from young, but he'd make love with her again before they slept.

She pulled away, and a warm, teasing light sparked from her eyes. "Only once more? I figured we'd stay in bed until someone came and rousted us out."

Ned laughed. "Sweetheart, we could starve to death, but we'll hold the rest of the world at bay as long as we can."

You've reached the end of *Marked by Fortune*. At the moment, I don't plan to expand it into a series, but you never know what the future might hold. Tantalus's child could make an interesting center point for a follow-up book.

If you enjoyed this cross between urban fantasy, high fantasy, and romance, you might enjoy the Earth Reclaimed Series. A snippet from *Earth's Requiem*, Book One of Earth Reclaimed follows.

Please take a moment to leave a review for *Marked by Fortune*. Do it now while it's fresh in your mind. Reviews mean the world to authors. Doesn't have to be fancy. A line or two will do it.

Resilient, kickass, and determined, Aislinn's walled herself off from anything that might make her feel again. Until a wolf picks her for a bondmate, and a Celtic god rises out of legend to claim her for his own.

Aislinn Lenear lost her anthropologist father high in the Bolivian Andes. Her mother, crazy with grief that muted her magic, was marched into a radioactive vortex by dark creatures. Three years later, stripped of every illusion that ever comforted her, twenty-two year old Aislinn is one resilient, kickass woman with a *take no prisoners* attitude. In a world turned upside down, where virtually nothing familiar is left, she's conscripted to fight the dark gods responsible for her father's death. Battling evil on her own terms, Aislinn walls herself off from anything that might make her feel again in this compelling dystopian urban fantasy.

Fionn MacCumhaill, Celtic god of wisdom, protection, and divination has been laying low since the dark gods stormed Earth. He and his fellow Celts decided to wait them out. Three years is nothing compared to their long lives. On a clear winter day, Aislinn walks into his life and suddenly all bets are off. Awed by her courage, he stakes his claim to her and to an Earth he's willing to fight for.

Aislinn's not so easily convinced. Fionn's one gorgeous man, but she has a world to save. Emotional entanglements will only get in her way. Letting a wolf into her life was hard. Letting love in may well prove impossible.

Books in the Earth Reclaimed Series:
Earth's Requiem
Earth's Blood
Earth's Hope

EARTH'S REQUIEM, FIRST PROLOGUE

Salt Lake City, Utah

Aislinn tried to stop it, but the vision that had dogged her for over a year played in her head. She squeezed her eyes shut tight. Mental images crowded behind her closed lids, as vivid as if they'd happened yesterday. She raked her hands through her hair and pulled hard, but the movie chronicling the beginning of her own personal hell didn't even slow down. She whimpered as the humid darkness of a South American night closed about her...

Her mother screamed in Gaelic, "Deifir, Deifir," and then shoved Aislinn again. She tried to hurry like her mother wanted, but it was all too much to take in. Stumbling down the steep Bolivian mountainside in the dark, she ignored tears and snot streaking her face. Her legs shook. Nausea clenched her gut. Her mother was crying too, in between cursing the gods and herself. Aislinn knew enough Gaelic to understand her mother had tried to talk her father out of going to the ancient Inca prayer site, but Jacob hadn't listened.

A vision of her father's twisted body lying dead a thousand feet above them tore at Aislinn. Just a few hours ago, her life had been normal. Now her mother had turned into a grief-crazed harridan. Her beloved father, a gentle giant of a man, was dead. Killed by those horrors that had crawled out of the ground. Perfect, golden-skinned men with long, silky hair and luminous eyes, apparently summoned through the ancient rite linked to the shrine. Thinking about it was like trying to shove her hand into a flame, her pain too unbearable to examine closely.

Aislinn was afraid to turn around. Tara had already slapped her once. Another spate of Gaelic galvanized her tired legs into motion. Her mother was clearly terrified the monsters would come after them, but Aislinn didn't think they'd bother. At least a hundred adoring half-naked worshipers remained at the shrine high on the mountain. Once Tara had herded her into the shadows, her last glimpse of the crowd revealed one of the lethal exotic creatures turning a woman so he could penetrate her. Even in Aislinn's near-paralyzed state, the sexual heat was so compelling, it took all her self-discipline not to race to his side and insist he take her instead. After all, she was younger, prettier. It didn't matter at all that he'd just killed her father.

...Aislinn shook her head so hard, it felt like her brains rattled from side to side in her skull. Despite the time that had passed since her father's murder, she still fell into these damned trance states, where the horror happened all over again. Tears leaked from her eyes. She slammed a fist down on a corner of her desk, glorying in the diversion pain created. Crying was pointless. It wouldn't change anything. Self-pity was an indulgence she couldn't afford.

Pull it together. The weak die.

Even though she wasn't sure why life felt so precious—after all, she'd lost nearly everything—Aislinn wanted to live. Would do anything to hang onto the vital thread that maintained her on Earth.

A bitter laugh bubbled up. What a transition: from Aislinn Lenear, college student, to Aislinn Lenear, fledgling magic wielder. A second race of alien beings, Lemurians, had stormed Earth on the heels of that hideous night in Bolivia, selecting certain humans because they had magical ability and sending everyone else to their deaths.

It was a process. It took time to kill people, but huge sections of Salt Lake City sat empty. Skyscraper towers downtown and rows of vacant buildings mocked a life that was no more. In her travels to nearby places before the gasoline ran out, Aislinn had found them about the same as Salt Lake.

Jacob's death had been a harbinger of impending chaos—the barest beginning. The world she'd known had imploded shockingly fast. It killed Aislinn to admit it—she kept hoping for a miracle to intercede—but her mother was certifiable. Tara may as well have died right along with her husband. She hadn't left the house once since they'd returned a year before. Her long, red hair was filthy and matted. She barely ate. When she wasn't curled into a fetal position, she drew odd runes on the kitchen floor and muttered in Gaelic about Celtic gods and dragons. It was only a matter of time before the Lemurians culled her. Tara had magic, but she was worthless in her current state.

The sound of the kitchen door rattling against its stops startled Aislinn. On her feet in a flash, she took the stairs two at a time and burst into the kitchen. A Lemurian had one of its preternaturally long-fingered hands curved around Tara's emaciated arm. He crooned to her in his language—an incomprehensible mix of clicks and clacks. Tara's wild, golden eyes glazed over. She stopped trying to pull away and got to her feet, leaning against the seven-foot tall creature with long, shiny blond hair, as if she couldn't stand on her own.

"No!" Aislinn hurled herself at the Lemurian. "Leave her alone."

"Stop!" His odd alien gaze met hers. "It is time," the Lemurian said in flawless English, "for both you and her. You must join the fighting and learn about your magic. Your mother is of no use to anyone."

"But she has magic." Aislinn hated the pleading in her voice. Hated it.

Be strong. I can't show him how scared I am.

Something flickered behind the Lemurian's expression. It might have been disgust—or pity. He turned away and led Tara Lenear out of the house.

Aislinn growled low in her throat and launched herself at the Lemurian's back. Gathering her clumsy magic into a primitive arc, she focused it on her enemy. Her tongue stuttered over an incantation. Before she could finish it, something smacked her in the chest so hard she flew through the air, hit the kitchen wall, and then slumped to the floor. Wind knocked out of her, spots dancing before her eyes, she struggled to her feet. By the time she stumbled to the kitchen door, both the Lemurian and her mother had vanished.

An unholy shriek split the air, followed by another. Aislinn clapped a hand over her mouth to seal the sound inside and clutched the doorsill. Pain clawed at her belly. Her vision became a red haze. The fucking Lemurian had taken her mother. The last human connection she had. And they expected her to fight for them? Ha! It would be a cold day in Hell. She let go of the doorframe and balled her hands into fists so hard her nails drew blood.

Standing still was killing her, so she walked into blindingly bright sunlight. She didn't care what happened next. It didn't matter anymore. A muted explosion rocked the ground. She staggered. When she turned, she wasn't surprised to see her house crack in multiple places and settle. Not totally destroyed, but close enough.

Guess they want to make sure I don't have anywhere to go back to.

Her heart shattered into jagged pieces that poked her from the inside. She bit her lip so hard it ached. When that didn't make a dent in her anguish, she pinched herself, dug her nails into her flesh until she bled from dozens of places. Fingers slick with her own blood, she forced herself into a ragged jog. Maybe if she put some distance between herself and the wreckage of her life, the pain sluicing through her would abate.

As she ran, a phrase filled her mind. The same sentence, over and over in time to her heartbeat. *I will never care for anyone ever again. I will never care for anyone ever again.* After a time, the words etched into her soul.

EARTH'S REQUIEM, SECOND
PROLOGUE

Ely, Nevada

Two Years Later

Rune paced from the kitchen to the living room and back again, hackles at half mast and tail twitching behind him. Marta, his bondmate and the woman who'd rescued him from a trap when he was just a wolf pup, was resting. At least he hoped she was. Something between a whine and a growl slipped past his clenched jaws.

Damn her, anyway.

Didn't she understand she'd been targeted by the dark gods? Ever since she took to spying on the Lemurians in Taltos, their underground city, things turned to rat shit. Something hideous happened on her last trip. He wasn't certain quite what because he wasn't with her, and she refused to tell him. Many moonrises had passed, and she was only just now beginning to talk and think normally.

Rune paused to stare out a large window. The front yard

was absolutely silent. So was the road fronting Marta's house, but then it would be since most of the humans were dead, and gasoline to make their cars run had long since run out.

He shook his fur out and came to a decision. Should he tell Marta now or wait until she woke?

She solved the problem for him. The sound of her footsteps made him spin to face the door into the living room. She was dressed to go out and had shoes on. Not a good sign.

"There you are." She favored him with a maternal smile, the one that made him want to bite her. She may have rescued him when he was too young to care for himself, but that was long ago.

"Here I am," he agreed and trained his amber eyes on the woman who meant everything to him.

"I'm leaving for a while—"

Rune's decision roared out of him. "Not without me, you're not. Never again. Look what happened last time."

"Be reasonable." She smiled again, and Rune felt magic prowl beneath her words.

He slapped up power of his own. "Reasonable has nothing to do with it. Last time they nearly killed you. I wasn't certain until yesterday you'd get enough of your memories back to be yourself."

"Neither was I." Her smile developed grim edges. She sank to the thick Oriental carpet and held out her arms.

Rune stayed where he was. "All the more reason to take me with you. You can merge your senses with mine. Together we're stronger. It's why we chose the Hunter bond."

"Aw, Rune." Sadness etched lines around her eyes and into her forehead. "You don't understand. None of us will get out of this alive, but we have to fight until we can't fight anymore. If we don't, it's like turning Earth over to those bastards, and I won't do that." She slapped the floor with the flat of her hand. "I won't."

"Neither will I." He gazed cooly at her. "Where are we going?"

"I can't take you with me. It's too dangerous."

"If you don't take me, you're not going, either." The wolf stood his ground, but it was shaky. She could order him, and he'd have to obey. It was how the Hunter bond worked.

Marta looked away, studying her hands. Her long coppery hair was in its usual tight braid, and she was dressed in loose-fitting black trousers and a black jacket, with stout lace-up boots. She was tall, almost as tall as the Lemurians, and she sat with her legs splayed in front of her.

Rune kept his gaze glued to her, willing her to capitulate. He was fully prepared to take her on in combat to keep her in the house, if she refused his company. "I'm not being stubborn," he said. "I need to be with you for me, not just for you. How do you think I'll feel if you don't return? How can I live with myself if you die in a place where I wasn't there to help you?"

"I could die anyway." She did look at him then, her clear green eyes filled with something he didn't have a name for.

"So could I, but if we're together at least we'll know we did everything we could for each other."

Marta nodded once. "All right. I don't have enough energy to argue with you. We're going to one of the mining camps to the west of us. Some humans are still alive, and they need my medical skill."

"How do you know anyone's alive?" he countered.

She shrugged. "Call it a hunch. I dream things sometimes, and this came to me not long ago. We'll do a travel jump. It's not far. If the place is deserted, I'll bring us right back." The same, sad smile returned. "With luck, we'll be home in time for supper."

"Ready when you are."

She got to her feet. "Are you going to come closer than that? I already said I'd take you, Rune. Bondmates don't lie to each other."

Shame filled him because she'd nailed his reticence. He didn't trust that she wouldn't trick him. He made his way to her side and felt her magic as she opened a portal for them to travel to the place she'd seen in her dream.

They rolled out into high, arid desert, and the remains of a mining camp sprawled about them, buildings falling into disrepair. Bullet holes riddled tin roofs and corrugated siding. Rune sent his senses spinning outward.

Nothing lived anywhere near here.

"Curious," Marta murmured. "I was so sure."

Rune's hackles hit full alert, standing on end the length of his back. "We must leave," he snarled. "It has to be a trap."

Before Marta could reply, another gateway opened a little way away. Bal'ta poured out. Marta flung magic at the disgusting creatures, minions of the dark, but she barely made a dent. They stood between five and six feet tall, with barrel chests, and their bodies were coated in greasy-looking brown hair. Thicker hair hung from their scalps and grew in clumps from armpits and groins. Ropy muscles bulged under their hairy skin. Orange eyes gleamed, and their foreheads sloped backward.

Rune had faced them before. At least they didn't have magic of their own beyond a shared intelligence. The flood had slowed, and he gathered himself for action. He and Marta could take them. They'd faced worse odds. Apparently she agreed, and he felt her merge her consciousness with his.

"I'll take this side," Rune growled and thrust himself into the thick of things, avoiding the cudgels and maces they used in battle. Rune knew to stay out of the line of Marta's magic. He sliced into one neck after another until he was coated in blood. The air was thick with the coppery stench of it. For some reason, Bal'ta avoided him. Something about his animal energy burned them, and he took full advantage of their hesitation.

He glanced at Marta from time to time, grateful beyond thought she was still on her feet. In addition to magic, she held a knife in one hand. A knife dripping blood. Dead bodies piled around both of them.

Rune danced to one side to avoid a cudgel aimed for him skull. He sent out a call for forest wolves, but none came to their aid. Maybe there weren't any living here—or maybe they didn't see the point in taking a stand in someone else's battle.

No matter. He and Marta were winning. Only a few Bal'ta remained. He'd begun to work his way back to his bondmate, when another gateway opened, this one black and edged with flames. A man sashayed through. Rune stopped cold, staring in disbelief. The remaining Bal'ta faded away from that gaping maw; in moments they'd summoned another portal and left.

Rune focused on the newcomer. It had to be one of the dark gods. No one else held that level of deadly beauty. Long dark hair streamed behind him, and he trained his shrewd dark eyes on Marta. She squared her shoulders and stared back.

"Kill him," Rune urged.

"I can't," she ground out. "Much as I'd love to."

The dark god tossed his shapely head back and laughed; the sound was disturbing, discordant. "Your bondmate is wise," he told the wolf. "She's clever not to get too close."

"Which one is he?" Rune demanded.

"You may as well ask me, since I'm right here." Dark eyes crinkled in chilly humor, and he mock bowed. "My name is Tokhots. I'm also known as the trickster." Dark robes fluttered around him, sashed in gray.

While Tokhots had been talking, Marta sidled farther from Rune and severed her connection with him. Worried, he tried to determine just what she was up to. If she planned an attack, he didn't want to be in the way and ruin things. Nor did he plan to leave her to the mercy of the dark god. Maybe if he kept Tokhots chatting...

"What do you mean by trickster? It's not a term I'm familiar with."

Tokhots did a funny little side step. "I play tricks. I'm funny. I'm a hell of a nice guy. If you got to know me, you'd—"

A ball of fire immolated one side of his robes. Tokhots'

pleasant expression shattered, and he batted at the flames—and at jolts of power Marta hurled his way. Rune wanted to launch himself at the dark god, but Marta's power kept him rooted in place.

Finally giving up on extinguishing the flames, Tokhots shucked his robe, revealing golden-hued skin beneath. "Bitch!" he spat and raced to Marta so fast he beat Rune, who was also headed that way at breakneck speed.

"Don't bite him," Marta shrieked. "His blood is deadly poison."

Rune aborted a leap in midair and crashed to the rocky ground. He'd been about to close his jaws around Tokhots' neck.

The dark god held a writhing Marta in his grip. "You can't hurt me either," he taunted. "One drop of my blood and you'll be deader than the shades that roam the countryside."

"What do you want with me?" Marta gave a mighty heave.

Rune thought she might free herself, but Tokhots tightened his hold. "You've become an inconvenience. I sent the Bal'ta as a diversion until I could get here."

"What happens next?" Marta's voice was steady, but Rune sensed her fear, and it filled him with fury. He worked his way closer to the pair, not moving very fast.

"That's for me to know." Tokhots laughed again.

Caution departed. Rune judged the distance and leapt. So what if he died? At least Marta would go free. The air around him thickened, holding him suspended above the ground. Darkness dropped over him like a curtain until he couldn't see. He thrashed against the magic holding him and plummeted to earth, landing hard on jagged rocks. Ignoring pain, he vaulted toward where Marta had been, still running blind in unnatural darkness.

She wasn't there. Neither was the dark god.

He still couldn't see, but he could smell and hear. He employed both senses, ears pricked forward and nose snuffling so hard it began to bleed.

Nothing.

Marta's scent was strongest right where he stood.

Rune threw his head back and howled his desolation to the skies. He'd failed. The dark god had his bondmate, and he had no way to go after them.

By the time the darkness receded, his throat was raw with grief. He called for other animals, birds, even insects, to tell him what they'd seen. If they knew anything, but no one answered.

Despondent, guilt-stricken, Rune put one paw ahead of another. No point in staying with the dead Bal'ta. Tokhots would never bring Marta back here.

The dark god had taken his bondmate on a oneway trip. Rune knew, as clearly as he knew anything, she'd never run by his side again. She was still alive, but her life force ebbed through their Hunter bond.

Soon she'd be no more, and it was his fault. If he'd been quicker, hadn't hesitated...

He shook his head hard and broke into a run.

EARTH'S REQUIEM, CHAPTER ONE

Aislinn pulled her cap down more firmly on her head. Snow stung where it got into her eyes and froze the exposed parts of her face. Thin, cold air seared her lungs when she made the mistake of breathing too deeply. She'd taken refuge in a spindly stand of leafless aspens, but they didn't cut the wind at all. "Where's Travis?" she fumed, scanning the unending white of a high altitude plain that used to be part of Colorado. Or maybe this place had been in eastern Utah. It didn't really matter anymore.

Something unnatural flickered at the corner of her eye and she tensed. Standing still bought trouble with a capitol T. She swiveled her head to maximize her peripheral vision. *Damn! No, double damn.* Half-frozen muscles in her face ached when she tightened her jaw.

Bal'ta—a bunch of them—fanned out a couple hundred yards behind her, closing the distance eerily fast. One of many atrocities serving the dark gods that had crawled out of the ground that night in Bolivia, they appeared as shadowy spots against the fading day. Places where edges shimmered and merged into a menacing blackness. If she looked too hard at the center of those dark places, they drew her like a lodestone. Aislinn tore her gaze away.

Not that Bal'ta—bad as they were—were responsible for the wholesale destruction of modern life. No, their masters—the ones who'd brought dark magic to Earth in the first place—held that dubious honor. Aislinn shook her head sharply, trying to decide what to do. She was supposed to meet Travis here. Those were her orders. He had something to give her. Typical of the way the Lemurians ran things, no one knew very much about anything. It was safer that way if you got captured.

She hadn't meant to cave and work for them, but in the end, she'd had little choice. It was sign on with the Lemurians—Old Ones—to cultivate her magic and fight the dark, or be marched into the same radioactive vortex that had killed her mother.

Her original plan had been to wait for Travis until an hour past full dark, but the Bal'ta changed all that. Waiting even one more minute was a gamble she wasn't willing to risk. Aislinn took a deep breath. Chanting softly in Gaelic, her mother's language, she called up the light spell that would wrap her in brilliance and allow her to escape— maybe. It was the best strategy she could deploy on short notice. Light was anathema to Bal'ta and their ilk. So many of the loathsome creatures were hot on her heels, she didn't have any other choice.

She squared her shoulders. All spells drained her. This

was one of the worst—a purely Lemurian working translated into Gaelic because human tongues couldn't handle the Old Ones' language. She pulled her attention from her spell for the time it took to glance about, and her heart sped up. Even the few seconds it took to determine flight was essential had attracted at least ten more of the bastards. They surrounded her. Well, almost.

She shouted the word to kindle her spell. Even in Gaelic, with its preponderance of harsh consonants, the magic felt awkward on her tongue. Heart thudding double time against her ribs, she hoped she'd gotten the inflection right. Moments passed. Nothing happened. Aislinn tried again. Still nothing. Desperate, she readied her magic for a fight she was certain she'd lose and summoned the light spell one last time. Flickers formed. Stuttering into brilliance, they pushed against the Bal'tas' darkness.

Yesssss. Muting down triumph surging through her—no time for it—she gathered the threads of her working, draped luminescence about herself, and loped toward the west. Bal'ta scattered, closing behind her. She noted with satisfaction that they stayed well away from her light. She'd always assumed it burned them in some way.

Travis was on his own. She couldn't even warn him that he was walking into a trap. Maybe he already had. Which would explain why he hadn't shown up. Worry tugged at her. She ignored it. Anything less than absolute concentration, and she'd fall prey to his fate—whatever that had been.

Vile hissing sounded behind her. Long-nailed hands reached for her, followed by shrieks when one of them came into contact with her magic. She snuck a peek over one shoulder to see how close they truly were. One problem with all that light was it illuminated the nasty things. Their backward sloping foreheads leant them a dimwitted look, but they were skilled warriors, worthy adversaries who'd wiped out more than one of her comrades. Their insect-like ability to work as a group using telepathic powers scared her more than anything. Though she threw her Mage senses wide open, she was damned if she could tap into their wavelength to disrupt it.

Chest aching, breath coming in short, raspy pants, she ran like she'd never run before. If she let go of anything—her light shield or her speed—they'd be on her, and it would be all over. Dead just past her twenty-second birthday. *That* thought pushed her legs to pump faster. She gulped air, willing everything to hold together long enough.

Minutes ticked by. Maybe as much as half an hour passed. She was tiring. It was hard to run and maintain magic. Could she risk teleportation? Sort of a *beam me up, Scotty,* trick. Nope, she wasn't close enough to her destination yet. Something cold as an ice cave closed around her upper arm. Her flesh stung before feeling left it. She snapped her head to that side and noted her light cloak had failed in that spot. Frantic to loosen the creature's grip, she pulled a dirk from her belt and stabbed at the thing holding her. Smoke rose when she dug her iron knife into it.

The stench of burning flesh stung her nostrils, and the disgusting ape-man drew back, hurling imprecations in its guttural language. She snaked her gaze through the gloom of the fading day, as she assessed how many of the enemy chased her. Aislinn swallowed hard around a painfully dry throat. There had to be a hundred. Why were they targeting her? Had they intercepted Travis and his orders? Damn the Lemurians anyway. She'd never wanted to fight for them.

I've got to get out of here.

Though it went against the grain—mostly because she was pretty certain it wouldn't work, and you weren't supposed to cast magic willy nilly—she pictured her home, mixed magic from earth and fire, and begged the Old Ones to see her delivered safely. Once she set the spell in motion, there'd be no going back. If she didn't end up where she planned, she'd be taken to task, maybe even stripped of her powers, depending on how pissed off the Lemurians were.

Aislinn didn't have any illusions left. Her world had crumbled three years ago. She'd wasted months railing against God, or the fates, or whoever was responsible for robbing her of her boyfriend and her parents and her life, goddammit, but nothing brought them back.

Then the Old Ones—Lemurians, she corrected herself— had slapped reason into her, forcing her to see the magic that kept her alive as a resource, not a curse. In the intervening time, she'd not only come to terms with that magic, but it had become a part of her. The only part she truly trusted. Without the magic that enhanced her senses, she'd be dead within hours.

Please... She struggled against clasping her hands together in an almost forgotten gesture of supplication. Juggling an image of her home while maintaining enough light to hold the Bal'ta at bay, she waited. Nothing happened. She was supposed to vanish, her molecules transported by proxy to where she wished to go. This was way more than the normal journey—or jump—spell, though. Because she needed to go much farther.

She poured more energy into the teleportation spell. The light around her flickered. Bal'ta dashed forward, jaws open, saliva dripping. She smelled the rotten crypt smell of them and cringed. If they got hold of her, they'd feed off her until she was nothing but an empty husk. Or worse, if one took a shine to her, she'd be raped in the bargain and forced to carry a mixed breed child. They'd kill her as soon as the thing was weaned. Maybe the brat, too, if its magic wasn't strong enough.

The most powerful of the enemy were actually blends of light and dark magic. When the abominations, six dark masters, had slithered out of holes between the worlds during a globally synchronized surge linked to the Harmonic Convergence, the first thing they'd done had been to capture human women and perform unspeakable experiments on progeny resulting from purloined eggs and alien sperm.

Aislinn sucked in a shaky breath. She did *not* want to be captured. Suicide was a far better alternative. She licked at the fake cap in the back of her mouth. It didn't budge. She shoved a filthy finger behind her front teeth and used an equally disgusting fingernail to pop the cap. She gripped the tiny capsule. Should she swallow it? Could she? Sweat beaded and trickled down her forehead, despite the chill afternoon air.

She'd just dropped the pill onto her tongue, trying to gin up enough saliva to make it go down, when the weightlessness associated with teleportation started in her feet like it always did. Gagging, she spat out the capsule and extended a hand to catch it, but it fell into the dirt. Aislinn knew better than to scrabble for the poison pill. If she survived, she could get another from the Old Ones. They didn't care how many humans died, despite pretending to befriend those with magic.

Her spell was shaky enough as it was. It needed more energy—lots more. Forgetting about the light spell, Aislinn put everything she had into escape. By the time she knew she was going to make it—apparently the Bal'ta didn't know they could take advantage of her vulnerability as she shimmered half in and half out of teleport mode—she was almost too tired to care.

She fell through star-spotted darkness for a long time. It could have been several lifetimes. Teleportation jaunts were different than her simple Point A to Point B jumps. When she'd traveled this way before, she'd asked how long it took, but the Old Ones never answered. Everyone she'd ever loved was dead—and the Old Ones lived forever—so she didn't have a reliable way to measure time. For all she knew, Travis might've lived through years of teleportation jumps. No one ever talked about anything personal. It was like an unwritten law. No going back. No one had a past. At least, not one they were willing to talk about.Voices eddied around her, speaking the Lemurian tongue with its clicks and clacks. She tried to talk with them, but they ignored her. On shorter, simpler journeys, her body stayed with her. She'd never known how her body caught up to her when she teletransported and was nothing but spirit. Astral energy suspended between time and space.

A disquieting thump rattled her bones. *Bones. I have bones again... That must mean...* Barely conscious of the walls of her home rising around her, Aislinn felt the fibers of her grandmother's Oriental rug against her face. She smelled cinnamon and lilac. Relief surged through her. Against hope and reason, the Old Ones had seen her home. Maybe they cared more than she thought—at least about her. Aislinn tried to pull herself across the carpet to the corner shrine so she could thank them properly, but her head spun. Darkness took her before she could do anything else.

ABOUT THE AUTHOR

Ann Gimpel is a USA Today bestselling author. A lifelong aficionado of the unusual, she began writing speculative fiction a few years ago. Since then her short fiction has appeared in many webzines and anthologies. Her longer books run the gamut from urban fantasy to paranormal romance. Once upon a time, she nurtured clients. Now she nurtures dark, gritty fantasy stories that push hard against reality. When she's not writing, she's in the backcountry getting down and dirty with her camera. She's published over 70 books to date, with several more planned for 2019 and beyond. A husband, grown children, grandchildren, and wolf hybrids round out her family.

Keep up with her at www.anngimpel.com or http://anngimpel.blogspot.com

If you enjoyed what you read, get in line for special offers and pre-release special reads. Newsletter Signup!

ALSO BY ANN GIMPEL

SERIES

Alphas in the Wild

Hello Darkness

Alpine Attraction

A Run for Her Money

Fire Moon

Bitter Harvest

Deceived

Twisted

Abandoned

Betrayed

Redeemed

Coven Enforcers

Blood and Magic

Blood and Sorcery

Blood and Illusion

Demon Assassins

Witch's Bounty

Witch's Bane

Witches Rule

Dragon Heir (Summer and fall, 2019)

Dragon's Call

Dragon's Blood

Dragon's Heir

Dragon Lore

Highland Secrets

To Love a Highland Dragon

Dragon Maid

Dragon's Dare

Dragon Fury

Earth Reclaimed

Earth's Requiem

Earth's Blood

Earth's Hope

Elemental Witch

Timespell

Time's Curse

Time's Hostage

Gatekeeper (Winter 2019 and spring 2020)

Shadow Reaper

Rebel Reaper

Untamed Reaper

GenTech Rebellion

Winning Glory

Honor Bound

Alice's Alphas

Megan's Mates

Sophie's Shifters

Wylde Magick

Gemstone

Lion's Lair

Unbalanced

STANDALONE BOOKS

Branded, That Old Black Magic Romance (paranormal romance)

Edge of Night (short story collection, paranormal and horror)

Grit is a 4-Letter Word (nonfiction)

Heart's Flame (post-apocalyptic romance)

Icy Passage (science fiction romance)

Marked by Fortune (post-apocalyptic coming of age story)

Melis's Gambit (historical paranormal romance)

Midnight Magic (paranormal romance)

Red Dawn (post-apocalyptic paranormal romance)

Shadow Play (historical paranormal romance)

Shadows in Time (Highland time travel romance)

Since We Fell (contemporary romance)

Warin's War (paranormal romance)

www.ingramcontent.com/pod-product-compliance
Lightning Source LLC
Chambersburg PA
CBHW070815190726
48292CB00006B/2018